# The Devil's Fragrance

Martin Fine

Eloquent Books
New York, New York

Copyright © 2009
All rights reserved — Martin Fine

No part of this book may be reproduced or transmitted in any form or by any means, graphic, electronic, or mechanical, including photocopying, recording, taping, or by any information storage retrieval system, without the permission, in writing, from the publisher.

Eloquent Books
An imprint of AEG Publishing Group
845 Third Avenue, 6th Floor – 6016
New York, NY 10022
www.eloquentbooks.com

ISBN: 978-1-60693-809-6   1-60693-809-6

Printed in the United States of America

Book Design: D. Johnson, Dedicated Business Solutions, Inc.

# The River Cydnus 41 BC

The silver oars glistened in the morning sun as they rhythmically rose from the placid waters. Droplets dripped, sparkling like diamonds as they splashed back down onto the shimmering surface. As if one unified body, all eighty oarsmen pushed forward. The oars dipped, parting the river, propelling the magnificent barge onwards. No common drummer pounded out a beat. This was no ordinary vessel. This was a royal barge.

No whips or harsh words were needed to maintain the cadence. Only the cream of a nation's oarsmen had been selected. They had practiced for long hours to perfect their motion. Each man selected not only for his strength but for his beauty—and each a eunuch. These were not slaves or prisoners. All had volunteered to have their manhood removed. It was a small price to pay to be of service to their queen—the most powerful ruler in the East.

The morning mist was beginning to dissipate. Along the shoreline the bank of the river was crowded with people. They had come to witness history in the making. They had come to see the most beautiful woman in the world. But they could see nothing. They could hear the titillating notes of distant pipes and the harmonic tones of the lutes somewhere out there on the river. The sound was growing. The barge must be drawing nearer.

There was fragrance in the air—lavender, frankincense, chamomile. The eyes and ears of the common people strained. Suddenly a cry disturbed the stillness. More shouts followed, then cheering, as the proud elongated bow cut through the blanket of mist as though opening a seductive curtain. The exquisitely carved head of the god Osiris, the protector of women, the goddess of plenty—protruded forth. Golden ears of wheat decorated the goddess's sides. Osiris, at one with Demeter—the complete mother—wife, sister, the all encompassing worshipped throughout the Hellenistic world.

Clouds of pink and green vapors wafted from the magnificent vessel. Magically, the veil of secrecy was lifted as the royal barge finally glided into full view. Gold and silver leaf adorning the dark wood of the hull gleamed in the morning light. An immense bright purple sail decorated with golden cherubs hung vertically from the main mast. Scantily clad youths of both sexes moved nimbly about the barge. Some were playing musical instruments; others carried platters, jugs or flowers.

"There she is," a voice cried out.

"Yes. Yes, I can see her too."

Obscured beneath a canopy of golden silk perched high up on a raised dais reclined a mystical figure. Four inky-black-skinned eunuchs, one at each corner, raised and lowered gargantuan ostrich plume fans in symphony with the pull of the oarsmen. Shadowy shapes moved around the fringes of the canopy.

On shore, the crowd was swelling by the minute, the noise deafening, as people cheered. They were running now, desperately trying to keep up, to follow this most wondrous of sights. The barge had only a mile to go before it arrived at its destination—Tarsus, where the Roman Emperor Antony was waiting.

The High Priest, Meryneith, seated behind the reclining figure, leaned forward before he spoke. "Majesty, we shall soon be there, within the hour. You are prepared?"

Cleopatra, Queen of the Nile, smiled. Inclining her head towards him, she brushed aside the golden silk veil partially covering her face. "Have no fear, Meryneith; I am more than prepared to meet the new Caesar. You have the potion?"

Meryneith bowed. "It is at my side ready to apply, Majesty."

Cleopatra laughed, the girlish sound muffled by the drapes. "Of course, Meryneith, Egypt can always rely upon you, just as she does on her queen."

"I fear Antony may not be as easy a conquest as Caesar. He is married. I am told he is of a much firmer character than Caesar."

"You forget. I have met with him on more than one occasion. It is only the circumstances this time which are different. History has a way of repeating itself. It is only seven years since you so cleverly had me smuggled into the Royal Palace of Alexandria wrapped in a rug to be so dramatically revealed to Caesar."

"You were younger, Majesty. It was the only way, with Pothinus's troops guarding all the entrances, to outwit your brother, King Ptolemy."

Cleopatra ran her hands down the silk front of her robe, feeling the hardness of her stomach muscles. Next, her fingers parted her breasts feeling their firmness. "Are you saying I'm old, Meryneith?"

"Good Heavens! No, majesty!" spluttered the high priest. "I was merely . . ."

"I'm joking, relax," she interrupted softly. "The fact is we need Antony. Egypt needs Antony. Just like before, we must secure a pact with Rome if we are to protect our Northern flank. Of the three so-called rulers since the death of Caesar, Antony appears to be the strongest. He is after all ruler of the eastern empire. Lepidus, who remains in Rome, is a foolish nonentity with no backbone. Octavius on the other hand, could become a threat, but as long as we can control Antony—well that's the plan isn't it? It is he who has called for this meeting. I am merely obeying his wishes."

"Majesty! But it is *you* who has chosen the time—the *manner* of your arrival. For five-hundred years Tarsus has been worshipped as the meeting place where Isis, the mother of gods, rules. You are Isis. You *are* a goddess."

The music suddenly changed. Six gold trumpets were now calling. The oarsmen reduced their stroke. From either side of the bow red jets of water erupted to splash into the mirror-like river. Scented petals, every color of the rainbow, were sprinkled on the surface by a dozen young maidens. The noise from the shore intensified.

Cleopatra moved. Maidens pumped up the cushions behind her. The black eunuchs continued their fanning. A maid readjusted her robe. Another passed her a golden goblet. She sipped the amber liquid. Noiselessly, in one perfect flow of movement eighty oars lifted, their silver tips reaching to the sky. Then, as one, they disappeared. The royal barge continued drifting forward. Its momentum slowed. The helmsman pushed with his steering oar. This was the most critical point of the entire three week voyage. Sweat covered his brow. His arms ached. He pushed—then pulled. He pushed again using the heavy oar to turn the cumbersome vessel.

The flow of water under the hull diminished. The royal barge slowly drifted sideways with the current broadside on to the landing stage. It was a perfect maneuver. Soaked in sweat the helmsman collapsed over his now useless steering oar. Pure white lines of braided rope were thrown to secure the craft. The music stopped. Flower petals ceased falling. All was silent.

"Your Majesty," Meryneith held out a gold tray. Posed upon it lay a small amethyst bottle. Carefully he removed the stopper. Cleopatra picked up the jar with her left hand. Placing her right-index finger over the top she allowed a drop of the amber liquid contained inside to flow onto her fingertip. Quickly, she dabbed her neck behind each ear. Returning her finger to the bottle she repeated the exercise. This time she touched the top of her cleavage, then allowed a drop to cascade down her stomach. Finally, she scented her wrists. She handed the bottle back to Meryneith.

She mocked. "That will do for the moment. I don't want to kill the man, do I?"

Ashore, a fanfare of trumpets blasted out. The clattering sound of armor grew as a column of men marched towards the barge. In front, his head adorned with a shining silver helmet from which projected a plume of scarlet feathers, strutted Antony. His body armor gleamed in the morning sun.

The trumpets ceased. A herald banged loudly three times on the wooden jetty with his mace, "The Emperor Marcus Antonius."

Cleopatra nodded. The gold silk shroud screening her was pulled back. She uncrossed her legs turning on her side. *The things I must do for my beloved Egypt*, she thought. She discretely smelt her wrist. She knew the secret fragrance would not let her down.

# Chapter One

## Chester England, the Present Day

The small courtroom was packed. The public seating was limited to primarily members of the alleged victim's family and friends. The only person supporting the accused was an old woman—his mother to be precise. Throughout the three-day trial she had sat resolutely bolt upright, glaring, dressed in the same shabby, outdated, green woolen coat. The same tatty yellow straw hat, with faded pink plastic roses, perched on her head. Black, straggly tufts of hair streaked with gray stuck out, giving the impression that hat and hair had been together for so long they were now inseparable.

The opposition, the alleged victim's supporters, in complete contrast flaunted the latest creations in vogue. It was summer, the hottest recorded July in decades. The UV warning factor was off the scale. This year flash flooding was not a problem. No rain had fallen for weeks. Water rationing had been imposed. The use of garden hoses was banned. Cars drove around dirty. Luscious verdant lawns were burnt brown and everyone was sweating, especially in courtroom B.

The solid old brick building was built long before the days of air-conditioning. Quite the opposite, cold was usually the problem; for this a system of antiquated radiators would gurgle and burp heated water in an attempt to stop the ink in the clerk's pen from freezing up in winter.

A series of electric fans had been procured in a futile effort to provide some form of relief from the heat, but all they succeeded in doing was to circulate the hot air whilst the droning noise they made added to the discomfort. The series of eight small windows inset high up on the outer wall necessitated closing after lunch and their black blinds pulled down in order to block out the sun's rays. It was as though the sun too, was trying to gain entry into this most unusual of trials.

The heat dictated to the fashion conscious supporters of the alleged victim that only the lightest and skimpiest of costume should be worn. Plunging golden cleavages, bronze shoulders, paler midriffs and long bare elegant legs were the order of the day. Outside the courtroom photographers lay in ambush to click, flash, then shout words of encouragement, none of which were really required: "Smile . . . Come on give us a bit of leg . . . more thigh . . . hold it . . . great."

But, within minutes of entering the courtroom and taking their seats mascara began to run. Tiny beads of perspiration appeared above lips and around the throat and neck. Hairless armpits became moist which necessitated their owners keeping their arms close to their body less the offending dampness be noticed. It all added to the discomfort. Graceful bare legs were crossed and uncrossed, bottoms shifted while tissues dabbed away at the offending perspiration inevitably smudging lipstick and staining facial creams.

Copious small bottles of only the costliest, purest mineral water or fashionable high-energy drink, each expensively packaged to resemble a giant baby's feeding bottle, were continuously sipped. Dehydration—"You must avoid dehydration"—was the buzzword. Bladders quickly filled up. Legs crossed and uncrossed. Teeth gritted. Concentration on what was being said or not being said waned. Eyes continuously searched the courtroom clock, willing it to speed up. Prayers were offered to any god who could persuade the judge to adjourn early.

The old lady in the outdated, green woolen coat and tatty yellow straw hat, with faded pink plastic roses, sat in the front row of the long wooden bench and glared. Completely oblivious to the panoply of young female beauty alongside her she glared down at the glamorous accuser and her council. She glared at the judge then the clerks. She glared at the jury. Never once did she appear to glare at her son, the defendant, except when he had taken the witness stand to be savagely attacked by the prosecuting council. As though immune to the heat, which was sapping everyone's energy, she just sat and glared. No perspiration, no discomfort appeared on her face, nor strangely enough did it appear on the defendant's.

Relief finally came. The judge had called a break in the proceedings. The small public gallery was upstairs. The toilets were downstairs. Then the real problem began. There were only two female cubicles. The men were adequately provided for, after all, in courts of law men usually outnumbered women twenty to one or more. "It is so unfair," the girls were heard to moan as they raced each other down the narrow wooden steps only to find themselves jostling for position in a queue.

"It's so unfair. All men have to do is pull it out then point it at the wall. They're in and out in seconds while we have to disrobe and squat. It's so unfair. Why don't they build more loos for women?" Of course what was not discussed was the need to spend a further ten minutes of precious time in reconstructing their damaged faces over the tiny cracked mirror. The back row was the luckiest. They could descend first. It was usually the fourth or fifth occupant who began to suffer the build up of smells, plus the lack of paper and soap.

But it was all worth it. "We've got to show solidarity with Kylie," they all agreed.

"I hope the bastard gets twenty years."

"Life—that's what he deserves."

"Cut his balls off if you ask me."

Outside, the press was waiting for them. More photographs, more poses; "One never knew if a casting agent or fashion house scout might be watching. Never miss an opportunity. Isn't that how Naomi Campbell, the lucky bitch, got started?" Lunch—food was not a priority. Pop a pill. Munch on a non-fattening health bar. It was essential to keep the weight down, the tummy tight and above all, guard against the celluloid.

Nobody watched the old lady in the outdated, green woolen coat and tatty yellow straw hat, with faded pink plastic roses exit the courtroom building. Few knew who she was, less even cared. Disappearing quickly around the corner she walked the two blocks to a small park where she sat herself down on a bench shaded under the canopy of a giant weeping willow tree. Out of her cavernous canvas bag she unfolded a red cloth tied at its four corners. Bread, cheese, home-made pickles were all laid out. Last, she removed a small glass perfume bottle. She unscrewed the top placing it down on the cloth.

Bringing her nose to the open neck she breathed in deeply. A bouquet of fragrances assailed her senses: first grapefruit, citron petit grain, then pine, sandalwood and finally absolute and jasmine. It cooled her body. It cleared her mind. Finally, using her right-index-finger she dabbed some of the potion behind her neck and ears. Not too much—it was important not to over do it—otherwise the affect would be cancelled. She just hoped her son remembered to do the same.

She would eat quickly, feed the remains to the ducks, then return to the courtroom. She could have visited her son—after all, he was not imprisoned—not yet. He had been allowed bail but they had agreed it was best they make no obvious contact. It was better that way. She could best support him from her position in the public gallery. She would have liked to have brought the toad to assist her but the possibility of having her bag searched and its subsequent discovery was not worth the risk.

The hour had quickly passed. Noisily, the plaintiff's supporters giggled and paraded themselves back into the courtroom. The old lady was already in her place ignoring them. They had previously asked themselves: "How has she managed not to die of heat wrapped up in that terrible rug of a coat?"

"I bet she must stink under all that."

"Probably hasn't washed for weeks."

"Months more likely."

"Must be a witch."

"That's right, a bloody old witch."

Then there was silence. The subject had been exhausted so the conversation changed to more mundane things: "Who was sleeping with who and which fashion house director was not queer?"

In complete contrast the plaintiff was dressed in a somber black suit. The white blouse buttoned to the neck. The skirt tailored just below the knee. She was hot, uncomfortable and completely overdressed but her council had insisted she dress with the maximum of propriety. "It will only help your case. Respectability is what the judge and jury will be looking for."

Not far away, perched in the defendant's box sat the defendant. A solitary bored court orderly sat behind him, a man who had great difficulty in keeping his eyes off the public gallery. The defendant's worn tweed sports jacket, with imitation brown leather patches sewn onto the elbows and cuffs, hung loosely off his narrow shoulders. A white shirt and brown tie concluded his drab garb. "Always best to dress down conservatively for the occasion," his defense council had advised.

Seated with his hands clasped gently on his lap, his bald head gleamed under the overhead light. Heavy, bifocal, old fashioned horn-rimmed glasses perched on his short stubby nose covering the upper part of his face. He showed no emotion. His eyes stared at the door through which the judge would enter. In spite of the heat or any nervousness he felt quite relaxed. It could be said he was even enjoying the trial. His mother's potion was working. The black drapes were drawn. The windows closed. The electric fans beat out their monotonous drone.

"All rise."

There was an instant scrapping of feet. The door at the back of the bench opened. With a flurry of red robes Judge William J. Sinclair swept into the room. He sat down. The room followed. Silence prevailed. The judge rearranged his papers. He looked up. The lamb curry he had enjoyed for lunch began to repeat on him. Already he was beginning to feel the heat. He hoped they could finish early. It was, after all, the final act.

"I now call on council to begin their closing arguments."

Courtroom B was in session.

# Chapter Two

## Paris, France

The bar was crowded. The dance floor packed. The Cameroonian disk jockey gyrated to the African beat grunting incomprehensibly into the microphone whenever the mood took him. Two young men squeezed their way towards the bar.

"Two Millers," Pierre held up two fingers and mouthed the word to the nearest girl serving. They watched her pivot around then stoop to open the fridge door. Her skimpy top rose exposing bare white skin. The low slung jeans revealed a red string thong underneath. The head of a snake was tattooed climbing out of her buttocks.

The bottles were banged down on the bar. The dream was suddenly broken. "Ten," she held up two hands. There was no sign of any wedding band. No offer was made to provide glasses.

"Cheers," Pierre raised his bottle.

"Cheers and good hunting," Jacques countered. The bottles touched with a click. They both drank. "Shit, that's good. The first is always the best."

"Come, let's move over to that far corner where there's a bit of space," replied Pierre. "We need to plan a strategy." They squeezed their way through the crowds and sat at an empty banquette.

"I never expected the place to be so crowded, not being July and half of Paris away on holiday."

"It's the air-conditioning," shouted back Pierre. "The Voodoo Lounge is one of the few fully air-conditioned bars. Everywhere else is sweltering on a night like this and anyway, this is where the action is. We might as well start here as anywhere."

"So, how do we go about this?" asked Jacques. "I've got the phials," and he touched his trouser pocket. "It all sounded so easy but now we are here . . . well . . . what now?"

Pierre glanced around the crowded room. "There's a table over there with six girls in a group, could be a hen party or something. Let's see if we can get a dance."

"With all six of them?"

"No, idiot, we'll ask only one at a time, but first we must prepare ourselves. Come . . . finish your beer. Let's go to the gents."

"See those two guys over there? No! Don't turn around, Samantha. I think their eyeing us up. Plucking up the courage me thinks."

"There're not bad looking. How old do you think they are twenty-five . . . twenty-six?" asked Bridgette.

"As long as they've got money?" added Susanne.

"Or their daddies?" remarked Simone.

"Prefer older men do you, Simone" and they all laughed. "I wonder if they're local. They don't look like tourists."

"Then they're definitely not rich or they would be sunning themselves on their yachts in Cannes instead of hanging around Paris. Shush, they're getting up. They've left their beers on the table. They're coming this way. Look down, everyone. Pretend we have not noticed them."

"Too late," laughed Bridgette. "They've gone to the loo."

They first went to a urinal. They took their time waiting for a third man to finish. Pierre looked around. "Come on. Quick! While it's empty, before anyone comes in—in case they get the wrong idea. Wash your hands," and he turned on the tap, "and the side of your face."

"Shit, there's no towel only a hot-air blower. I should have thought of that, still, it will just have to do." Turning his face he placed it under the nozzle. Pierre followed suit. Jacques removed two glass phials from his trouser pocket. He placed them on the washbasin. "Number One or Number Two? You call."

Pierre picked up the two glass phials. "Green or yellow, what's it to be? Yellow I think," and he handed the phial to Jacques.

"Number two it is." Jacques eased off the small rubber stopper. He poured a drop of the yellow liquid onto the palm of his left hand then quickly smeared it onto the side of his face. Changing hands he repeated the procedure. The small phial was half empty. "Your turn," and he returned the phial to Pierre.

Next, they combed their hair before flicking up the collars of their open-neck casual-shirts. Pierre opened his mouth to flash his teeth. "Right! I'm ready. Let's go," he declared. They re-entered the noisy room. One glance confirmed that the table of six girls was still seated.

"Good evening, ladies, may we be as bold as to ask if one of you beautiful creatures would accompany us to the dance floor." Pierre bowed sweeping his arm. The girls giggled. "Come now, gracious ladies, take pity on us mere male mortals, so besotted by your magnificence."

More giggles followed and the girls looked at each other. "If you dance with one you must dance with us all, those are the conditions," commanded Samantha.

Pierre looked at Jacques and winked. Again he bowed. "We rise to your challenge, mademoiselle."

"Do you now." Bridgette, who was seated in the middle, pointed at Simone. Go on, you're the nearest, Simone. You and Crystal go first." The girls hesitated. The boys offered their hands. Reluctantly, the girls stood up. Pierre led the way.

"What's your name?" Shouted Jacques as they both began to gyrate to the rhythm of the music.

"Crystal," came the reply.

"Please to meet you, Crystal," and Jacques smiled. Further conversation became impossible as the beat intensified.

Finally the heavy African tempo gave way to the more melodic sounds of Tracy Chapman. The DJ mumbled something over the sound system. The pace began to slow. Jacques took hold of Simone's hands. Their bodies touched then politely moved away as they danced slowly to the ballad. Jacques turned his cheek to ensure his partner could smell the fragrance. There was no obvious response.

Bob Marley took over. It was time to leave the dance floor. The two couples returned to the table. "Can we buy you ladies a drink?" asked Pierre.

The girls glanced at each other. "No thanks, we're all going Dutch," replied Samantha. "You're welcome to join us, but first, you must now dance with Julie and Susanne."

"What about you, Bridgette? You're next," retorted Crystal.

"While you girls are deciding I'm going to get a beer. We'll be back in a moment. Are you sure I can't bring anyone a drink?" Jacques winked at Pierre. "You go to the bar while I try the other phial."

Three minutes later Jacques returned. Pierre was still holding out a ten-Euro note in an attempt to get served. "Here, take this. I'll get the drinks," and he slipped the small phial into Pierre's hand. "Remember to wash off all traces of the first fragrance. Jacques took his place at the bar counter. A woman standing next to him turned to look at him. Her nose twitched.

"Two Millers please," the barmaid with the tattooed snake on her lower back swiveled around. She bent down to reach for the beers. The snake moved. She banged the two bottles down on the granite bar counter. Frothy gas poured out of the top to dribble down the neck. Jacques handed over the banknote. Their hands touched. The girl smiled. She hesitated. Her nose twitched. For a fleeting second a curious expression came over her face then she pivoted towards the electronic cash screen. She tapped in the order. The cash drawer opened as the receipt was being printed. She threw the money into the drawer before closing it. She ripped off the receipt and turned to face Jacques. Her hand shook slightly as she handed it over. Their fingers touched again. Her nose twitched.

Pierre pushed his way forward. The woman standing next to Jacques turned again. Ignoring her partner she smiled sheepishly at him and then Pierre. Her nose twitched. Her partner called. Turning to face him she blushed. The two boys maneuvered their way through the crowd back to the girls. "I hope I haven't overdone it. This one seems much stronger."

Jacques sniffed Pierre. "No, seems all right, but it does appear to be richer. In this one I used more vetivert, which gives it a woody fragrance."

They placed their beers on the table. The girls looked at them; this time more closely. "We thought you weren't coming back. We thought we'd scared you away," announced Bridgette and the girls laughed.

"A gentleman's word is his bond," countered Jacques. "So, which lovely lady is next?"

Pierre was leaning over Susanne. "I think it's me." Taking his hand she jumped up. Julie followed.

The South African band, Jaluka, was pounding out their sound. The floor was packed pushing the dancers closer to each other. It was inevitable. Bodies touched. In spite of the air-conditioning the dancers perspired. A girl started to rub up against Pierre, as she twisted and turned alongside him. She laughed then winked at him. A bead of perspiration appeared on Susanne's upper lip. Her nose twitched. She moved closer to him. Their arms found each other. The pace of the music intensified but their movements slowed. They kissed. Her tongue was in his mouth as she thrust her body closer to his. Her hips pushed into his loins in time to the music. Pierre felt a hardening coming on. She was arousing him. They're mouths pulled apart. They both sucked in the hot air.

Pierre stole a glance at Jacques. The same was happening to him except his partner had brought her leg up between his thighs. Somehow they were still spinning around in time to the music. Susanne's mouth returned to smother his face, a hand broke away. It began to rub his crutch, next it fumbled with his zip. "Take me away and fuck me. I want to feel you inside of me *now*," she muttered pulling her mouth off his. Out of the corner of his eye Pierre saw Jacque's partner pulling him off the dance floor. Somewhat mesmerized the two couples rushed towards the exit. Nobody looked back.

# Chapter Three

## Grasse, France

The boardroom was sterile white. The walls were painted glossy white except for one which was made of glass. No pictures, be they of the roaming countryside, or even of the many successful products launched over the years, broke the monotony. Grayish tiles covered the floor. The long boardroom table was imported from Murano in Italy; manufactured out of a solid sheet of white toughened glass. The accompanying white chairs were constructed from a molded plastic. They were uncomfortable—deliberately so. "Minimalism is the way to go. It helps to focus the mind." This was the instruction given to the designer in conjunction with the Feng Shui advisor selected by the Chairman's latest mistress.

One by one they filed in each selecting their usual place. The larger chair at the head of the table remained empty. It was reserved for the Director of Marketing, Jean-Luc Picard. He would arrive late—five minutes "To give the troops time to settle down," he liked to tell his secretary.

Hervé Duronzier, Head of Merchandising, was the first to speak. "Does anyone have any idea how long this meeting is scheduled to last?"

Mutterings of "Don't know. Who cares" and "about half an hour" echoed around the room.

"Well I've got one hell of a day. Can you believe it? Production has informed: there's a problem with the screw-top of the mimosa range bottles. After all the meetings we've had to finally come up with a design. Now it looks as though we'll have to start all over again. It bloody well pisses me off." Hervé whipped a lilac silk handkerchief from inside his jacket cuff to dab the bead of perspiration that had appeared on his forehead. Retaining it in his hand he gesticulated to the room. "And as if that isn't enough the wretched printers have buggered up the spelling of our La Coque promotion to run next month at Au Printemps."

"What have they done?" asked Edmond Bajulaz, the Head of Market Research.

"What have they done? What have they done?" cried Hervé. "They've only printed La Coque as *La Cock*," and he banged both fists down on the table in frustration.

"That is a bugger up," remarked Denise Vergé, trying desperately to contain her smile. Looking down she opened the white leather-bound folder embossed in gold with the company's name—Essence de la Grasse.

"You can laugh. It's all right for you in management. You don't have to deal with the buyers," retorted Hervé, and he touched the pink rose attached to his pale blue suit as if to comfort it.

The door to the boardroom opened. Jean-Luc Picard marched in closely followed by his secretary, Madam Pommé. "Gentlemen, lady, good morning. Where's Christine Guérard?"

"She sends her apologies. She's meeting with Air France to discuss their winter duty free promotions," offered Madam Pommé.

"Yes, of course, very well then. I know you are all frightfully busy." Hervé raised his hand. The lilac handkerchief fluttered while Hervé's mouth opened.

Jean-Luc cut him short. He too raised his hand. The ten-carat diamond ring on his little finger glistened in the artificial light. "Yes, I know all about, your problem, Hervé, but we are not going to talk about this now. I have a far more pressing matter, The Chairman . . ."

Denise Vergé could hardly contain her laugher as she discretely coughed into her hand. Jean-Luc shot her a frustrating glance.

Hervé squirmed in his chair. "*Nothing* could be a greater disaster than the mimosa bottles."

Jean-Luc ignored the utterance. The heavy gold identity-chain on his wrist clattered against the glass tabletop as he lowered his arm. "The Chairman . . . The Chairman has asked me to call this meeting as a matter of utmost urgency. The board is very concerned. We are losing market share in both the female and male perfume and cologne markets."

Hervé's mouth dropped. Perspiration clung to his brow. Denise Vergé sat bolt upright. A sudden shock of possible retrenchments ran through her brain. Edmund Bajulaz leaned forward staring at Jean-Luc. Forced early-retirement, a reduced pension and his crippling mortgage bond became top of mind. The others present around the table concentrated on his every word. It did not come as a surprise. Rumors about possible cost cuts had been circulating for months. Job losses would be inevitable.

Grasse, located only fifteen kilometers from Cannes in the south of France, had been the world's perfume capital for over 200-years. The rolling hillsides virtually exploded with the fragrance of citronella and tea rose. A handful of houses created the fragrances for the world's top fashion names.

The ever-spiraling oil prices, not to mention power shortages, were fuelling worldwide inflation. The consumer's disposal income was diminishing at an ever-increasing rate. The American economy was in recession, again. Money, which might previously have bought expensive perfumes, was being channeled elsewhere. The constantly-changing electronics market was siphoning off customers. Computers, digital cameras, portable DVD-players, cell-phones and all the 1001 accessories which go with them was where the money was being spent in the duty-free shops.

Customers were purchasing cheaper products. The market was becoming very price conscious. The classical brand names were all feeling the pinch—even Chanel, Dior, Givenchy, Guerlain, Gucci, Hèrmes, Cardin, Balmain and a host of other top names were reporting a drop in sales. It was not as though the public had stopped buying perfumes. The fact was the global market was growing by eight percent per annum. New markets; China, Eastern Europe and South America were opening up. The problem was the traditional American and European markets were down-trading. Cheaper fragrances, manufactured using artificially created essences in laboratories, were outselling handmade traditional perfumes. Lobbyists, and an armada of animal-rights activists, had ensured that popular perfumes no longer contained glands from the male husk deer or the perineal gland of the civet. Even ambergris, the Rolls Royce of base notes, was deliberately boycotted.

The fact that these new *cheaper* fragrances had little or no staying power did not seem to deter the consumer. They just had to use more of it. Perhaps it all had something to do with the disposable society in which the modern world now lived. Everything seemed to have a limited life span and this had flowed into the traditional world of perfumery.

The longevity of a good perfume was traditionally obtained by using the resin of trees, such as frankincense and myrrh, or even lichen, such as oak moss growing on the bark. Balsams, on the other hand, obtained by cutting and bleeding the bark, provided a cinnamon or vanilla scent. But these traditional methods were expensive, which all added to the cost of production.

Effleurage, the classical French method of extracting essences from flowers, was no longer used. The earliest alchemists had invented the process of coating glass plates with clear neutral fat or oil-soaked rags, onto which the flower petals were laid. Once it was deemed, that all essence had been extracted, a fresh supply of flowers was introduced. The process could be repeated 10-15 times until the fat had become saturated with the volatile products. It was both costly and time consuming but it produced the best results.

Today, solvent extraction had replaced *effleurage*. Hexane, a liquid solvent, was circulated over the flowers inside a hermetically sealed container to dissolve the natural oils. A sticky substance called *concrete* was formed, which when immersed in ethanol (pure alcohol), dissolved the wax resulting in a highly aromatic liquid—absolute. Quick, efficient and cost affective 'but not yielding the same result' claimed the purists.

Jean-Luc was in full stride. He knew he had everybody's undivided attention even Hervé's. "So, you see we are not alone. Our competitors, Fragonard, Mollinard and even Galimard are all feeling the pinch. The market is changing and, if we are to survive, we must meet these changes."

"Couldn't we consider cutting prices to increase sales—cheaper packaging perhaps? After all, the cost of the bottles and boxes of some of our creations is treble the cost of the actual contents," suggested Denise Vergé.

"Over my dead body," shouted Hervé Duronzier, banging his fist down hard on the glass table. The water jug next to him jumped splashing water over its brim. "I suppose that is want you want anyway. Even the village idiot knows merchandising *is* the product. It starts with the packaging. It must be seductive, promising, daring the buyer to open it to see what is hidden inside. Then, like opening a Fabergé Egg, a priceless jewel is revealed, tantalizing, teasing, appealing, irresistible. Now there is no going back. The bridges have been burnt. The point of no return has been passed. There is only one thing left—to open this most wondrous of objects and to breathe in its heavenly nectars." Hervé sat back in his chair perspiring. Gasping for air he dabbed his brow with the lace handkerchief content he had labored his point.

Denise leaned forward in her chair. At twenty-nine she was half his age—a graduate of the Sorbonne, where she had mastered in business science and marketing. A newcomer to the perfume industry, she was appointed not just because of her natural good looks and charm, but for possessing modern business acumen. The board, much to the chagrin of the traditionalists, deemed it prudent to appoint someone from outside the closed-confines of the industry. Almost from day one she found herself crossing swords with the purists and Hervé ranked as a super-conservative traditionalist in her book.

"I suppose that is why Chanel No. 5, in its plain white box and square unadorned bottle, has been the number-one best seller since 1921, grossing over a billion dollars."

Hervé glowered at her. "Chanel . . . Coco Chanel . . . what could you," and he gesticulated his manicured fingers in her direction, "possibly know about her?"

Before he could continue Jean-Luc shouted him down.

"Enough! Enough I say. Petty squabbling will get us nowhere."

"She started it."

"That is enough, Hervé. I do not want to hear any more. Yes, packaging. We need to look at that too. Where we can save money but *not,* and I shall repeat, *not* cheapen the image of the product. Remember," and he focused his gaze on Denise. "Discounting is a very dangerous game to play in a top-end market like ours. The superior brand must always carry the heavier price tag. If you aspire to drive a Ferrari, a Lamborghini or a Bentley you must pay the price. There are plenty of other cars just as fast. Some might even be prettier and more comfortable but they do not carry the badge. That is what the driving-connoisseur is paying for.

"Twenty-year-old Remy Martin is just that. Like fifteen-year-old Glenfiddich Single Malt Whisky it means that when you sip the amber nectar it has lain for all those years in casks of oak. The imbiber is transported to another world— one of dusty cellars, old men with long-flowing blue aprons and elongated tasting glasses. These products can never be discounted. To do so would be to destroy them. If you cannot afford them, if you cannot subscribe to them, there is always a cheaper alternative on the market.

"Gentlemen, Ladies, as the marketing department we must be creative. It is the opinion of the Board that the time is opportune for us to create a new exciting brand of perfume. Like our competitors we supply the base product to the established fashion houses. They put their name to it. Many prepare their own packaging and marketing material. However, their changing fortunes affect our business. When they do well we do well. When they do badly . . . well, we all know the answer to this one."

Jean-Luc removed a blank sheet of white paper from his folder. He held it up for all to see. "What is this?" Nobody answered. "This . . . is a sheet of white paper. It is blank. There is nothing on it. This is where I want you all to start. You must have no preconceived ideas. Now write this down . . . all of you," and he glanced especially at Hervé.

"Our mission—is to conceive a range of perfumes for the future which must become our top selling brand into the next decade. All got that," and he glanced around the table. "Good. How are we going to do this? Edmond, as Head of Market Research you will drive this. You will go out into the market. You will conduct research which informs us: What fragrances does the modern-day consumer want? What colors turn them on most? What price are they prepared to pay? What should it look like? There are more, many more questions, which I'm sure you will come up with. Split the research into age groups. The young adults of today will be the middle-aged consumers of tomorrow. Will they continue to support Gucci, Lagerfeld, Hugo Boss and Ralph Lauren's Polo Brand, or will they move, if so, to what brand?"

"What about production, do they have any particular senses they are working on?" asked Edmond.

"That is exactly my point." Jean-Luc again held up the blank sheet of paper. "Instead of us creating some magical new fragrance then spending hours deliberating what shape bottle we should use—how it opens and closes—whether the box should look rustic or eastern, we will have all the answers to tell production."

"What's the budget? How much is allocated for marketing, over and above the launch? We all know how costly this is."

To emphasis his point Jean-Luc picked up the blank sheet of paper again. "Like I said, you tell us, Hervé. But what I can say is we shall not try to compete with Lacroix's C'est La Vie". He turned to face Denise. "Forty million dollars they lost. Our industry is famous for blowing away vast sums of money in launching a new fragrance which nobody wants."

"Cher, Sophia Loren, Pelé the footballer, and Armani's Giò, are just some of the names which spring to mind," offered Edmond Bajulaz.

"Don't forget Amphibia. A scent with green notes, as though naming a perfume after Kermit the Frog would sell. I told you all at the time. I remember saying . . ."

"Thank you, Hervé; I believe you have made your point. The fact is: this new range will be market driven not product driven. So, unless you have anymore questions I suggest we close this meeting." He glanced at his secretary. "How's my diary look same time next week?"

Madame Pommé glanced up from her notes. "It's clear, Monsieur Picard."

"Good! So there you have it. First report back meeting in one week."

"That doesn't give me much time," complained Edmund Bajulaz.

"Enough for a progress report," replied Jean-Luc.

# Chapter Four

## Chester, England

There was no relief in the heat wave. If anything it was hotter than ever. It was the fourth and final day of the trial. The morning session had opened with Judge William J Sinclair's summing up of the case then, the jury departed the courtroom to make their deliverance. Bets circulated amongst the packed public gallery.

"They'll be back within the hour with a guilty verdict."

"I'm not so sure. I think they'll take longer than that."

"What happens if they are split? Does that mean a retrial?"

The old lady in the outdated, green woolen coat and tatty yellow straw hat, with faded pink plastic roses, sat patiently at the end of the front row. She waited for everyone to leave before she quietly made her way out, down the stairs and out of the courtroom. Outside in the sunlight the press was busy photographing the alleged victim's followers. Ignoring everyone she walked purposely away towards the river.

The old Roman walls of the ancient town of Diva Castra, established in 79 AD, guarded the approach to the river. Groups of obedient foreign tourists, their necks straining under a burden of cameras; their stomachs extended by the obligatory moon bag carrying all their worldly possessions, trailed behind their tour leaders. Some guides were dressed the part of a Roman centurion carrying mock shields and spears. Other groups comprised parents tugging along recalcitrant children. Every now and then the guides stopped to point out some salient feature or to convey some priceless piece of historical information.

She paused for a moment to check her time against the famous Eastgate Clock. Sitting proudly, high up on a sandstone arch, built to commemorate Queen Victoria's diamond jubilee—a time when the sun never set on the British Empire. It was twenty-two seconds fast.

It was a beautiful July morning—hot, and the school holidays. Every craft which floated had been put to use ferrying visitors up and down the busy river. Large streamlined river cruisers vied with tiny motorized boats for space. Long pencil-thin rowing boats speeded past on the opposite bank. The sound of the Coxswain's voice to "Pull" echoed across the river. The ice cream vendors were out in full force. It was Christmas Day for the river's birdlife as they feasted upon the comestible delicacies thrown to them by excited holidaymakers.

The old lady in the outdated, green woolen coat and tatty yellow straw hat, with faded pink plastic roses stood to watch a dozen white swans glide elegantly by. Nearby, two mothers, occupying a bench overlooking the river, offered to make space for her to sit as they watched their children playing down by the water. The old lady thanked them. The bench was one of the few shaded from the sun by the overhanging branches of a willow tree. She sat at one end grateful to take the weight off her feet. The walk from the courtroom had lasted half an hour. It would take her the same amount of time to return. She could not afford to be late. She must be there when the verdict was returned although she felt she knew what the outcome would be.

Fumbling inside her cavernous canvas bag she extracted a cell phone. Next she removed a spectacle case. It snapped open to reveal a pair of old tortoise-shell glasses. Adjusting the spectacles on her nose she peered closely at the phone. It was switched on. There were no messages. She rarely used it. She had little use for one. Her son had given it to her. He had demonstrated how it worked and all the different functions it could perform, none of which interested her. "Use it for emergencies," he had said. "You'll never know when you'll need one."

She was using it now. This was an emergency—her son's wretched trial. Deliberately, she had befriended the clerk of the court. At first he had been cold and aloof wanting nothing to do with her. His red runny nose, persistent nagging cough and sore throat, indicated to her he was suffering from severe hay fever and possibly summer flu. There was a lot of it about. The pollen count, like the UV factor, was the highest recorded in years. On the second morning of the trial she arrived early baring a small jar of cream and bottle of green liquid. Reluctantly, he had taken it from her promising to use it immediately.

Perhaps it was the irritating parade of young female flesh and their constant banter of trivial remarks or their callous flirting with the press which upset the Clerk. It might have been the old lady's medication which had soothed his tortured sinuses but by the afternoon he had befriended her. Naturally, he must be seen to be impartial; "But these young girls these days . . . you know the way they dress . . . well, it's scandalous . . . no wonder there is such an increase in rape."

The old lady could only agree with him. "How correct you are," she had replied, "and how nice you keep your courtroom. It is so clean and tidy considering the types that frequent it." Unlike the others, no complaints about inadequate female ablutions came from her mouth.

"Of course I'll phone you, love," he had said, "once the jury has reached a verdict. There's usually a delay, sometimes up to an hour before they're returned to the courtroom. I'll send you an SMS, that'll give you plenty of time to get back. You're going to the river; you say . . . well, you enjoy yourself. With a bit of luck there should be some breeze down there. I'd love to come with you but I've got to stay here."

The old lady placed the phone on her lap. She did not wish to risk placing it back in her bag lest she failed to hear it. Her eyes glanced at the morning's paper, which one of the mothers had discarded on the floor. She asked politely if she may borrow it.

The headlines bored her. The opposition in parliament was accusing the government of failing to do anything to stem the ever-increasing flow of illegal immigrants. A school in Birmingham was being investigated for refusing to teach the English language. Mohamed al-Fayed was claiming fresh evidence had come to light which proved the Royal Family had contacted Russian hit men to kill his son and Lady Diana. She turned to page two. Another Catholic priest was accused of committing unlawful acts with choir boys in Washington. The new English soccer coach had begun English lessons and was not unduly worried about the team's recent loss by five goals to Greenland.

It was on page three. "Verdict expected today in top fashion model rape trial. Will Archibald Crumpet be found guilty? What really happened on that spring night in March? How did this man have sex with top fashion model Kylie Moon?" The old lady put the paper down. She looked out across the busy waters. A pleasure cruiser, loaded with waving passengers, was chugging up river. One of the mothers seated next to her was calling to the children—to stop whatever it was they were doing. A picture of Archibald, her son, flashed into her mind. Such a good boy he would never rape a woman. He could never hurt anyone. Just look at the way he doted over the cats. Anyway, soon this wretched thing would be behind them then they could both go home to the cottage in Beeston—she to her garden and Archibald to his antiques.

She returned to reading the paper. "The question the jury must ask is: did top fashion model and beauty queen, Kylie Moon, willingly have sex with a bald-headed, potbellied, middle-aged man, half her size, in the back of a Ford Transit Van down a leafy country lane? Or did the accused forcibly drag her into the vehicle in order to have his evil way? How come the alleged victim showed no sign of any bruising? No forensic evidence has been produced that any drug or intoxicating substance was used? We leave it to the judge and the jury to decide."

There was a picture of the van as well as Archibald walking up the stairs to the courtroom. His baldhead was hidden under the hat she had told him to wear. It was to cover his scalp from the sun. The poor boy had always suffered from delicate skin. The slightest rays of the sun turned him red as a lobster.

The old lady put the paper down. The women were calling to their children to come. They were finally leaving. The old lady was about to consult her pocket watch but one of the mothers answered her unasked question. "Come, Timothy and Julie, its twelve o'clock and time for us to go." Protests emanated from down by the water's edge.

The Clerk had informed if no verdict was reached by midday, which was unlikely, then the court would not be called back before two o'clock. The mothers and children were departing. She held out the paper to them. "Keep it, we've finished with it," the woman replied.

Reaching once more into the depths of her bag she brought out a plastic container. With difficulty she pulled off the airtight lid to reveal her lunch—egg mayonnaise sandwiches on whole-wheat bread. A young couple sat next to her. They had not asked if she minded. Typical of youth today she thought—inconsiderate no thought for others.

Slowly she munched her sandwich while all the time looking out across the river. There was so much activity, not like in winter, when the ducks and swans had the whole place to themselves. These days she rarely visited Chester. She had no reason. The fact was she hardly ever left the confines of her cottage and her rambling garden with all its hidden secrets tucked away in the Cheshire countryside.

She worried about her son. She had made him his favorite lunch—two rounds of tinned tuna sandwiches, a hard boiled egg and a slice of her own home baked Melton Mowbray Pie with Branson Pickles to go with it. She had to admit: he was coping very well—the naughty boy. She had warned him enough times. "Be careful use it sparingly—too much and . . ."

Cigarette smoke was drifting towards her. The young couple was smoking. They must only be in their late teens she thought—the silly idiots. At least Archibald had never smoked not that she would ever have permitted him. He was such a quiet boy—a man really—soon approaching fifty-five, that made her? She shuddered.

He had never married. She had seen to that. He had had his share of girl friends over the years. But the moment one of them showed any sign of turning a casual relationship into something more permanent she had quickly stepped in and put a stop to it. Well she had to. She needed him at home with her. That was the way it was supposed to be.

A young family walked in front of her towards the river. They stopped halfway. The father threw a brown chequered rug to cover the grass. The mother put down a wicker picnic basket. Two boys and girl began to help unpack the food. How nice, she thought, how very-well behaved. Archibald had always been polite. He still was. His only weakness was women. She blamed her long-departed husband. It was his fault. The poor boy had inherited his insatiable appetite for members of the opposite sex. It was all in the genes—not hers.

At first she had learned to ignore her husband's philandering ways, but when he started to bring his harlots back to the cottage—her cottage—well, she had to put a stop to it for Archibald's sake. The boy was only five when his father disappeared. Nobody in the village was surprised. None of them liked Cornel, except that Henderson woman, the one he had been conducting a clandestine affair with. As far as the world was concerned her husband had run away, deserting his young son and poor wife. Everyone had been most considerate. Many had come to comfort her.

"Don't worry," they had said, "there's plenty more fish in the sea."

"You're still young."

"Mr. Right will come marching around the corner any day soon. You mark my words."

She did mark her long-dead neighbor's words. Mr. Right never did arrive, not that she cared. There was young Archibald to bring up. The years passed. Archibald grew into a nice young man. He had always exhibited an interest in history. On leaving school he had gone to work in the village with Mr. Jones who restored antique furniture. Jones had died over ten years ago. He had no family so her son inherited the small antique shop. The business continued as usual. It was no goldmine but provided a regular income. She turned her head to study the high city walls behind her built all those years ago. Archibald would have loved to be here now. He could probably tell her so much about the history. He was such a clever boy. She hoped he had eaten all his lunch and remembered to dab his skin with her cooling potion. It would also help to calm him should those nasty people say bad things about him again.

She reached into a bag. This time she withdrew a plate, then a knife and finally a juicy fresh peach, picked from her garden that morning. Using the knife she carefully cut a slice. She brought it to her mouth. A droplet of fresh juice dropped down onto her coat. She ignored it. Her mouth filled with peachy flavors. This year had seen an exceptional crop. The two trees had thrived. By right they should have died a long time ago, but for some reason they survived, producing bumper crop after bumper crop year after year. She had planted them as young saplings just after her husband disappeared all those years back. She chuckled to herself. It must be the fertilizer I used; at least the bastard has done some good in our lives.

Her reverie was suddenly disrupted by the ringing of the phone. She dropped the peach. Her sticky fingers fumbled to pick it up. She pressed a button. Nothing happened. The shrill noise continued. She pressed another button. There was silence. Gently, she lifted the phone up to her spectacles. Squinting her eyes she sat staring at the damn thing.

She thought the symbol of a little yellow envelope had appeared in the top right corner of the minuscule screen. That meant she had received a message. She froze. What button should she touch? They were all so close together. They said nothing to her. If she pressed the wrong one the message might be lost forever.

"Can I help you?"

It was the young girl seated next to her.

The old lady said nothing. The young girl shifted closer to her. "Come . . . let me help you."

For once the old lady was too embarrassed to speak.

The girl reached out for the phone. The old lady did not move. The girl's voice was soft and kind. Gently, she took the phone from the old lady's hand. "You've got a new message." The girl's thumb moved mysteriously. "Here, shall I read it to you or would you prefer to read it yourself?"

"You read it," the old lady replied.

"Court back in session two-thirty" and the girl handed the phone back. "It's stored in the memory so you can recall it again. Would you like me to send a reply for you?"

The old lady shook her head. "No thank you, you're most kind," and she dropped the phone into her bag. It was time to leave. Wearily, she stood up. From her bag she removed another peach. She offered it the young girl. "Here, have this, I misjudged you."

The girl took the peach in her hand. "Ooh! It's lovely. Thank you so much," she replied, but the old lady was already making her way back to the courthouse.

"I wonder what she meant by 'I misjudged you,'" asked the young boy.

"No idea," replied the girl. "Shame, the poor old soul reminds me of my grandmother. She too battles to use the phone my father gave her."

"Does your grandmother go around in an old winter coat in the middle of summer?"

"No silly" and she cuddled up closer to him. "Strange, I never noticed what she was wearing."

The old lady walked steadfastly across the grass back towards the town. "Silly me," she mumbled to herself. "I've never received a phone message before."

The windows were closed. The blinds were drawn. The courtroom was as hot as ever. She was early. She took her usual place and waited. One by one the accuser's entourage noisily made their way up the stairs. The prosecuting team was next, followed by the jury. The old lady carefully studied they faces. They were different this time. The look of anxiety, of carrying some onerous burden, was gone. They appeared more relaxed somehow content. They had reached a decision—the right decision.

Her son entered, closely followed by the bored-looking court orderly. A hush fell over the packed courtroom. All eyes watched him take his seat. Then, as if on cue the conversations continued, this time louder. The old lady looked down towards her son, for a second their eyes met and she knew he had taken her potion. Like her he was cool and calm unlike the rest.

The door behind the judge's bench opened.

"All rise."

The moment of judgment had finally arrived.

# Chapter Five

## Paris, France

Pierre Nimier placed the small glass phial in his hand. He studied it carefully holding it up to the light. "It's darker more golden," he remarked. Carefully, he wrapped it in a sheet of bubble wrap before placing it gently in his shoulder bag.

"Yes, I've used more ambergris and added nutmeg to the top note as well as mimosa for the middle note. It's more concentrated, so use it sparingly. It's all I've managed to make. Let's see if this one works the same."

Pierre grinned, "So do I. What pity you can't come. Are you sure?"

His friend, Jacques Gavotte, shrugged his shoulders. He rubbed his hands down the front of his stained white laboratory coat. "I've got to complete this last distillation and clear everything up." He turned gesticulating at the muddled array of glass bottles, pipettes, beakers and jars which cluttered the large dining room table. "Phone me tomorrow on my cell. Let me know how it went—if there was any reaction. I'll be at the laboratory all day, so will not get back here until tomorrow evening."

Pierre turned. He walked towards the apartment door, slid back each of the five bolts and pulled hard on the handle. The heavy door opened. "Are you sure you won't come? It's better with two."

"No, you go. It will take me at least three hours to finish and anyway I'm still recovering from the other night."

Pierre left the room closing the door behind him. He heard Jacques slide the bolts as he began his descent of the staircase. The small garret flat located in the 5ème district of Paris was a popular area for students to find cheap accommodation. The Sorbonne was around the corner as well as numerous cheap bars and cafes. On the negative side an ever-increasing number of immigrants had moved in over the past decade many from North Africa. Crime had risen and with it the inevitable problem of growing racial tension.

The flat suited Jacques who having completed his PHD in chemistry had been offered a position by the university in their research department. One of the giant pharmaceutical companies had engaged them to conduct research into how the body's olfactory senses relate to pheromones, the biological substances which affect biorhythms. It was a massive project. It could take years—forever, just as long as the money continued to roll in.

For a warm Sunday evening the streets of Paris were relatively quiet. July and August were strange months. Half the city's population took the month of July for their annual vacation while the remainder took August. This left Paris deserted. Businesses and shops closed for either of the two months. Paris was abandoned to the tourists while its citizens headed north, south, east or west, anywhere, just so long as it was out of the city. It was Pierre's favorite time of the year. He loved the city, the vibe, the excitement the constant action.

He was born in the sleepy historic town of Bayonne, only a few kilometers from Biarritz, down in the south close to the border with Spain. Famous for its chocolates his parents ran a small patisserie. Like many in the town they rose early and were in bed by eight each night. His father was a fifth generation Basque and sympathized with his Spanish cousins across the border. Unlike them he had no desire for Bayonne to become part of a separate Basque state but remained proactive in supporting the use of the Basque language, the only indigenous non-Indo-European dialect spoken in Western Europe.

Much to his father's regret Pierre did not support these views. He showed no interest in learning the family trade and joining the business. This he left to his younger sister. After leaving school he chose to travel, "To broaden my education" was his excuse. Two years of trekking around the world, sleeping in youth hostels and under tents brought him into contact with a diverse bunch of humanity.

On finally returning to France—penniless, two weeks at home in Bayonne was sufficient time for him to realize his future lay farther north in the big city—Paris. A series of jobs: waiting at tables, cooking pasta in an Italian restaurant, delivering pizzas helped him to survive until one day, in a bar in the fourth arrondissement, he met Jacques. They had nothing in common. They came from different backgrounds yet somehow they immediately hit it off. Jacques was an academic, born of scholastic parents. He had never traveled out of France, not even across the border to neighboring Switzerland. It was Jacques who suggested Pierre enroll in a computer course. It would give him the basic certificate with which he could obtain a job in the ever-expanding IT industry.

Tall, good looking, energetic with a permanent suntanned complexion inherited from his Basque parents Pierre quickly moved up the ladder. Unlike conventional industries young technicians working in the computer world changed jobs and allegiances overnight. Technology was advancing in massive leaps and bounds transforming the business world. He found himself working with all the big international system providers—Dell, IBM, Oracle, Panasonic, HP to name but a few. They all competed to obtain the next big installation, the next big upgrade. It was dog eat dog, and like the wild dog there were days of plenty when the entire pack ate well but then inevitably followed days of hunger. Together with two colleagues, Pierre formed their own company offering their services and technical knowledge as independent consultants to both suppliers and customers alike.

The money he earned enabled him to raise the deposit on a small two-bedroom flat two streets removed from the futuristic-looking Parc André Citroën, where his office was located. His knowledge of chemistry was basic—four years of high school. However, Jacques's dabbling in fragrance manufacture had fascinated him. The more Jacques told him of the research he was doing the more interested Pierre became.

The home laboratory had started because of a dare. It was a Friday night. The two young men had found themselves at a stag party. A friend of Jacques's was getting married the following day. The habitual stripper had completed her lackluster act of removing her clothes. With the money safely tucked into her purse she had made a speedy exit under the watchful eye of her six-foot-eight protector. The conversation became embroiled around the subject of women. Why, on the one hand, did they all play so hard to get, while on the other, when finally conquered they became so possessive, sometimes, almost impossible to ditch? What was needed was an aphrodisiac drug—something which turned them on today, but allowed them to forget all about it tomorrow. Jacques was a chemist. The question was asked: surely the university could spend some of its time searching for such a substance rather than spending all its resources searching for a cure for cancer or aids? After all, there were plenty of other research centers in the world doing just that.

From the flat they had staggered off to a bar, then another. The more the beer flowed the easier it became to solve the world's problems. Finally, on being asked to leave by the proprietor of a shady cellar bar in Montmartre the dye was cast. Jacques, assisted by Pierre, would astound the world by producing the perfect potion—"the Devil's fragrance" they would call it.

That was six months ago. Jacques, egged on by Pierre, for reasons he never really understood, began to experiment. Necessary equipment was purchased; some of it was *borrowed* from the university laboratories. The raw materials were easily obtained from local markets and pharmacies – other, less common ingredients, were again *borrowed*.

They had produced a mélange of exotic smells. On more than one occasion Jacque's concierge had threatened eviction when obnoxious odors had poured out under the door. Some of the aromas were actually pleasant and when placed in a fancy-looking bottle, which they acquired from local flea-markets made quite acceptable gifts. But no "woman slayer" had yet evolved until last week.

The air was warm. Heat still rose off the tarmac adding to the discomfort. Pierre thought of taking the Metro perhaps to the Champs Elysées. There would be thousands of tourists strolling along this famous boulevard, shopping, window-shopping and enjoying refreshments at one of the many overpriced cafes and bars whilst they watched the world pass them by. Tomorrow was Monday, a busy day, the start of a new contract. Pierre needed to be up early and at his best if they were to commence the upgrade of the bank's data storage system. The job was scheduled to take ten days but he felt if they could burn the midnight oil the task could be completed before the weekend. This would not only earn him a hefty bonus but would enable him to enjoy some leisure time. No, he decided he could not afford a late night.

His feet pounded the pavement as he headed towards the Metro Maubert Mutualité. He checked his watch. It was already seven-thirty. He hesitated. The River Seine was only one block away. There would hopefully be a breeze. His mind was made up. He waited with a crowd of pedestrians for the traffic lights to change so he could cross the wide Boulevard St-Germain.

The temperature was the same by the river but the glistening black water had a physiological affect. It allowed the overheated Parisians and tourists to think they were cooler. Large restaurant boats glided down the Seine with every window open to encourage the manmade breeze. Their wakes threw aside plastic bottles, stained white blocks and bubbles of polystyrene foam that littered the river, pushing the debris to the side of the quay where it bobbed up and down with soiled sheets of plastic.

A professional dog-walker led a string of well-manicured dogs on their evening sojourn. Their owners were no doubt sunning themselves on the beaches of Corsica or the Côte d'Azur. Toy poodles struggled to keep up with their taller cousins. Pekinese waddled. Pugs shuffled along while on the outside, two elegant Egyptian greyhounds strutted nobly with their long snouts arrogantly projected forward. Two focused Basset Hounds pounded the pavement, their long wet black noses sniffing and analyzing a mélange of odors, while their floppy ears brushed the ground channeling the smells. Every now and then the pack would stop as one after another an anus strained to deposit its load. From the walker's backpack a plastic bag would suddenly appear, together with a small scoop, and the offending poop would be removed to be deposited in the nearest refuse container.

Elderly couples strolled sedately. Young lovers meandered, their arms intertwined, hands touching bottoms or bare midriff. Pierre walked not concerned where he was heading or even what he intended to do. The plan had been to test out the latest batch, which Jacques had spent the entire weekend producing. It amazed Pierre just how great a quantity of raw ingredients were required to produce a tiny phial of perfume, not to mention the time it took.

He was approaching the Garden of Sculptures. An empty bench came into view. Pierre sat down to take in the scene. His stomach informed it required some attention. He thought of catching the nearest metro home. He could grab a pizza or takeaway from the corner shop next to his apartment. It stayed open until ten. If he retraced his steps there were plenty of small bistros and places to eat.

From his bag he removed the small phial. Carefully, he unscrewed the glass stopper. Intending to dab a little of the golden liquid onto his fingers it half-emptied onto his hand. There was nothing for it to but to dab his cheeks and neck. There was still enough for his forehead. He replaced the top and returned the phial to his bag. Jacques was correct. This second batch did smell stronger. He smelt his hands then rubbed them on his trousers. He hoped he hadn't overdone it.

Another dog-walker was approaching. This time a man strained to control two Dobermans, an Alsatian, a Border Collie and three other exotic breeds, whose names Pierre could never remember. The lead Doberman's nose began to twitch. Canine heads turned to glare at Pierre seated on the bench. The dogs were twenty meters away and closing fast. The Doberman howled. The others quickly followed. The man tugged at the leads like an Eskimo trying to rein in his huskies except these dogs were under no load. The man shouted. The dogs barked. Pierre sat transfixed as the wild pack advanced upon him. From out of his pocket the walker fumbled for an object placing it in his mouth. Suddenly, the dogs stopped barking. Their pulling ceased. The Doberman whined. The Alsatian whimpered. They turned in circles trying to understand where the shrill noise, which was so disturbing them, was coming from.

Having finally got the pack under control they hurried past. The walker shot a worried glance at Pierre. The Doberman bitch looked curiously at him as its nose continued to twitch. A woman waved to the man. He acknowledged her as best he could. The woman approached the bench. She glanced at Pierre who moved over to the left indicating she was welcome to join him. He estimated her to be the wrong side of fifty. Her dark her was pulled back and tied in a knot. Thick makeup which had melted in the heat caked her face. Pierre was about to leave but the women addressed him.

"So hot, I wonder for how much longer this heat wave will continue?"

Pierre grunted, "No idea."

The woman turned to face him. "Still, I love Paris when half the city is away. Are you local?"

"I was born in Bayonne but I now live in Paris, the 15ieme."

"5ieme, all my life," she replied.

She moved closer to him. Her nose twitched. Pierre smelt stale garlic on her breath. Two massive melon-like objects rose up and down on her chest. The thin flowery dress revealed a brown wrinkled skin, dried up from too many hours exposed to sunlight. Once upon a time she had been quite good looking. She was probably paying the price for too much rich French food and too little exercise.

Her hand touched his. He tried to withdraw it. She pulled it closer to her. "May I?" She said nonchalantly. "You have such beautiful hands. Hands are the most fascinating part of a man for me."

Pierre resisted. He tried to stand up. But too late, he found himself pinned down. Her lips, heavily coated with ruby lipstick, were smothering his mouth. She had taken his hand and was forcing it up between her fat thighs. Pierre gasped. He kicked out forcing her weight off him.

"What's wrong?" she spluttered. "Don't you like me?" One of her breasts had fallen out.

"Disgusting."

"Really! What is the world coming too?"

Pierre heard the voices. An elderly couple hurried by pushing a child in a small carriage. "We should look to calling the police." The voices disappeared.

With a final shove he pulled himself up. He grabbed his bag and ran.

*"Baisse moi, je t'adore,"* she screamed.

Pierre doubled his pace. He prayed nobody would recognize him. There were two things foremost on his mind. One; was to put as much distance between himself and that wretched women, the other—to find some water with which to wash off the perfume.

# Chapter Six

## Grasse, France

Denise Vergé loved living in Grasse. She adored its vertiginous hills, its steep alleyways and narrow streets. In winter it was frost-free protected from the icy winds. In summer the fragrance of mimosa, jasmine, lavender and herbs filled the air. Since the later part of the nineteenth century Grasse had been the world capital of perfume, almost every perfume molecule owed its origins to the town.

She had never thought that one day she would find herself working for one of the oldest perfume houses, let alone relocate to Grasse. Born in the north of the country near Saint Malo, she had always lived close to the sea. On graduating she had been tempted to join a firm of business consultants. The job had entailed traveling overseas, especially to Africa, a continent she had never visited. The travel appealed to her. She was in two minds whether to accept when a head-hunter approached her with the offer of Business Manager for Essence de la Grasse.

They had provided her with a first class railway ticket to visit the town and factory. A chauffeur driven Mercedes had met her off the train at Cannes Station and driven her the fifteen kilometers to Grasse where she was met by the Chairman, Alan Thulier. She new nothing about perfume only that the cheap brand she used was made by an opposition company. They told her that was an asset. The company needed fresh blood, fresh ideas. The industry was changing. What they wanted was someone who looked at the business with commercial eyes—someone who was not bound by the traditions and constraints of the perfume industry.

All that was two months back, she had so much to learn about the trade. It would not be easy. Many resented her appointment going out of their way not to cooperate but she had made one good friend—Michel Ramonet—The Nose.

Aged seventy-four he had dedicated his entire life to the creation of exotic odors, as he liked to refer to his many fragrances. She was on her way to meet with him. She gasped as she entered the first of the production block buildings. It was certainly not her first visit but each time, breathing in the mephitic cloud of noxious chemical fumes, disturbed her. The outer room was kept noticeably cooler in order to keep the neatly packed sacks of raw materials fresh.

She paused to read the labels: ginger from the Indies, vanilla pods from Zanzibar, petit grain from Paraguay, coriander and oak moss from Morocco, rosewood from Brazil and other substances she had never heard of. Pushing open the double doors she entered a small area which separated the next room. Steam heated the air. Workers wearing protective white clothing were shoveling an earthy brown substance into an extractor. Exotic senses filled the air—blackcurrant, lemon, rose, seaweed, wood shavings—assaulted her nose. An array of strange equipment bubbled, steamed, gasped and dripped away in a mélange of vats, boilers, pipettes, flasks, bains-maries. Technicians moved in between the rows busy checking dials, testing meters, verifying temperatures, switching valves. It was all so chaotic yet so organized.

At the far end of the building the offices stood on two levels. She opened the first door closing it immediately behind. The bubbling and hissing sounds disappeared. The air was cooler with no exotic smells. "He's upstairs expecting you." The secretary never once took her eyes off the computer screen.

"Thank You." Denise climbed the steel staircase. Her shoes clattered on the steps announcing her arrival. There was one door. She knocked once and pushed it open. Michel Ramonet, the Nose, the master olfactor, was seated behind an enormous marble-top desk. The side wall of the office was constructed of glass enabling the occupant to observe the myriad activities taking place below on the factory floor.

On seeing her enter he stood up. Denise suddenly realized how small a man he was. He wore a simple green knitted cardigan over a white shirt. An old fashioned purple bow-tie bobbed around his neck as he spoke. "Mademoiselle Vergé, you are most welcome." Offering his hand in greeting he moved away from his desk to meet her. He pointed to a couch. "Why don't we sit there? It's far more comfortable than at the desk. Can I offer you something to drink, some coffee or tea perhaps?"

Denise politely declined his offer. She sat on the leather couch pulling down the hem of her black skirt to just above her knees. From her attaché case she removed her personalized executive notepad together with a pen. "It is very kind of you, Monsieur Ramonet to make the time to see me. I really appreciate it."

He sat himself down on the easy chair facing her. "It is all my pleasure, Mademoiselle. Now I take it from your phone call you would like me to tell you a little about how I create a perfume. Have you got twenty-years to spare?" He laughed and gesticulated with his hands. "No, of course you haven't, but I must warn you, once I get started, well, it's difficult for me to stop. You might be here all night—trapped, a prisoner listening to the ranting of an old man," and again he laughed out aloud.

Denise smiled, "Monsieur Ramonet, I am all ears."

"*Merveilleux,* so let me begin, but where? The perfumer's world is one of contradiction, the creation of a fragrant smell to replace an odious odor. It can conjure up purity or sensualism—exotic spices or cool citrus—baked vanilla or subtropical roses. It is a concomitant list of infinite possibilities from a fragrant whiff to a malodorous pong. There are perfumes soft and fresh as a baby's skin, green as an orchid, or golden as the sun.

"A true bouquet scent is intangible yet it is there. You cannot see it but, you can smell it. You can even *feel* it so therefore it must be tangible. It will provide an aura of well being. It will enhance the confidence of the wearer. Our sense of smell propels us on a mystical journey. When a new scent is first experienced we have no idea where it will lead us."

He stood up and walked over to the window then, turning to Denise, he continued. "A man must sense a woman before he sees her. When the door of her apartment opens a whiff of her image must pervade the nostrils. He will then know her before he meets her face to face. Our olfactory senses play an intrinsic part of a successful libido. When I think of perfume, I see and smell freshly cut flowers the language of love and romance. Their narcotic fragrances sweep me off my feet. My mind plays with their exotic images—the curvaceous rose—the vulva of the orchid so resembling a receptive female genitalia. I'm not embarrassing you am I? My wife tells me off when I get so carried away."

"Not at all," replied Denise. "Quite the contrary, I find your description of perfume most fascinating."

"Why thank you, if you don't mind, I shall remain on my feet. I feel I can best communicate when I am moving, somewhat like a flower bending in the breeze calling to the honeybee to come and pollinate it. Did you know our earliest ancestors used their sense of smell as a necessary tool of survival, a talent, which we have long lost the need to do. Like the animals they could smell the rain in the wind or follow the scent of the herd. Smell is part of our makeup. Why do we sweat? Simply to communicate—communicate what?—Fear, terror, or basic animal attraction. Why does the female body, which is glabrous, still persist in growing hair under the armpits and down at the crutch? Hair helps to expedite the flow from the sweat glands and to retain it as an aid to procreation. In other words, these natural body-odors act as a catalyst enhancing our sexual activity. Human sweat is nature's pheromone. It calls to a member of the opposite sex. Come . . . here I am . . . take me or conversely can I take you?"

"Sorry, what do you mean by phero . . . mon? You've lost me."

"Pheromone is a chemical substance secreted and released by an animal to attract response from another. The domestic canine bitch goes on heat and within minutes every male dog in the neighborhood is barking mad with frustration. "Let me out . . . let me at her," they howl. She's sending out a message, which they are receiving. Dogs, as you know, have one of the most powerful noses in nature. They think, analyze and make decisions with their noses.

"Perfumers have been experimenting for thousands of years in an attempt to create a pheromonal perfume using the excretions from flowers that attract pollinators in the hope of coming up with an elixir which will stimulate a sexual reaction. Some say Cleopatra used a magic potion to entrap her men. Others, that Casanova and the Marquis de Sade, made use of such a substance. Personally, I don't believe it is possible."

"Are you then saying it is impossible to create a perfume which could act as a powerful aphrodisiac?"

Michel smiled. "Nothing is impossible. In my lifetime I have witnessed man walk on the moon. I can talk to someone, even see them, on the other side of the planet without any wire or cable connecting us. No, nothing is impossible but, perfumers, chemists, even alchemists, have been experimenting for years to find the elixir of life. One hundred years ago perfumers had about 100 ingredients to play with from which a fragrant perfume could be created. Today," and he waved his arm towards the factory beneath him, "we can choose from 600 naturally occurring substances plus as many as 3,000 synthetic ingredients." He paused for a moment before continuing. "No, even if I could produce such a fragrance it would be wrong to do so."

"Why do you say that?"

He moved away from the window and closer to her. "Because it would not be a perfume it would be a drug. Imagine the chaos, the damage it could inflict. It would redefine the meaning of rape. I am afraid our present civilization, the type of people we have to live with, could not handle such a substance"

"However, our natural sense of smell has been artificially changed over the centuries. Natural body odors have been replaced by artificially created fragrances. These new odors are designed to play on the imagination. I suppose I can best define them as having three stages: The very first whiff we call the *top note,* which soon evaporates, but then we move to the *body note.* This is the heart and soul of the fragrance and in a good perfume should linger for up to an hour. Finally, we come to the *dry-out note*; being redolent it should linger for many hours. This tenacity to linger is what the customer is really seeking when they select a fragrance. The change from each stage should be concomitant, almost melodic in flow.

"A skilled perfumer is a composer and conductor, as well as a full symphony orchestra, all combined into one. He or she must first select the notes to be used then group them together in a melodic flow. A central theme must be created to flow through the composition.

"A symphony of ambrosial essences is best built from the ground up, which means laying the foundation of what we call a *base note.* This becomes the essence of the fragrance. These syrupy liquids are usually dark in color and sometimes come over as overpowering to the uninitiated. Sandalwood, angelica, labdanum, oak moss, benzoin and of course, musk and civet secretions all make strong *base notes.*

"The abdomen of the male musk deer, an inhabitant of the lower wooded slopes of the Himalayan and Atlas mountains, contains a spherical pouch. Inside this sac are found small grains, which when dried emit a powerful scent that can last for years. History is full of legends of the aphrodisiac power of musk.

"Another, more readily available animal is the civet. Although commonly referred to as a cat it is related to the mongoose and originates from Abyssinia, Borneo and Bengal. They are now bred in large numbers to supply the trade. A perineal gland, located in both the male and female posterior, produces a soft fatty substance. As little as ten drops of civet to two ounces of alcohol are all that is needed to make liters of perfume. Civet is by far the most popular base ingredient as it blends with almost everything enhancing the other essential essences."

"I thought we were moving away from using these animal by-products?" asked Denise.

"We are. Animal-rights lobbyists have steered public awareness to boycott perfumes made using these substances. However, because no synthetic material has yet been found which acts so powerfully there will always be a market for people who want, and can afford, only the best. Civet and musk essence is incredibly expensive to use to make the *base note* but like caviar there will always be a limited market.

"The function of the *base note* is to anchor the fragrance so as to prolong its life. It must fix the bouquet to the skin allowing the other constituents to slowly evaporate. The resin benzoin and the gum balsam have an adsorptive effect, because their molecular construction when boiled retards the evaporation of the other essences.

"Alternatively, oak moss and labdanum have a low volatility so evaporate more slowly yet do not upset the other chemical elements. However, it is the animal essences namely musk, civet, ambergris and castoreum which form the most powerful synergic compounds. These mystical ingredients generate the power and aging capacity of the fragrance. Care must be taken that the aroma does not overpower the person to stink out the room—often the case in so-called new-generation flavors.

"Of biblical fame, frankincense from the bark of the *boswellia* tree generates a soft flowery odor, which blends well with citruses. A vegetable equivalent to husk, which is currently gaining notoriety, due to the current trend away from animal products, is ambrette seed from the hibiscus plant. The dried fruit releases large seeds, which when crushed render rich, sweet oil not dissimilar to brandy."

Down below the factory lights were extinguished. Now, only a glow remained. Michel glanced quickly at his watch.

"Good heavens, I have been rabbitting away for more than an hour. I do hope I am not boring you."

"Far from it, Monsieur Ramonet, I am most grateful for your time but if you wish to leave I can always come back."

"No, not all, just because the majority of the workforce has finished for the day does not mean we have stopped production. Come here and see." Denise stood up. She smoothed down her tight-fitting skirt and joined Michel at the window. "Look, the vats are still boiling and the stills continue to steam. The process continues until we have managed to squeeze the very last drop of fragrance. Just like the wine maker at harvest time we cannot rest until the finished product is in the bottle. Speaking of wine . . ." and he approached the large cupboard, which formed part of the wall behind his desk. "It is time to enjoy that other great gift from nature. Will you join me in a glass . . . red or white?"

Denise hesitated.

"Come, I won't take no for an answer," he pursued.

"I prefer white."

"*Très bon*, let me see what I have here." She watched as he slid open the wooden paneling to reveal a refrigerator. He opened the door. A light immediately came on. His hand danced around the shelves, "How about a Château Grillet from Rhône? It's a bit young, really needs a few more years in the bottle."

She watched as he expertly removed the cork. "I thought that *noses*, if I may call you that, refrained from drinking alcohol."

He laughed out aloud as he poured the wine into the glass. "When you reach my tender years there are many things which one should not do. I never drink of course if I am *nosing*". He handed the glass to her whilst raising his own. "Good luck. I wish you a long life in our bizarre world of smells."

"Thank you," she replied, before savoring the fruity explosion of viognier grapes which rolled around her palate.

Michel took another sip before placing the glass down on the edge of his desk. "To continue on our journey through perfumery: most inhalants are substances, which are sniffed in order to facilitate a behavioral effect and are volatile organic substances. The traditional alchemical process of separation, purification, recombination and fixation has been made easier by the use of modern synthetics. Synthetic or inorganic substances may contain odoriferous elements but they do not contain any *real* body or *life force*. The power of a natural essence is because it is emanating from a *living* substance.

"Distillation allows the extraction of high-quality essential oils from a large variety of basic substances. In a concentrated alcohol form it becomes an essential diluent and fragrance carrier. The preferred method of distillation with water enables those substances that have a higher boiling point to be volatized when their vapors are mixed with steam enabling it to be preserved in a purer condition.

"All fragrances make use of essential oils, which are classified by their volatility being their speed of vaporization. Examples of highly volatile oils are: anise, basil, bay, bergamot, bois de rose, cardamom, fir needle, grapefruit, lavender, lime, lemon, orange peel and silver pine. Less volatile are: carrot seed, cedar-wood, chamomile, cinnamon and clove. Further down the scale comes: ambrette seed, angelica root and cognac. The orange tree in fact yields four distinctive oils: essential oil of orange from the fruit rind; absolute and neroli from the flower, finally petit grain from the leaves.

"I apologize if I'm becoming a bit too technical but I'll give you some notes which will help you better understand the process. You can study them at your leisure. If a drop of pure essential oil is placed upon a sheet of white paper it will eventually evaporate without leaving a trace. However, if the oil is adulterated a tidemark will remain to indicate its former presence.

"A semisolid wax referred to as "concrete" is the bi-product of the distillation of natural flower oils. They have become the main ingredient in the manufacture of solid perfumes because of their staying power. However, by removing the waxes the concrete becomes an alcohol-soluble concentrated liquid. 190-proof ethyl alcohol is still the preferred medium in which to blend the essences, although some of our competitors like to boast they are using vodka, particularly for their male fragrances."

"Are flowers still the main ingredient necessary to make a good perfume?"

"That's an excellent question and one which I am often asked. Yes and no is my reply. It all depends. Flowers: Freesia, gardenia, heliotrope, honeysuckle, lilac, lily of the valley, orchid and violet may all rein as beauteous wonders of nature but resist all forms of scent harvesting. Part of the mystic allure of flowers such as jasmine, tuberose, lilac and orange blossom is a substance called indole, which emits a putrid smell of decay and faeces. It is this substance, which contributes the sensual element to a fragrance—too much and it will take over but insufficient will pass un-noticed.

"It is the rose, in all its myriad forms, the symbol of love and concupiscence that immediately stimulates all five senses. Growing profusely in most temperate climates each hybrid reacts differently in how it surrenders its personal fragrance. Shy, timid, nervous and always delicate, the petal easily bruises. It is best picked in the early morning while the bud is still contemplating whether to open. Rose absolute willingly joins with other essences and the wide selection provides panoply of fragrances with which to play with.

"Of the narcotic essences jasmine is the easiest to work with. 90-kilos of flowers will produce a mere 1 1/2-kilo of jasmine absolute, yet in spite of its puissance, it complements rather than subjugates the other bouquets. Nicknamed the poor man's jasmine, ylang ylang growing in the Comoros Islands, has become a popular favorite. An aphrodisiac in its purest form it combines easily to enhance the overall power of the fragrance."

"I heard somewhere that nutmeg is also an aphrodisiac?"

"An excessive intake of nutmeg can result in hallucinations. The ancient Romans used to carry grated nutmeg around in little silver containers to sprinkle into their wine. Rastafarians and other marijuana smokers use it if their supply of hashish runs out. From the middle-ages up to the last century it was recommended that rubbing nutmeg oil onto the male genitals increased virility. It could be said that nutmeg was the first Viagra, but I digress.

"From distilling the freshly opened flowers of the bitter orange tree an essential oil, neroli is produced, which has been used by perfumers for centuries. However, this dark orange liquid is expensive to produce but it is to perfumery, what the Rolls Royce is to the automobile industry. It is intense, yet cool and sophisticated while imparting a powerful passionate flavor.

"Spices, which are a favorite in the kitchen, are also popular in the laboratory: allspice, ginger, black pepper and cinnamon to name the most frequent used. Clove bud oil contributes a warm, woody-spice tone which when blended with vanilla produces a carnation fragrance. On the other hand, cinnamon oil made from the bark of the tree must be treated with the greatest respect. Its powerful golden color, which reddens with age, is tenacious and will overpower all other essences if not used sparingly.

"The ever-popular lavender absolute gives us the elegant dark green color as well as a spicy pungency, which marries so well with other essences, namely: labdanum, patchouli, vetivert, pine needle and clary sage.

"Citrus essences are piquant, light and fresh: sweet orange essence is readily available so is used in cheaper fragrances. Personally I much prefer the rich yellowish sweet odor, which comes from the peel of the pink grapefruit. Blood oranges on the other hand render overtones approaching raspberries and strawberries. However, if one wants to be subtle then petit grain oil made from the green twigs and leaves of the bitter orange tree offers a woody-herbaceous undertone to the flowery orange bouquet. I use this predominantly when making a male fragrance."

"How about lemon? So many perfumes today seem to favor a lemony smell."

"No, I do not use lemon or lime. I leave this to the industrial chemists to scent their detergents. Other oils, which I sometimes play around with if I wish to introduce a hint of green, are: spearmint, galbanum—from the ferula family, which gives us parsley and fir needle oil."

Michel paused. He moved over to his desk to refill their glasses. A drop of wine landed on the desk top. Using a tissue he quickly wiped it up. "One of the advantages of having a marble top it does not stain."

"I was wondering about that," remarked Denise.

"Marble or granite is a popular surface with perfumers and wine makers to work on. I chose white because of course it serves as the perfect neutral color against which to measure delicate shades."

Denise consulted her watch. "Good heavens, it is fast approaching seven o'clock. I have kept you all this time, Monsieur Ramonet."

"Not all, my dear," and he drained his wine glass. "As I said, it has been all my pleasure. Now, I'm going to give you some notes to read." He turned to reach behind his desk. Denise watched as he opened a drawer from which he removed a small file. "Take this," and he handed it across to her. "May I suggest you return, say tomorrow, and we can continue this talk downstairs? I can show you some of the raw materials as well as explain better the various processes."

# Chapter Seven

## Chester, England

"Will the foreman of the jury please stand?"

There was a shuffling of feet. A short, middle-aged woman wearing a blue floral dress stood up. Silence ruled throughout the courtroom. Not a sound not a titter came from the public gallery. Journalists posed, ready to run out to make their precious phone calls once the verdict was announced. The old lady in the outdated, green woolen coat and tatty yellow straw hat, with faded pink plastic roses stared down from her usual place in the gallery. The prisoner in the dock showed no emotion. The young attractive plaintiff leaned forward on her elbows, ears straining.

The judge asked solemnly. "Have you reached a verdict in the case of Archibald Jeremiah Crumpet versus Kylie Samantha Moon?"

"We have, Your Lordship."

"Are you unanimous in your verdict?"

"We are, Your Lordship."

The clerk of the court stepped forward. The foreman of the jury handed him a folded sheet of paper. The clerk walked towards the judge's bench where he passed the precious object to the judge who glimpsed at it briefly.

"Will the defendant please stand?"

More shuffling, a chair scraped back on the wooden floor. Archibald Crumpet stood up as did the police guard seated behind him. The guard towered over him giving the impression that Archibald was even shorter than the five-foot-four he claimed to be. His hairy knuckles grasped the brass rail of the box. The light from the overhead neon strip light bounced reflections off his baldhead. His expressionless eyes stared at the judge. Up in the public gallery his mother glared at the foreman of the jury.

The silence returned. Judge William J Sinclair turned in his chair to face the foreman. "Do you find the defendant, Archibald Jeremiah Crumpet, guilty or not guilty on the charge of rape?"

The foreman lifted her head. All eyes focused upon her. Her mouth moved. It was suddenly dry. She looked towards the Judge conscious of the great responsibility she bore.

"We the jury find the defendant *not guilty*."

The courtroom exploded in a cacophony of human voices. The plaintiff turned to her council then burst into tears. Instinctively he placed his arm around her to comfort her.

"The bastard is guilty."

"It's a miscarriage of justice."

"No ways."

The shouts boomed down from the public gallery.

"Not guilty, I said," screamed the news reporter to his paper taking the opportunity to use his cell phone in all the noise. A second reporter had already sent a prepared SMS to his editor.

"Silence... silence in court." The judge repeatedly banged his gavel.

A sudden hush descended disturbed only by the sobbing of the plaintiff, who was now joined by her supporters in the public gallery. Paper tissues were being freely distributed as moist eyes were carefully dabbed to avoid smearing mascara.

Throughout the uproar, which lasted only two minutes, but seemed an eternity, the old lady in the outdated, green woolen coat and tatty yellow straw hat, with faded pink plastic roses continued to stare down. This time her eyes were transfixed on the judge. Archibald, the plaintiff, remained immobile in the dock his hairy fingers continued to grasp the brass rail. His eyes showed no emotion.

"Archibald Jeremiah Crumpet, you are a free man. You may step down." Turning immediately to the jury the judge continued. "Ladies and gentleman of the jury, I thank you for your time and for your deliverance. You are now relieved of your duties." With a thump the judge closed his large file shoving it under his arm. He stood up.

"All rise," shouted the clerk.

Pandemonium filled the courtroom. Members of the press pushed and shoved their way out in a desperate race to file their stories. Long bronze legs hovered on stiletto heels. Manicured hands smoothed down tiny skirts, finger tips touched hair to ensure all was perfectly in place. The visitor's gallery was quickly emptying except for one person who remained staring—her eyes had shifted to her son.

"I don't believe it. It can't be true. How can I live this down?" sobbed Kylie Moon clutching a white linen handkerchief in a tight ball.

"I'm sorry. We did our best but I did warn you the evidence against the defendant was inconclusive. We can appeal of course . . ."

"There's no point. How can anyone possibly believe that I would willingly go with a creep like that?" and she spat the words out lifting her head towards Archibald.

"You can go now. You are free to go, sir." The policeman tapped Archibald on the shoulder.

"Am I? Oh yes, I suppose I can." Slowly he turned around releasing his hands from the rail.

The policeman opened the side door of the dock. "You can go this way, sir. There's no need to go back downstairs."

"Thank you," Archibald hesitated. He glanced up to look at his mother. Their eyes met. "I'd rather go down if you don't mind . . . perhaps wait a little."

The policeman hesitated. "Well, if you prefer to, sir."

Together they descended the stairs. "I'll escort you out through the back way. It's much quieter, less chance of the press hounding you."

"That's very kind of you, Officer, but I'd like to wait for my mother to join me. Can I just sit here?" Archibald pointed to one of three steel chairs arranged in the corridor.

"If you wish, sir, but I'll have to remain with you."

"Oh I am sorry. Am I keeping you?"

The policeman smiled. "No sir, not at all. I don't knock off for another hour."

A minute passed. Nobody spoke. Both men stared at the blank grey wall. The officer stood up. "Do you mind if I ask you, sir? Did you really fuck this Kylie model? Of course you don't have to answer me now that the case is over like."

Without hesitating Archibald replied, "Yes I did."

Another minute's silence passed between them. "What was it like?"

"How do you mean?" responded Archibald.

"Well, you know," and he winked. "She's got a great body. Every man would like to give her one. Did she pant? Did she grunt? Did she just lay back? What was it like with her?"

"So so, her breasts are a bit on the small side but she gives a very good blow job."

"Jesus, she didn't?"

"She did. That was before we did it properly."

"How did you meet her?"

"You heard at the trial," answered Archibald softly. "I met her in a pub, we chatted and she went with me in my van."

"How did you manage that? What's your secret?"

Archibald shrugged his shoulders, "Charm, personality?"

Kylie Moon, dressed in a stylish black suit tailored exclusively for her by Jenny Button, was escorted to a waiting car shrouded by her defense team who defiantly fended off the barrage of news reporters.

"Are you going to appeal the verdict?"

"Will you make a statement?"

"No comment," shouted back a lawyer.

"Will the verdict affect your newly signed contract with Essence de La Grasse?"

"Is it true that Vivienne Westwood will no longer use you if you loose the case?"

"Miss Moon has nothing to say at this moment in time. A press statement will follow once we have received a full transcript of the trial."

"Does that mean you do intend to appeal the verdict? Can we quote you?"

"I said *no comment*, now please clear the way." They pushed their way towards the waiting car.

"Miss Moon . . . Miss Moon I know he raped you. I know because he raped me. I think I know how he did it."

Kylie stopped to look at the voice. A young girl with short black hair wearing jeans and a t-shirt was waving frantically at her. They had reached the car. The rear door was being opened for her. Her lawyer looked towards the girl. "If you know something, young lady, phone my office," and he fumbled into his jacket pocket for a business card.

"No wait," shouted Kylie. "Let her come. Let me talk with her."

"It could be some kind of cheap publicity trick. Let us first check her out," interjected the lawyer.

Kylie slid across the car seat. "Let's take a chance. If she's obviously lying then we can throw her out. I've got a feeling." She called to the girl. "What's your name?"

"Lisa."

"Come on then, Lisa, jump in."

The girl pushed through the crowd. She slid alongside Kylie. The lawyer followed shutting the door. The limousine pulled forward. The welcoming breeze of air-conditioned air wafted through the car.

"Well, Lisa, what's your story? It had better be good. I'm in no mood to play games."

# Chapter Eight

## Cheshire, England

They drove in silence neither wishing to speak. They had waited a good half-hour before the friendly policeman had shown them out through the rear entrance of the courtroom. The press and the entourage from the public gallery had long departed. He had deliberately parked the small Fiat two blocks away. It had been his mother's idea. She did not want the car to be associated with them. The white panel van had been traded in the minute the charge of rape had been raised against him.

"Archibald."

"Yes, mother."

"You know you will have to be very careful in the future."

"Yes, mother."

They drove on in silence for a further five minutes.

"Archibald."

"Yes, mother."

"I don't think you should go out for a while, not until this wretched thing dies down and is forgotten,"

"Yes, mother."

"Stay away from Chester. Rather do your socializing in Manchester. Do you understand, Archibald?"

"Yes, mother."

"Do you still have any potion left?"

"No mother," he lied, hoping she had not discovered where he had hidden the bottle in his shop.

"Good! Because I'm not going to make you any more."

"Mother!"

"Well at least not for the moment. It's too risky. You cannot take the chance. I'm worried that this last one may pursue the case farther."

"How can she? I'm acquitted. I've been proved innocent in a court of law."

"Why on earth did you choose to do it with such a high profile tart like that? It was just plain stupid. Rather stick to ordinary girls when you get one of your urges."

They drove on in silence. The traffic thinned as they left the main Manchester road to meander off through country lanes, which would lead to the tiny Cheshire village of Beeston. He pulled into a service station. "I need to buy something from the shop. Do you require anything, Mother?"

"Some ice cream, just some ice cream, buy your favorite, raspberry ripple."

"Very well, mother."

Ten minutes later they came to a stop outside the wooden farm gate, which blocked the entrance to the small three-hundred-year-old cottage. Archibald jumped out to open the gate. He drove through, parking the Fiat outside the old barn. His mother squeezed herself out of the car. "Bring my bag, there's a good boy, Archibald?"

"Yes, mother."

He opened the boot. His mother turned the key in the front door. "Methuselah, Salmanazar, Balthazar, Nebuchadnezzar—there you are my babies." Four black cats purred before her, their long tails curled upwards flickering from side to side. One by one they elegantly strutted forward to rub themselves against her skirt, one against each leg. "Out you go now, on patrol, make sure everything is all right." The lead cat, Nebuchadnezzar, turned its head to look at her. Its emerald green eyes glistened. It meowed. Its long aristocratic whiskers quivered then as though acknowledging her instruction. The cat strutted forward followed by the other three through the open door.

Archibald, carrying his mother's bag, witnessed the four cats strut out of the cottage door. They ignored him. Nebuchadnezzar followed by Methuselah turned left while Salmanazar and Balthazar turned right.

"Mother, I need to go to the shop. I must check up on how Mrs. Wainright is doing."

"I'm cooking a chicken for dinner . . . with roast potatoes, cauliflower and broccoli . . . your favorite. I thought we could celebrate. We can even have a glass of my mulberry wine."

"What time, mother?"

"Make sure you are back before seven. I need your help in the garden."

He checked his watch. It was four-fifteen. He had plenty of time to accomplish what was on his mind. "Very well, mother."

Archibald closed the front door. He walked to the gate, opened it, and then drove the Fiat through. Leaving the engine running he closed the gate. Four pairs of cat's eyes followed his every movement. Fifteen minutes later he parked outside the small antique shop in Main Street. The sign above the door engraved in wood proudly announced the name: "Donaldson Antiques—Old Collectibles Bought and Sold—Furniture Restored." He had never bothered to change the name when he took over the business.

The door opened with the clanging of the bell. "Good afternoon, Mr. Crumpet. How did it go? Do tell me. I'm dying to know." Mrs. Wainright, a feather duster in her hand, walked forward to greet him.

"Innocent . . . completely innocent," he replied.

"I knew it. I told my Robbie there was no way *you* of all people, could do such a terrible thing. The nerve of that wretched woman, to accuse someone like *you.*"

"Thank you, Mrs. Wainright, that's very kind of you and how's the business been?"

She put down the feather duster on a small lacquered Chinese side table. Oh! I almost forgot to tell you, such was my worry. I sold the two Wedgwood figurines yesterday and this morning a lady came in and put down a deposit on the Edwardian writing desk. I've written it all up in the book and the money is in the tin box."

"Excellent, now you run along home to your Robbie. I won't need you until Saturday. Can you do Saturday morning for me?"

"I don't see why not. Are you sure you don't want me to stay until five? It's no trouble."

"No you go. I've a few things I need to attend to."

Mrs. Wainright hurried to the back of the shop where she collected her bag. Archibald waited until she left and the bell clanged as the door opened and closed. He walked into the back room, his office and workroom. Chairs and tables in various state of repair, cluttered one wall. He sat down at his Victorian desk. He inserted a key in the lock before rolling up the front shutter. From his pocket he removed his cell phone. Pushing his heavy, bifocal, old fashioned horn-rimmed glasses firmly up his nose he scrolled down the phonebook memory. Placing the phone down; he wrote a number on a sheet of scrap paper. He switched off the phone, removing first the battery then the sim card.

From another pocket he produced his purchase from the garage. Ripping open the packaging he detached a second sim card belonging to a different phone company which he inserted into the phone. Following the written instructions he punched in all the numbers to activate it. Finally he was able to dial the number he had written down.

"Sam, its Archie, how are you? Good . . . you heard the news . . . yes free . . . innocent . . . of course . . . listen, can you come round? Yes, now . . . help me celebrate. What do you mean you can't get away? I'll make it worth your while. Good . . . say half an hour. Great . . . see you then."

On terminating the call he repeated the process of exchanging the sim cards finally secreting the new one in a drawer in the desk. It was something his defense council had said. "Did you ever make a call to the plaintiff? Be careful how you answer. Remember, under recent legislation, phone companies are required to store a record of all calls for up to six months. The courts can subpoena the records and use them against you." The thought that the police might still be monitoring him worried him. His mother was right. He must not take any chances.

A mock-Napoleonic chaise-lounge lay against the wall beside the desk. He pulled it out. From the drawer of a Welsh-dresser he removed a red sheet. He threw it over the chaise. He took off his jacket and hung it from a coat hanger on the wall. He undid his tie and opened the top button of his shirt. Seated back at the desk he opened the last of six narrow sliding drawers on the first row. His fingers felt for the wooden button which he pressed, firmly. A clicking sound rewarded him. Standing up he leaned over the left side of the desk. A secret compartment was revealed—from it he removed a basket containing two bottles.

A door led to the bathroom which he had installed on taking over the business. The existing small toilet had been extended out into the backyard creating sufficient space to install a full-size bath as well as a separate shower, toilet and washbasin. After urinating in the toilet he rolled up his sleeves then gave his face and hands a thorough wash. From the bottle basket he picked up a plain round bottle with an ornate glass stopper. Taking a ball of cotton wool from the sink he poured a small drop onto it. The immediate smell of nutmeg permeated the air. Gently, he dabbed his genitals with the cotton wool stopping only to add more of the oil. He felt the beginning of an erection coming on. Putting the first bottle away he pulled out a second matching bottle. This time it was only a quarter full. Using a clean, smaller ball he placed it over the open top before tilting the bottle to allow a minute drop of the yellowy-green liquid to permeate the pad. First he patted his neck, then his throat, finally his wrists and hands. After smelling the pad he squeezed it over his half-erect penis then rubbed it around his crotch.

The used cotton wool balls were flushed down the toilet. He zipped himself up, looked in the mirror before running his hands over his baldhead. The bottles were returned to the secret compartment in the desk before he re-entered to the shop. He noted immediately the empty space on the Edwardian sideboard where the two Wedgwood figurines had stood. He made a mental note to look in the storeroom to see what he could replace them with.

The door opened. The bell rang. He checked his watch. It was five-thirty. He only had an hour. "Archie, where are you? It's Sam."

He stepped out from behind a series of display cabinets filled with valuable porcelain and cut glass items. "Hi, thanks for coming . . . just a moment." He moved passed her towards the door. First he flicked the hanging "open" sign to "closed" next he shot the bolt closing the door.

He touched her hand. "Come, let's go into the back. Would you like a drink?"

"Not so fast, Archie, I think you owe me some money."

"Are you sure, love?"

She hesitated. Well, I couldn't find the money in my purse when I got home last time."

"Strange," he muttered. They entered into the back. 'Sit yourself down, a glass of wine, sweet white?"

She nodded her head. Her nose began to twitch. Archibald removed an opened bottle from the refrigerator. With a pop he pulled out the cork. He poured two glasses passing one to her. Their hands touched. "Money please, remember, I'm a working girl."

"One hundred? It's only for the hour."

"That'll do. It's been a while where have you been? I was about to cross you off my list."

"Don't do that, love." Archie sat down next to her on the chaise. "You've got such lovely hands," and he picked one up bringing it to his face. Her nose twitched. Subconsciously, she uncrossed her legs. The light summer dress rode up revealing more of her thigh.

"The money, can we get that over before we start?" She said somewhat uncomfortably.

"Yes of course." Archie leaned closer to her. "Can't I have a kiss, just a little one?" Their lips touched. She resisted. Half-heartedly she attempted to push him away. Her nose twitched. She pushed herself onto him. Archibald rubbed his face over her mouth. She removed his glasses. They dropped off the chaise onto the floor.

"God," she gasped. "What is it about you?" One hand fumbled for the zip of his trousers while the other began to tug at the elastic of her knickers.

# Chapter Nine

## Paris, France

"*You* ran away from a woman. I don't believe it."

"You should have seen her—smelt her breath. It's not funny I tell you."

Jacques looked up from his laptop wide-eyed. "I'm trying not to laugh, believe me." He rolled his chair back slapping his legs with the palms of his hands. "When you first phoned me on Monday evening I thought you were joking. Shit, I wish I'd been there to see you."

"I wish you had. I don't know what you have put into this concoction but there is definitely something which turns women on in a big way. What started out as a joke amongst us now scares the living daylights out of me. I'm not sure if I want to go on with this."

Jacque stood up. "You want to quit? You can't—not now—not when we're on the edge of the greatest discovery in perfumery history. Christ, chemists have been searching for thousands of years for an aphrodisiac fragrance." He walked over to the window. "Pierre, have you any idea what this," and he pointed to the dining room table cluttered with chemical apparatus, bottles and jars, "is worth? A fortune, a bloody fortune—there's more money to be made if I can perfect this than Bill Gates and that kid who came up with Face Book put together."

"You really think so, Jacques."

"Look, I've hit on something extraordinary. The problem is: I'm not sure exactly what it is. Our playing around with different ingredients to produce a sexy smelling perfume has come up with a chemical compound which somehow stimulates the female sex hormones. I'm no expert but what I do know is that men and women excrete both male testosterone and female estrogen. Obviously, in women it is estrogen which dominates. The production of reproductive hormones is controlled by a feedback system between the hypothalamus pituitary axis and the gonads. It's possible I may have stumbled across something which accelerates or triggers this action."

"So what precise ingredient do you think it is?" asked Pierre.

"That's the problem. I don't know. It's what I'm trying to find out. If I can isolate it then I can begin to understand it better." He returned to the computer. "Look here." Pierre leaned over his shoulder. "The horizontal line of this spreadsheet shows the ingredients. I used ambergris, nutmeg, mimosa, vetivert which gives it the woody fragrance, cinnamon, pepper, sandalwood oil, ylang-ylang, lavender, citrus amber and spicy fougère. I used a heavier concentration of ambergris. The vertical axis shows the quantities. The problem is it's not scientific enough. Because each ingredient is acquired from outside I've no control over the exact composition of each batch. I have to assume the labeling and chemical composition is correct which of course it's probably not. Plus, the exact time and temperatures involved have not been properly noted. To be quite honest I never for one moment thought we would achieve a result like this, so far it's all been a bit of a game."

"I see the problem," responded Pierre. "It's like looking for a needle in a haystack."

"No, that's easy. You can use a metal detector," added Jacques. "This is more like trying to find a specific flower hidden somewhere in the middle of the Amazonian jungle."

"Yes, I see your point. I read somewhere—I think it was in a National Geographic—there are still hundreds of undiscovered plants and that the natives produce drugs from them to cure illness more effectively than our modern drug companies."

"The Amazon rainforest, I wrote a paper on it as part of my doctorate. There are an estimated 80,000 species of plant. More are being discovered each day. Just imagine, by combining two of these plants, which work together they produce a healing or hallucinogenic drug. Theoretically, this should require the testing of each possible combination. This equates to 3,700,000,000 possibilities. We must ask ourselves just how did primitive tribal shamans discover what we call ayahuasca—a powerful hallucinogenic drug made from combining the leaves of a particular shrub with a certain type of creeper? When swallowed this magical compound has no affect. It simply passes through the body because an enzyme in the stomach renders it harmless. But, when inhaled as a vapor, it releases dimethyltryptamine, a hormone secreted by the human brain.

"It would take modern day botanists and chemists equipped with the latest electron microscopes and state-of-the-art equipment decades to arrive at the precise formula. Yet, Stone Age people possess the knowledge—surely not by chance?

"There's so much more. Numerous poisons are used to smear on the tips of blowpipes—curare, is one such drug. It attacks the nervous system relaxing the muscles. Again, taken orally it has no affect but must be entered into the blood. The animal dies and the meat is not tainted. The Amazonian hunters use over 40 variants of curare—each performing a specific function. From whom and how did they acquire this advanced knowledge? The question remains unanswered."

"Jacques, you said you used extra ambergris in this last batch. What exactly is it?"

"If only I could get my hands on regular supplies of ambergris. For me, it is the Rolls Royce of naturally occurring compounds with which to provide the base note to build up a fragrance. It is arguably the finest of fixatives binding together all the different raw materials which perfumes contain. But more than this it somehow holds the delicate fragrances together and prolongs their life."

"But what exactly is it?"

"What is it you ask? If you are walking along a lonely beach and you happen to stumble over an aromatic waxy pellucid *rock* with a somewhat marbled exterior, pick it up bring it home. It could be ambergris. On the other hand it probably isn't.

"Ambergris is a by-product of the stomach of the sperm whale. Their basic diet is squid of which they consume copious quantities when they can find it. Squid being composed of soft flesh except for the beak does not require mastication. However, the sharp beak remains a problem as it floats around the massive interior of the whale's stomach. Unlike most mammals whales, for reasons only known to them, do not simply poop it out. They vomit vast quantities of it. In the gut of the whale, ambergris is a black, semi-viscous foul smelling liquid. On contact with sunlight and air it quickly oxidizes becoming hard. It smells foul but floating around on the sea matures it.

"The first task the perfumer performs is to soak it in alcohol for several months. Over time it becomes velvety. Its smell can be described as stale tobacco, truffles and even human sweat. To illustrate its power one tiny drop on a sheet of absorbent paper, dried, folded and placed in a book will retain the smell for forty years.

"Unfortunately, for the trade, but fortunately for the sperm whale, trade in ambergris has been banned for years. Now, the only source can be obtained from that which washes up on selective beaches such as on the island of Socotra in the Indian Ocean, off the coast of Yemen and Somalia, or, when a dead whale washes ashore. You can't simply buy it, and even if you could, the price is extortionate. Fortunately, this supply," and he pointed to a small mustard bottle, "is *borrowed* from the lab."

"So what happens now? How much do we have?"

"With the phial you brought back, plus what I still have in the flask," he stood up to examine a beaker on the table, "say not more than 200-ml. I plan to take at least half of that back to the lab. There, I can analyze it using the lab's equipment and see if I can reproduce it using head space technology." He turned to face Pierre. "By placing a few drops in a stainless steel container I suck out the air creating a vacuum. Half an hour later the exudation is drawn off into a gas chromatograph. This will analyze and hopefully generate the exact formula of the composition. It works with flowers but I'm not sure if it will work with a liquid."

"Ok, so assuming you can capture the exact formula, this means it can be easily reproduced in much larger quantities," added Pierre.

"Yes, but that is only the beginning. Before any drug company or cosmetic house brings a new product onto the market they first have to thoroughly test it. This can take years. The product has to pass stringent tests to show it is not detrimental to health. You know the furor raised by the animal rights activists. Once this hurdle is overcome the next is to test it on humans before it would even be considered by any of the myriad authorities.

"The fact is: I'm not sure if we are dealing with a perfume or a drug. Assuming I can reproduce it and can patent the formula, what would be our next step? Should we approach one of the top pharmaceutical companies or rather a perfume house?"

"How about going it alone? Start small, you know and grow from there. Could you trust one of the big firms not to steal it for themselves? They could drop us on the grounds that it is unsafe then, send it off to one of their plants on another continent and we would never know. The other possibility is to sell it outright, after all, if we make a few hundred million Euros each we can both buy a villa in Monte Carlo, a yacht, a couple of Ferraris and retire young."

"You forgot the jet."

"Sorry, yes a jet and a helicopter for when the roads are crowded."

Jacques laughed. "I wish it were that easy. Who would have that sort of money, certainly not the established organizations?"

"I was thinking more of the new money in this world. What about the Chinese or the Arabs? The Saudis have more money than they know what to do with and then there are those super rich Russians—oligarchs they call them I think."

Jacques stood up. He walked over to the window to look down on the street three floors below. He stretched his arms in the air. "I need some fresh air. Come, help me clear up. Before we start spending the money we haven't yet earned we need to do some testing of our own." Returning to the table he picked up the small phial holding it up in the air. "Enough here for two more tests. Where shall we go? I think a different location tonight."

# Chapter Ten

## Cheshire

The silver-grey Jaguar slowed as it turned off the road. Two giant, black, wrought iron gates barred the way. The driver pressed a concealed button and silently they opened. The car glided 50-metres up the gravel driveway to come to a halt under an impressive porte cochère. The front door of the large house opened. A woman, somewhere in her early sixties, stepped out. Dressed in a smartly cut pink suit she walked briskly towards the car. The lawyer exited first. The woman acknowledged him but her eyes were fixed on the young woman who followed. They embraced each other the younger of the two towering over the older woman.

"I am so sorry, darling. It must be terrible for you," the older woman sobbed. She stepped back to look at her daughter. A second young woman was getting out. "Who is this, Kylie?" The mother looked surprised.

"This is Lisa."

"Oh!" replied her mother. She held out her hand. "You're a friend of my daughter are you?"

Lisa hesitated taking the hand. "Not really I . . ."

"I'll explain in the house, mother. Shall we go in?"

The driver remained with the car while they followed into the house. "Shall we have some tea down by the lake? Your father will not be back from Manchester until seven. He has heard the news."

They entered a large lounge. At the far end French windows opened onto a spacious garden. A slate path dissected a well-manicured lawn leading to a white wooden pergola. A green metallic garden table was posed in the middle with eight matching cushioned chairs. Twenty feet away a lake glistened in the afternoon sun. The mother indicated with her hand where the guests should sit. A young maid approached the table.

The mother spoke. "What would you like, Mr. Jefferson, some tea, coffee, or perhaps a fruit juice?"

"Tea would be nice, Mrs. Moon, thank you."

"And you Miss . . ."

"Lisa . . . a juice thank you," replied Lisa.

"Did you get that, Maria?"

"Tea, juice and for you, Madam? Asked the maid in a strong Spanish accent.

"My usual, and bring some cakes, not that my daughter will be tempted."

"So, Mr. Jefferson, what went wrong? Why did we loose the case?"

The solicitor paused for a moment before responding. "I did warn before going to trial. Rape can be a difficult thing to prove if there is no evidence of bruising or signs of a struggle."

"But my daughter was drugged."

"Yes, Mrs. Moon that was the foundation of our case, but with what? The fact that Kylie, Miss Moon, did not report the fact for well over twenty-fours made it impossible to conclude what substance was used.

"But that's the whole point, she was drugged surely . . ."

"Mother," interjected Kylie. "There's no point in us going all over this again. Mr. Jefferson and Mr. Tomlinson did their best. The fact was, the jury preferred to believe Crumpet than me. That's it. The case is closed."

"But surely," and she looked directly at Tomlinson, "we *must* appeal. Demand a retrial. Do whatever is necessary to clear your name. Your father will expect nothing less."

"I did discuss this briefly with Miss Moon," and he turned to look at her.

Kylie sat forward in her chair. "No, mother, I do not want to go through all this again. The publicity for one—it is simply not worth it."

"But we cannot just sit back and do nothing—let the bastard get away with it."

"Mother! Calm down. Lisa here has a similar story to tell. I want you to listen to her."

"Very well," replied Mrs. Moon, "if that's what you want."

"Lisa, tell mother what you told us in the car."

Lisa cleared her throat while moving forward in the chair. "Well, Mrs. Moon, my name is Lisa Evans. I work behind a bar at a pub near Congleton, The Plough, you might know it."

Kylie watched her mother grimace. She was clearly not impressed.

"It was a Monday night, some months ago. Monday is usually a quiet night. Normally I would have been off but Marjorie, the landlord's wife, asked me to cover for Pauline who always does Mondays. When we're busy we never have time to talk to a customer but like I said, it was a slow Monday. It was about nine-thirty when this little guy comes in. He ordered a glass of sweet white wine. He chose to sit at the bar and not at a table.

"I never gave him much thought. He just sat there keeping very much to himself. You see he certainly wasn't my type—too old and bald." Lisa watched a frown come over Mrs. Moon's face. "Not that I ever date customers that is," she added quickly. "Anyway, at ten-forty-five I called last orders. There were only three tables occupied, one was a local, the other two were couples. It was then he asked if he could buy me a drink. He looked harmless enough so I poured myself a cider. People started to leave. Taking a tray and a cloth I cleared the tables. I washed the glasses, tidied up the bar and called to Marjorie who was in the restaurant bar that I was closing. She replied she would come through to cash me up. It was then I went over to the man seated at the corner of the bar. I asked him if he would please finish his drink and leave as the bar was now closed.

"He asked me if he could quickly see the locket hanging around my neck as his mother possessed one very similar.

I thought nothing of it." Lisa put her hand to her chest and pulled out a gold chain upon which hung a purple stone. "Its amethyst, supposed to transmit calm and control anger, as well as being an aid to chastity, although a fat lot of good it did me."

"It's very beautiful. Where did you get it?" asked Kylie.

"My mother gave it to me as a twenty-first birthday present."

Conversation ceased as the maid arrived bearing a heavy ornate silver tray which she placed on the table. Without asking she poured the tea. From a crystal jug she poured freshly squeezed orange juice into two glasses which she handed to the girls. She was about to offer cake when Mrs. Moon stopped her. "Thank you, Maria, you can leave us now."

Kylie looked at Lisa, "Please continue," she asked.

"The man, I didn't know his name at that stage, touched the stone with his fingers to examine it. His fingers brushed my hand and as he leaned forward I got a strong smell of his aftershave. It was then I began to feel funny."

"How do you mean? Can you explain it to us?" asked Kylie.

"It's difficult to say. I sought of felt a warm feeling come over me."

"Hot flushes," interjected Mrs. Moon.

"Sort of . . . I'm not quite sure. Anyway the man, Crumpet, sat back on his stool, downed the remains of the wine and sort of smiled at me. I don't know why but somehow I couldn't keep my eyes off him. I remember locking the till and flicking off the bar lights. I fetched my bag, shouted to Marjorie that I was leaving, then walked through the darkened bar to the door. He stood there, opened it, and waited for me to come. I arrived at the door. I remember smelling again his strong after shave."

"What did it smell of? Can you describe it?" pleaded Kylie.

"It's difficult. I'm not very good at remembering smells. It was sort of musky with tones of wood, almost forest . . . yes, that's right possibly fern."

"I too remember a woody, perhaps leathery odor," added Kylie.

"Anyway," continued Lisa, "the next I remember is him leading me to this white van parked in the far corner of the car park."

"Did he use force to get you to accompany him?" asked Jefferson.

"No, that's the strange thing I went willingly, something I would never normally have done. Remember I didn't even know his name."

"Did he talk to you?" continued Jefferson.

"Not a word."

"So how did he communicate with you?"

"He didn't . . . I mean . . . I don't know."

"And, what happened then?" persisted Jefferson.

Lisa looked at Kylie.

"Go on, you have to finish the story, Lisa."

Lisa hesitated. "Well, we made love. I don't know what came over me."

"Did he use a condom?"

"No."

"Are you quite sure?"

Lisa glared at the lawyer.

"I'm sorry. I had to ask you. It is important, so what happened when the . . . lovemaking . . . the act was finished?"

"We lay there for a bit then he made me arouse him and we did it again."

"And you did all this willingly?"

Lisa smiled. "Yes, I suppose you could say I actually enjoyed it."

Mrs. Moon was about to speak but Kylie interrupted her. "How did he end it? What happened next?"

"We dressed and he escorted me to my car, which was parked on the other side of the car park."

"Did he say anything? Ask you for your phone number or anything?"

"No, nothing. It was as though we both knew it was over, never to be repeated."

"He never contacted you and you never saw him again, is that correct?" asked Jefferson.

"Two days ago I happened to pick up a newspaper. His picture was on it with the story of Kylie accusing him of rape. I recognized his face immediately. I'd practically forgotten the entire incident. It had happened. There was nothing I could do about it. But on seeing his face the memory of that night came flooding back. I needed to find out if what happened to Kylie is what I experienced. I tried to enter the court but they wouldn't permit me. They said it was full."

Kylie stood up. She picked up the jug of orange juice, "Some more Lisa?"

"Thank you, yes please."

Having refilled the glasses she replaced the jug on the silver tray. She turned to face her mother. "What Lisa has just told us is practically what happened to me. This bastard is using some form of hallucinating drug or aphrodisiac to trap his victims."

Mrs. Moon poured more tea for Jefferson. She cut a small slice of carrot cake for herself. "Do help yourself, Mr. Jefferson." She sat down. "So what are we going to do now?"

Jefferson put down his cup. "Legally speaking, I am not sure what we can do. Lisa's case is no different to Kylie's. The victim, if I may use this expression, went willingly with Crumpet. No physical force, no evidence of bruising, no torn clothing, no blood in fact nothing for the police to open a case other than the victim's statement."

"But what about this drug he used?" Argued Mrs. Moon, "surely that must count for something."

"It wasn't sprayed. It was not injected. It was not even dissolved in a drink or placed in food."

"But, Mr. Jefferson, it was smelt—the willingness to submit to Crumpet's carnal demands was induced through a strong perfume—that's a drug," argued Kylie.

"You are probably correct," agreed Jefferson. "Without having obtained the substance and having it chemically analyzed by a forensic chemist it would not stand up in a court of law. The only possible solution which comes to mind is if Lisa were now to charge Crumpet with rape. A court order could be obtained to search his premises on the hope of finding such a concoction."

"Wait a minute," cried Lisa. "There's no way I want to go through what Kylie has just experienced, exposing my private life in public and anyway, I simply could not afford the legal costs."

"I am sure my husband would agree to help."

"Thank you, Mrs. Moon but no. Surely, there must be other girls out there who have experienced what we have been through. Couldn't we maybe advertise? Try to get them to join us in a fresh case?"

"That idea has occurred to me, Lisa, but we must be very careful. For a start the publicity is the last thing Kylie and her family seek. Secondly, we might quite possibly attract all kinds of weird characters who would only jeopardize our case. And, thirdly, if we were able to bring a case to court without this substance it would be difficult to prove. Any half-rate defense council would be able to claim victimization against you because of this case we have just lost."

"Bloody Hell," shouted Kylie, "so that means the bastard has not only got away with it but is free to do it again and again."

"Shouldn't we at least inform the police? We could ask them to keep an eye on him," suggested Lisa.

"We could, but with the evidence we have I doubt if they could justify the manpower. They have far more serious crimes to investigate. The problem is we are not dealing with a pedophile or a viscous rapist. Crumpet has not physically injured his victims. Forgive me for saying this but both of you have indicated you willingly participated in going with him." Kylie was about to object but Jefferson raised his hand softly. "Please . . . here me out. Legally, pursuing this through the courts is not an option at this moment in time. We need proof, solid evidence which will convince a jury to have the man put away.

"The question is: how do we obtain this proof? There is I believe only one way. We need to hire a private investigator to look into the affairs of this Mr. Crumpet and to monitor his movements on a daily basis. It will not be cheap. It could last several months and, at the end, we still might not find the evidence we seek."

"Do you know such a person, Mr. Jefferson?"

"Yes, I do, Mrs. Moon. There is an agency whose services we have called upon from time to time. They are discrete. They do not come cheap but they are thorough. Would you like me to contact them on your behalf?"

"Let me first discuss the matter with my husband. Where is this . . . agency located?"

"Manchester."

She stood up. "If you will all excuse me, I have heard enough about this filthy business for one day. Kylie, will you show Mr. Jefferson and Miss Evans out when they are ready to leave? We will talk more about this with your father over supper tonight."

# Chapter Eleven

## Grasse

Raindrops hammered the green tiles bouncing and running down the pitched roofs. They slopped into the overflowing gutter before cascading down onto the street below only to splatter once more before being swallowed up by the ever-growing stream. Cars battled their way through the narrow streets like battleships cutting a wake through an angry sea. Their tires flung out torrents of water in a giant wake drenching any brave pedestrian foolhardy enough to have ventured outside.

The weather had changed. A ripple on the Polar front, way out in the north Atlantic was pushed upwards by a steady stream of warm subtropical air. This bulge quickly became a moving wave drawing the colder air ever-upwards, until it too rapidly cooled—a depression was born. Stretching for over one thousand miles, fifty-knot winds roared down the Irish Sea creating waves of up to twenty-meters high. Heavy banks of nimbostratus cloud darkened the sky finally releasing their voluminous quantities of water. The channel ports were closed. The Atlantic seaboard all the way to the Straits of Gibraltar was boiling like a caldron. Thunderous waves crashed ashore threatening sea defenses as the huge surge sucked back, built up, then thrust forward with increased vehemence.

Gale force winds blew the water-laden clouds eastwards. The weather bureau had predicted it. The cows and sheep in the fields knew the rains were coming. Noses turned upwards to the sky to smell the approaching moisture. Ancient instincts told brains to seek higher ground. On farms free range chickens scampered to corral their young to find cover.

The first heavy drop of rain landed onto the dry earth with a silent thud. For a minute or so it claimed its place in history by the tiny impact crater it created. But, just as suddenly, a second drop of rain, quickly followed by another and another, fell to earth. Now the dull thud of each raindrop was replaced with a resounding plop. The place of that first crater has been obliterated forever.

The dry soil quickly opened to allow the life-generating water to enter. Its hard exterior softened quickly to welcome the invader. Soon the surface became gooey. The land was transformed into a quagmire. It was not too long before the earth's tolerance to absorb the rain was reached. Small puddles rapidly grew in size. Called by an unknown force to reach the lowest level they ran becoming a small stream. Dry riverbeds were resurrected. They swelled and grew as more and more water found its way into them; always surging forward carrying with them the season's dead leaves and branches. The river became a torrent continuously gathering momentum. Soon the dry riverbanks could no longer contain it. Like an adolescent child it needed more space to grow. The waters clawed and stripped away at the earth that insisted on confining it, as its strength grew it surged forward carrying everything with it.

Yesterday's worry was drought. Today it was flooding—too much too soon. Farm dams were filling too rapidly. In the towns, drains were overflowing. Low-lying streets were becoming flooded. A winter storm had arrived in the middle of summer—why? Global warming was the cause. The weather patterns were changing. Some blamed the ungodliness of present day society. Everybody blamed the government.

Jean-Luc Picard, Director of Marketing, at Essence de la Grasse stared out of the boardroom window. The sky was overcast. Rain cascaded down the windows limiting visibility. The normal beautiful view of the Grasse countryside was hidden. The board meeting was not going well. It matched the weather. Sales were down. Blame it on the financial crisis in the United States. Blame it on the ever-rising oil price. Blame it on a war in the Middle East. Blame it on the Japanese encroaching into the perfume market. Blame it on the government. Jean-Luc listened as the Financial Director, Eugène Delacroix, droned on with his financial report.

"The fact is we shall not meet our budget for the second year in succession. Now, if you will turn to page three you will see the revised figures. The impact on the bottom line is drastic. A drop of 10% in sales impacts as a reduction of 45% in the net operating profit and that is—only if we are able to contain costs."

There was silence in the room as the figures were studied. The Managing Director, Charles Seberg, was the first to speak. "Thank you, Eugène, for the bad news. It is obvious we cannot just sit back and do nothing. Sales?" He posed the question directly at Jean-Luc. "What do you intend to do?" Sitting back in his executive chair at the head of the table he glanced at his heavy gold Rolex watch before tucking it under the cuff of his light-blue Calvin Klein suit. The meeting was taking longer than planned. His diary showed he had a luncheon appointment in Cannes at the celebrated Auberge de Chevalier followed by another meeting with the bankers—at least that was what his secretary had written down. The lunch part was correct. He was dining at the Auberge with Madeleine, his latest mistress. The fact she was younger than his youngest daughter by two years did not trouble him.

The problem distracting him was where to take her for the afternoon. The company flat in Cannes was out of the question. Hotels were too risky. They required registration and he could not take the risk of running into any of his acquaintances, let alone one of his wife's numerous friends. If she caught him cheating again he knew the consequences—divorce, the scandal he could cope with but the cost? He looked up at Jean-Luc. "Sorry, could you repeat that?"

"I said, I propose bringing forward our advertising campaign using that British model, Kylie Moon, as the new face of Essence de la Grasse. We plan to mirror Estèe Lauder who ran a very successful campaign using Elizabeth Hurley a few years back."

"What about that South African film star, Sharon Crowther? I thought we were signing her," asked Charles Seberg.

"Her agent is demanding six-million for a two year contract."

"Dollars?"

"No, Euros."

"Mon Dieu, that's crazy."

"That's what I said, Sir. There are a number of other possibilities but our advertising agency feels that Kylie has the perfect face. Apart from her natural beauty she exudes class. The fact she has a degree in natural sciences proves she is intelligent. It adds further weight. She is not just another sexy dumb bimbo."

The Managing Director discretely checked his watch. The problem of where to bed Madeleine lay prominent on his mind.

"The agency is proposing we use her profile together with endangered animals such as cheetahs and pumas. This will have a broad appeal. We might consider making some form of donation to the World Wild Life Trust."

"Hasn't this Kylie model been involved in some sort of rape case? I seem to remember reading about it... in the newspaper, I think."

"I sincerely hope not, Eugène. Otherwise, we may have to change our plans. I'll check with the agency as soon as this meeting is over," replied a worried Jean-Luc.

He couldn't get Madeleine's magnificent cleavage out of his mind. "Let's move on shall we? What news do you have of the market research on the new range of products?"

Jean-Luc opened a file in front of him. "It's too early to tell yet. We've had some luck however. We've been able to tap into a survey conducted six months ago through Buyer's World. They focused on the purchasing habits of transit passengers at the top twenty international airports. There is quite a lot of interesting information particularly why certain brands sell better than others. A lot has to do with positioning and also the accessibility of samplers." He glanced down to select a page. "Did you know there is a tendency today of younger women to spray their throats and cleavage whereas older women spray their wrists when testing a fragrance?"

Madeleine had a mole in the centre of her cleavage. He had called it her third nipple which had made her giggle.

"I should be able to report back with our proposals in time for the next board meeting. Other than that our big store campaign is on target. Our prize of a holiday for two in Cannes combined with an educational visit to our factory has been well received by the sales staff. There are a total of fifty-eight stores in ten different countries participating."

The yacht! That was where they could go. He would just have to be careful how he entered Le Yacht Club de Cannes. He could use the chandlery entrance. The keys were kept in the marina office. Madeleine would have to remain out of sight for a few minutes.

There was silence in the room. All eyes focused on the head of the table. They were waiting for him to speak. "Yes... well... thank you, Jean-Luc." Charles Seberg glanced down at the agenda. "Production—that's your baby, Serge." He sat back in his chair. His stomach rumbled. The thought of lunch filled his mind. Better have something light, perhaps perch or the duck bigarade. It was a specialty of the Auberge. Best to avoid meat and limit myself to only half bottle of Chambertin, otherwise I might fall asleep and that would never do.

"The problem with the Mimosa bottles has been sorted out. The supplier sent the wrong tops. Routine maintenance will take place on the three extractor plants over the next month. We will be shutting them down one by one."

"Will that affect production of any of our products?" Enquired Eugène Delacroix.

"No, but I'll liaise with stores to ensure we are holding sufficient stocks before we commence the shutdown. This brings me to our stock levels of base materials. I enclose the current inventory for your perusal." Leaning across the table he handed out a computer printout.

Charles Seberg took his copy. He began to scan the long list of products together with the quantities currently held but his mind was elsewhere—Madeleine. He wondered if she would be wearing those ridiculous black-lace-string panties. He enjoyed taking them off with his teeth. She would giggle and wriggle complaining his moustache tickled her stomach. He glanced at his watch. He needed to conclude the meeting within the next half hour. He was driving himself. Chauffeurs talked.

"You will note that our stocks of ambergris are very low. The world shortage has driven the price through the ceiling. Ambrette Seed is also very scarce since the volcano in Martinique destroyed the fields. We have been buying seed from Madagascar but the quality is very inconsistent. We may have to resort to India, but this will put the price up even further."

Eugène Delacroix interrupted. "Sorry, Serge, but considering the financial restraints shouldn't we be turning to our laboratory to come up with a synthetic alternative. After all, we have invested many millions of Euros in the latest scientific equipment not to mention the salaries we pay out each month. I think the time has come to make better use of this asset."

Serge Laurens, the Production Manager looked at the Managing Director before responding. "If it is the wish of this board that we break away from our hundred-year-old tradition of only using natural ingredients then so be it. However, I have no idea how Michel Ramonet and his team will react to such a move. You would have to clear this with him yourself, Charles."

Charles Seberg, the Managing Director, was in a trance. The thought had occurred to him that he should phone the marina office at the yacht club and have them fill the yacht's Jacuzzi. He wasn't sure if he could remember how it was done. Normally there was always a crewmember present to perform such a mundane task. His eyes glanced at the window. The rain was continuing to bucket down. The Jacuzzi was under cover on the stern deck but might it be too cold?

"Charles . . . Charles I said "You would have to clear this with him yourself."

"Quite . . . yes," he replied suddenly returning his focus to the meeting. "I do not think we should make any decision now . . . rather let's leave this for another day. *Tempus fugit* as they say. We need to press on. Is that all from you?"

Serge Laurens nodded that it was.

"Good, so that brings us to any other business . . . around the table." His eyes moved quickly from one member to another. Everyone knew his dislike for being surprised by any item which had not already been forwarded to his secretary for inclusion on the agenda. In most cases a phone call or a brief meeting usually solved the matter. Denise Vergé, the new Business Manager spoke.

"Thank you, Monsieur Seberg. I have a point for discussion."

Madam Marguerite Bise, the Managing Director's secretary, scowled at the young women who now held the floor. She blamed herself for this breach in etiquette. She knew her boss needed to get away to attend a very important meeting with the company's bankers in Cannes. She should have warned this young woman just how things were done. It was too late now. This new position of Business Manager had been the Chairman's initiative. She knew her boss was not completely in agreement with this appointment but, when the Chairman called . . . well only a fool would choose to disagree. His family after all, did own sixty-two percent of the company.

"I've been studying our I.T. systems and I have some suggestions to put to the board."

"Will this take long?"

"No, Monsieur Seberg, I shall be brief." Without waiting for a response she continued. "The company is currently working with four different computer programs. We have the accounting package—the inventory system—marketing runs their own programs—distribution is yet another. This results in an enormous amount of work being duplicated not to mention time being wasted."

Charles Seberg glanced at his watch. He did not want to be late picking up Madeleine. She would be waiting for him on the corner outside her flat in the student quarter of Cannes. If the rain continued and he was delayed she would be soaked. The thought of her young full breasts pushing out against a wet T-shirt began to arouse him.

"To improve efficiencies, which will considerably reduce operating costs, we need to have one integrated system." She paused to glance at Eugène Delacroix. "I have discussed this briefly with Monsieur Delacroix. The problem is each of our systems was procured at different intervals. Each has a different service provider resulting in four service contracts. To be quite frank two systems are quite outdated. The individual service providers have already tendered to upgrade their programs, which is not a cheap exercise."

"Didn't we discuss this, two months ago?" asked Serge Laurens.

Madeleine was going to be wet. He was about to respond but Eugène beat him to it.

"We did, but no decision was reached."

Denise noticed the managing director had closed his file. He was beginning to fidget. "Let me come directly to the point. I called in each of the service providers. I informed them what our requirements were: one integrated computerized system. After each of them had extolled the virtues of their own product I told them to go away—to work together—only return when they could tell me how each system can integrate with the other. I know for a fact this will not happen. Therefore, I request the board's permission to go out to tender for a new integrated management system. There will of course be an initial capital cost but the savings in time, labor and efficiency will recover this outlay."

Madeleine was getting in his car. Her sopping rain coat fell open revealing . . .

There was silence in the room. Eugène Delacroix spoke. "I confer with Denise. We have discussed this before on several occasions. Now we have Denise on board I believe we should let her drive this project."

Charles Seberg sat upright. "Excellent . . . yes . . . I agree." He glanced quickly around the board table. "All in favor . . . good." He nodded to his secretary. "You've got that, Madame Bise?"

She nodded, lifting her HB-pencil in confirmation.

He stood up. "If you'll excuse me I have an urgent meeting in Nice."

# Chapter Twelve

## Paris

It was Jacques's idea. Together they walked up the Avenue George Cinq passed the famous five-star hotel which bore its name. Their attention was drawn to a flotilla of black limousines which pulled into the reserved parking in front of the entrance. Liveried footman stepped forward to open the rear doors. Tall, mean-looking men dressed in tight-fitting dark suits jumped out of the front. They talked softly into microphones which disappeared inside their jackets. Curled strands of wire led to an earphone. Menacingly, they stamped forward clearing space for the car's occupants. Mushroomed between phalanxes of burly black suits the car's occupants quickly disappeared inside the building.

"I wonder who that was."

"Must be important, a diplomat perhaps?"

"Possibly. Just think, Jacques, it could be us in a few years once the formula is perfected."

Pierre laughed. They had stopped outside a small expensive boutique. "I like that dark suit with the blue-striped shirt and red tie, *très chic*."

"But I don't like the price. Come . . . for the moment we will just have to stick to *Prix Unix* to buy our wardrobe."

They continued walking up the road. The lights, sounds and crowds on the Champs-Elysees grew louder with each step. Cars of every description hurled down the six-lane boulevard on both sides in opposite directions. Their lights gleamed like cat's eyes as they flashed passed. Built by the Emperor Napoleon, wide enough, so a full battalion of his army could march in one line it was now perhaps the most famous street in the world—and one of the most expensive. Gargantuan billboards strategically placed high up on the corners of buildings flashed like leviathan television screens. Daring the world to drive this car—wear this perfume—drink this drink—invest now in your exclusive place in the sun—fly this airline and you too qualify to become a super-jetsetter.

Money. Spend spend spend was the message shouted out from the giant Virgin record store to the potpourri of dazzling fashion stores, shoe shops, computer mega-stores plus every modern necessity essential to maintain a contemporary, trendy, healthy lifestyle. When the shopping became too much then the exhausted consumer could fall back on a myriad bars, cafes and restaurants. Wine bars, Wimpy hamburgers, Kentucky Fried Chicken, Asian noodle bars, German sausage houses, Starbucks Coffee—every multinational fast food outlet worth their salts was represented. Only the traditional French bistro or grander auberge was missing. The astronomical rents compounded with unrealistic labor laws had ensured the demise of the traditional French cuisine once and for all.

They needed to cross over. Traffic lights changed to red. A flotilla of cars screeched to a sudden halt. An armada of pedestrians made the precarious crossing to the centre aisle. Sandwiched in the middle of sixty people the two young men waited patiently for the lights to change. The air was full of conversation—English, German, Italian, Spanish, Chinese, Japanese, Russian, Arabic, Greek and occasionally a smattering of French could be heard spoken by the diverse crowd.

Fifteen minutes later they were walking up the Rue Balzac leaving the noise and bustle of the Champs Elysees behind them. Finally, they stopped outside a large nondescript building. All was in darkness except for a narrow doorway on the side, lit with garish pink lights.

"Are you sure?"

"Come on, we've come this far . . . might as well go the whole hog."

Two large apparitions dressed in black suits blocked their approach. "Lift your arms," they grunted. Both Jacques and Pierre obliged. A handheld metal detector was run over their bodies. There was a sudden ping. "What's that, remove it *slowly*?" Pierre reached into his trouser pocket and brought out a small Nokia phone. The apparitions stepped aside.

They entered a brightly lit foyer. A third apparition asked to see their membership cards.

"We're not members. We're from out of town," lied Jacques.

"Pay the cashier."

They were directed to a cage on the side behind which sat a young man. He was wearing a pink, tight-fitting T-shirt with the phrase "La Reine Rules" screen-printed across the chest. Numerous rings pierced his ears, lips, eyebrows even his tongue. He smiled. "Forty Euros, please." A speech impediment prolonged the please implying a snake was spitting out the words. Pierre nervously took out the money and pushed in under the grill.

"Thanks, is this your first time, boys?" hissed the man.

"Yes," replied Pierre.

The man handed across a receipt. A dozen rings, plain, dazzling, large and small cluttered his thin fingers. "Enjoy," and he winked at them.

Together they descended the red carpeted stairs down into the bowls of the building. Pink and white LED lights flickered from the ceiling. The crooning voice of Michael Franks became louder. Their eyes made out a long bar which ran the full length of the far wall. Pink, green and mauve back-lighting lit up the numerous shelves crowded with exotic bottles of every description. Banquette seats with low tables encompassed a small glass dance floor upon which couples danced closely. They thread their way around the floor towards the bar.

A muscular barman wearing a black string-vest approached them. Black curly hairs clouded his chest up to his neck. "Two beers, please."

The barman frowned. "We only serve beer with a chaser."

Jacques looked at Pierre. "I prefer wine if that's the case."

"White or red?"

"White, Chablis, if possible?" Replied Pierre.

Neither spoke as they quietly sipped their wine while taking in the atmosphere. Their eyes gradually became focused to the darkly lit room. Table lamps glowed dimly emitting a muted red light from each table. The glass dance floor reflected a soft kaleidoscope of multicolored lights which changed and pulsated to the throbbing music. The room was half-full. A dozen couples groped their way around the floor. The music suddenly changed. Freddy Mercury was begging to be set free. Some couples left the floor while others jumped up. A middle-aged man, with balding grey hair and a large round belly, dressed in a white Elvis-type jacket, began to perform his John Travolta routine. His younger partner giggled and shouted encouragement as the man attempted to jump higher and bend lower in discord to the music.

"Do you see what I can see?" Whispered Pierre.

"Yes," replied an embarrassed Jacques. "Fancy a dance, darling?"

"Fuck Off," responded Pierre out of the corner of his mouth.

Freddie Mercury was enjoying riding his bicycle as more couples entered the room. "Like another?" asked Pierre.

Jacques nodded his head.

Pierre waved to the barman, "Same again, please."

"I need a crap."

"Turn you on do I?" ridiculed Pierre.

"Some hope; try to behave yourself while I'm gone."

Pierre paid for the wine. He turned his back on the floor and began to study the bar. The brightly lit shelves boasted a myriad of exotic bottles. Some he had never seen before. There were two barmen working. They appeared to have divided the bar between them. Pierre decided he had "hairy armpits" to serve him as the other barman wore a white shirt. His head was shaven.

"Is this seat taken? Good. Mind if I join you?"

Pierre turned around. A smallish man exquisitely dressed in a lightweight beige suit sporting an enormous purple cravat under a crisp white shirt had posed himself on Jacque's stool. At first glance Pierre estimated the man to be somewhere in his mid-fifties or early sixties. Pierre was about to speak when the barman came waltzing up.

"Good evening, Monsieur Lucian, and how are you . . . the usual?"

The man waved a manicured had in the direction of hairy armpits. Light danced, reflected from a large diamond ring. "And bring an extra glass for my friend here."

The barman spun around. Pierre was about to speak. The man held out his hand. "Hi, I'm Lucian, pleased to meet you."

Instinctively, Pierre took the hand. It was damp and limp. Hairy armpits returned carrying a silver ice bucket which he banged down on the bar. From it he extracted a bottle of champagne. With great dexterity he skillfully peeled off the decorative foil to reveal the wire holding down the cork. With a twist of his fingers he unscrewed the wire discarding it behind the bar. Next, he gently tipped the bottle whilst squeezing the top of the cork between his finger and thumb. With a gentle pop, followed by a hint of gas, the cork was removed. Finally, he poured a drop into a tall champagne flute.

"Excellent, as always, Perrier-Jouët Belle Époque, I adore the flowery bottle as much as the champagne." The diamond flashed again as a finger pointed to Pierre's empty glass. "*À votre santé.*"

"*Santé*," responded Pierre. Their glasses clinked.

Lucian took several sips. He smacked his lips. "The first taste is always the best, before the palate becomes complacent—don't you think?" Before Pierre could reply he continued. "Your first time at La Reine Rules?" Again he gave no time for Pierre to respond. "I can always tell. I'm here most nights. I'm almost part of the furniture." And he giggled loudly, "aren't I, sweetie?" Hairy armpits nodded his agreement and topped up the glasses before moving off to attend to another customer.

"I live in a cute little apartment just around the corner with just my little Max to keep me company. He's ever so cute and intelligent. He always tells his daddy when its time for wee-wees and walkies. But I am so rude, as is my habit. I am monopolizing the conversation. Do tell me, dear boy, all about yourself. I want to know *everything*." Lucien leaned forward placing his hand gently on Pierre's thigh.

Somewhat shocked, highly embarrassed, Pierre froze staring at the offending hand. He did not hear Jacques return.

"That's nice. I'm away five minutes and you're picking up every man in the house."

Pierre looked at Jacques—mortified. Lucian immediately withdrew his hand. He touched the side of his face with it. His mouth dropped. "Oh! I am so sorry. You never said you were taken. I feel such a fool."

"Relax," replied Jacques. "What's that you're drinking—champagne?"

Lucian leaned over to pull the bottle from the ice bucket. "Come. Have a drink." He snapped his fingers in the air to attract hairy armpit's attention. "Another glass," he mouthed.

"Excellent, is it a special vintage?" asked Jacques, savoring the taste.

Lucian showed him the bottle with its beautiful engraved white flowers. "Perrier-Jouët Belle Époque. Every year I buy thirty cases. I put them in my cellar and forget about them for five years. Champagne peeks at seven years so I make sure I always drink the wine when it is coming into its best. After all isn't that how life should be lived?"

The cut of the beige suit, the enormous diamond ring, 360 bottles of expensive champagne, Jacques was struggling to calculate the cost in his head.

"Why don't you pull up a bar stool? Or, why don't we go and sit over there?" Lucian pointed to an empty banquette seat next to the dance floor.

"Why not," replied Jacques winking at Pierre. "I'm sure we'll be much more comfortable."

Lucian called to hairy armpits. "Send the bucket over together with another bottle, Sweetie."

Sir Elton John was blowing a candle in the wind as they sat back in the lush red velvet seats. Lucian placed himself in the middle. More people had entered the room. "So, who are you boys? Where are you from? What do you do with yourself when you're not drinking champagne with an old man?" And he chuckled away to himself.

Pierre looked at Jacques. Jacques looked at Pierre. Neither spoke.

"Come along now, don't be shy. I'm beginning to think you both might be straight—that would never do now would it?"

Jacques laughed. "There's not much to tell really. I'm a research scientist at the Sorbonne and Pierre here is in computers. What do you do, Lucian, when you're not drinking champagne?"

He touched his lips with his index finger. The large diamond glittered. "That would be telling too much, after all, we have only just met and anyway, I asked the question first. So tell me, what is it you are researching?"

"I'm conducting research into how the body's olfactory senses relate to pheromones, the biological substances which affect biorhythms."

"Mon Dieu! What on earth is that? It sounds positively disgusting," laughed Lucian loudly, waving his hand in the air as though to emphasis the point.

"It's all to do with smell. How different substances, when smelt, affect the body by causing chemical reactions, which can change metabolism even cause organ failure. A typical extreme example is nerve gas or mace."

Lucian leaned closer towards Jacques. Their body's touched as he lifted his right arm exposing his wrist. "Here, Mr. Scientist, what can you tell me about this?" Jacques had no choice but to smell the man's wrist.

"It's strong. I'll give you that. I'm no expert in men's deodorants but I can detect lavender, possibly jasmine."

"Not bad . . . close, myrrh is used in the base note. It generates the slight balsamic odor, the hint of masculinity. I wouldn't want to be wearing a girl's perfume now would I?" He giggled loudly. "You won't find it any shop. I have it created exclusively for me by L'Artisan Parfumeur located at Montparnasse."

"Interesting," remarked Jacques. He fumbled in his pocket and removed a small phial. Pierre stared with horror. Jacques caught his gaze but ignored it. Carefully, he removed the top allowing a drop of the liquid to fall on his left wrist. He replaced the top then tested it to make sure it was properly sealed before returning it to his pocket. He held out his wrist to Lucian. "Tell me . . . what do you think about this?"

Lucian gently held Jacques's wrist to his nose. He sniffed several times before reluctantly releasing it. "Mimosa, possibly nutmeg . . . I'm not sure." He lifted up Jacques's hand this time cradling it in his own before bringing it up to his nose. "Sandalwood . . . Oak moss, am I getting close?"

"Possibly."

"Go on. Tell me. Where did you get it? I like it. I like it very much; very masculine, but not too butch if you get my gist."

Jacques pulled his hand away. He glanced quickly at Pierre. Lucian reached for his champagne. He downed the glass. Pierre topped it up. Perspiration appeared on Lucien's brow and above his lip. He pulled out a red handkerchief to dab his forehead. "It's getting frightfully hot in here," he muttered. He moved closer to Jacques. This time he grabbed Jacques's hand pulling it up to his face. Pierre watched in horror as Lucian rubbed his nose on Jacques's wrist. Jacques tried to pull his hand away but Lucian held tightly to it. His other hand reached across to fondle Jacques's thigh.

"Not here, not now," gasped Jacques as he struggled to rise.

Pierre was already on his feet. "Look, I think we should go."

Lucian stood up. He grabbed Jacques's arm again. "Yes . . . yes, you're right. We should go. My flat is only around the corner."

"But . . ."

"Come . . . there is no time. We must go now."

Too frightened to force Julian's vice like grip off him without creating a commotion, the three men pushed their way around the dance floor, through the crowds, and up the stairs. Pierre managed to whisper in Jacques's ear. "As soon as we are outside we must make a run for it."

Jacques nodded his agreement.

They had arrived back at the cashier's cage. One of the giant apparitions stepped forward. "Leaving now, Monsieur Bourboché?"

"Yes, Frank."

"To your apartment, Monsieur Bourboché?"

"Yes, that's right," gasped Lucian.

They had reached the doorway. Jacques could feel the cooler night air on his face. They stepped out onto the street. The apparition followed. Jacques craned his neck to see.

"Hey, why are you following us?" asked Pierre nervously.

Lucian hugged Jacques tighter. "Don't be scared, darling, he works for me. He'll come with us to the apartment to make sure we're all quite safe."

"I don't understand?" asked Pierre.

"Didn't I tell you, darlings? I own *La Reine Rules*," and he tried to kiss Jacques on the cheek as they walked along. "I am the queen, who rules," and he giggled loudly. "Ooh, that perfume is divine. You must tell me where you get it. I'll make it worth your while, and you." He put his right arm out to pull Pierre closer to him.

# Chapter Thirteen

# Manchester

They chose to take the train from Altringham to Manchester. It was easier than driving—trying to find their way around a city, which neither knew very well—plus the nightmare of parking. From Piccadilly Street Station they caught a tram to Salford Quays. Public transport—it was a new experience for Kylie and she enjoyed it.

A week had passed since her fatal day in court. The story of the trial was now history. The media had soon switched their attention to more juicy topics. There was the high court judge photographed in a compromising position with a convicted male prostitute. There was the cabinet minister unable to explain clearly how he came into possession of a five-million pound house in Surrey, registered in his wife's name of course. Pop stars, sports celebrities, well-known television and film faces were photographed denying all knowledge of the illegal drugs found on their premises and of course there was always the Middle East to provide horrific stories of bestiality.

They came from two very distinctive backgrounds. Kylie was brought up in the stockbroker belt of Cheshire, in a mansion of a house with servants, overlooking a large lake or mere as it was referred to locally. On the opposite side, practically on the horizon, stood the Mere Golf and Country Club—eighteen championship holes, health hydro, tennis, squash and everything fashionable for the well-healed mink and manure Cheshire elite to indulge themselves. Educated privately and *finished-off* in Switzerland, before entering Oxford where she graduated with a degree in natural sciences, her striking facial beauty and tall thin stature had long captured fashion photographers' clicking lenses. Father's contacts, not to mention money, had further helped to accelerate her career in modeling haut couture.

Lisa came from a very different world. Her mother was only seventeen at the time of her birth. Her father, she vaguely remembered him, had disappeared just before her fifth birthday. Her mother had moved in with Dave. Lisa was never quite sure what her *stepfather* did for a living. He was home more than at work. When she was eight he disappeared for two years. "Gone to sea," her mother had explained. But her friends at school in Runcorn understood—everybody in the town knew—her *stepfather* was in prison, not that Lisa cared. It was perhaps the best two years of her childhood. Her mother no longer sported a black eye or had difficulty in explaining away her bruises. The small council house in which they lived was quiet. It no longer smelt of stale beer, sweaty socks and cigarette smoke. But, the two years quickly passed and Dave returned.

He never married her mother. They never really saw the point. Her mother held a solid job as secretary to one of the managers of Unilever. It was her escape. She paid the rent, bought the food, while struggling all the time to provide for Lisa as the girl grappled with school and adolescence. Dave drifted from one job to another with increasingly long periods of inactivity in between. Everton Football Club, racehorses and greyhounds preoccupied his mind when it was sober enough to focus.

At seventeen Lisa left home. Dave's final drunken attempt to seduce her when her mother was at work was the final straw. Lisa went to live with a friend. She got a job with Tescos. The money was poor but she could survive. Marks and Spencer attracted her. They offered more prestige and better wages. She was beginning to move up in the world, then came the cuts. Sales were down. Restructuring they called it. It was necessary to refocus the business. This meant less staff. They explained it so nicely—LIFO—last in first out. She was young. She had her whole life in front of her loads of opportunities awaited her.

At nineteen she had grown into a pretty girl, not stunning, but attractive. Unlike most of her friends she chose not to become too closely involved with boys. She did not trust them. There was good money to be made in waitressing. She learnt the hard way. The hours were long, the work tiring but if you smiled and went that extra mile the tips made up for it. Then, a summer season job in Jersey, making beds, waiting at tables attracted her.

When the hotel closed at the end of the season they offered her a contract for the next year at almost double the money. They wrote her a flowering reference. She was twenty. She now knew what she wanted to do with her life. She had discovered her vocation. On returning to the mainland she found work as an assistant manager in a restaurant located in a busy shopping centre on the outskirts of Chester. The hours suited her. Three nights a week she supplemented her income by working at the Plough, sometimes in the restaurant, other times behind the bar. She enrolled on a three-year correspondence-course in business management. Any spare time was occupied in studying.

Once a month she met with her mother, never Dave. His name was no longer mentioned. It baffled her why her mother stuck with him. She assumed there must be some deeply hidden masochistic reason. The battered housewife syndrome she had heard it called on a radio station. At twenty-two her life was in order. She enjoyed her job. She was learning about the business. The studying stimulated her mentally. The occasional arms-length date or night out with the girls completed her life. The future looked good until—that night in the van in the car park of the Plough.

"Nobody, who has *not* experienced what we went through, can possibly understand."

"I agree, Kylie," answered Lisa. "It's the feeling of being dirty, unclean. No matter how hard you scrub you just can't erase the memory—the smell."

The tram rattled along the track. They could now clearly see the canal. Sitting on the upper deck they were pushed together as it rounded a bend. They had met twice during the week—"planning the campaign," Kylie had pronounced. In spite of their different backgrounds they quickly discovered they both shared a lot in common. Where Kylie was headstrong, ready to jump into a situation headfast, Lisa was more cautious. The tram was slowing down. They had arrived at the station.

Quickly they both descended. "Have you been here before?" asked Kylie.

Lisa shook her head. "He said to meet him outside the Lowry at eleven. What time is it now?"

"We're early. It's ten thirty, time to have a look around."

"Check out the rendezvous," responded Lisa.

"The Manchester ship canal was opened in 1894 and soon became the busiest port in the country after London. The Salford Quays was the heart of the complex. Ships and barges brought cargo from all over the world into the many giant warehouses. Throughout the sixties and seventies trade dwindled to a mere trickle. The Salford Lock finally ceased operating in 1982. The area became desolate and run down. Today the Salford Quays is home to new businesses, luxury apartments. It is thriving and booming once more. In the heart of the Quays lies the world famous Lowry dedicated to . . ."

"That's where we're meeting him," interrupted Lisa.

Together they walked away from the brass plaque following the signs. They chatted freely. Lisa was fascinated by Kylie's travels, the places she had visited and the famous names she casually mentioned. They soon arrived at the Lowry.

"Of course, the artist L S Lowry. He painted those famous matchstick figures and those dreary dull North of England factory scenes."

"I quite like some of his work. He must have been seen as quite abstract in his day." Lisa picked up a brochure from a stand.

"Let's sit over there outside the café. Fancy a drink or something?"

"Cappuccino would be nice, thank you."

Lisa sat browsing through the brochure while Kylie went off to the self-service counter. She returned three minutes later with Lisa's coffee and a plain mineral water for herself.

"Lowry's people introduce the variety of the artist's singular, special vision. Early drawings demonstrate his mastery of traditional life-study training. At the heart of the exhibition, however, are Lowry's crowds. Paintings such as *Britain at Play* and *Going to the Match* team with life and energy. Without the streets, factories, the tenements and the open, public areas Lowry's people would have no purpose." Lisa stopped reading to sip her coffee. She put the booklet down on the table. "I'd like to go in once we've concluded the meeting. Might as well as we are here. I'm not one for art galleries but there is something fascinating about his style."

"That's fine by me." Kylie glanced at her watch. "It's five minutes to eleven, we'd better prepare ourselves."

Lancelot Slim, Lance, to only his closest friends, whom he counted on one hand, had watched the two girls descend from the tram. The Commander, as his subordinates and numerous acquaintances called him, followed them from a safe distance. They were not expecting anyone to follow them so surveillance was easy, not that this would present a problem to someone who had spent his entire life living in the shadows.

Dressed in a brightly colored summer shirt, which he chose to wear outside his grey flannel trousers, he looked very much a tourist. Middle-aged, possibly bordering on retirement, he blended in with the summer visitors. Half an hour ago he had changed out of his Harrington Brothers, lightweight blue suit, hand crafted for him by the small private Manchester tailor, who only took on new *gentlemen* if, they were recommended by an existing client. His suite of offices occupied the entire floor of a seven-storey block overlooking the lock. No name, no signs, indicated what business was conducted behind the closed doors. The top floor had been selected because the flat roof with its raised edge helped to hide the numerous satellite dishes and aerials so necessary to the successful running of his organization.

He studied the two girls as he followed them. The taller must be Kylie Moon, the international model. The way she walked, her pose, told it all. Men of all ages were drawn to steal a second glance. There was a mystical magnetism drawing their hungry eyes towards her. The other girl was not unattractive but just another pretty girl of sorts. Kylie's black hair was worn tied back in a bun, almost maiden-like. She wore pastel, three-quarter length trousers and a silk, long-sleeved blouse. Her body was completely covered unlike the latest trend where girls of her age liked to expose buttocks and tummy buttons. Large, wraparound dark glasses partially hid the top half of her head. Lisa, the shorter one, wore jeans, tight fitting, which emphasized her girlish figure. The sleeveless red top struggled to meet the heavy leather belt which hung low on her waist. The strap of a black brassiere was visible on her upper back.

The Commander waited for them to sit down. The model went off to purchase drinks. The smaller girl was reading a brochure. He ambled over to the counter and ordered himself an orange juice.

"Mind if I join you two ladies?"

The model looked up surprised. "We are expecting someone actually."

"Yes, me, I believe." Lancelot Slim pulled up a chair and sat down.

They shook hands; his grip was firm and hard. Lisa stared into his steely-blue eyes. Kylie studied his short cropped grey hair. They both subconsciously came to the same conclusion. This was not someone you would wish to make an enemy of.

Lancelot broke the silence. "Well ladies, here I am. I deemed it prudent to meet first in the open here. It is so less formal than a stuffy old office. Your solicitor, Mr. Trevor Jefferson, has briefed me about the unfortunate incidents and of course I am conversant with your recent case, Miss Moon. However, I would like to hear it directly from you."

Kylie glanced at Lisa. "Shall I?"

Lisa nodded her head.

Kylie sipped her water. She looked around nervously. Lancelot leaned forward on the table. "Please speak freely, nobody can here us and I do not require every detail just the basic facts."

"Do you know the Deansgate Arcade in Chester?"

Lancelot indicated that he did.

"It had been a long day. We had been shooting . . . filming a series of ads for Vogue. The theme was leather and the magazine wanted to use the Tudor-style backdrop of the architecture. It was ten o'clock by the time we had finished. Naturally, we had drawn a crowd of curious onlookers. They were kept away by security guards. We were on the upper level. The lighting boys were beginning to dismantle their equipment and I was ready to leave when a group of teenage girls asked for my autograph. There were about six of them. I stopped and concentrated on signing everything that was thrust in front of me."

"Is that usual?" interrupted Lancelot.

"Sometimes it happens. One gets use to it really. Anyway, a man . . . Crumpet, of course I never knew his name, thrust his way forward asking me to sign a book. He insisted I use his pen. I thought nothing of it. I took his pen. I tried to write my name but the pen was dry. I handed it back to him and was about to use my own when he blew on it then shook it. He handed it back to me and as he did so he leaned forward, our hands touched and I smelt a strong perfume, aftershave I suppose. I signed my name, handed back the pen and again our hands touched briefly. He thanked me and asked if he could walk down with me. He was very polite and anyway the rest of the team was following.

"We had arrived at the lower level when he began to tell me about his young niece. She wanted to be a model and could I offer him some advice as to what steps she should take. Again, I couldn't help but smell his perfume. The strange thing was it seemed to draw me closer to him. It was as though I needed to smell more of it. The next thing I knew we were walking towards the car park together. I could see my car but some force . . . I can't describe it, drew me closer to him. Before I knew it I was getting into the front of his van." She stopped. "Must I continue . . .? I'd rather not."

Lancelot leaned back in his chair. He smiled. "No, of course if you don't want to—just a few questions though. He drove off and at some stage you willingly got out and went around to the back of the van."

Kylie nodded her head.

"Am I correct in saying he did not use force or verbally threaten you in any way?"

"Yes."

"Were you fully conscious the whole time? Were you aware of what you, or should I say, *he* was doing with you?"

"Yes, that's the strange thing. I suppose in a way I participated willingly, yet somehow I didn't. It was as though my body was removed somehow distant."

"After the act, what happened then?"

Kylie drained the last of her water. "I . . . we got dressed. He drove me to my car. I got out and drove home to my parent's house."

"Did he use a condom?"

"No, that's how I was able to get his semen stains on my underwear."

"Tell me what happened when you went home. What did you do?"

"I was tired. I felt strange. My parents were in bed. I went to my room took a shower, made myself a hot chocolate and went to bed. But I could not sleep. I tossed and turned. I switched on the television before finally dozing off."

Lancelot studied Kylie. He then turned to Lisa. "Did you experience similar after-effects . . . the same sort of feeling when you eventually went home?"

"Yes, I did. I felt very depressed almost suicidal."

Lancelot sat back. His hand touched his forehead. "It is obvious he is using some sort of hallucinogen to create a feeling of well-being almost euphoria in conjunction with an aphrodisiac. Such drugs do exist but I have never heard of one used in this way, at least not so effectively. So, what exactly do you want me to do? Have him beaten up? Catch him and castrate him?"

"Would you really do that?" asked Kylie.

"It can be done, not by me of course, but there are people who earn their living in such ways. I certainly would not advise it no matter how tempting a course of action it may seem. So, what do you truly want?"

It was Lisa's turn to speak. "We know," and she looked at Kylie for confirmation. "We are probably not the only women he has taken advantage of and, he will continue to play his evil games until he is caught or, someone puts a stop to him. We've discussed with Mr. Jefferson the legalities of preparing a fresh case using me, but without proof, without obtaining a sample of the substance and having it chemically analyzed it would be a waste of time. We want you," and again she looked at Kylie, "Mr. Slim to obtain it."

Lancelot ran his fingers through his short-cropped grey hair. "Can I get you, ladies, another drink?" He waved his arm in the air. One of the counter hands came forward from behind the buffet.

"Yes, Commander."

"Sally, would you be an angel and bring me another juice." He pointed to Kylie.

"Water, plain please."

"Cappuccino, thanks."

"Breaking into a private residence then stealing a substance in order to use it in a case of law would not win your case—assuming that is—we were able to find it in the first place. The problem is we do not even know what we are looking for. The answer is surveillance—at least eighteen-hour surveillance. It is not easy. It is not like on television and in the movies. It can take months—years even. A dedicated team of three would be required. They would have to work very carefully and not draw attention to themselves. Such professionalism does not come cheap."

Kylie handed over a sheet of paper. "Crumpet lives with his mother at this address. He owns a small antique shop in the village of Beeston, near Tarporley."

Lancelot took the paper, studied it briefly, folded it and placed it in his trouser pocket. "Here is what I propose. We can do what I call a preliminary investigation to start with. I'll appoint a man to visit these addresses. He will scout the layout of the land and prepare a report as to how big a team will be required. Sometimes one person at a time will suffice. It all depends upon the habits of the suspect being followed. For this I will charge £2,000 together with a cost estimate for an extended period. Now how does that sound to you?"

Lisa looked at Kylie who replied immediately. "Can I give you a cheque now, or do you prefer cash?" and she reached for her bag.

"Not so fast," replied Lancelot. "It takes a few days to set something like this up. First, I will send you a contract together with a pro-forma invoice. If you're happy with the conditions you sign it and return it to me with your cheque."

"Do you have a card?" asked Lisa.

Lancelot produced a slim leather wallet from which he produced two white embossed cards. He handed them across the table.

"Commander Lancelot Slim, Chairman, Special Services International." Lisa turned the card over. It was blank. "What exactly does Special Services International do?"

Lancelot smiled politely. "Many things, young lady, many different things."

"Such as? Can you be a little more specific?"

Lancelot paused before replying. "Let me say my organization, which has been established for over thirty years, performs a variety of functions. We investigate. Isn't that what brings you both here today. We find missing people. The British Government is one of our major clients. Normally, I would not involve us in a case such as yours. I would respectfully decline and my office would refer you to other agencies. However, after what Trevor Jefferson, your solicitor informed me I became intrigued.

"We underestimate the power of smell. My organization includes a dog division. Apart from Alsatians, which we use for guarding and protection assignments, we have cocker spaniels especially trained to smell out hidden explosives. However, the deadliest weapon in our arsenal is Fred and Joe—two bloodhounds. They possess the most powerful noses in nature. Their short stubby legs enable their oversize heads to travel fast centimeters above the ground hour after hour in search of a scent. Other dogs would quickly tire. Every now and again they would have to raise their heads to rest their tired neck muscles. This is when they loose the scent. The bloodhounds' long ears trail along and help to funnel the smell towards the nose shutting out other confusing scents."

The girls laughed.

"Smell has the power to suppress the left side of our brains, the rational lobe, while stimulating the right lobe, the area evoking memories and emotions. Of our five senses sight, sound and touch are physical but taste and smell are chemical. I read somewhere that the human nose is capable of recognizing some 500,000 different aromas. I for one have difficulty in identifying ten. Many gases used by security forces worldwide to disperse unruly crowds contain obnoxious odors. If you want to empty a crowded room strong body pong will usually do the trick. Yet, human sweat is supposed to be nature's aphrodisiac.

"Anyway, I deviate. If this Crumpet character has devised, or got his hands upon a chemical or substance, which can affect the type of character change in female human behavior which you describe; it is important we investigate it, and if necessary neutralize it."

"Why?" Kylie asked somewhat surprised.

"If such a substance exists just imagine the terror and chaos that could result if it fell into the hands of terrorists."

# Chapter Fourteen

# Banbury

The ground was still damp. The early morning sun had not jet burnt off the night dew. Terry Bagshaw lay flat on the groundsheet. The camera-binoculars were trained on the cottage 100-yards away. It was the second day. Yesterday had been spent driving the countryside then walking around surveying the small farm. Robertson's Book of British Birds—the edited edition—was stuffed into his stalking-jacket. That was his cover except his knowledge of birds was less than basic. He would be hard pressed to differentiate between a common garden sparrow and a robin if put to the test.

The countryside, the fresh country air, the solitude; it made a difference from the normal surveillance of sitting in a car watching, or pavement pounding after some prurient individual who was cheating on a partner. The front door of the cottage was opening. Terry refocused the binoculars. Four black cats came strutting out in a straight line, one after the other. Half way to the farm gate they stopped. Two turned right while two turned left. They then continued walking, this time in pairs. "Well I'll be damned," Terry muttered under his breath. The door remained open but there was no further sign of life. He checked his watch. He pulled out his notebook. He began writing, "Door opened. Six fifteen—four black cats exited."

Inside the cottage Archibald Crumpet was in the bathroom. His mother was downstairs in the kitchen.

Terry shifted his body. Turning on his side he reached for the thermos flask. Using the cup-top he poured out the steaming coffee. From a plastic container he removed a cheese sandwich. Slowly he began to chew it. His partner, Jennifer, had made them for him the previous night. They had had an argument. Her hints on marriage were becoming more pronounced. She was thirty-two. It was time they considered a family. They had been together for four years. Her parents were pushing. They wanted grandchildren. He had heard it all before. It was not that he did not love her. It was just that he avoided being rushed into things. Perhaps that was why he liked surveillance work. He'd been doing it for eight years now since he left the army.

There was a movement. Terry put down the coffee. He swallowed the last bite of sandwich and refocused the glasses. The cats—the bloody cats had returned having circled the property. It was uncanny. He thought of recording it but control would only laugh if they ever read it.

"Archibald, your eggs are on the table."

"Coming, mother," he shouted from up the stairs.

She heard the bathroom door slam, then his bedroom door open. She loaded more logs into the wood-fired oven. Using both hands she struggled to lift the first of three large black iron pots onto the range. She connected the hose to the tap placing the open end into the first of the pots then turned on the water. The hose was Archibald's idea. For years she had spent hours pouring water in from an old enamel jug. The wooden stairs resounded to the sound of Archibald's boots.

"Your eggs are getting cold."

He said nothing. She plonked a tin teapot on the kitchen table covered with a woolen cozy she had made herself. He was busy tackling the bowl of Shredded Wheat, his favorite cereal. She turned around. Methuselah had walked back through the door and stood staring at her. Archibald broke the top off the first of his boiled eggs. His mother joined him at the table. She poured his tea then a cup for herself. She walked over to the stove. The first pot was sufficiently full so she moved the hosepipe to the second. Archibald was cracking the top of his second egg. His mother pushed the neatly cut plate of toast closer to him.

"You've not eaten your soldiers."

"I will now," and he dunked the first finger of toast into the runny egg.

Terry stood up and stretched. He was confident nobody could see him. He had purposely chosen the raised patch of ground backed by a clump of trees. He had a clear view of the front of the cottage as well as one side. The sun was much higher in the sky. It was already warmer. Sprinkling shivers of light glimmered through the branches. Something hooted. Terry's heart stopped. Swinging around he craned his eyes. There was nothing just silence, while before there had been a cacophony of bird calls. The hoot sounded again. Something made him look up. Twenty feet above perched on a branch an owl stared down at him. Terry cursed.

"Don't you shit on me you . . . you cunt." He murmured under his breath. He tried to remember, "Are owls dangerous?" He seemed to recall they killed mice and small rodents but did they attack men? Robertson's. He could discover what type of owl it was. He pulled out the bird book. There were more than twelve different species. He looked up. He looked at the pictures. He looked up again. He flicked over the pages. "Barn Owl—pointed off-white heart-shaped facial disc outlined with golden buff." The owl moved. Terry turned over the page. "Wood Owl—The large brown eyes are highlighted by a circle of dark plumage which in turn is surrounded by white edged plumage. Could be I suppose."

Terry closed the book. Barn or Wood either was close enough. There was a flutter from above. The owl flew off. Terry returned to studying the cottage. "Jesus," he swore. "I could swear that black cat is staring at me. Can't be?"

Archibald had finished his eggs. He was busy smearing marmalade on his toast. His mother was talking to the cat. "What is it?" he asked.

"Methuselah wants to show me something. In a minute, my big boy, I'll come and have a look when Archibald has finished his breakfast."

"He's probably caught another rat and wants to flaunt it in front of you, mother."

Some more tea, dear?" She did not wait for him to answer but dutifully topped up his cup. "Will you be in the shop all day? Or will you be going out?"

"I'm not sure, mother, probably not."

"Then will you be home for lunch, Archibald?"

"I don't think so, mother."

The second pot was almost overflowing. She rushed to the stove to move the pipe. "Shall I make you some sandwiches then?"

"That would be nice, mother," and he rose from the table to return to his bedroom.

Methuselah was meowing loudly. She patted him on the nose. "Clever boy . . . there's a clever boy." First she removed the breakfast dishes then, from the larder, she brought out a large chunk of yellow cheese, some tomatoes and an onion. In less than five minutes three thick sandwiches were ready. Home made pickles, two apples, two pears and a slice of her blueberry pie followed the sandwiches into a wicker basket. Archibald clunked his way down the stairs.

"I'm off, mother, is there anything you require from the shops?"

She placed her hands on her hips and thought for a minute. "You could buy some nice chops from Mr. Jones. Do you fancy chops tonight? You're not planning to go out are you?"

"No mother."

"Good, here's your lunch and ask Mr. Jones for a large bone for Methuselah and the team."

"Very well, mother," and he pecked her on the cheek.

Terry checked his watch. His notebook was open in front of him. He lowered the binoculars, picked up his pen and began to write. "07:05 subject at door of cottage. Subject leaving in blue Fiat."

She ignored Methuselah's repetitive cries. "I must get the pots going first," she told the cat. "I've so much to do today. Mrs. Braithwaite wants more of my arthritis cream for her shop and Mr. Alsek has ordered more of my ligament oil. Why don't you go out and check on the others while I gather the herbs?" The cat crooked its head, meowed then strutted out purposely through the open door. She went into the back garden.

The previous day, Terry had reconnoitered *the wilderness* or jungle which comprised the acre of land behind the cottage. From the farmer's field all he saw was untidy bushes and strange looking trees and shrubs. It meant nothing to him.

With a large basket under her arm containing her secateurs she marched out through the back door. Nothing was written down but she knew instinctively what was required. Basil—she snipped away, red bergamot, chamomile flowers, coltsfoot, horsetail, rosemary, nasturtium leaves—the basket was soon full.
   Returning to the kitchen she placed each bunch of herbs into separate piles on the kitchen table. Wormwood—coriander, fennel herb seeds, verbena, blessed-thistle, dandelion and finally the female flower of the cannabis plant, of this she picked extra. "I might as well bake some muffins," she mumbled to herself. The second basket was full. This time she looked for her heavy gloves. One more trip to the garden for nettles. She needed a lot.
   Methuselah was standing, crying. "Right, my big boy, show mummy what you've caught." She followed the cat out of the front door.

Terry lay on his stomach. There was movement at the door. "07:25 Subject, old woman, coming out, following black cat," he wrote in his book.

Methuselah stopped at the gate. He called out. Balthazar strutted into view followed by Salmanazar, and Nebuchadnezzar.

There was a flutter of wings, quickly followed by a loud hoot. Terry looked up. The owl had returned to the branch.

The old lady followed the four cats to the open gate. She stood legs apart, arms on hips, staring out across the lane over towards where Terry was hiding. There was movement in a far tree. "My goodness, Oliver, you're up late this morning." The cats meowed. The owl hooted. "So that's what the fuss is all about, Methuselah, you clever boy." She reached into the pocket of her apron and removed a small round biscuit. Bending forward she offered it to the cat. Methuselah took it from her hand then rubbed himself against her leg. She patted him on the back and scratched him behind his ears. He purred loudly then strode off with his black tail erect flicking from right to left. The other three cats followed suit.

"We seem to have a visitor, well; you children know what to do. Mummy's got a busy day." She turned to walk back to the house. The owl left the tree. The four cats crossed the lane and quickly disappeared in the under growth.

Terry put the binoculars down. He glanced at his watch. He decided to wait another hour then he would pay a visit to the antique shop. He doubted if anything was going to happen here today. The question troubling him was how he was to gain entry to the cottage if the old lady never went anywhere.

# Chapter Fifteen

# Paris

"The film shoot can take place at the Palais de Versailles. It isn't necessary to fly Kylie Moon to Africa to capture the right atmosphere. All we need is a studio. The animals can be superimposed even computer generated if necessary. The main thing is for a decision to be made one way or the other. Are we using Kylie, yes or no?"

Jean-Luc Picard wasted not time in replying. "I don't see why not. I've discussed her recent court case with our Chairman and MD. They are of the opinion that *you* gentlemen should make the call. After all, it was *you* who recommended using her in the first place. However, the Chairman has asked me to raise the question again: "Do we really want to go the animal route?"

Georges Rouault, the Creative Director of Hands On Advertising, smiled. Leaning back in his chair he raised his arms in the air as though stretching. The chair pivoted forward with a bang. His hands hit the round table. "We've given this a great deal of thought. The most successful advertising in most people's opinion is the Calvin Klein Obsession campaign—a tangle of bodies—two men and a woman or is it two women and a man. Some people have denigrated it calling it obscene others have praised it. The fact is it worked. It raised awareness amongst the man and woman in the street. To the consumer Obsession became top of mind. Our challenge in launching a new fragrance in an already overtraded, oversupplied market is to take something which people don't really need and turn it into a product they cannot live without. How do we get their attention? How do we create public awareness—shout louder—more often—become controversial by offending a minority? Spend bucket loads of *your* money?

"The answer we feel is reading current trends. What's on peoples' minds today—global warming, over population, the environment, care of the planet? It's all these things rolled into one. That is why we are proposing; endangered wildlife, together with a beautiful face as the platform from which to launch our new campaign."

Jean-Luc looked towards his colleagues. Their eyes met. Nobody spoke. "Thanks, Georges I think you have more than answered our chairman's query. Let's move on shall we?"

"So be it." Georges turned to face his assistant, Marguerite Bise. "Marguerite, as soon as we finish this meeting contact her manager. Email him our standard contract. I want to start this assignment as soon as possible, while it is still quiet before the holidays are over.

"I believe Kylie Moon is tomorrow's face. She's young; her career has only just started. She's well-educated and highly intelligent. It's only a matter of time before some Hollywood director discovers her and whisks her across the Atlantic. If this happens, the impact on our advertising campaign will be blown out of all proportion."

"I didn't know she could act."

"She probably can't, Jean-Luc, but when did this ever prevent anyone from becoming a superstar."

They all laughed.

"Either way, unless she goes off the ropes like half of them, and starts smoking dope or some such thing she has a lucrative career ahead of her. A key factor is we are acquiring her before she hits the big-time. The fact is: she probably wants this assignment more than we need her. That's why we can obtain her services for considerably less than the other names we have banded about."

"Is there a clause in the contract to cover us if she does something illegal which could affect our good name?"

Georges looked at Denise Vergé who until that moment had remained silent. "Yes and no is my response. If for instance she was convicted in a court of law for some felony which we deemed to be detrimental to our image we could terminate the contract and even sue. The problem is these things become quite protracted. Reality usually dictates we pull the adverts and move on. However, don't forget we would probably not be the only company using her face to promote its products, although we will be the only cosmetic house."

Again he turned to Marguerite. "You know I'm having second thoughts about the location. She must come here. We have the studio. I can even get my hands upon a tame cheetah, a leopard and a panther, if that is the route we want to go."

Pushing back his chair he stood up. "Let me show you what we propose. I'd like us to move to the projector room."

Georges indicated with his hand the direction. The marketing agency was located in what was once an old warehouse close to the Pompidou Centre. Sixty years dirt, grime and paint and been removed from the walls to reveal a rich brown brick, which when cleaned and treated gave the cavernous loft a warm feeling. The rusty old steel girders supporting the ceiling were painted dark silver. Decked wooden floors created different levels allowing a subtle degree of privacy for the different offices. From the boardroom-space they descended three steps leading to a lower level which was made private by heavy black curtains hung in a U-shape. A large plasma screen filled the far wall. Offset on the left was a lectern. Facing the screen were eight executive chairs arranged in two rows of four.

Jean-Luc, Denise Vergé and Hervé Duronzier from Essence de La Grasse occupied the front row while Marguerite and two other agency personnel sat behind them. Georges went directly to the lectern. He pressed a button. Behind them the curtains closed encapsulating them in a curtained box. The lights dimmed. The screen lit up with the company's logo.

"So far we have only discussed the basic outline of the campaign. I've prepared a number of concept slides for you to have a look at but before I go into that I first want to outline the principles of this campaign."

Georges touched the laptop on the lectern. The picture on the screen changed, the heading—media, appeared on the screen. He began to elaborate on the subject.

Pierre Nimier arrived at the offices of Hands On Advertising early. He pressed the bell and announced himself to the receptionist. With a click the door opened. Ignoring the lift he climbed the stairs to the second level. The girl on reception showed him to a small boardroom. After offering him a coffee she explained that his meeting with Denise Vergé would take place as soon as the present one finished. Pierre thanked her and immediately began to prepare himself for the meeting.

The phone call from Dell had come three days ago. They had successfully negotiated to supply Essence de La Grasse, the famous perfume manufacturer, with all new hardware for a management operating system. They wanted to subcontract Pierre to help with the installation. It was short notice but they asked that he meet with Denise Vergé, the Business Manager. She was in Paris for the day to meet with the perfume house's advertising agency.

Pierre turned on his laptop, while waiting for it to boot up he checked through the three presentation packs prepared by Dell. Having picked them up from their office on the way he had not yet had time to study them. Half of France was still on holiday so there were only a handful of people remaining in the office. Normally, a whole team would have been present. Skipping through the first ten pages which contained the usual fancy blurb about the company—how good it was and the long list of satisfied companies they had serviced—he arrived at the crux.

The type of server, capacity, security, access information, number of terminals and back up—it was all there. He called up the program on his computer. Any questions fired at him which were not clear in the presentation would hopefully be answered in the comprehensive files. He checked his watch.

There was still forty-five minutes to go. He needed this time to bring himself up to speed. He wondered if he would get the opportunity to mention Jacques and his amazing discovery. They had agreed there was no harm in dropping a subtle hint. They had already discussed the possibility of negotiating with an established perfume manufacturer.

The screen in the presentation room went blank. The lights came on. Georges stepped away from the lectern and stood directly in front of his audience. "So, there you have it. To sum up the campaign featuring Kylie Moon; we propose to use a series of ten photographs. Five will feature her at one with nature—the flowing mountain stream—the fragrant green pine forest—the shimmering arctic glacier—the field of multicolored flowers and the rich golden-brown rolling desert sands. I rather like the "At One with Nature" theme. We must just check that nobody has used it before.

"The animal scenes will feature a cheetah, a puma, a leopard and we'll possibly use a Siamese cat and a French poodle or similar. This will provide us with two distinctive angles—one, the purity of nature—care of the environment etc. The other will intimate the prurient, sensual, seductive theme—the controlled savagery of nature. Once the portfolio is complete we can choose which themes best promote the individual products. We will feature them primarily in airline magazines and at airports as close to the points of sale as possible—Fair Lady, Vogue, Elle, as well as the usual glossies."

"How about cinema, before the main feature?" asked Jean-Luc.

"We can, but I'm never happy with the way the advertisements are presented. There is always a terrible crackling or embarrassing pause between frames. They somehow never seem to get it right. Television, as I mentioned, does not prove cost effective. It is too expensive and quite frankly reaches too large an audience. Airlines, airports and of course the large departmental stores are where the customer can be most impressed to make a purchase.

"I will finalize the production cost by . . ." and he looked towards his assistant, Marguerite Bise, for support.

"Two weeks max," she responded.

"We are already in possession of the schedule and costs for the printed media. It is just a case of preparing a spreadsheet for showing frequency. I will also include the twenty major airlines we have identified. Twelve have already indicated their interest. If we advertise in their duty free magazines they guarantee to carry our products."

"Thirteen," added Marguerite, "Qatar Airlines have just confirmed."

"Good and we'll chase the others. All that remains is for you to advise us which specific products you want to feature. I take it we are talking about the existing range and not the new one planned."

"Yes, that is correct. We are still some way from launching but would we use Kylie Moon for that?"

"Good question, how long is 'still some way?'"

"A year, possibly two, certainly no longer."

"How long did you say Kylie's contract is for?" asked Denise.

"Two years."

"Then shouldn't we include the possibility of using her to launch the new range, if as you say, she might become very big?"

Georges looked again at Marguerite. "Make a note, that's an excellent point. Do you have any other questions?"

"Costs?" asked Jean-Luc.

"The production cost is of course a one-off. This, I will have finalized within two weeks. It should not vary too much from the draft budget figure you already have. The insertion costs which of course depend upon frequency will correspond with the spreadsheet. It is entirely up to you how much you want to spend and when."

"Who owns the production material?"

"You do, Denise, that is, Essence de La Grasse owns the copyright. You have commissioned it. You have paid for it. It is yours to do with what you like. You can choose to place your own advertisements directly."

The room became quiet.

"Good, if there are no more questions then I shall close the meeting."

Jacques and Marguerite escorted them back to the reception. "There's a Monsieur Pierre Nimier waiting to see you, Mademoiselle Vergé," informed the receptionist. "He is in our small boardroom."

Denise turned to Jean-Luc. "That's the guy from Dell. I arranged to meet him here while we are in Paris. Do you want to join me?"

"No thanks, Denise, I am off to visit Au Printemps and our other main outlets with Hervé. Phone me when you have finished and we can meet up somewhere before we catch the six o'clock Rapide back to Cannes."

Pierre was studying the figures when the boardroom door opened. The secretary entered followed by Denise Vergé. Pierre stood up. Subconsciously, he ran his fingers down the edge of his tie, an article of clothing he hated wearing, particularly in summer, but it was important to create the right impression. He had owned the black suit for two years. He had bought it originally to wear at a friend's wedding, since then this was only the third time it had seen the light of day.

"Monsieur Nimier? Denise Vergé," and she held out her hand.

Pierre liked what he saw. The grip was firm, businesslike. She was much younger than he thought. He half-expected to meet some middle-aged spinster not an attractive young woman more or less his own age.

"Can I bring you some coffee?" asked the receptionist.

"That would be nice, but I don't want to impose on you," replied Denise.

"That is no problem, and for you, Monsieur?"

"Coffee will do nicely, thank you."

They sat down eyeing each other across the round table.

Denise opened the conversation. "Thank you for meeting me here at such short notice, Monsieur Nimier."

"Please call me, Pierre."

"And I'm Denise."

Their eyes met embarrassingly. He particularly admired her long black hair.

"I'm in Paris for the day for a briefing by our marketing agency so I took the opportunity to meet with you. Dell informs you will be responsible for the installation and setting up of our new system that is of course assuming my board approves the purchase."

"Yes, that is correct. I work with Dell's technicians. They are primary responsible for ensuring all the hardware and software which they supply works to the specifications. My role is to assist with the interface. I remain on site much longer to iron out any snags which inevitably will crop up."

"How long does this all take?"

"It depends. Normally, we allow two weeks but sometimes on the request of the customer I am asked to remain longer. Do you employ a qualified IT person?"

"No, not really. The company is very conservative. It is over a hundred years old. Tell me, have you ever visited Grasse and what do you know about the perfume industry?"

The door opened. The secretary entered carrying a tray, which she placed down on the table between them.

"Thank you very much, you can just leave it."

The girl left the room. The door closed. They were alone again.

Denise picked up the coffee pot. "Milk, sugar?"

"White, with two spoons, please?"

Denise poured the coffee and pushed the cup towards him, together with the milk jug and sugar basin.

"Thanks." It amused Pierre she had not poured it for him, so much for women's lib, he thought. He waited for her to sip her coffee before he tried his own. He put the cup down.

"You asked me about Grasse. No, I do not recall ever visiting it. The closest I have been is Cannes, I believe. However, I do know it is the heart of the French perfume industry and that your organization is one of the biggest. In the middle-ages Grasse was famous for its tanneries but the stink of urine, the principal tanning agent, was so obnoxious that people began to grow lots of flowers to disguise the smell. The tanneries themselves began to perfume their leather so that is how it all began."

Denise laughed. "I'm impressed, not many people know that. I myself only learned of it after I started working there. Perhaps you should take me through your quotation."

Pierre slid a glossy folder across the table. She picked it up opening it on the first page.

"I suggest you turn to page ten that's where the real substance starts. Pages 1-9 you can read at your leisure. Would you like me to take you through it or are you happy to study it first?"

There was no reply. Pierre was able to observe her more closely. He liked the way her long black hair fell across the side of her face as her head fell forward. A white hand, red nails immaculately manicured, pushed the hair back in one quick reflex action. Heavy black eyebrows gave her eyes a slight sunken feature. His initial image of a middle-aged business spinster wearing layers of thick makeup had been happily shattered. She had turned over the page.

"The gigabytes, WXGA display, Geforce and all the technical jargon which you people love to throw at us means very little, but the cost . . . ?"

"The system is not cheap, but you are purchasing the latest technology. Most of the components are manufactured in Europe and the units are assembled here in France unlike other products which may be cheaper because they come from China or Korea. Reliability and backup support must be paramount to choosing the right system."

"And when it crashes?"

"Bang! Like a plane into the ground everybody dies."

Denise looked up in surprise.

Pierre smiled, "Every system crashes at some time, power fluctuations, a local environmental change, human error all contribute. What is of importance is how quick the system can be reactivated and how little, if nothing, of the data is lost or scrambled. That is where I come in to make sure all the necessary protection is in place. Normally, I would spend several days visiting the site to understand the individual needs of the various interfaces."

Denise returned to studying the document. She asked nonchalantly. "Do you do much traveling?"

"A fair amount."

"Your family doesn't mind?"

"I'm not married." He wondered why she asked such a question.

Denise closed the file. "I first need to study this so I can prepare a report for the board. Assuming approval is given, how soon could you visit Grasse?"

Pierre turned to consult his computer. "Let me check my diary. This is a big installation so I can give it priority." He paused for a moment. "Next week—there is nothing I cannot reschedule. When do you think you can confirm?"

"A couple of days I'm scheduled to meet the Chairman and MD on Monday. As soon as a decision is made, one way or the other, I will phone you."

"I look forward to that. Perfumery has become somewhat of a hobby of mine so I would be fascinated to visit a real plant."

Denise smiled. "How strange, having perfume as a hobby. Have you made some yourself?"

"Sort of, I'll bring a sample down with me to show you."

# Chapter Sixteen

# Beeston

"I think the truck has arrived, Mr. Crumpet. I'll call our Robbie to come and give a hand."

"Thank you, Mrs. Wainright, they're early. I'll go outside and attend to it immediately."

Archibald Crumpet left his desk at the back of the shop to open the double receiving-doors. It had been a busy day rearranging everything to make space in the shop. The new consignment was the property of Mrs. Hamilton-Ford. At eighty-six, a widow of ten years, her surviving two children had finally won their battle to have her committed to an old age home. This meant they could finally sell "The Grange" the family home, sitting on two acres of prime land which a hungry developer had been eyeing for the past three years.

It had been a battle. The old lady had not gone without a fight but the onset of Alzheimer's disease had been the deciding factor which convinced the family lawyer it was in her best interest. The old house was to be demolished to make way for yet another medium-density housing estate. Although the pictures on the brochure, together with the prices, suggested it was to be an exclusive up market development, the brief to the architects had been to pack in as many one-storey units in the available space as the planning laws permitted.

The local historical and cultural society was perturbed but they had no teeth. The two children were happy. They stood to make a considerable sum of money, far more than if they had merely sold the house. The architects were happy. The contractors were happy. Even the local Labor council was happy considering the increased rates the development would bring to their coffers. Archibald was especially happy. He had achieved the perfect deal. His mother knew Mrs. Hamilton-Ford. Over the years she had supplied some of her medicinal remedies, not only to the family, but to a menagerie of dogs, cats and even horses. But that was all in the past.

On hearing of the development she nagged Archibald to find out what was happening to all the wonderful antiques. Both children and developers were in a hurry to dispose of everything. The minute the old lady departed the entire contents of the house was to be auctioned then the bulldozers could move in. Time was money. Archibald had convinced them that by holding a rushed-auction the more-valuable items would never achieve their full potential. He offered the perfect solution. He would take the choice pieces and sell them in his shop for a small commission—less expenses of course. The deal was done. His shop was about to be restocked without him suffering the indignity of asking the bank manager for an overdraft.

The men were already opening the doors of the large green furniture van as Archibald stepped outside.

"Afternoon," cried the foreman. "Where do you want all this?" He handed over a clipboard containing the inventory.

"Just start to unload the big items in the road please. I'll take it from there."

Mrs. Wainright appeared from around the corner. "My Robbie is on his way, Mr. Crumpet."

"Thank you," he acknowledged.

There was so much more than he had first imagined. He used Robbie, who brought along his eldest boy and two friends, to place the most valuable items of furniture directly in the shop, which Mrs. Wainright immediately attacked with dusters and polish. The less valuable pieces soon began to fill the outer room. Canteens of silver cutlery with carved bone handles, boxes containing cut glass decanters, wooden crates packed with antique porcelain were unceremoniously dumped on the floor.

They were fast running out of space. He would have liked to reassemble the giant George III four-poster bed. It was one of the best examples he had ever encountered. The drapes of course were not original but he estimated them to date from the late Victorian period. The thought of romping with Sam on it sent a shiver down his spine. He made a mental note to phone her it had been more than three weeks since their last encounter. Three weeks without sex. He felt the urge coming on. He would have to do something about it and soon.

"Mr. Crumpet, can we move this?"

Archibald jumped. Snapping out of his reverie he turned to confront Robbie.

"This lounge-thing, can we shove it in the back to make more space?"

It was the mock-Napoleonic chaise, the one he used with Sam. They were correct. It was in the way but, if it was relegated to the back of the room he would have nowhere to . . ."

"Mr. Crumpet, sorry to disturb you, but could you come to the front of the shop for a moment? I need help with a customer."

"Push it up against the wall, Robbie. I use it from time to time." He almost said what for but the words died away as he walked away into the shop. Two young girls were standing by a George V1 armoire.

"Oh here's Mr. Crumpet. He'll be able to help you much better than I can." Mrs. Wainright disappeared to continue with her dusting.

One of the girls was admiring a set of six sherry glasses. The girl turned to face him. She smiled. He froze. He estimated her age to be not more than seventeen. She wore one of those stupid tight-fitting strapless tops. Boob-tubes he had heard them called. It exposed a beautiful young cleavage as well as her midriff. Skin-tight hipster-denims left nothing to the imagination. Her friend wore similar but lacked the flawless complexion of her friend. He swallowed deeply. "How can I help you?" he asked.

The girl looked into his eyes. Hers were the clearest of blue. Her natural golden-blonde hair was shoulder length. He could smell the freshness of it. She used an apple-scented shampoo. Pointing to the sherry glasses she asked, "Can you tell me about those six glasses? I'm looking for something like that for my mother's birthday."

She had a beautiful clear voice to match her youthful complexion. Archibald picked one up and handed it to the girl. Their fingers touched. "It's quite heavy," she gasped.

"It's Austrian, early twentieth century. That period favored the heavy base with the darkened glass."

She handed the glass back to him. Their fingers touched again. "Do you have any . . . less . . . lighter?"

Her chest moved with her breathing. His eyes were riveted to the top of her breasts as they pushed into the thin material trapping them. He wondered if she had big or small nipples. Small pointed, he thought, judging by the shape. He struggled to reply. It had been over three weeks.

"Yes . . . yes, I do, but they've only just arrived. I have not yet had time to unpack them. When is your mother's birthday? How soon do you need them?"

"Not for another week. You see we were in the vicinity. I've just passed my driving test so Jenny and I decided to go for a drive."

His eyes lit up. Seventeen was the minimum age to drive a car. A plan quickly formulated in his mind. When could you come back, tomorrow?"

She looked at her friend who was shaking her head.

"The day after, or how about Saturday, say lunchtime?"

Again Jenny was shaking her head. "What time on Saturday?"

"Round about one o'clock?"

"Can we make it later? I've got swimming Saturday afternoon."

He visualized her diving into the pool. A tight black costume hugging the contours of her body while her long arms reached out her legs . . .

"Sorry Mr. Crumpet, the men are wanting you."

He turned. "Thank you, Mrs. Wainright tell them I'll be along shortly.

"Tell me . . . err?"

"Carmine."

"Carmine, what a lovely name." He watched her blush. What time on Saturday can you come?"

"Not until after three, will that be too late?"

"No that's perfect. I'll have at least four more types of sherry glass for you to choose from."

"Will they be very expensive, more than these?" She pointed to the six Austrian glasses.

He gave her what he thought was his best fatherly smile. "No, in fact I can promise you they will be a lot cheaper. You see, because you are coming especially I will give you a preferential discount. You are obviously a young lady of taste."

She turned to her friend. "Are you sure you can't come, Jenny?"

Jenny shook her head again. He held out his hand. "See you, Saturday, three o'clock then."

"Thank you, Mr. Crumpet."

"Call me Archie," he replied.

"Archibald, you're late. I've had to keep your dinner warm."

"Sorry mother, it's been a busy day. The Hamilton-Ford furniture arrived."

"Oh good, I often wonder how poor Mrs. Ford is doing. Such a shame she had to leave the big house. It's been in the family for generations."

But Archibald did not hear. He was already in his room relieved his mother had not observed the DVDs he was carrying under his arm. He hid them under a stack of Home and Garden magazines. He took off his tweed sports jacket and slipped on a blue pullover his mother had made for him. He entered the bathroom washed his face and hands and descended the stairs.

He sat at his usual place at the kitchen table. His mother was busy at the stove. "I've got a surprise for you, Archibald, or rather should I say Oliver brought us a present."

"Oliver?"

"Yes Oliver. He brought us a rabbit."

"A rabbit?"

"You like rabbit. I've cooked it with prunes and some of my elderberry wine." She placed a large white plate in front of him—steaming mashed potato, carrots and broccoli from the garden and chunks of rabbit swimming in a deep-red sauce. He needed no further encouragement. She joined him. Her plate was smaller. She sliced the loaf posed on the wooden board passing it to him. They ate in silence until both had finished.

The meowing of a cat disturbed the calm. She stooped to touch Methuselah. The other three sat in line. "Has mummy got something special for you?" From her plate she picked a rabbit bone handing it to the cat. "Archibald, pass me your plate." She scraped the remaining bones onto her plate. Salmanazar was next. The cat took the bone and strutted off. "The boys have been busy today. They've something to tell you, Archibald. Haven't you?" She looked towards Methuselah for confirmation. The cat purred loudly.

Archibald looked up. "What mother?"

"A man was spying upon us."

"Really, did you see him?"

"No, but Oliver did, then the boys chased him away." Archibald buttered another slice of bread. He was deep in thought. "You must be very careful, Archibald. Promise me you will do nothing silly."

"No mother."

She stood up from the table to clear the plates. "Would you like tea?"

He rose grating his chair on the stone floor. "No thanks, mother, I'm going to my room. I managed to obtain a couple of DVDs of the Antique Road Show. Id like to watch them if you don't mind."

"Just keep the volume low."

"Yes mother."

He left the kitchen. His mother abhorred television. She refused to even listen to radio. She had forbidden him to bring one into the house claming it destroyed the natural equilibrium. He could have persisted but then the internet changed everything. She accepted reluctantly, the need to have a computer otherwise he would have to spend more hours in the shop when he could be at home with her.

On entering his room he closed the door, turning the key in the lock as quietly as he could. His room was big with a low ceiling which would have hampered the movements of a tall person. His single bed occupied one wall while an old doctor's style desk occupied the far wall. Two bookcases, crammed with novels and old auction catalogues completed the mess. Two heavy antique wardrobes contained his clothes next to a neglected exercise bike. He sat on the bed to kick off his boots. There was a clang. Leaning down he checked he had not chipped the chamber pot under the bed. He also confirmed he had remembered to empty it that morning.

For a moment he forgot where he had hidden the DVDs. He switched on the computer frustrated at the time it took to boot up. He opened the blank cover of the first DVD and removed the disk. Another minute passed before the title flickered onto the screen "Confessions of a Girl Guide". His hand felt for the handle on the side of the chair. He pulled it. The chair inclined back to its maximum. In a field two young guides, with massive breasts were struggling to erect their tent. A beefy scoutmaster entered the scene to assist them. One of the girls was told to hold the pole which she accomplished in an erotic matter. The other guide was pulling on the guy rope while the scoutmaster hammered in the stake. He slipped. They rolled together on the grass. The tent collapsed. Her breasts were dangling free. He began to kiss them. In a half-hearted attempt the girl pretended to fight him off. Suddenly the second guide appeared. Miraculously she was naked. She moved towards the other two who were now kissing passionately. The camera zoomed in on her fingers as they began to play with her pubic hairs.

Archibald frantically tugged at the zip of his trousers. He undid his belt then pulled down the front of his boxer shorts. He imagined seeing Carmine's angelic face. The scoutmaster was now kneeling. Both girls were tugging to pull down his shorts. The blonde took him in her mouth. The scoutmaster's naked buttocks filled the screen as he began to gyrate. Archibald was out of control. "Saturday . . . Carmine," he gasped.

# Chapter Seventeen

# Manchester

It had not been a good morning. At the very last moment the South African Government had impounded the plane. In spite of meticulous paper work, plus the greasing of a multitude of greedy palms belonging to an army of petty-government officials all the way to the Minister, there had been no smooth departure. The cargo was not his responsibility, not his money—thank God. His role was simply to ensure its trouble-free departure to its ultimate destination—The Comoros Islands.

Since obtaining independence from France in 1975 there had been nineteen coup attempts—twenty if the cargo plane stuck in Cape Town was to be included. The tiny archipelago covered a miserly 719 square miles of land sprinkled over a greater expanse of ocean. With a total population of 600,000 the Comoros boasted three presidents. Unable to unite amongst themselves the three main islands, Grand Comore, Anjouan and Moheli had each declared their own independence then came together under a sort of united federation. Still, three presidents required three palaces, three governments, three personal security forces, three assemblages of sinecures to rule over their coconut trees and cassava plantations.

The red phone on his desk rang. His secretary informed: "Cape Town on the line they are using Skype."

Lancelot Slim grunted then put down the phone. Swiveling around in his high-back chair he turned to his laptop hitting the Skype program button. Hastily he placed the headphones on his head while struggling to find the right outlet in which to plug in the connection. The face of Simon Manning filled the screen then the voice crackled.

"Simon, I read you. Start from the beginning. What the hell is happening down there? Is this mission on or not?"

For fifteen minutes he listened saying nothing. Finally, he spoke. "Simon, get the hell out of Cape Town. Destroy all files. Make sure you leave no trace between this organization and that plane. Yes . . . leave via Namibia it's safer," and he terminated the connection. Next he picked up his Nokia communicator. He searched for a number then touched the dial button. Whilst waiting for a reply he stood up from the desk and walked over to the window. Down below the sun glistened off the dark water of Salford Lock. Pedestrians were going about their daily business. All was normal, peaceful.

Finally the call was answered. "David, it's Lancelot, we need to talk *now!* Yes, phone me back on the secure line." Terminating the connection he picked up the red phone. "Joyce, no calls no interruptions I'm expecting an important call. What's that? Terry Bagshaw is in your office? He's injured? All bandaged up. Look, tell him to wait," and he put the phone down.

Lancelot walked back to the window to enjoy the view. It always relaxed him. He hoped David Symington-Jones would not delay in returning the call. The trouble with these young Foreign Office career-boys was that they all suffered from illusions of grandeur. They lived under the impression they were all-powerful as they each fought their way up the career ladder to become a Permanent Secretary or Ambassador in some far corner of the former empire. One minute they promised you the earth. There was nothing they could not do for you. The next moment, if plans did not turn out the way they were expected, they denied all knowledge of your very existence. Today, a plan had gone horribly wrong.

Lancelot had never wanted to become involved in the scheme. It was foolhardy from the start. The days of running military coups in Africa, or on islands off the mainland, were long gone. The Mark Thatcher fiasco involving the Central African Republic was still fresh in everyone's mind. A dozen or so mercenaries were still paying the price. They were dying slowly in African jails as a result of it. The idea to *remove* the President of the tiny island of Moheli because of his growing ties with Iran and Muslim extremists had been ill-conceived in Washington. The French had declined, so it was left to the British to put together a plan of sorts—not that they must be seen to be directly involved.

The black phone rang. Lancelot picked it up. "Yes, David, the line is clean. Where are you? In the Minister's office . . . good. The plane has been grounded. It's sitting at Cape Town International Airport. So, you'd better get your ambassador to talk to the South Africans. Best send it off to Ascension where it can refuel before coming home."

There was silence as Lancelot listened. "You ask, *What went wrong*?" His voice raised a tone. "I would assume the South African Government changed their minds. You know how fickle these people are. They say one thing then do nothing . . . no, not like us. We say one thing and do the opposite. Look, there is no point in prolonging this. The element of surprise has gone. The mission is stillborn. You must just use your Whitehall powers to have the plane released. I'm still billing you for my expenses."

He replaced the black phone. "Damn," he muttered. He remembered Terry Bagshaw was waiting to see him. Joyce had mentioned something about him being injured. He picked up the red phone. "Joyce, send Terry in please."

Terry Bagshaw limped into the office. His head and hands were swathed in bandages. What little of his face was visible looked terrible. Lancelot stood up beckoning him to take the seat in front of his desk. "What the hell happened to you? Who did this?" He asked gravely.

"Four bloody black cats."

"What?"

"Four black cats."

Lancelot sat down behind his desk. "You'd better start at the beginning. Take your time. Do you want a glass of water or something?"

"No, I'm fine thank you. Joyce made me some tea. Where to start? It was the second day of the Crumpet surveillance, the morning actually. I spent the first day reconnoitering the area to get my bearings. I selected a grassy knoll hidden by trees 100-yards in front of the cottage from where I had a clear view of the front entrance and the left side leading to the back. I swear there was no way I could be seen. Christ, I've done this thing too many times. Anyway, I was in place by 05:30. At 06:15 the front door opened and four black cats walked out in a straight line. Just before the gate they stopped, splitting into two groups. One turned left the other right."

"What, one cat turned left and–"

"Two turned left the other two right, walking in single file as though they were bloody patrolling. Twenty minutes later the subject exited. He went straight to the blue Fiat and drove out. Another twenty minutes passed when the old woman stepped out following the four cats."

"Sorry, Terry, you've lost me. I thought you said the cats disappeared into the grounds."

"They did but they came back and re-entered the open door of the cottage."

"All at once or individually?"

"Like I said, at the gate they split, two going left, two going right. It must have taken them about fifteen minutes before they returned—still, one following the other but converging together at the same time."

"How bizarre?"

"You're not joking, Commander. Anyway, the next time I see them is when the old woman comes out following them. She walks up to the gate and looks around. I swear: there was no way she could have seen me from that distance even if she was using binoculars. I was flat on the ground peering through grass and before you ask there was no sun reflecting on my binoculars."

"Was anybody else around?"

"No, apart from a bloody owl, which chose to sit on the tree above me."

"Are you absolutely sure?"

"On my mother's life."

"Go on."

"She stood for about two minutes then went inside. I didn't see what happened to the cats until the bastards attacked me."

"They what?"

"I'd planned to stay an hour then visit the antique shop. I was trying to figure a way to get into the cottage, without being seen of course. There was no sign of any dog. Ten minutes must have passed then they rushed me."

"The cats?"

"The bloody cats. I heard nothing not a rustle. Something jumped on my back then bit into the back of the neck. At first I thought it was the owl. I jumped up then a black shape jumped on my face."

"Jesus Christ! It's miracle you didn't loose your eyes."

"That's why the back of my hands got the worst of it. All I could do was run as I tried to pull them off me. I must have covered about ten yards when suddenly they all let go. I was bleeding profusely. All I could do was quench the blood, gather my things and get the hell out of there."

"Well I never," replied Lancelot.

# Chapter Eighteen

# Paris

Jacques Gavotte was tired. He was also frustrated. He felt he was stuck in a rut. Work had become boring. Hour after hour, day after day, week after week, month after month doing the same thing—testing. His dream of being the next Pasteur, of discovering some new miracle drug and becoming world famous had somehow dissipated. Pharmaceutical research was proving monotonous. At first it was exciting to work with the latest equipment money could buy with people at the cutting edge of science, but now, he was no longer sure.

Then there was his personal experimentation with fragrances. He had not touched it for a week. Pierre was his business partner. Together they were going to become billionaires. But, he was the one doing all the work. He was the one spending all his spare time mixing herbs and distilling potions. If anything did come out of it he should be the one to reap the rewards. It was his work, his labors, his genius not Pierre's.

Pierre was away on business in Grasse. Reluctantly, Jacques had agreed to Pierre taking with him a small phial of the potion. He just didn't have the strength to say: "No! It's mine not yours". The problem was: the last two batches he had made did not produce the same results. There was an element missing. Something had escaped him.

The film was boring. He switched channels. Football, more football, a quiz game—the French loved these. He did not. Another movie, same drama, same sex, same beautiful people, same violence just a different name—he left it on. Standing up he picked up the tray—another tasteless frozen TV dinner—lasagna, it had said on the jacket. He threw the empty container into the rubbish bin. It was full. The cutlery he slid into the sink. It too was full. He checked the time. It was nine o'clock. He thought of going out. This was after all Paris. There were a dozen bars within a short walk of the flat. He could use some of the fragrance to pick up a girl. Have a good time. Bring her back here and enjoy a night of wild sex. He looked around at the uncontrolled mess. Dirty clothes lay strewn around. His bed had not been made for a week. What was the point?

He went to the fridge. It was empty except for some brie—long past its sell-by-date—a carton of milk, two over-ripe tomatoes, some brown limp lettuce, sauce bottles which he had long forgotten what they contained, a half opened tub of pâté and two beers. Taking a beer he slammed shut the fridge returning to his seat in front of the television.

He must have dozed off. The half-drunk bottle of beer was flat. The movie was different. There was a knocking at the door. It had woken him. He stood up. At the door he peered through the spy hole. There was a man dressed in a black suit. He looked official.

"Who is it?"

"*C'es La Sûreté*. Open the door."

"The police? What do you want?"

Jacques began to slide back the bolts. He left the safety chain on as he peered through the gap. The man waved what looked like an official ID-badge. "Inspecteur Maurice," a gruff voice answered.

Fear ran through Jacques's body. Could it be about one of the girls he had seduced with Pierre? Had she come to lay a charge of rape against him—surely not? With a trembling hand he released the safety chain. The door crashed open with a loud bang. Jacques found himself propelled backwards. A large shadow loomed over him. He struggled to his feet but a huge fist had grabbed his shirt pulling him upwards. He tried to lash out with his feet but something sharp smacked across his face. The blow brought tears to his eyes but he was not crying. Terror filled him. It was a robbery, a violent robbery.

The shadow propelled him to a chair. There was more than one of them. More hands gripped his arms forcing them back behind the chair. He screamed as a bolt of pain ran through his shoulder blades then the pain eased. Someone was tying his arms to the chair now his feet. He looked up.

An elderly, short, bald, fat man, immaculately dressed in a double-breasted beige suit worn over a pink shirt, stood with his arms folded. A matching pink handkerchief sprayed out of his breast pocket. An enormous diamond ring sparkled on his finger. He rocked backwards and forwards on the balls of his small feet.

"Hello darling, surprised?"

Jacques did not know what to say. It was the queer from the club. What was it called, La Reine Rules? Just as they had arrived at the entrance to his apartment. Jacques had screamed run. Pierre needed no further encouragement. They had both broken the man's firm grip and ran. The security guard had followed but his master soon called him back. They headed towards the Champs Elysees and found themselves not far from the Metro Charles de Gaulle Etoile into which they entered jumping onto the first train. The direction did not matter.

"You ran away. Why did you run away, darling?"

Jacques tried to answer but his mouth was dry.

"It's rude not to answer Lucian Bourboché, isn't it Monty?" The man grunted. A second slap to the side of his face sent Jacques flying but the second man was ready to catch the chair as it pivoted over.

The side of Jacques's face was stinging. "What . . . what do you want?" he croaked.

"She speaks, at last she speaks." Lucien rocked faster, backwards and forwards on the balls of his feet. He unfolded his arms and began to rub his hands together.

"What do I want? What I want? We shall come to that but first; I do *not* like to be made a fool of. Do I Monty?" There was another grunt. Jacques braced himself for the blow. It didn't come. He opened his eyes, but this time the smack came from the opposite direction. His face was burning.

Lucien began to pace around the room. "You're not very tidy are you?" He stooped to pick up a discarded sweater, which he quickly dropped again. "Such dirt, such filth and this?"

He had stepped out of Jacques's line of vision. "What? I can't see you." His head was jerked backwards and the chair swiveled. Lucien was walking around the large dining room table with its clutter of chemical apparatus. He picked up a glass flask removed the stopper and smelt the contents.

"Phew." He picked up another, "that's better." Leaning against the table he turned to face Jacques. His arms were folded. "Do tell me, dear boy, what exactly are you doing here?"

Jacques tried to reply but his mouth was too dry. "Find him a glass of water," ordered Lucien. Monty went to the sink. He rummaged in it until he removed a dirty glass which he filled with water from the tap. Jacques gulped down the water.

"Enough," barked Lucien. The glass was immediately withdrawn. "So, you were about to say."

Jacques spluttered then coughed. "I've been making some perfumes; experimenting with different scents . . . you know . . . it's nothing really, just a sort of hobby."

Lucien moved closer towards him. He thrust his face in front of Jacques's nose. "Do you like it?"

Jacques gasped. The man's perfume overwhelmed him. His nose failed to analyze the fragrances.

"Don't you remember? You said you liked it—lavender, narcissus, freesia, hyacinth and of course a heavy overtone of myrrh. I told you it was made especially for me by L'Artisan Parfumeur in Montparnasse. You see I *own* that company and now I want your formula, understand?"

"Where is the perfume you wore the night you came to *my club?*"

"It's gone. There's nothing left. It was only a small quantity."

"Then make some more."

"That's the problem I have tried but it just doesn't come out the same."

"You're lying, isn't he, Hugo?"

The shadow nodded in agreement.

Lucien unfolded his arms. From his jacket pocket he removed a flat silver box. He flicked it open. "You don't mind if I smoke in your apartment? Good." Jacques had said nothing. Hugo came forward and immediately lit the cigarette. Lucien made a show of inhaling then exhaling allowing the smoke to waft towards Jacques. Each time he blew on the lighted edge so the tip glowed a fiery red.

"We can do this the easy way or the hard way. Personally, I prefer the hard way. It's much more fun. Isn't it boys?" Lucien giggled loudly. He handed the glowing cigarette to Hugo who took it carefully in his large hands. "Have you any idea the temperature of the tip of a glowing cigarette?"

Jacques tried to reply but his mouth had dried up again. The cold sweat of fear was soaking his body.

"I thought you didn't but then neither do I," giggled Lucien.

Suddenly, Jacques found his head held in a vice like grip. Hugo brought the cigarette close to his left-cheek. Jacques could feel the heat. He spluttered trying desperately to say something. The grip was released. The cigarette was pulled back. Sweat poured down his face.

"We'll start on your cheeks, two or three little burn holes, then your eyes. Do you fully understand?"

"Yes, yes, for God's sake take the wretched stuff. I don't want anything more to do with it."

"Where is it?"

"Top drawer left . . . cupboard." Jacques's eyes stared towards the far wall.

Hugo pulled out the drawer bringing the entire contents to Lucien. "Is this it? Is this all?" Lucien waved the small phial in the air.

"Yes, yes I swear that's all I've got."

"Can you make more?"

"I told you. I've tried, but for some reason the last two attempts were not the same."

"Where are your files?"

"In the laptop."

Lucien waved for Hugo to bring him the computer. He placed it on the table. "Password?"

"Rosemary."

"Capitals or smalls?"

"Smalls."

"Damn! Spell it?"

"R.O.S.E.M.A.R.Y. one word."

"File?"

"My Documents—perfume—test one onwards—twenty-six was the one which worked."

"Do you have any written notes, back up files?"

"Nothing in writing, the backup CD is in the computer."

Jacques heard the laptop closing down. Lucien snapped the top shut. He handed it to Hugo. "Good, shall we go then?"

Monty was untying his arms then his legs. He pulled Jacques up roughly. "Keys?" he grunted.

Lucien adjusted the pink silk handkerchief. He checked his cuffs then pivoted around. Just before the door he stopped. "I'll leave with Hugo. You bring our friend. Make sure you put out all the lights and lock the place properly. We don't want to give the impression he has been kidnapped, now do we?"

# Chapter Nineteen

# Berlin

Gerhard Bock paused to stare at the 65-foot-high Brandenburg Gate, designed in the neo-classical style by the architect, Carl Gottard Langham, in 1791. It represented to him the heart and soul of the city he once loved, then hated, but now loved again. Not just Berlin but the history of Germany evolved around the monument. Despoiled by the Emperor Napoleon in 1806 when he seized its majestic crowning statue, the Goddess of Victory. It became the Government strong point, when loyal Berliners rallied to the call and defeated the left-wing communist uprising in 1919. Then came 1945.

For twenty-eight years, two months and twenty-seven days it stood proudly defiant, in a no-mans-land separating East from West. The multitude of scars from Russian shells and allied bombs, a constant reminder of what his father's generation had cost the nation, by supporting a fanatical Nazi dictator. However, it was the night of November the 9th 1989 which was indelibly printed on his mind. There was nothing he could have done even if he had wanted to. The people just came. It was the beginning of the end, or rather, was it the end of the beginning? The unthinkable had happened. Ten thousand East Berliners walked through the crossing at Invalidenstraße singing and dancing into West Berlin while he and his guards sat back and watched—powerless.

But all that was in the past. It was confined to history. Now there was a new generation of Germans growing up who had never experienced a wall dividing the country breeding two separate cultures. Leaving the Brandenburger Tor behind, he walked purposely down the wide Unter den Linden towards the Palast der Republik. So much had changed since the collapse of the wall. His world of omnipotence had disappeared with the rubble of the wall as they pulled it down section by section. He knew the system was wrong. The German Democratic Republic was bankrupt both financially and spiritually.

The wall had been constructed, "As an anti-fascist protection wall to save the people from the morally depraved Federal Republic, which was threatening to invade," but Gerhard knew only too well it was to stem the tide of East Germans fleeing to the West. He had risen quickly through the ranks of the State Police, the Staatssicherheitsdienst, or STASI, as they were better known. He had never married. There was no need. His job entailed extensive traveling, monitoring and controlling hundreds of agents. Many were women and were only too eager to share their bed with him.

The dull concrete government buildings had long disappeared. Modern, glass-fronted windows presented the latest fashions and consumer goods. He stopped outside the impressive Volkswagen showroom. A crowd had formed to marvel and stare at an exotic purple sports car. It was raised on a circulating dais. Craning his neck he read the sign: "The Bugatti Veyron—16.4 liter engine—1000-brake horsepower, 16 cylinders—top speed 250 miles per hour." There was no price indicated. He moved on. Across the road was the dull mass of the Palast der Republik the former seat of Government. Once, the magnificent 1,200 room palace of the Hohenzollerns had stood there, a building resembling the famed palace of Versailles. British and American bombs had severely damaged it but the German Democratic Government in its rush to divorce itself with the past had leveled the site. The former spacious lustgarten had been turned into the vast impersonal space of the Alexanderplatz. How many times had he endured a protracted political rally in its 5000-seat auditorium?

He continued walking. The wide street thronged with people. Fashionably dressed women strutted; their hands burdened with expensive-looking shopping bags. Students bore books under their arms. Businessmen, dressed in ubiquitous black, carried briefcases. Lovers, with arms entwined around each other ambled freely. Mothers pushed along their babies in high-tech push-chairs. Teenagers shouted into cell phones as they rushed past. Old people moved sedately. A roller-blading youth roared past. Something was missing.

He was almost there. He would be early for his meeting. That was good. He was closing in on the famous Fernsehturn Tower, at 365-metres, the second tallest building in Europe, built in 1969 as a proud monument to the glory and superiority of East Germany. Sunlight glistened off the steel cladding of the dome. From where he stood the embarrassing shadow of a giant cross was not visible. This phenomenon had caused much embarrassment to the old regime. They had spent a fortune to try and remove the affect but without success. In the end they just pretended it did not exist. Then he remembered what was missing.

Police. There were no police watching, stationed at 50-metre intervals along a deserted thoroughfare. No military vehicles patrolled up and down with their machineguns cocked—just in case. He turned left off the Unter Den Linden quickening his pace. He still had a way to go.

Fifteen minutes later the drab hulk known as the Hohenschönhausen came into view. Distant memories—the ones he had tried so hard to suppress—filtered back. Visions of dark, filthy, soundproof cells located in the basement. Screams of tortured bodies filled his mind. It had officially been referred to as the Central Investigation Prison. It now lay deserted—an embarrassment to past deeds.

The corner café, two blocks to the east was still there. Some things had not changed. Dowdy, high-rise, characterless apartment buildings, their plaster peeling and shutters missing or hanging from one hinge at a precarious angle remained as though trapped in a time warp. So far, this corner of northeast Berlin had eluded change.

Old men, survivors of a bygone era, sat on rusting chairs around paint-bare tables. Foul smelling cigarettes dangled from the corner of their mouths. Empty beer glasses, dirty coffee cups littered the tables. Some played cards, others chequers. Two tables were engrossed in playing a game of chess. Gerhard chose to enter the dirty room. It was less crowded, practically deserted and more private.

He studied the old man behind the bar trying to remember his face but it had been a long time—more than twelve years, he thought. The old man shuffled towards Gerhard. Yes, it probably was him; the same grimy, open-neck shirt, the badly frayed collar, the rolled up sleeves and the faded blue apron. The somber grey eyes—the outlet to the soul—they recognized him, but the man was confused; a lifetime of secrecy, the fear of being betrayed, dread of saying the wrong thing, horror of being arrested, trepidation of being interrogated.

Gerhard saved him the embarrassment of asking. He ordered a König. The barman gratefully shuffled off. Ten minutes passed. An elderly man dressed in brown, baggy, corduroy trousers pulled up to his chest by a pair of heavy leather braces walked slowly in. He looked smaller. It must be the permanent stoop he had developed, thought Gerhard, curvature of the spine or something. The blue shirt had once fitted him, but the man had shrunk with time, not the shirt in the wash. Gerhard motioned with his hand for the man to sit next to him. "It's been a long time."

Wilhelm Voigtländer was puffing. His breathing was heavy. He gasped for air as though he had just climbed a mountain. It was a minute before he replied. "Yes, Colonel, it's been a long time."

The elderly barman was watching them. A look of recognition appeared on his face as he heard the name Colonel. He did not smile.

"What will you have, a beer?"
"Yes, Colonel."

Gerhard raised two fingers then pointed to his glass. The old barman jumped into action.

"Have you eaten yet?" It was a pointless stupid question. He knew the answer.

Wilhelm shook his head.

They sat neither speaking both watching the barman struggle over with the beers. A customer clutching a newspaper entered and sat at a table against the far wall. The beers were banged down. "What have you for lunch today?"

"Zum Nussbaum."

"Pork knuckle, excellent, bring us two." Gerhard allowed Wilhelm to savor his beer before he spoke. He was going to ask how he was faring but his shabby appearance and gaunt features told him everything. Like so many retired state employees of the former German Democratic Republic, Wilhelm was struggling to survive on his meager state pension, which inflation had gobbled up. He had once been the custodian of one of the STASIS' most secret and bizarre departments. In addition to the miles of underground files recording every trivial detail, collected from thousands of spies about practically every citizen, there was one further secret source of information—smells.

Early on in his career he had spent time at Lobetal, thirty miles northeast of Berlin. It was here dogs were bred and trained to perform various functions for the STASI and the border guards. By the time the wall was pulled down over a 1000 dogs were employed on border duty. Many were *cable-dogs* attached to a cable strung between man-high posts on ten-foot leads. But it was the sniffer-dogs which most interested him. Once presented with an article of clothing or even a material touched by a suspect, the dog could be trained to memorize the smell. Months or even years later if the suspect was apprehended the dog could be used to verify the smell thereby placing the person at a particular place. The problem arose on just how to preserve the smell. Millions of glass vacuum jars were used to store bits of material, a shoe, fibers, toenail clippings, a dirty tissue, anything relating to the subject. The air was then sucked out. The jar was sealed and stored away in a secure place.

"Do the honey files still exist?"

The question did not surprise Wilhelm. He was expecting it. Why would Colonel Gerhard Bock of the former STASI seek him out after all these years? With the collapse of the wall in 1989 the Colonel had disappeared. Rumor had it he had fled the country. No doubt he had stashed away money to provide for such a day unlike the millions of his fellow countrymen who found their lives changed not all for the better. Some years back he had heard from an old comrade that the Colonel was living in England and was working for some high-flying security company.

"They may. Then they may not. It's been a long time, Colonel."

"You were in charge right up to the end."

Wilhelm shrugged his shoulders. He was not sure if that was a statement or a command. He sipped his beer. Silence. It was always prudent to listen. Let those in authority do the talking. Old habits die hard.

"I'm interested in the work done on disguising hallucinogenic drugs using perfumes. You do remember?"

Wilhelm smiled inwardly. They had spent over ten years experimenting, everything from sodium thiopental to nerve gasses. Unwittingly, he had become an expert in using the power of smell to induce personality change. They had tried it first as an interrogation tool but it had proved ineffective. Hundreds of experiments were conducted on prisoners to see how certain substances could affect mood swings. They had even manufactured or rather doctored, perfumes to help erotic spies entrap their vulnerable victims. But then the wall came down and his little empire collapsed.

The pork knuckles arrived together with a mound of steaming potatoes and sauerkraut. Gerhard asked for more mustard. The conversation would continue when their plates were empty.

"If the files still exist I know of someone who would be interested in buying them."

Wilhelm sat back. Deep in thought he sipped his second beer. So that was what it was all about. This was why the Colonel had reappeared after all those years. He wanted something. Nothing had changed.

"They might exist. It's been a long time."

Gerhard reached into his inside jacket pocket. He removed an envelope placing it slowly and deliberately in front of Wilhelm. "There are 5000-Euros in there, that's just a start. Wilhelm was about to pick up the envelope but Gerhard quickly removed it. "So, we have established they do exist. Now tell me. What's left? Where are they?"

"In Leipzig."

"Where in Leipzig?"

"Hidden. I found a place big enough to hide the more important material."

"When were you last there?"

"Five . . . six months ago."

"How do you know the place has not been discovered?"

"Unlikely."

"So, I want you to take me there." Gerhard pulled the envelope from his pocket. This time he placed it in Wilhelm's hands. "It's all there you can check it if you want."

Wilhelm shoved the bulky envelope into his trouser pocket. "That's a deposit . . . for taking you there . . . to cover expenses. What's hidden inside is mine. It's my pension. The Honey Files are worth a lot more than 5000-Euros."

"How much more?"

"100,000-Euros."

"That's a lot of money."

"No it's not and you know it. I just want enough to live on. I don't have much time left. At least let me enjoy my final years."

"Another beer?" Gerhard waved to the barman. "Let's celebrate our partnership shall we? When can we go then . . . tomorrow?"

"No, not tomorrow. I need a few days to make the arrangements."

"What arrangements?"

"I can't leave Berlin for three days."

"Busy man, are you?"

Wilhelm said nothing. He had been waiting for this day—the day when someone would come and offer to buy his secret. He never guessed it would be the Colonel, but like the rest of them, they were not to be trusted. But Wilhelm had a plan.

# Chapter Twenty

## Grasse

It was his third night in Grasse. Tomorrow, he planned to return to Paris. The trip had been successful, more than successful and tonight was only the beginning. He could have completed the assignment yesterday but she was the reason for him extending another day. The setting was her choice. He was her guest, in her hands, in more ways than one. The venue was perfect. It was a balmy Mediterranean summer evening. They dined in the garden of the Auberge at a corner table. The flickering candle generated all the necessary light. Lavender, rose petals, mimosa and other fragrances scented the air.

They had shared an endive and dandelion leaf salad sprinkled with slivers of Cantal cheese as a starter. She had recommended the main course. It was a specialty of the house—Lapin à la Moutarde—rabbit braised slowly in Dijon mustard with shallots and button mushrooms accompanied with rich buttery cream potatoes.

He broke off another chunk of baguette using the bread to mop up the last of the sauce. He closed his knife and fork on the empty plate. She was still eating but was not far behind him. He sipped the Marsannay La Côte, again her recommendation, "The only decent rosé wine of the Côte d'Or," she had explained. "They use Pinot Noir, start the fermentation then stop it once the perfect tinge of pink is achieved. Then they filter off the liquid and recommence the fermentation. It's quite a process."

He had not commented. He had always assumed that rosé wine was made by simply mixing red with white until the desired color was achieved. He picked up the bottle first topping up her glass before his own. The bottle was empty.

"That was a delicious meal, Denise. I can't say I'm a great lover of rabbit but that was really something special."

She put down her knife and fork then wiped her lips with the white linen serviette. "I'm glad you enjoyed it, Pierre. Good food has always been a weakness of mine. I enjoy cooking. Do you?"

"I specialize in microwaving TV dinners and one minute boil-in-the-bag," he replied all serious.

She laughed. "My mother and father liked to entertain a lot. I used to help my mother in the kitchen whenever they invited guests. I suppose that's how I became interested. But enough of me, how do you feel about the installation?"

The waiter arrived to remove the plates. Expertly, he crumbed down the table. "Some dessert?" he asked.

"I'm full," she replied, "but you have some dessert, Pierre."

"Crème Brûlé, it is light and freshly made this evening," tempted the waiter.

She smiled at Pierre. He loved the way her lips curved outwards.

"Make it two," commanded Pierre taking charge.

"And the wine, sir?" The waiter picked up the empty bottle.

They looked at each other, "Perhaps just a glass of white," he suggested.

She nodded in agreement. The waiter vanished leaving them together.

"Don't worry about the installation. It's fairly straightforward. The data transfer will take a day or so. We'll run the new system in parallel with the old until we are happy all staff are fully trained then it's just a matter of turning off all the old switches."

"You make it seem so easy. It's just that I have so much riding on this. I'm new to the company and there are many of the older generation who resent my joining. I wouldn't put it past some of them to deliberately make the changeover difficult."

"Like your Monsieur Hervé Duronzier."

She laughed. "That old queen, has he given you a hard time?"

"Nothing I couldn't handle." They both laughed. "He made it very clear he is against computerization of any kind. What was it he said? "Takes the soul out of creativity". It is fear of being left behind, of failing to keep up with the pack. I've come across someone like him in practically every company where I've been contracted to install a new system. I tell you what, within a week your Monsieur Duronzier will be singing its praises."

"I hope you're right. It will certainly make my life easier. But what makes you so confident?"

The waiter arrived bearing two wine glasses, which he placed before them. Simultaneously, they raised their glasses together.

"Santé."

"Cheers." Their glasses touched.

He put his glass down first. "I've promised Monsieur Duronzier that I shall spend extra time with him to make sure he is up to speed. It is our little secret."

Denise put down her glass and laughed. "You'd better be careful. It sounds as though he might fancy you."

"I'm sure he does."

"You're a devious character, Monsieur Nimier. I shall have to watch you." They both reached for their wine glasses again. Their fingers touched. He lightly held her hand. She did not resist.

"I'd like that. I'd like that very much," he replied.

"Two Crème Brûlé," the waiter had returned. Suddenly their hands withdrew to their respective side of the table.

The meal was over. The other diners had departed. The waiter had started to make all the subtle hints that it was time for them to leave. Adjacent tables had been stripped of all cutlery and linen. Chairs were being upturned and placed on distant tables ready for the garden to be swept in the morning.

They were holding hands. "I suppose we had better go. I'll call for the bill." She waved to the waiter who within seconds placed a folder in front of her. He offered to pay. She wouldn't hear of it. It was a company expense.

"Denise, I've got something to tell you. I'm not sure if I should but what the hell, in for a centime in for a franc."

Fear gripped her stomach. The wonderful evening was about to be shattered. He was about to tell her: He was married—no, worse, he was engaged—no, he was queer. No! He was *à la voile et à la vapeur*. AC-DC was how the British called it. Not bothering to check the bill she placed her credit card on the plate knowing the waiter was hovering in the distance. All she wanted to do now was to go back to her flat. Men, they were all the same. He was talking about a chemist friend, Jacques. He *was* gay.

Pierre moved to take her hand again. She withdrew it out of range. "Denise, would you believe if I told you that Jacques had discovered a perfume, a formula really, which acted as a real aphrodisiac. It is so powerful that were I to dab some on my skin you would be unable to resist me."

Her attitude was changing. A wave of relief flowed through her body. A great weight was lifted off her shoulders. She pinched herself—silly bitch, she thought. "An aphrodisiac, you said, really?"

"Denise, I am not joking. I'm serious. Is there anyone in the company I could show this to?"

"Try it on me," she laughed.

The waiter returned holding a portable credit card transactor. She busied herself imputing her pin number. The waiter left the garden. They were alone again. From his pocket Pierre produced a small glass phial. Carefully, he removed the top. He held his forefinger on the open hole and inverted the phial. He touched her cheek with his finger. "Smell that."

She took his hand placing her nose millimeters from his finger. "Nice, very nice. I should of course be able to analyze the fragrances but to be honest I haven't a clue. My forte is business management but I'm trying to become as knowledgeable as I can about perfumery. He withdrew his hand. This time he dabbed a drop of the liquid onto the back of it.

"Try again," he smiled. He watched her take his hand. This time she allowed her nose to touch his skin.

"Like I said, it's a very pleasant fragrance. We must ask our celebrated nose, Michel Ramonet, to have a look at it." She put down his hand. "Come, we had better go or they will lock us in."

He lifted his hand, "Try again. Humor me." She obliged. He watched closely as her nose twitched. She picked up his hand again. This time she held it more tightly. Her nose touched it rubbing up and down. He felt her tongue beginning to lick the skin. He pulled the hand away from her. There was a glass, half-full of water, remaining on the table. Leaning to the side so the water ran onto the floor he poured some of the water over his hand before drying it with a serviette. He looked back at Denise, her nose was twitching. There was a dreamy look in her eyes. Taking the damp serviette he soaked it with the remaining water and handed it to her. "Wipe your nose, your mouth, quickly, do as I say." She obliged. Her nose finally stopped twitching.

"Oh my God! What on earth came over me? I feel . . ."

"Sexy," he replied for her.

She shifted her body uncomfortably on the chair. "Yes, terribly sexy. I still am, I think," and she reached for his hand. He gave her the other one.

"I told you. It's amazing but it terrifies me. I too feel like you but if this relationship is going to go anywhere it must not because of this," and he pointed to his pocket.

Denise arranged for them to meet with Michel Ramonet the following afternoon. It meant Pierre would have to delay his return to Paris for another twenty-four hours, which was a bonus to him. He could have taken the 18:00 express but the thought never occurred to him. Michel Ramonet—the nose—the master olfactor, was seated behind his enormous marble-top desk as they entered his office. Dozens of assorted glass jars were lined up in front of him. He stood up as they entered.

Denise introduced Pierre who wasted no time in telling his story. Michel smiled. "The dream, the fantasy of every budding Casanova, is to obtain the elixir of life, the magic potion which reduces every female to a quivering wreck. It is a well-researched story dating back to the beginning of time. The wicked wizard, the witchdoctor, the old hag stirring the magic black pot as yet another rat's tail or frog's skin is dropped in.

"However, on a more serious note, I have no doubt such substances have existed from time to time. Many archaeologists, Egyptologists, to be precise, believe the ancient Egyptians used perfumery to perform many functions not just to remove a malodorous odor. There is a school which believes they inherited this knowledge from older, more ancient civilizations possibly the Moans. It is documented that Cleopatra seduced Caesar and Mark Antony using a special fragrance. What few images of her that exist show her to be quite a plain, if not ugly woman, contrary to the popular belief that she was a stunning beauty. But I digress, come, show me your magic potion."

Pierre handed Michel the small glass phial. He held it carefully between two fingers under the light on his desk. "Nice color, a deep amber yellow." He shook the phial. "A cursory glance shows no undissolved particles. Your friend obviously understands the principles of thorough distillation." He removed the top bringing the open phial under his nose. He inhaled quickly. They watched him as he concentrated his olfactory senses. Two, three minutes passed he said nothing.

Finally he lowered his head to look at them. "It's very concentrate, probably 95% pure. I detect ambergris, nutmeg, mimosa, vetivert which gives it a pleasant woody fragrance, cinnamon, pepper, sandalwood oil, ylang-ylang, lavender, citrus amber and possibly spicy fougère. I suspect ambergris has been used for the base note. I can detect quite a lot, but, as for its aphrodisiac powers, that I cannot say. I would be interested to learn where your friend obtains ambergris. These days it is very difficult to come by. Many countries have barred its use. To sum up, the fragrance is strong, its masculine, its appealing, its very good but it is no different really to a thousand other fragrances currently on the market. Its commercial potential would depend of course upon a very large marketing budget."

Pierre looked somewhat deflated. The examination had been so quick, so clinical, precise and to the point. He was not sure what he had expected—a chemical analysis, electron microscopes, centrifugals—was that it? "Monsieur Ramonet, I appreciate your time and your expertise but could I ask you to indulge me by conducting a small experiment?"

Michel shrugged his shoulders. "Why not? What do you propose?"

"Monsieur Ramonet, I would like to dab my hand with the fragrance and have a lady smell it. Would that be permissible?"

"I'll be the lady," volunteered Denise.

"No, not you, it must be someone neutral."

Michel smiled. "I have a number of young ladies working with me who are quite accustomed to loaning their noses for such experiments." He stood up from his desk and walked over to the window which overlooked the factory below. "Now let me see, who have we got today?" They heard him mumble to himself. He returned to the desk to pick up his phone. "Can you ask Madeleine to pop and see me for a second?"

Pierre placed some perfume on the back of his hand. He shielded it from Denise as they waited. The door to the office opened and a young girl dressed in a white lab coat entered. She was petite with short cropped black hair. "You called for me, Monsieur Ramonet?"

"Thank you, Madeleine. I would like your expert opinion on a fragrance."

"I don't know about expert," she replied somewhat embarrassed, "but I'll try."

Pierre was about to present his hand but Michel stopped him. "Please give me the phial?" Pierre handed it to him. "Madeleine, tell me what you think, first impression, that's all I want, no complicated analysis."

He passed her the phial. She removed the top and inhaled deeply before closing it. She closed her eyes in concentration. "Strong, perhaps a bit too powerful, sandalwood, lavender, vetivert or tuberose probably ylang-ylang used as the top note." She returned the phial to Michel.

"Overall, would you buy it for your boyfriend?"

"If I had one, it would depend on the price."

"Thank you, Madeleine, please take a seat. One more test if you don't mind." Michel nodded to Pierre who stood up and moved towards the young technician. "The body test." Pierre offered his hand. Instinctively, she clasped it holding it close to her nose. She sniffed. "Less harsh, mellower, I wonder if it contains civet."

"Keep smelling," commanded Michel.

Madeleine obliged. This time she took longer. As she lifted her head her nose began to twitch. Pierre felt her grip harden on his hand. For a moment nothing happened then her head dipped. This time she began to rub her nose against the skin. Her face had become red. Pierre tied to remove his hand but Madeleine resisted. Michel jumped up. "Madeleine," he called. With a glazed look in her eyes she slowly turned her head. "Madeleine," Michel shouted again. "Drink this," and he thrust a glass of water at her. Pierre pulled his hand away. He walked purposely over to a small hand washbasin and ran the tap over his hands.

Pierre returned carrying a damp cloth. "Wipe your face with this."

"Are you OK?"

"Yes, I'm sorry, Monsieur Ramonet. I really do not know what came over me." She turned to face Pierre. "I do apologize, I . . ."

"Think nothing of it, I'm grateful for your help," he replied.

Denise noticed a profound change had come over Michel. A solemnity had replaced his usual buoyant disposition. "Madeleine, you can go now. I will see you later. I would prefer you not to discuss this incident with anyone."

"Certainly, Monsieur Ramonet." She stood up, nodded to Denise and Pierre, and walked out of the room.

Michel picked up the phial. "May I analyze this? This is not a perfume. It is a very dangerous drug?"

# Chapter Twenty-One

## Beeston

The shop had never carried so much stock. Archibald had never been so busy. It had taken his mind off his other problems. Although he had tried not to show it, the fact a stranger was watching the cottage perturbed him. Cataloguing the furniture and the bigger items was easy but the panoply of crockery, cutlery and glassware had taken longer than he expected. He had even resorted to taking some of the smaller pieces home with him. The internet had proved a reliable source of information to help identify some of the less familiar objects.

Of particular interest was a collection of six small white porcelain figures. Each caricature was of a Chinese peasant holding a whistle which actually sounded when blown. He was amazed to discover they dated back to the mid-seventeenth century. Blonde de Chine had been their official description and the price—minimum £1,000 each. His original estimate had been £50.

A Worcester, gold leaf on blue limouge enamel plate, was a particularly beautiful item. He had put a price of £200 on it wondering if that was too much. Thirty minutes research revealed it was made by Thomas Bott in 1865 and would fetch a conservative £1,750 if auctioned.

But it did not stop there. What he considered to be a hideous large green teapot decorated with pineapple leaves, which his mother adored, turned out to be a 1765 Wheeldon Tea Pot predating Wedgwood in Staffordshire. Repairs had been made to the handle but it could still command £4,000. He had already emailed a number of collectors two of whom had replied showing interest.

The Hamilton-Ford collection turned out to be more diverse and valuable than he had first expected. An outhouse on the estate had revealed a coarse six-foot wooden coffer. Made from roughly hewn planks it had darkened with age. Two heavy old iron hinges were still intact but the crude locks were long-broken. Used for storage it had contained dirty Hessian sacks. The estate's elderly gardener who inherited the job from his father was unable to throw any light on the matter. The old trunk had just been there for as long as anyone could remember. At first Archibald was inclined to leave it with the rest of the junk which did not interest him but, something changed his mind. It wasn't even on the inventory. He thought perhaps his mother might make use of it. It was after all very solid. He now glanced at it in the shop window. He had worked hard cleaning it up. The dirt and grime and been scrubbed off, the wood fed with a mixture of oil and polish. A quick phone call to an acquaintance, who specialized in restoring old furniture, was sufficient to bring the man running to the shop. He had immediately bought it and would return to collect it in a week's time. The label advertised it as SOLD—£3,000—coffer—circa 1685.

"I'll be going now if that's alright, Mr. Crumpet? It's one o'clock."

He was busy at his desk trying to solve the mystery of a bronze head. He was convinced it was Austrian, probably late-nineteenth-century but he could not be certain. He'd bought it for only £30 at a car-boot sale. He would have to get a second opinion. "What's that you said, Mrs. Wainright?"

"I said its one o'clock, Mr. Crumpet, time for me to go."

He left his desk and proceeded into the shop. "Thank you, Mrs. Wainright you be off, have a nice weekend with your family."

"It's Saturday," she replied, "are you not closing now, Mr. Crumpet?"

"No, no I'm expecting an important customer. I promised to stay open until she arrives."

"Oh it's a lady is it," she said all knowingly.

"I said a *customer*," he replied somewhat abruptly. He watched her leave. The shop was empty. On the few occasions over the years when he had stayed open on a Saturday it usually proved to be a futile exercise. Today was different. He was expecting Carmine.

He returned to the back room. Although packed tight with furniture the space surrounding his desk was clear. He pulled the mock-Napoleonic chaise away from the wall. It stood in front of his desk. There was just enough room to walk around it. From a drawer in his desk he pulled out the purple sheet. A round circular stain made him realize he had forgotten to take it to the launderette.

The ringing of the shop bell disturbed him. "Damn," he muttered under his breath. There was still much to do. He needed to arrange the sherry glasses. His face lit up. A young attractive woman had entered the shop. She was inspecting a large mahogany dresser. "Can I help you with something?"

"Thank you, no . . . not for the moment I'm just browsing."

"Please feel free." He moved to the sales desk in the shop pretending to busy himself. The women looked respectful enough but you could never tell. The temptation to slip a valuable item into a handbag was all too easy. He studied her out of the corner of his eye. Attractive, brunette, hair neatly trimmed to above the shoulder. She wore three-quarter-length, tight-fitting white trousers which showed off a slender figure. She carried her handbag over her chest which hid her breasts. The security mirror hidden high up in the ceiling provided him with a clearer view of her cleavage. He checked the time. It was 13:30. He hoped she wouldn't stay too long. He was worried Carmine might arrive early. He still had preparations to make.

She had returned to the mahogany dresser and was pulling out the drawers to closer examine them. "Excuse me . . . what can you tell me about this . . .?"

He stood up. Moving towards her he announced: "A beautiful piece, mahogany, of Scottish origin, late-nineteenth century. The style is that of George Walton although I regret it is not a genuine Walton, possibly manufactured by one his contemporaries." He moved closer. She was wearing a heavy perfume—jasmine he thought. He liked what he saw—large mouth, sharp nose strong jaw, nice complexion not too much makeup. He caressed the furniture running his hand over the red Venetia surface. "Note the rounded edges. The rippling fountain-like corners are typical of the period."

"What an unusual centre-drawer?" He liked her voice. It was gentle, possibly a slight touch of Irish.

"Yes it's enormous." He pulled it out. "Note the depth. Have you any idea why?"

"Not the foggiest?" Yes, there was definitely a touch of Irish, South he thought.

"This piece of furniture was originally designed to stand in the hallway of a not too modest house. They called it a lun-chest. On his entering, the servants would have taken their master's coat, his cane, then his hat and gloves. In Scotland they called the fashionable man's hat a lun. Further south we referred to it as a stovie—the ridiculously tall top hats as illustrated by Dalziel and Townley Green in the Charles Dickens novels. Isambard Brunel, the famous engineer, was always photographed wearing a stove-pipe hat. You see the drawer was designed to accommodate the hat."

"How fascinating . . . and the price?"

"£4,000."

"I need to think about it."

"Of course," and he moved away.

It was 13:50 and the woman was still browsing. He knew she was not going to buy anything. He could sense it. She was probably just killing time while possibly waiting for someone. She was approaching his desk. He looked up.

"Is this all the furniture or do you have more in the back?"

He stood up. "Lots more. Is there something specific you are looking for?"

"Through here," she called, stepping towards the door leading to the back.

"Yes . . . but . . ." He did not want her to enter. The mock-Napoleonic chaise covered with the red sheet—she would see it. It was too late. He followed behind her. "It's a bit of a mess. I also do restoration here."

She had stopped at the chaise. Her hand touched the red sheet. "How sexy."

"It's just come in . . . returned from a film shoot . . . I'm often asked to loan out items for period pieces." It was the first thing which came into his head. "Unless you can be more precise . . ."

"I am sorry, you're quiet correct. I shall have to return with my husband. We've just bought an old farmhouse outside Congleton. He's determined to furnish it with chunky old furniture."

He followed her back into the shop. She walked through it only pausing to admire some silver candlesticks resting on a table. "Those are nice." She had arrived at the door. She pulled at the handle. The bell rang then she turned around. "Do you have a card Mr. . . .?"

"Crumpet."

"Mr. Crumpet."

He returned to the desk in the shop and fumbled around. "Here you are."

She took it from him. "Do you have a website?"

"I'm afraid not. I am thinking about it though."

Turning on her heels she walked towards the door. "Thank you, I'll be in touch," and the door clanged shut behind her.

He watched her depart then ran to the window. She was parked across the road, a black Discovery. She opened the car door. He heard the engine start. He checked the time again. It was 14:10. Returning to the inner room he fussed over the mock-Napoleonic chaise, creating more space around it. He turned the sheet to try and hide the stain. It was time to prepare. Seated back at the desk he opened the last of six narrow sliding drawers on the first row. His fingers felt for the wooden button which he pressed, firmly. A clicking sound rewarded him. Standing up he leaned over the left side of the desk. His secret compartment was revealed. Then the phone rang in the shop.

He hurried to answer it. By the time he got there it had stopped ringing. He picked up the phone anyway. The line was dead. He returned to his desk. The phone rang again. Cursing loudly he ran back. This time he was in time but it was a wrong number. The clock on the shop desk informed it was 14:24.

He cleared a space on a table then, carefully laid out the four sets of sherry glasses. One set badly needed dusting. Another minute was lost as he tried to find where Mrs. Wainright had hidden the polishing cloths. Returning to the back room he removed the glass bottles from the rack. He undid his belt, dropped his trousers, pulled down his Y-fronts and using cotton wool freely moistened his genitals with the perfume. Next he undid his shirt buttons so as to dab his hairless chest with more potion. The clatter of the front door bell made him panic.

Dropping the cotton wool he frantically buttoned his shirt leaving the top two buttons open. There was no time to hide the bottles. Struggling to tuck in the shirt he hurried out into the shop. His eyes lit up when he saw Carmine standing there. Her hair was damp. She was wearing a blue tracksuit. He assumed the badge belonged to her school. She looked even younger. This pleased him.

"Sorry, I'm a bit early, hope you don't mind."

"Not at all come, let me show you what I have." He shooed her to the table. They stood together. He moved closer. "Take a look." She picked up the first sherry glass and studied it closely. He studied her. He wondered what she was wearing under the tracksuit—nothing he hoped. He doubted it. Maybe she wanted it as much as he did. Maybe she sensed the real purpose of the visit. He wondered if she was a virgin. He hoped she was that would really make it special. She had put the first glass down and was now examining the second in the series. He moved closer. The normal detumescent feeling was beginning to arouse him. She did not react. He put his face closer to hers. She moved away. Something was wrong. His hands, his face, in his rush he had forgotten to use the perfume on them. He stepped back. It would only take a minute.

Returning to the back room he reached for the bottle. The door bell rang again. "Shit shit shit," he cursed. He put down the bottle. A horrible thought crossed his mind—she'd gone. He rushed back into the shop. A tall well-built man, casually dressed had entered. Archibald called out. "Sorry, we're closed." The man ignored him and continued to walk forward. "I said we're . . ."

"Hi Dad, you took a long time parking."

Archibald froze.

"Dad, this is Archie, whom I told you about."

The man approached closer. He was tall, standing well over six-feet. He towered over Archibald.

"Please to meet you. The name's Bradley, Detective Superintendent Donald Bradley."

Archibald's heart skipped a beat.

"Nice place you have here," remarked the man.

"Look Dad, what do you think about these?" Her father held the glass delicately in his hand holding it up to reflect the light.

"It's nice, but it's your choice, Carmine. It's your money you're spending."

"But will mum like it?"

"If you chose it, she'll love it." He turned to face Archibald. "What can you tell us about this set?"

Archibald coughed. Subconsciously, he fastened the top two buttons on his shirt. He struggled to find his voice. "The style is classic, Georgian hexagonal facetted, particularly the fluted bowl over a baluster stem. I can't be sure of the maker but it could be any one of a dozen from that period."

"How much are they?"

"They are priced at £45 each but I promised your daughter a discount. You can have them for £30." Archibald was depressed. Now he just wanted to get rid of them both.

"That's very kind of you. Haven't we met before, Mr. Crumpet? Your face is somehow familiar."

"I don't think so," stuttered Archibald, "in fact I'm sure."

"Dad, I'll take them."

"Don't tell me, Carmine. Tell Mr. Crumpet here."

"Thank you, Mr. Crumpet."

Archibald clapped his hands. "Excellent, I'll find a little box for them. Grateful for an excuse to leave them he hurried to the back room. The mock-Napoleonic chaise covered with the red sheet was the first thing he saw. "Damn damn damn, buggary bug," he kicked a leg of the chaise in frustration.

He returned holding a small box stuffed with tissue paper. One by one he expertly wrapped each glass in the paper before gently placing it in the box. She handed him the money—£180 in crisp twenty-pound notes. He was taking no chances not with her father being in the police force. At his desk he wrote out a receipt which he handed to her. Her father towered over him. She thanked him and turned to leave. Archibald forced a smile. Midway towards the door her father stopped. "I definitely know your face, Mr. Crumpet. It's puzzling me. Have you ever helped the police with their investigation into stolen goods?"

Archibald shook his head vehemently.

Her father scratched his head. "Strange, I pride myself; in my line of work I never forget a face."

The bell announced their departure. Archibald ran to the door double-locking it; next he reversed the open sign. He was about to bring down the burglar grill when a thought crossed his mind—Sam.

He ran back to the inner room and searched in a drawer for his other phone. He dialed Sam's number. It rang and rang. He was just about to give up when the phone was answered.

"Sam . . . Sam its Archie, I wonder if . . ."

A man's gruff voice answered. "If you're one of Sam's little pricks you can go and fuck yourself. She's no longer on the game."

The phone went dead. Archibald found himself sitting on the mock-Napoleonic chaise staring at the phone in his hand. "It's so unfair," and tears poured down his face.

# Chapter Twenty-Two

# London

Lancelot Slim sat back in his chair as the waiter placed the steaming-hot cast-iron plate in front of him. There was no need to be cautioned about the heat. The glazed sirloin steak had been grilled to perfection—rare. The chef had expertly carved it into perfectly balanced one-inch strips, which allowed Lancelot to continue using chopsticks although he would much have preferred a knife and fork. Crisp brown onion rings, fresh bean sprouts and exquisitely decorated buttoned mushrooms completed the dish. He was going to enjoy this.

They had started with a selection of sushi. Nori, nigiri zushi, makizushi, sashimi—the names meant very little to him—although he did appreciate the artistry which went into their presentation. However, slithers of raw tuna, mackerel, salmon and star fish eaten with vinegary rice, dried seaweed and accompanied with strips of pickled ginger, soya sauce and that green mustard which exploded on impact was not his idea of a *good* meal.

He dipped the first morsel of steak into the sauce provided. "Excellent, melts in the mouth. What was it you ordered for me?"

"Gyüniku Teriyaki, which is beef marinated in a sweet soya sauce." Takao Fujimoto nodded his head as he speared a crisp Teppanyaki prawn following it with Harusame, transparent noodles. With his mouth still full he boasted, "Your English beef is good but nothing compares with our Kobe beef.

"What makes your Kobe beef so special, apart from the price?"

Takao poured himself more sake wine. "When you make your promised visit to Japan I will take you personally to a farm to see for yourself. Once the highbred calf is weaned from its mother it is fed a special diet of rice, rice bran and beans. Specially trained animal masseuses massage the animal daily using shochu, a muscle laxative, which is not unlike your local gin. This kneads the accumulating fat through the muscles. From two and a half years beer is added to the diet to increase their bulk. They are usually slaughtered just after their third birthday when they are considered to be in their prime and the meat at its most tender."

The two men continued to eat in silence until Takao, who was the first to finish spoke. "Seeing as you enjoy sushi so much I shall also take you, Commander, to a restaurant in Tokyo specializing in Fugu."

Lancelot looked up. "That's not that poisonous blowfish is it?"

*"Fugu wa kuitashii, inochi wa oshishii.* The literal translation is: I would like to eat fugu but I would like to live."

"Is it really that dangerous?"

"Commander, every year dozens of people die within minutes of eating the fish because it has not been properly prepared. From October to March the liver and ovaries are infected with a lethal toxin. There is a special way of removing them without contaminating the flesh. A fugu chef has to undergo years of intensive training and pass numerous exams before he is licensed to prepare the dish so I assure you it is quite safe."

"If you say so, Takao, but I think I'll stick to my Kobe beef. It sounds safer."

They finished the meal with *Shincha*, freshly picked new tea leaves, flown in from a private tea plantation in Shizuoka located 110-miles south-west of Tokyo. "The company owns it," explained Takao. "We use a significant amount of tea in many of our cosmetics." Cradling the tiny round rice cup in the palm of his hand he blew on the surface to cool it. "We

Japanese drink as much tea as you British. How do you find the *Shincha*, Commander?"

The Commander studied his cup. "Lovely fragrance, deep golden color, I'm not really a tea man, Takao. Coffee is more my poison but I am enjoying this."

"I shall have to educate you, Commander. The brewing of *Shincha* is an art. It is important that the water be 150°F. If it is boiling then the leaf is scorched and the flavor will be impeded. The leaf must be exposed for not more than two minutes to ensure the clarity of the liquid. Too long and it will sink in the pot. Too short a time and the leaves will float on the top. Perfection is when they float suspended near the bottom. And yes, the cups must also be heated to 150°F."

"Thank you, Takao I shall try to remember that."

The thin parchment wall slid to one side as a young Japanese waitress entered the private dining salon. She bowed respectfully. "Yes, you can remove everything. Just leave the tea. Sorry, Commander, would you like a whisky or brandy to finish?"

"No thank you, Takao, not at lunchtime. I have had a most memorable meal. It was good of you to bring me here."

"It is my pleasure entirely. When you phoned my office to say you would like to discuss some business I thought this would be the perfect setting. For how long are you remaining in London?"

"I go back tomorrow. I'm staying the night at my club."

"You British and your clubs," laughed Takao. "So, what business do you wish to discuss with me, Commander?"

"Takao, I have been asked to investigate something quite strange. Does the name Kylie Moon mean anything to you?"

Takao shook his head.

"Well, I shall not bore you with all the details. Suffice to say Kylie Moon is a top British fashion model who claims she was drugged by a perfume which compelled her to have willing sex with a stranger. Another girl has come forward with a similar experience. We have a suspect under surveillance. It is possible his mother manufactures the substance. Assuming we are able to lay our hands on a quantity, would this be of interest to your organization?"

Takao sipped the last of his tea. "Commander, you never fail to fascinate me. You come across the most interesting people in your chosen profession. If you're not saving errant diplomats from their crapulent ways you are discovering wonder potions. My organization, Shiseido, would be most interested in acquiring such a substance, if indeed it does exist. We have come a long way since our foundation as a humble pharmacy in 1872. As you know, we are now the largest cosmetic manufacturer in the world. However, this is something we prefer not to boast about. Few people know we own the Issey Miyake and Jean-Paul Gautier brands. If you succeed in obtaining a sample I shall certainly have our laboratory at Boulogne-Billancourt in France analysis it. However, I'm sure there is more to this than just your interest in some exotic love potion."

"Money. If such a substance exists it will be worth a great deal of money. In the wrong hands it could reap havoc on innocuous people. Imagine an invading army or occupying power. They would not have to rape the female population the women would be queuing up to be seduced. It puts a whole new meaning on the word soldiering. Men would gladly volunteer to fight. On the other hand imagine the money to be made if you were to produce a range of men's toiletries which could affect women in such a way."

"Interesting, Commander, does this substance work the other way? How does it affect men if worn by a woman?"

"I don't know as yet. It's still early days. Have you ever heard of The Honey Files?"

"No, what are they?"

"Apparently, the STASI, of the former German Democratic Republic, experimented with drugs and smells to induce and inhibit human behavior. With the collapse of communism the files were assumed lost or destroyed. However, an associate of mine believes the more important documents may have been preserved. He is currently trying to track them down. They may reveal nothing. On the other hand this associate believes that a considerable amount of knowledge exists which may prove very revealing. Again, such information could be of extreme interest to a cosmetic company such as Shiseido."

"Why Shiseido? Have you approached anybody else—any of the big pharmaceutical companies for instance?"

"Because I know you. Because I like you. Because you buy me such nice lunch."

Takao laughed loudly. "Of course, forgive me for asking."

"To answer your questions, Takao, No, I have not spoken to anybody else. As Director of European Operations you are very much your own man. You make the decisions not Tokyo. We have known each other for a number of years ever since I first helped you with that little problem, so naturally you are my first port of call."

Takao smiled. "The world is a strange and wonderful place. If it had not been for our chairman's itinerant daughter becoming mixed up with that crowd of drug-taking misfits, who hatched the plot to ransom her in return for a very large sum of money, we would not be sitting here now. You managed to find her safe and sound, when the police had practically given up. Yes, I suppose we can trust each other. So what exactly do you propose?"

"A partnership 50:50, I supply the material, the raw product, plus any files or formulas that kind of thing. You then turn it into a money-making product."

Takao turned to face Lancelot. He held out his hand. "I can shake on that. Perhaps we should order a whisky to toast our partnership. Is 24-year-old Royal Salute to your liking?"

# Chapter Twenty-Three

# Leipzig

The countryside had changed or had it? Gerhard Bock was undecided. Was it fourteen or fifteen years since he had last made this journey? In those days he would have driven the two-hundred or so kilometers from Berlin. The old trains of the German Democratic Republic were unreliable, as well as being dirty and shabby, even though his rank and position guaranteed a private compartment. Some poor family could easily be relegated to sitting on their suitcases in the corridor if necessary—all it took was the clicking of fingers.

Leipzig had been the capital—his *head office,* the Runden Ecke, served as the headquarters of the Stasi. In this drab monolith of a building literary millions of files had been stored containing notes and photographs. Every possible piece of information was gathered by the 91,000 official employees spread throughout the Republic and indeed the world. Spies spied upon spies, neighbors upon neighbors, husbands upon wives, children upon their parents. There was no limit to the level of distrust sewn. The files contained laborious bits of information about a suspect—or citizen—their preference in toothpaste, what side of the bed they slept on, how often they bathed, when they had sex and with whom, their favorite foods, their friends, what they said, even what they did not say. There was no limit to the trivia collected all neatly filed away in miles of underground corridors—just in case.

The countryside was now green. The train had stopped briefly at the uninteresting town of Dessau. Now it was speeding to Leipzig. Gerhard checked his watch. He would arrive in twenty minutes. Far in the distance something caught his eye. Protruding out from a clump of trees, standing tall and foreboding stood a watch tower. The majority had long been removed but this sinister sentinel of the Cold War had somehow survived. He craned his neck to catch the last glimpses of it as the train sped on. He turned to glance at the other passengers. The business man opposite was engrossed in reading his newspaper. The young couple seated next to him was obviously on holiday possibly even honeymoon.

The watchtowers. They had been built not just along the border but across the entire country to observe—to control all movement. Memories, which he had long tried to suppress, flooded his mind—interrogations, screams, death and always the stories the lies told to appease the interrogator, leading to another arrest—more lies—and so the cycle continued. The clatter of the train on the tracks jerked him back to reality. All that was in the past. It was history; still he had to be careful. It would not do to be recognized. He had made a new life for himself—in the West. The old enemy had embraced him or rather the files he had brought with him.

It was 1990, six months after the collapse of the Berlin wall. People were either in a state of euphoria or shock. He knew exactly who to contact in British intelligence, after all they had been on opposite sides of the chessboard of Cold War politics for years. They weren't really interested in the East German spies operating in London, these they already knew. It was the American dossier which they were so keen to get their hands upon.

Ever since the sixties, following the disastrous discovery that George Blake, Kim Philby, Guy Burgess and Donald Maclean, all top-ranking members of MI5, were Russian spies the Americans had distrusted their main ally. On the outside the CIA gave the impression it was business as usual in cooperating with the British when in reality they tried to infiltrate them, withholding vital information even sewing disinformation when it suited them.

It was the file on Sir Roger Hollis, the former Director of MI5, which most interested them. Was he really the Soviet

Mole, "Ellie"—the Russian's super spy? There were many things which the KGB kept to themselves, not everything was shared with their STASIE cousins, but over the years, snippets of information had come Gerhard's way. Sometimes it was a harmless passing remark, other times a minute cross-reference. Many many pieces were missing from the jigsaw but over time a picture of circumstances began to emerge.

The deal had been simple. In return for a British passport, a new identity and not an uncomfortable sum of money he had selected those files which were of most interest to MI5. The *debriefing* had lasted almost a year. He had deliberately played the game of stretching it out for as long as possible, but eventually like the habitual sponge he was rung dry.

Before terminating his services they had discreetly put him in touch with a private organization—Special Services International. The Chief Executive, Lancelot Slim, took an instant liking to him, employing him to perform specific undercover tasks. Although past the normal retirement age he kept himself fit by exercising, every day if possible, in the gym when not on a mission.

After returning from his last visit to Moscow he had briefed the Commander in his office on the latest changes taking place in the Kremlin. Putin was becoming bolder. The assassination of the ex-KGB operative, Alexander Litvinenko, by doctoring his coffee in a public restaurant with radioactive isotope polonium-210 had incensed the British Government. The sorry pictures of Litvinenko dying an agonizing death in a London hospital had outraged the British public. The police were thorough in their investigation. They had traced the deadly isotope to Andrei Lugovoi, an employee of the Russian Government. They were demanding his extradition to face the charges of murder, but Putin was refusing to cooperate. The question being asked was why? What did Putin have to hide? Had he in fact ordered the kill?

Some of his former KGB acquaintances were resurfacing; be it under a new guise. The possibility of a second Cold

War warming up was a real possibility. While the West was preoccupied with its war against terror the Russian bear was beginning to come out of hibernation. However, all was not what it seemed. There was another side to the coin. Polonium-210 was produced in every country which possessed a nuclear reactor; of particular interest were China, Pakistan, India and North Korea. The polonium-210 could have come from any of these countries. Although lethal it was not the ideal substance with which to assassinate a subject. There existed a dozen other toxic substances which killed more efficiently and without leaving a trace. The official British version was that Litvenko was a political refugee. Could he have been a clandestine purveyor of the deadly substance and through careless handling contaminated himself?

The Commander had shown surprise. He had actually whistled out aloud as Gerhard related the story. His body language had tensed. He had written the odd note then deliberately, so Gerhard thought, moved the subject on.

It was late afternoon verging on evening. Gerhard had brought the Commander a bottle of Stadium Export Vodka, the very finest, distilled twice from pure grain. As the bottle emptied the conversation flowed. The Commander had informed about the bizarre story of Archibald Crumpet and how he had succeeded in *seducing* a top fashion model. They had both laughed—"the lucky bastard"—they called him.

Gerhard reminisced about "The Honey Files" and how the STASI had spent years in collecting smells. They had experimented in doctoring perfumes to make the wearer more attractive or seductive. They had even tried unsuccessfully to create a *truth* fragrance which would compel the wearer to divulge inner secrets. There was a chemist who ran the operation. "Wilhelm Voightländer," he thought the man was called. "We seconded him from the Karl-Marx-Universitä, probably died years ago," he remembered saying. So secret had been the operation they had established a laboratory on the outskirts of Leipzig in the countryside. He had visited it once but that was a long time ago. "Everything came to a grinding halt in 1990. The place has more than likely long been dismantled."

A change had come over the Commander. He demanded to know if the covert laboratory still existed. Gerhard doubted if it did but, if Wilhelm Voightländer was still alive, there was a chance he might have retained some of the more important files. The conversation had continued long into the night. Food had been brought in. The Stadium Vodka was emptied. The Commander asked—ordered him to go back. "Try and find this, Voightländer character. If these files still exist we should try and obtain them. There could be serious money to be made if they prove to be real."

The train was beginning to slowdown. The green countryside had changed to a suburban monotony. Dull grey buildings, many abandoned, their outer skins still pockmarked with the shrapnel of a long-lost war came into view. More railway tracks intertwined. They were approaching Leipzig. The squealing of the brakes intensified. The train gave a slight jerk. They had arrived under the cavernous curved-beam roof of the Hauptbahnhof, for years the largest railway terminal in Europe, built to glorify the might of East Germany. Gerhard began to gather his thoughts—how best to handle Wilhelm Voightländer.

Leipzig, once the former capital of the German Democratic Republic—the home of German music—Bach, Mendelssohn, Wagner, had all lived there to write many of their greatest masterpieces. The former regime had encouraged the arts, providing of course the artist toed the party line. The university was still in the forefront of research and learning. The Gewandhaus had been home to the orchestra named after it since 1843.

Gerhard wasted no time in leaving the train. He had no interest in the three floors of glitzy shops built into the station structure. Dressed in a local, plain khaki shirt and black corduroy trousers he wanted to blend in. There was no point in attracting unwanted attention. He was just another middle-aged local tourist. For good measure a Walter PPK was strapped to his right ankle. He would have prepared to have carried a 9mm-Glock, his preferred handgun, but the Walter was light and flatter making it easier to hide. A light summer jacket together with the money and three more foldaway bags filled the travel bag, which he threw over one shoulder. He did not intend to stay the night. The last train to Berlin departed at 20:00 and he intended to be on it.

He noted a Holiday Inn across the plaza—if he needed accommodation it was as good a place as any—three-star, middle of the market, appealing mainly to overseas tourists. He crossed the busy Willy-Brandt-Platz. What had it been called before? Karl Marx or was it Walter Ulbricht-Platz? It no longer mattered.

So much had changed. Many of the drab institutional buildings of the former regime had disappeared. New gleaming shopping complexes, tall glass-fronted office towers, intermingled with elegant old townhouses, survivors of a golden age. Many were now utilized as corporate offices or up-market shops. He was in another world. People, just like Berlin, thronged the streets. Dressed in a kaleidoscope of bright colors, young and old went about their business as though they did not have a care in the world. Again, there were so few police visible.

They had agreed to meet at a small café located not far from the Altes Ratheus. The colorful cobblestone square lay in the heart of the city guarded by the slanted 16th-century clock tower with its four bright-blue faces. Two people were leaving a table. Gerhard hurried to capture it, much to the distaste of a young couple who had similar thoughts. He ordered a coffee and waited. He was early which suited him.

The waiter brought the local delicacy, an open Bemme sandwich topped with smoked Plockwurst. It was garnished with sauerkraut and pickled cucumber. Many years had flown since Gerhard had last savored the local, dark, whole-grain bread seasoned with fat and pepper. Today it was served with myriad of toppings. He had chosen the traditional sausage made from beef and pork. He was enjoying his second Gose, the local top-fermented wheat beer with oats when he noticed an old man slowly making his way across the cobbles.

Wilhelm Voightländer sat down with a sigh. Gerhard noticed his breathing was worse than at their previous meeting but this time he was wearing new clothes. Somehow they helped to make him appear younger.

"Can I get you something?"

Wilhelm pointed to Gerhard's glass. "I'll have one of those."

They said nothing. Gerhard waited for the beer to arrive. "How far is this place?"

"Did you bring the money?"

"It's in the bag," and he leaned over to lift it up. "It's quite heavy. I hope you can carry it alright."

Wilhelm ignored the sarcasm. "Show me?"

Gerhard placed the bag on his knee. He removed his jacket followed by the three folded bags. "Satisfied? You can count it if you want."

Wilhelm stretched over. His trembling hand rummaged amongst the bound, crisp bundles of new 100-Euro notes. He removed his hand and finished the beer. Gerhard called the waiter. He paid the bill. The old man stood up.

"It's not far. We'll take a tram."

Slowly, they walked across the cobble-street towards the Museum Der Bildenden Künste where Leipzig's art treasures were once stored. They did not have to wait long for the tram. Gerhard helped Wilhelm onboard. They sat together on the nearest seat. Wilhelm had already bought the tickets.

Twenty minutes later after numerous stops the tram rattled to a creaking halt on the eastern outskirts of the city. Gerhard observed this was one part of Leipzig where the new building frenzy of unification was yet to reach. He wondered if it ever would. They walked slowly down a narrow leafy road. Old houses dating back before the war indicated that once upon a time this had been a fashionable suburb. Some residences had fallen into total decay, most lacked paint, roof tiles—gutters hung precariously. A wooden shutter banged in the breeze. A cat chased another across the unswept road. An old Trabant trundled towards them belching out dense clouds of black smoke.

Gerhard had stepped back in time. A distant memory of visiting the filthy antiquated factory in Zwickau, located a thousand kilometers south of Leipzig, where the cars were once made flashed through his mind. Not that *he* had ever driven one. The Trabant had been East Germany's answer to the Beetle. Even though it had been a criminal offence to criticize them everyone told the joke about paying the full price only to be told there was a ten year waiting list. The dour salesman would dutifully write down the delivery date—"Friday June 15th ten years from now". The eager customer would look up and plead, "Please not. On that day I am expecting the plumber."

"We're almost there," panted Wilhelm.

They turned left into another nondescript road except this time it was narrower, the buildings smaller. Wilhelm stopped outside a house. It was no different to any of the others. The front gate was missing. The small garden was overgrown with weeds. An old kitchen cooker lay rusting on its side, next to it a rotting sofa. All that remained were its coiled springs sticking up from a decomposing wooden frame. They climbed up three wooden stairs which lead to a small bare veranda. Many planks were rotten and would not support his weight if stepped upon. All windows were shuttered. From his pocket Wilhelm extracted a set of keys. He fumbled for what seemed an eternity. The key grated in the lock. The handle turned. Wilhelm used his shoulder to help push open the door.

Gerhard followed. It was dark and musty inside. Wilhelm shuffled over to a table. There was a scratching sound then a paraffin light lit up the room. Gerhard gasped. Wilhelm went back to the door and locked it securely behind him. He turned to face Gerhard. "Surprised?"

For once Gerhard was speechless. Despite the outer decay the room was spotless. Everything was in its place. The furniture was old—very old—it probably dated back to before the war. In complete contrast to outside there was no dust no decay. Wilhelm lifted up the lamp. Gerhard could make out old framed portraits hanging on the walls. In a far corner stood a cupboard, ornate crockery, silver jugs and crystal wine glasses crowded the shelves. A very old Bavarian-style three-piece-suite complete with crisp white linen arm covers was positioned in front of a large granite fireplace. Logs were neatly piled ready to light.

"Follow me."

Wilhelm led Gerhard into a corridor. The floor was wood with a carpet, a runner, down the middle. All doors leading off were closed. Gerhard was tempted to open one. Then, they were in the kitchen. An ancient wood stove dominated one wall. Copper pots, pans, strange cooking utensils from a bygone age hung neatly from hooks. A well-used kitchen table, its surface worn with years, decades, of scrubbing stood in the centre. Gerhard touched it with his fingers. It was spotless not a trace of dust. He was about to ask, but the old man had gone through a door. Gerhard followed. It was the pantry except the shelves were bare. Wilhelm did something. A wall moved. They descended a flight of narrow stone stairs into a cellar.

"Hold this." Wilhelm handed the paraffin lamp to Gerhard. As he lifted the lamp Gerhard could see they were at the entrance of what appeared to lead to a series of rooms. Shadows of distant shelves flickered in the lamplight. Gerhard turned to his left. Wilhelm was pulling at a cord. On the third pull lights flickered, a generator spluttered, coughed and finally began to rumble. A series of electric light bulbs suspended from bare wires hung from the ceiling. They were in a cave carved out from the solid bedrock. It seemed to stretch for miles. With a bang the door through which they had entered at the top of the stairs closed. Gerhard gasped. "I don't believe this."

# Chapter Twenty-Four

## Paris

"Men and women excrete both male testosterone and female estrogen. Obviously in women it is estrogen which dominates. The production of reproductive hormones is controlled by a feedback system between the hypothalamus pituitary axis and the gonads. There must be something in the formula which excites or accelerates this process. The problem is I've not been able to correctly identify what it is."

Lucien Bourboché paced up and down the cramped room like a caged tiger. He dabbed at the perspiration building up on his forehead with a blue handkerchief, which he then thrust back into the top pocket of his pale-yellow suit. "Open a window. It's hot as hell in here. I don't know how you can work in this heat."

Herbert Siebert rose from his wooden chair. Turning around he pushed up the window. A draft of warm air wafted into the cluttered room. But still Lucien Bourboché continued to ambulate. "I don't understand. You've been working on this for four days. You told me if I brought you a sample you would be able to analyze it. So! What's the problem?"

"Why don't you sit down? Stop getting yourself worked up. I'll try and explain. Here, spray some lavender water on your face. It will help to cool you down." From his cluttered desk he handed across a small spray bottle. Lucien grabbed it and began to liberally douse himself. "Would you like a mineral water?"

Lucien nodded that he would.

Herbert stood up. He stepped over to the far wall and opened a cupboard. Inside was a small fridge. Returning with a cold bottle of Evian he poured the contents into two crystal tumblers.

"The boy's computer lists the ingredients together with quantities. Unfortunately, it does not specify process times. Remember, he's not manufacturing his own absolute let alone the concrete with which to blend the perfume. We can only guess their origin and subsequent strengths, let alone if they are harboring some hidden substance."

"Did you not ask him?"

"Of course. Some ingredients he bought locally most came from the university. He can only guess where they acquired them from."

"But surely . . .?"

"I can hardly pack him off to the university to ask where everything came from, now can I?" Herbert was frustrated. For three days he had conducted experiment after experiment. He had tried every possible test to discover what created the reaction. Each of his fifteen own attempts had failed. He had successfully emulated the smell—that was easy—but the catalytic affect it produced still eluded him. Closeted in the tiny office, which served as a laboratory above the shop, L'Artisan Parfumeur in Montparnasse, he had done his best.

He knew his employer, Lucien Bourboché, was an unscrupulous bully. He was fine when he was getting his own way but when things went wrong—it was best not to be there. Fortunately, he saw him only when Lucien wanted a special fragrance to be manufactured for one of his many friends. Otherwise Herbert ran the business his way. Lucien was a creature of the night who rarely surfaced during the day and when he did, he would inevitably be in a foul mood like now. In spite of his posturing he knew little about perfumery. This suited Herbert. For eight years he had crafted fragrances for an elite market which believed they were buying an exclusive handmade product. They were in a way. But more often than not he simply added a little of this to a little of that to a bulk aldehyde. This was nothing more than a strong chemical which artificially reproduced specific odors. The customers expected to pay a high price. It was what Lucien demanded from his business. The fact that Herbert could thus make excessive profits enabled him to participate in them unknown to Lucien. Skimming off the top he had heard it called in an American film.

Lucien had calmed down having finally placed himself in the chair facing Herbert. "So what's in this stuff? What have you found?"

"He is using ambergris with sandalwood as the base note. The middle note contains nutmeg, mimosa, vetivert, cinnamon and pepper. Ylang-ylang, lavender, citrus amber and spicy fougère make up the head. I've reproduced the exact odor. I have precisely followed his recipe but for reasons which elude me I have not yet been able to duplicate the required result. You told me you tried out the fragrance at the club."

Lucien clutched the blue handkerchief in his hand. He used it first to dab his face then began to fan himself. "My God! You should have been there." Herbert sat back listening, grateful he had not attended and that Lucien at last seemed more relaxed. "Well, my dear, you know we put on a little cabaret after two. It helps to keep the place going just when people think about leaving. Giorgio, the Brazilian dancer—gorgeous body—hung like a bull, splashed some of the boy's perfume around his manhood. At first the act went as normal. He dances around gradually undressing building up the excitement until all that remains to remove is the skimpiest of briefs. When finally he exposes himself he allows some of the audience to touch him even kiss him but he is expert at moving around.

"Well, the place practically erupted. The first two men he approached refused to release him. Before we knew what was happening they had him pinned to the floor. Finally we were forced to use Hugo and Monty to pull them off."

"Did you try it with my mixture?"

"Oh yes, but it did not achieve the same reaction, that's why we must be certain the boy is holding nothing back. Are you sure you thoroughly interrogated him?"

"*I* have *not* interrogated him. Your goons did that. And, I am quite sure he has told us everything."

"So he is of no further use to us?"

"I would say that. I suggest you let him go. The sooner you remove him from the basement here the better. I only hope he doesn't know where he is. The last thing we want is for the police to come marching in to arrest us all on a kidnapping charge."

For a moment Lucien sat saying nothing then he rose. "Right, leave that to me, but what do you intend to do now, Herbert?"

"I have an idea, Lucien. I'll need to do further research. I am convinced the sexual reaction is triggered by some enzyme which the mixture unlocks. The perfume element merely holds and transports it."

Lucien walked towards the door. He pulled on the handle. Hugo was dutifully standing outside in the corridor. "Hugo," he called out, "you can take our visitor home. Herbert has no further use of him, is that correct, Herbert?"

"Yes Lucien, please get rid of him."

Lucien turned again to face Hugo. "You heard the man, Hugo, but first I want you to take me home. It's time to take Max for walkies."

Herbert waited for the sound of footsteps descending the stairs to dissipate. He stood up, moved to the door, closed it then returned to his desk. He picked up his telephone directory and flicked through the pages until he found the number. The call was answered almost immediately.

"Department of Antiquities—I want to speak with Professor Raymond Chapel . . . its personal. Tell him Herbert Sibert is calling . . . yes I'll hold."

Two minutes passed before the Professor was on the line. They briefly exchanged pleasantries before Herbert was able to make his request. "Raymond, remember you telling me awhile back about the sealed urn which was found in a recent tomb excavation in Egypt? Yes, that's correct; the one you believe belonged to Cleopatra's High Priest. You said it still contained traces of a powerful perfume. Do you still have it? Good. Is there any chance I could examine it?"

Pierre was worried. Jacques was not answering his phone. The university had not seen him. They were also trying to contact him. He had not reported for work for four days. Pierre continued to ring the bell outside the front entrance of his apartment. Finally, his efforts were rewarded. An elderly woman appeared through the frosted glass. He at last heard a voice.

"Yes... yes... what is it? Stop ringing that infernal bell."

There was the clunking of a bolt. The heavy street door opened to reveal a small rotund woman dressed in a faded flowery dustcoat. Her short brown curly hair was streaked with grey. Short bristles peppered her chin. A Gitanes hung precariously from the corner of her mouth.

"What do you want?" She coughed causing ash to fall from the cigarette.

"My name is Pierre Nimier. I'm a friend of Jacques Gavotte... on the third floor. Can you let me in? I'm worried about him."

"If he's not in you can't enter. Those are the rules." She began to close the door.

"Look this is serious he's not answering his phone. He's not been to work. He may be ill."

"That's not my problem." The door moved to shut again.

Pierre placed his foot forward preventing the door from closing.

She protested. "Hey! You can't do that I'll call the police and have you arrested."

"Call them," shouted back Pierre. "He might be dead for all you know. His body could be already rotting away."

She hesitated. The door moved. "Do I know you?"

"Of course you do. You've seen me hundreds of times in and out of Jacques's apartment."

"I've got to be sure. I'm only doing my job."

Pierre bit his lip. There was no point in upsetting the old concierge. She was paid a pittance by the landlord to *look after* the tenants—*spy on* would be more appropriate. She shuffled backwards. "Close the door behind you." Pierre obliged. "Wait there." The old woman opened a door beside the stairs. The blast of a TV soap opera filled the small foyer. She returned clutching a bunch of keys. "I'm not supposed to do this you know." Pierre said nothing.

He was about to mount the stone staircase which curved its way up to the top of the five-storey building but she had already opened the creaking cage door of the lift. There was barely room for the two of them. Pierre held his breath as the door banged shut. The floor shuddered then with a groan the lift jerked upwards. In all his visits he had never used the lift. It was quicker to take the stairs and safer.

Finally, the lift shook itself to a reluctant halt ten centimeters too high. The concierge struggled to pull open the door. Pierre held it as she stepped down. He followed and the door crashed shut with a loud bang which echoed throughout the building. For what seemed an eternity she fumbled with the keys to open the apartment but finally they were in. Everything looked normal. The place was a mess. Congealed plates and glasses clogged the sink. Dirty clothes lay scattered over the floor and across pieces of furniture. One chair stood in front of the dining table. It looked somehow out of place. The bedroom was unkempt.

Pierre walked around. Jacques's mobile lay on a side table next to a half-empty bottle of beer. He picked it up. The battery was flat. "You mustn't take anything," barked the old woman.

Pierre ignored her. He muttered out aloud. "Why would he go out without his phone? That's not like Jacques."

"Well he's not here. There's no body . . . satisfied?"

"Pierre turned to face her. "No I'm not. Something is wrong. Jacques would not just disappear like this."

"Look," she replied. "The rents paid in full to the end of the month. If he isn't here that's not my problem. Now you must go. I can't stand around here all day. I've got things to do."

Pierre, deep in thought, looked around the room. Something was missing. "His laptop? Where's his laptop? It's missing."

Jacques sat on the bare mattress with his back against the cold hard wall. For the millionth time his eyes searched the bare walls of his prison for some kind of meaning. Eight meters by six meters of plain dirty white painted bricks. Twelve meters up a skylight provided his only means of air. Even if he could have reached it; it was barred on the inside. The bucket, his toilet, stank with the morning's excrement. He stank. Forced to wear the same clothes for five days he dreamed of taking a shower or soaking in a hot soapy bath. The stubble on his face only added to the discomfort.

A solitary light bulb dangled from a dusty old cord. At least he could turn it off at night when he tried to sleep. And sleep he had. There was nothing else to do. At first he had pleaded with them to let him go. He promised, he swore not to tell a living soul. They could keep his computer. They had his precious phial so what was the point in keeping him. He had told them everything. Then he pleaded for some books, magazines—something to read to help kill the boredom, but they weren't listening.

In the morning the door was opened. He carried out his slop bucket and emptied its contents down a filthy toilet. There was a sink with a bar of cheap soap. The water was cold but he made the most of it. Never again would he complain about having to take a cold shower. They provided a towel for him to dry himself. Then, back to his prison. A baguette, a carton of milk was his breakfast.

Sometime during the day they would return. The ritual of the slop bucket would be repeated. Now he actually looked forward to it. It gave him something to do. A takeaway meal—it varied—chicken, beef, some cheese—food had never tasted so good.

For the millionth time he stood up taking four paces. Touch the wall, turn, four paces, touch the door, turn. What time was it? It was still light outside but that didn't mean anything. They were still in summertime. The days were long. The questions had stopped. How long was it now—two—three days neither of the two men had come to ask him about the perfume. He had told them everything again and again. So why were they still keeping him? What was the point?

The key scratched in the door. Jacques turned to face it. His heart beat louder. It was too close to breakfast and too early for dinner perhaps they were finally coming to release him. Euphoria swept through his body. The door opened. The same two men stood there. Hugo and Monty they were called. In a strange way he had actually grown to like them. Hugo entered first. His face was grim. He raised his right hand. He was wearing black leather gloves. He pointed a dark shiny metal object at Jacques. Jacques smiled. He was about to ask if they had come to take him home. His mouth opened. There was a plop. Simultaneously something pierced his forehead. Darkness descended. Jacques's legs collapsed and he fell to the ground like a rag doll.

Monty wheeled in a large laundry basket. Hugo removed the glove from his right hand. He placed his finger on Jacques's carotid artery. There was no pulse. Together they picked up the lifeless body and shoved it into the basket. Jacques's legs stuck out. Monty pushed them back in then slammed down the lid. Using two leather straps he secured the top. Without speaking they wheeled it out closing the door behind them.

# Chapter Twenty-Five

## Manchester

"It is still early days, Kylie. All I can say at the moment is we have Crumpet under surveillance. So far he has done nothing out of the ordinary. I assure you as soon as we find some concrete evidence you will be the very first person I shall contact. Congratulations . . . so you are off to Paris . . . you'll be there for at least a week. Yes . . . no problem . . . phone me as soon as you return."

Lancelot put down the phone. He buzzed Joyce, his secretary. "Any news from Gerhard? No, he has not contacted me either, most unusual. It's been five days now. I am beginning to worry. Keep trying his mobile. Yes, show Sandra in."

Sandra Robinson entered his office. He stood up. They shook hands then both sat down facing each other across the desk. Sandra reached into her bulky bag and removed a note book. She crossed her legs flicked open the book and waited for Lancelot to begin the conversation.

"You have some news for me?" he asked.

"Yes, Commander, not a lot, at least it's a start."

"The cats did not get you then?"

"No, but they are really scary. How is Terry by the way?"

"Somewhat cut up. His wounds were only superficial thank heavens. There should be no permanent scaring but I think it is his pride which has suffered the most."

"Good, I'm pleased to hear that." She picked up the notebook. "On Saturday I visited the antique shop. It's quite the Old Curiosity Shop. He stocks some interesting items and, he appears to be knowledgeable about the pieces he is selling. I made out I was scouting around for big antique furniture to furnish a farmhouse my husband and I had just bought outside Congleton. So if I need to return I could take Terry or someone with me to add credibility to the story.

"In the back there is a large room full of stock. He also uses the space for restoration purposes. At first he did not want me to enter, but I was too quick for him. On opening the door the very first thing I saw was a hideous chaise. It's one of those long couch-like things with a back and only one side. The top is decorated with hideous gold scroll. I'm not very good at describing it. It's the type of furniture Josephine would display herself before Napoleon or Cleopatra would flaunt herself upon."

"I get the picture, Sandra."

"Good. The strangest thing was a bright red linen sheet had been thrown over it as though it was about to be used."

"Interesting," remarked Lancelot.

"I did not ask him but he volunteered the information that it had just been returned by a film company who had borrowed it. The way he said it convinced me he was lying. Anyway, I left soon after. Just to be safe I made a show of driving off. Down the road I turned and parked in a different space but with a clear view of the shop. A car pulled up in front of me. A young girl got out. A man, I presume was her father, remained talking on the phone. After five minutes he joined her. I jotted down the registration number and guess what? After checking later I discovered it was an unmarked police vehicle. The driver is," and she referred to her notebook, "Detective Superintendent Donald Bradley from the Manchester CID."

"Coincidence?"

"I don't know. Maybe Crumpet was expecting the girl to arrive on her own. That would explain the seductive couch scene or possibly it is just a coincidence. Fifteen minutes after they left the shop Crumpet drove home. I have placed a bug on the vehicle. He did not leave his mother's house until Monday morning when he returned to the shop. It's too risky to stake out the cottage. The mother is weird. The way she communicates with those cats makes me believe she possesses some kind of supernatural power."

"What makes you say that?"

"I am coming to that. On Monday, after Crumpet had left, I waited a few hours then called on the cottage. The minute I drove up the four black cats were standing watching my every movement. I tell you I was terrified opening that farm gate and walking up the drive to the front door. I had dressed in my leathers, only a small part of my face was exposed. In my pocket I carried a can of mace.

"I knocked on the door and the old woman eventually came out. All the time the four black cats sat in a semicircle behind me staring up, as though ready to block my escape. I explained I was passing and couldn't help but admire the cottage. I showed her a card I had specially prepared. It claimed I was from the Historic Country Homes Association. My story was I was collecting data on old properties and would she mind showing me around. I explained that if it was inconvenient I could return on another day. At first she was recalcitrant then I mentioned I was a cat lover."

"Are you?"

"Absolutely not I can't stand them. I complimented her on the four little bastards standing behind me. This did the trick. Before I knew it I was sitting at her kitchen table drinking herbal tea with four black cats purring sweetly at my feet."

"Well done, so you managed to take a look around."

"I certainly did. Overall, I spent two hours with her. I shall not bore you with the details of the property other than to say it is almost three hundred years old. She is growing an amazing assortment of plants and herbs, including marihuana." Sandra reached into her bag. She brought out a small plastic food container placing it on the edge of the desk. From it she removed a paper serviette inside of which there was a small cake.

"Have a marihuana scone, Commander. I saved this one especially for you."

Lancelot picked it up. He sniffed it before breaking a small piece off. "Not bad, a bit dry." He put it down. "I think I'll save the rest for later if you don't mind."

Sandra continued. "All in all, Mrs. Crumpet has quite a kitchen-cupboard-industry going for her. She manufactures, in small quantities of course, all kinds of homeopathic remedies which she sells to any number of health shops. It took awhile but I managed to steer the conversation around to her son. Her husband disappeared when the boy was only five although she said something very strange." Again Sandra referred to her notes, "he was never very far away. I tried to get her to expand on that but she shut up like a clam. The cottage was hers. She was born there. She raised Archibald on her own. I asked if he had ever married and if he had a regular girlfriend, again she refused to be drawn on the subject.

"What about her cats?"

Sandra read out the names—"Methuselah, Salmanazar, Balthazar, and Nebuchadnezzar—"the boys" she calls them. She talks to them—no, she communicates with them. She tells them to do something and they do it. I have never experienced anything like it."

"Do you think she ordered the cats to attack Terry?"

"Absolutely, there is no question about it."

"So what do we do now? How can we lay our hands on this mystery fragrance?"

"Assuming she keeps a quantity in the cottage, which I somehow doubt, it would be near impossible to locate. It would take an army to conduct a proper search. For a start I doubt if any written records, recipes, or that kind of thing exist. She doesn't watch television or listen to radio. In fact, other than Archibald's room, I did not see a single book—no newspapers or magazines. All knowledge must be stored in her brain."

"That means we would have to kidnap and torture her to obtain the information."

"Only if your hit team could get beyond the cats."

"Oh yes, the cats, so that eliminates that course of action, pity. It looks as though we shall have to concentrate on Archibald."

"What, wait for him to find a fresh victim?"

"Something like that perhaps we can fast track it by finding a young attractive woman, someone whom he will not be able to resist."

"Who do you have in mind?"

"I rather think I am looking at her."

Archibald Crumpet drove slowly around a multitude of second-hand car dealers' parking lots. He knew exactly what he wanted. The idea had first come to him on Saturday evening. He had arrived home in a filthy mood. The cats sensed it immediately and for once they kept their distance. His mother perceived it too. She scolded him so he ate his dinner quickly then disappeared up to his room. He downloaded an old film made in the sixties. It was the story of a bunch of dope-smoking hippies who drove around America having sex and fun in an old beat-up camper van. The film was trash but it inspired him.

His mother had forced him to sell the van. The Fiat was tiny. Bringing woman back to the shop was hopeless. Sam was different but now she too was gone. He needed wheels—the right type of vehicle, which he could conceal from his mother in a hired garage. It would be safe out of sight and most important, his mother need never know.

"Sam Wright Cars Always Right" the gaudy neon sign flashed on and off. Archibald stopped the car. He got out and walked into the yard. Thirty to forty vehicles all of which had seen better days displayed their prices on the windscreen. It was the Volkswagen Camper Van which had caught his attention. Painted a dark green with faded orange flowers, from the outside it could have been the very vehicle used in the film. £1,499 was the price displayed on the windscreen. Archibald walked around the vehicle. He tried the door. It was locked.

He looked around the deserted lot. Tucked away at the back was a wooden garden-shed-like office. He tapped lightly on the door. He was rewarded with a gruff "Enter." A fat man bordering on obese was seated behind a tiny cluttered desk. Cigarette smoked coiled upwards above his perfectly round head, bald, except for a solitary strand of greasy black hair which was plastered across his dome. The man put down the girlie magazine.

"Can I help you?" He said somewhat disdainfully as though annoyed at being disturbed.

"Yes," replied Archibald. "I'm interested in the camper," and he pointed in the direction as though the vehicle could be seen through the flimsy wooden wall.

The man dropped his burning cigarette into the already overflowing ashtray. With a scratching noise his chair scrapped back on the wooden floor followed by a loud thump as it smacked into the rickety wall behind. The shed shook. As he stood up a role of his ample stomach fell onto the desk. Leaning forward he held out a stubby paw. "Sam Wright is the name, right cars is me game. The Camper—excellent vehicle, a pedigree of the open road it is." He wobbled towards a large wooden cabinet which occupied practically an entire wall. Pulling it open he rattled about, "Camper . . . camper . . . camper. Here they are," and he extracted a bunch of keys. "Come Sir, follow Sam and what's you're good name, sir."

"Archibald Crumpet."

"Archibald, mind if I call you Archibald, or is it Archie or Arch. Once you become a customer of Sam Wright you're a friend forever."

"Archie will do fine, thank you."

"After you, Archie."

They both hesitated at the tiny door each waiting for the other to descend.

"So the open countryside, the fresh air, far away from the maddening crowd—that's what you're seeking and the Volkswagen is the perfect vehicle to accomplish this in."

Archie touched the rust above the wheel arches with his fingers. He walked around to the back. There was rust on the air vents of the engine cover. Sam was busy trying to open the driver's door. He appeared to be having trouble. "Locks a bit stiff," he explained. "Of course that's always a good thing, makes the car more difficult to steal."

"What year is it?"

Sam ignored the question. The door finally opened. Sam moved quickly around the front to the other side. His stomach fought to remain inside his shirt as the buttons strained. He opened the passenger door and then the sliding door. "Come, get in, and roll around a bit. This is where the real action is with this type of vehicle." Archibald crawled in. One side of the camper was neatly shop fitted with small drawers and cupboards. Cigarette burns had left their mark on the cheap plywood. A heavily stained quilted mattress completed the remainder of the interior. Frilly red lace curtains covered the side and back windows. Archibald liked what he saw. He crawled forward and slid behind the wheel. Sam handed him the keys. "I think the ignition is the middle one."

It was the last of the three. Sam struggled to climb into the passenger seat. With a gasp and a plunk he landed causing the Camper to rock on its suspension. They were blocked in by a grey Ford Sierra. Nervously, Sam looked towards Archibald. "The battery might be flat," he mumbled. Archibald rattled the gear stick to check they were in neutral. He turned the ignition key. Lights came on the dashboard. The milometer showed 220,000 miles. He rotated the key again. The engine turned with difficulty. He tried again and again. Archibald pumped the accelerator peddle. The battery seemed strong but appeared to be loosing the fight. Suddenly, there was a loud bang from the back then the engine fired. It spluttered, coughed then the familiar Volkswagen air-cooled engine-sound burst forth.

"These motors run forever," remarked Sam showing more confidence. "They need little servicing and of course spare parts are no problem."

"How old is she?"

"Late-82, I seem to recollect. I have the papers in the office of course."

Archibald revved the engine. Sam looked apprehensive. "You'll have to put some fuel in if you want to take it on the road. I'll have to move the Sierra."

"What's your best price?"

"£1,499, as you probably know, Archie, quality campers like this are far and few between. They sell faster than I can acquire them. They're practically becoming vintage, real collectors' vehicles, the price will only appreciate. You're looking at a real bargain."

"Do you MOT and all that? What sort of guarantee do you give?"

"That's an extra charge. I can offer you insurance to cover the first three months if anything goes wrong. How do you intend to pay?"

"Cash, but I first want to drive her."

The Sierra had to be pushed out of the way. The battery was flat and in spite of attempts to jump start it the Ford refused to start. By the time Sam had locked up his shed of an office another half-hour passed. With his dealer's number plates attached to the vehicle they drove off together.

An hour later the deal was finally struck. £1,299 cash and Sam would organize the paperwork.

# Chapter Twenty-Six

## Grasse

It was early evening. Most management and staff had already departed for home. Only the night technician remained tending to the bubbling brews and infusions taking place in the factory below. Seated around Michel Ramonet's desk were Denise Vergé and Madeleine. Michel was reading from a computer printout.

"Our cursory analysis of Pierre's fragrance shows nothing out of the ordinary. Present are Ylang-ylang, citrus amber, mimosa, vetivert, lavender, cinnamon, pepper, nutmeg and ambergris. There is however a protein present which could be musk but we need to send a sample away for further analysis."

Madeleine was also studying the laboratory report. "I think we should exclude the normal elements and focus only on those which can produce medical changes to the body's chemistry, particularly estrogen."

"I was thinking the same, Madeleine, but perhaps we should broaden the scope a little. A standard fragrance works on our olfactory senses. What we have here indicates definite homeopathic qualities. The fact that sexual arousement is accelerated by touch leads me to believe this."

"What exactly do you mean, Monsieur Ramonet? I thought homeopathy only worked through pills and tablets and is a fairly recent discovery."

"Far from it, Denise, homeopathy is as old a form of healing as acupuncture. Ancient civilizations had long discovered its practical uses. It is as though modern medicine conveniently chose to forget or ignore it. It was only in the 1920's when Rene-Maurice Gattefosse noticed that essential oils penetrated the body through the skin. Many oils are natural antiseptics nearly every ancient civilization had knowledge of their healing properties. For example, lavender oils were used to treat burns and open wounds. Various oils possess individual properties and react with the body differently. Some are anti-bacterial, others anti-biotic, another is anti-inflammatory. It is how we choose to use such oils which determine their value. Some oils work as mood enhancers such as a sedative, slowing down a specific bodily function while others act as a stimulant. Wealthy Egyptians, Greeks and Romans believed passionately in the therapeutic power of bathing in fragrant oil.

"The Medici family who ruled Florence from 1434 to 1737 promoted the study of perfumery primarily to disguise the stench of a medieval European city with all its malodorous odors. However, there are many stories, some of which may be true, of how they used specific fragrances for seduction purposes. Sybarites impregnated sponges with musk, amber and civet which they freely dabbed on their bodies to induce sexual arousement."

"What exactly is musk and civet? I think I know what ambergris is," asked Denise.

"Certain animal proteins contain powerful enzymes. We use these to fix a perfume. On their own they can smell quite foul. However, when mixed with a pleasant smell they sort of take it onboard but not only that, they reinforce it. They provide the vehicle, the protein, to carry the essence onwards. This is the longevity we strive to put into our top perfumes. That is what makes them so important. The problem is only a few specific animals produce these substances. The Musk deer is one such creature. The male secretes a reddish-brown substance from glands in its penile sheath. This it uses to mark its territory. It is a business card which hopefully a female in the vicinity will pick up. The glands, the size of a walnut, producing this substance are removed."

"How horrible, the poor animal, does it die?"

"No, Denise, not necessarily, but that is why we no longer use musk. Artificially produced musk is now made in the laboratory but regretfully, it is not quite as affective. It is derived from aleuritic acid, a compound made using the lac resin produced by insects. *Opium* by Yves Saint Laurent, *Bal à Versailles* by Desprez, *Notes* by Jean-Paul Gaultier, *L'Air du Temps* by Nina Ricci are just a few top-selling perfumes which contain musk. The best musk comes from China and Tibet. At first it smells faecal. Its chemical composition is close to human testosterone.

"Civet is very similar except it is an excretion from the anal glands of an Ethiopian cat. The buttery excretion is scraped on a regular basis. However, civet is rarely used today except in the Middle East, although Jean Patou uses it in *Joy*."

"And Desprez in their *Bal à Versailles* and of course let us not forget Chanel No 5" added Madeleine.

"There might be a trace of musk in Pierre's fragrance but we do know that ambergris has been used. Today, because supplies are so erratic and expensive not many perfume houses are using it. Givenchy uses it to make *Amarige* and Jil Sander uses it in her *Jil*.

"I wonder where his friend obtained his supply of ambergris. It's not a substance which is readily available."

"That's a valid point, Madeleine. Denise, can you ask Pierre that question when you next speak with him."

Denise nodded that she would.

"OK, what other substances can we isolate, which could affect sexual behavior? We have found quantities of sandalwood and nutmeg in the fragrance. Sandalwood contains a steroid not dissimilar to testosterone. Courtesans in India rubbed their breasts and pubic parts with a concentrated sandalwood paste believing it stimulated their male partners. The Ancient Egyptians used it for embalming. Certain Christian cults use it for religious fumigation purposes. Sandalwood retains its powerful sweet smell for years. Elizabeth Arden uses it as their base note in their *White Diamonds* and *Black Pearls* which they market under the Elizabeth Taylor brand."

"I seem to remember their early marketing campaigns suggested the formula was based upon a secret seductive recipe once used by Cleopatra, hence using Elizabeth Taylor's name," contributed Madeleine.

"Then we come to nutmeg, used in every modern-day kitchen to spice foods it can, if excess quantities are absorbed, induce hallucinations. It is the veritable cook's LSD. Its illusionary powers were known to the Chinese, Indians and the courtesans of Imperial Rome. It was common practice for them to carry a small ivory box containing grated nutmeg to sprinkle over wine. This put a whole new meaning to becoming inebriated. A seventeenth-century doctor, William Salmon, prescribed rubbing nutmeg oil on the genitals to increase size and sustainability during sex. One hundred years later nutmeg was the basis of a compound given to married couples who were experiencing difficulty in conceiving children. More recently in America the notorious Black Activist, Malcolm X, boasted he used nutmeg in prison to achieve a high when the authorities confiscated his stock of marijuana."

Michel put aside the printout. "You see, Denise, although today we have literally thousands of ingredients to choose from, with which to blend our fragrances, the very best perfumes can only be made from traditional well-proven ingredients. A cheap mass-produced product may be powerful when the bottle is first opened but unless a strong fixative is used the perfume will quickly dissipate. Although gums, resins and balsams, such as myrrh or galbanum, are more commonly used nothing compares with nature's animal products. Our problem of course is these products have either been outlawed, thanks to animal-rights activists, or have simply become too expensive to use except in the very top-of-the-range fine-fragrance perfumes. Because this market is so small large producers such as ourselves have left it very much to the small private perfumeries to cater to this small niche market.

"Madeleine here can tell you. We would like nothing more than to produce top of the range perfumes using only the purest extracts and fixatives. Unfortunately, we are no longer a creative driven company, but like most modern business, we find ourselves market orientated. It is the marketing department which more than often dictates whether a range of cosmetics should be citrus, floral, amber, woody or even leather fragrant. As you well know the style and quality of the bottle, the box it is wrapped in, often costs much more than the contents.

"Then we come to the health and safety factor. International regulations now govern the use of all powerful oils. Every product which we produce must be one-hundred-percent guaranteed non-toxic. It must be tested and retested to ensure it does not initiate or aggravate any of the thousand-and-one allergies which modern man is susceptible to. Any slip, any mistake, could cost the company millions in litigation."

Denise leaned forward in the chair. Her right hand swept her long black hair away from her eyes. "So where do we go from here? Do we simply say to Pierre, thank you but no? Take your potion to one of our competitors, who might decide to run with it. I'm looking at it purely as a unique business opportunity. Remove the pleasant smells and we are left with a substance which possesses powerful aphrodisiac qualities. I am not for one moment suggesting this should be released into the market to enable men to seduce every woman who smells it. This mysterious substance can be put to medicinal use, perhaps to help alleviate people with sexual disorders. What I am saying is that if you feel it is too risky for us to use then perhaps we can patent the formula but sell it on to a pharmaceutical company."

"Denise, you have a point. I was not thinking on those lines. Like you," and he looked at both women, "I am curious to discover what triggers this catalytic emotional change. Madeleine, we need to run more tests but we shall have to do this outside of our normal work schedule. As of this moment only the three of us know about it. For the moment, let's keep it that way, until we are sure we can replicate what is in this phial," and he picked it up in his hand. "Unfortunately we do not have very much to work with. Let us just hope it will be enough."

# Chapter Twenty-Seven

# Leipzig

As the generator coughed then spluttered into life the silence in the cave was replaced by a steady throb. A long row of bare light bulbs dangled from the end of short cables attached to an electric wire which ran the entire length of the ceiling. They flickered intermittently casting strange shadows as far as the eye could see. There was just sufficient light to facilitate navigation between the never-ending lines of shelves. A quick glance revealed to Gerhard that the cellar of the house had been extended into the bedrock to make a tunnel. The ceiling was not more than 3-metres high, carved as a dome, the highest part being the centre along which was attached the electric wire. Wooden shelves stood floor to ceiling. The tunnel was just wide enough to support a row of shelves against each wall with a double row running down the centre.

Wilhelm picked up a heavy industrial torch. He handed it to Gerhard. "Take this, use it sparingly in case the generator trips."

"Where are the files?"

"I'll take you to them. They are further down but first my money."

Gerhard placed the bag on the stone floor. He unzipped it, removed his jacket then three tightly-folded collapsible bags. "Count it if you wish."

Wilhelm knelt on the cold stone floor. With shaking hands he lifted up a neat bundle of 100-Euro bills. He quickly flicked through them."

"Nine bundles containing 10,000, one bundle containing 5,000. It's all there. You don't think I'd cheat you do you?"

Wilhelm said nothing. With difficulty he stood up. "This way," and he began to walk down the narrow aisle. Gerhard followed closely behind.

"This cellar, did we carve it?"

Wilhelm coughed. "No, it was the Nazis. In March 1944, when all but Hitler and his inner circle knew the war was lost, the Einsatzab Rosenberg, who were responsible for collecting all the Nazi's *acquired* works of art, had this tunnel constructed to store their precious paintings, jewellery as well as gold and silver bars. A small army of slave laborers was used to carve it. The house was demolished then rebuilt once the tunnel was completed. In January 1944 the British and Americans began their saturation bombing raids on German cities. The Einsatzab Rosenberg needed somewhere safe to hide their booty. Certain high-ranking officials also believed that by hiding everything in secret tunnels, not only would they protect it, but they could use the contents for their own nefarious purposes once the war ended. They never banked of course on the Russians occupying Germany as far west as Berlin."

"How did you know about it?"

"I was born here. My father once owned an antique shop in Leipzig. In 1939 he was employed by Goering to follow the conquering Wermacht into occupied Europe to appropriate all valuable works of art for the new Germania. Those items not selected by Goering were stored first in Berlin and later in Leipzig."

"What happened when the Russians came?"

"At first nothing, but you know what it was like. There were no secrets. It was only a matter of time before someone spoke out. Fortunately for my father he was well-connected with the new administration, so in return for disclosing the contents of the cellar he managed to retain the house."

"And you've lived here ever since?"

"On and off."

"When did you move all this lot here?"

"I started in 1988 six months before the Wall came down."

They had passed row upon row of dusty cardboard boxes which were now replaced by grimy glass jars.

"What are these?"

"Smells," replied Wilhelm.

Gerhard stopped to closer examine a row. "What's in them?"

Wilhelm turned to face him. "Each jar carries a label, inscribed on it is a number. This corresponds with one of those files we have just passed. In each jar is a personal possession either worn or touched by the subject in the file. It contains their smell. See, this jar contains an item of clothing, this one a comb, this a sock and this, paper tissues. A trained dog, when given the smell, could use it to identify the person if caught in a police trap. It could prove they were in a particular place at a certain time connecting them to some previous illegal activity."

"And you've kept this all these years, for what?"

"You're here aren't you?"

Wilhelm continued down the cellar. They had traveled a hundred-meters when he stopped. He pointed to a brown cardboard box, the size of a small suitcase. "That's what you've come for."

Gerhard put his arms around the box. In a cloud of dust he pulled it off the shelf. "Shit its heavy," he muttered. Placing it on the floor he first removed the top; a series of box files and bulky brown A4-envelopes confronted him. "Is this everything?"

"Yes," replied Wilhelm. I suggest you bring it to the front where the light is brighter. The mass is just correspondence. You know us Germans we file everything. Nothing must ever be thrown away. I assume it is only the results which interest you."

"Well I certainly don't want to carry all this back with me."

They returned to the entrance where at the bottom of the steps stood a small wooden table with a lamp and chair. Wilhelm switched on the lamp. He picked up the bag containing the money and began to climb the stairs. "That should make it more comfortable for you. Take your time. I'll go upstairs and make us some tea."

"You stay here with me. You don't go anywhere," barked back Gerhard.

"Very well, if that's what you want." Wilhelm sat halfway up the stairs watching Gerhard flicking through the files. Twenty minutes passed and a small pile of loose sheets began to grow on the desk while the bulk of the contents were discarded on the floor.

"What's this? Refer sample PZFL/83/11"

"Let me see." Slowly Wilhelm descended. Gerhard showed him the document. "That's the entrapment file. We manufactured a strong perfume which was given to agents in the field. It was to help them seduce a subject. Did you never hear of it?"

Gerhard chose to ignore the question. "So, does a sample still exist?"

"Give me the paper." Gerhard handed it too him. "It should be here, let me see if I can find it." He shuffled off down the narrow corridor. Minutes later he returned clutching two small dusty bottles. Their tops were sealed with wax over a rubber cork.

"Fantastic." Gerhard grabbed the bottles. He rubbed away the dust before holding them closer to the light. One bottle contained a pale lime-green liquid the other, a golden ochre. "That's it. I've got what I came for." Gerhard opened out a foldaway carrier bag. Quickly he stuffed in those papers which he had chosen to retain. Ripping loose sheets from the discarded pile he wrapped them round the bottles as protection.

"Can we go now? Are you finished?" Wilhelm was standing at the top of the stairs clutching the bag of money.

"One final thing," replied Gerhard.

"What's that?" But no answer was required. Wilhelm found himself staring into the barrel of a Walter PPK aimed at his chest.

"You didn't really think I was going to pay an old man like you €100,000, now do you?" Gerhard squeezed the trigger. The explosion rebounded throughout the cellar. Gerhard's legs collapsed. The impact bowled him over causing him to fall back against the wooden door at the top of the stairs. The money bag remained firmly in his hand. A rattling sound followed by a second bang, resembling a crash, echoed down the tunnel. Gerhard stared at the iron portcullis, which had suddenly descended from the ceiling two feet in front of where he was standing. He was imprisoned.

"What the . . . open this thing . . . can you hear me . . . come on . . . I'll get you to a hospital. You can't enjoy the money if you're dead."

There was no reply. The lifeless body just lay at the top of the stone steps with the portcullis separating it from Gerhard. "Shit shit shit; there must be a way of opening this thing." Gerhard picked up the torch he shone it first on Wilhelm. The chest was heaving slightly—or was it? He could not be certain. The light moved to the wall. It shone over a small square metal plate, out of the centre of which, protruded a round green object. "There's a button sticking out. That's it. The old bastard must have been standing next to it. He probably meant to hit the button trapping me down here but I was too quick. That was why he was so keen to stay at the top of the stairs. A long stick might do the trick. I need to find something long enough to reach the button."

Holding the heavy torch in his hand Gerhard turned around. "Think . . . think man there's got to be something I can use." Only the steady thumping sound of the generator could be heard.

# Chapter Twenty-Eight

## Paris

The two men stared through the security glass at the funeral vases. Their concentration was disturbed by a group of school children. After first telling them all to be quiet, or the outing to the museum would be immediately cancelled, the young teacher attempted to explain the significance of the exhibits. It was a futile exercise.

"Come, we'd better escape to the sanctity of my office."

Herbert Sibert followed his friend, Professor Raymond Chapel, out through the crowds which were beginning to crowd into the Egyptian room. They walked briskly down the long corridor. Using his security pass he opened an unmarked door and Herbert found himself in area of the Louvre rarely visited by the public. The Professor offered no explanation as to the activities taking place in the rooms they passed. Technicians dressed in white dust coats poured over ancient-looking objects. Statues, tall, big, small of all shapes littered the floor space. Catalogues, files and books covered every available surface. They spilled out of bursting bookshelves to be piled up on the floor.

The Professor's office lay at the end of the corridor. Herbert followed him through an anteroom where two young girls where so engrossed with their computer screens that neither looked up to acknowledge their presence. The office was no different. The Professor sat behind his cluttered desk. Herbert moved some books off a chair. He searched for somewhere to place them.

"Stick them on the floor. I don't often receive visitors. We're terribly tight for space."

Herbert sat down relieved to take the weight off his feet. He looked around trying to take in the myriad artifacts which filled the small room.

"So, Herbert, are you still creating exotic fragrances for the rich and famous?"

Herbert smiled. "Yes, I suppose I still am, although I must say I am beginning to think about retirement. The thought of spending my time in the fresh air as far away from the noise and pollution of Paris becomes more inviting every year."

"But what would you do with yourself—sit and watch the flowers grow? You have no children?"

"No. But my wife loves gardening and I would like to devote more time to my painting—talking of wives, before I forget." He reached into his jacket pocket and pulled out a small decorative bottle which he handed to Raymond, "A little something for Catherine. I hope she likes it. Tell her the only other woman to wear this fragrance is the wife of our new President. It would be prudent if she refrained from wearing it in her presence."

The Professor took the bottle. He held it up to closer examine it. "That's very thoughtful of you, Herbert. I'm sure Catherine will be delighted and as for her not embarrassing our new President's wife I fear there will be little chance of that. Now what is it you wanted to discuss with me?"

"Raymond, the last time we met, I think it was when we had dinner together. You mentioned something about discovering a tomb which you believed was that of Cleopatra's high priest."

"Meryneith, we believe he was called, yes that's correct but what of it?"

"I seem to recollect you telling me about the sealed jars containing a perfume-like substance. Would you still have them by any chance as I would very much like to analyze the contents?"

"If they were here I would be only too happy to oblige but unfortunately we no longer have them. In fact we never really did. You see although we part-financed the dig the Department of Egyptian Antiquities now forbids the removal from Egypt of all such artifacts. However, I do have a chemical analysis of the contents. I'm sure I can make you a copy but what is your interest, if I may ask?"

Herbert waited a moment before responding. He needed to gather his thoughts. "What can you tell me, Raymond, of the myths that Cleopatra used an aphrodisiac to seduce her lovers? Is it just fantasy, or in your expert opinion, could there be a level of truth?"

"That's a strange question, especially from you, Herbert. You're not thinking of trying to create something on those lines, are you?"

"No, of course not it's just . . . it's just that . . . look it's difficult to explain . . . a substance . . . a fragrance has come into my possession which does appear to produce some erotic feelings."

"Marvelous," joked the Professor. "Perhaps you can share some with me before I become too old and you make your millions out of it."

"I only wish it were that easy, Raymond. The fact is although I have the so-called formula, I have been unsuccessful in reproducing it. Therefore, I thought if I could compare it with this Egyptian substance I might discover some trace element which I have so far overlooked."

The Professor reclined in his chair. Removing his spectacles he wiped them with a white handkerchief before returning them to his nose. "Now let me see, Cleopatra was Macedonian, the last ruler of that dynasty. Strangely enough we believe she was the first monarch of a three-hundred-year-old dynasty to actually speak the language of the people she ruled over. Although born in Egypt, her culture and background was more Greek than Egyptian, not that my colleagues in Cairo will ever admit. Therefore, any such potions she used probably owe their origins to Athens rather than Thebes. Be this as it may, Archaeologists first discovered oily unguents in 1922 when Howard Carter opened the tomb of Tutankhamen. Amazingly, after 3,000 years they still gave off a powerful odor. We now know they used oil called kyphi, which translated means, "Welcome to the Gods". It is derived from a Himalayan plant of the valerian family which produces rhizome, an underground root-like stem bearing both roots and shoots. However, Kyphi had more than religious uses. It could lull one to sleep, alleviate anxieties, increase dreaming, eliminate sorrow, treat asthma and act as a general antidote for toxins."

He paused to retrieve a file from which he began to read. "Cubes of incense were prepared by mixing ground gums and plants with honey, similar to a technique used by the Babylonians and later adapted by the Romans and Greeks. Today the substance is used both as a stimulant and an antispasmodic. Chemical analysis reveals their spikenard contained: iris root, tree resin, peppermint, henna, juniper, cinnamon, honey, cassia as well as traces of unidentified grasses. To prepare these substances, the Egyptians used genuine laboratories where they employed techniques such as cold-pressing, high temperature maceration in olive, sesame, or almond oil, as well as a technique resembling a form of distillation. However, the most sought after odors remain those of the lotus, the lis, and the iris. Receptacles of various shapes contain all the ointments placed into the tombs: rounded belly receptacles or majestic goblets characterized by a large opening, covered with a flat cork and a cloth. All sorts of stones are used to this effect but Alabaster dominates."

"Can you give me a printout, Raymond?"

"Better still I can give you a paper—written by one of my postgraduate students as part of their doctorate on oils and potions as used by the ancient Egyptians." Picking up the phone on his desk he dialed a number. "Angelique, be so kind to print out a copy of your Egyptian oils thesis . . . yes . . . *now* if you don't mind. Kindly bring it to my office . . . thank you.

"Back to Cleopatra—where was I? Yes, did you know she bore four children? The eldest, Caesarion, was fathered by Caesar and executed by Augustus his great-nephew. To

Antony she bore a girl, Cleopatra Selene II, then two boys, Alexander Helios and Ptolemy Philadelphus. On the death of their parents Antony's wife, Octavia Minor, took them in and brought them up in Rome. Strangely enough we hardly know what Cleopatra looked like as no authentic statues, carvings or busts exist. Why was this you think? Some scholars believe it was because she was not a very attractive woman—ugly in fact, if the coins baring her profile are anything to go by.

"So how come she was able to successfully seduce both Caesar and Antony who of all people became quite besotted by her? Could it have been her great intellect? I hardly think so. No, I rather believe she could have been aided by the use of some powerful aphrodisiac. Remember, she was always a mysterious woman. Rulers in those days did not attend public functions where their faces became a popular feature. Most lived closeted lives shielded away in their royal palaces by an army of priests and sycophants."

"So you are saying Cleopatra used some form of drug to entrap her lovers."

Raymond smiled. "Don't put words into my mouth. I said *could* have used some form of aphrodisiac. The emphasis is on could. Some of the oils found in Meryneith's tomb were different to previous finds. The size of his sarcophagus and the number of artifacts buried with him point to him being a once powerful man but not a pharaoh, mark you. Not a lot is known about him—where he was born—how he rose to his position and in fact what happened to him after Cleopatra's dramatic death. He appears to have remained very much in the shadows but we do know that Cleopatra relied heavily upon him. He may even have had some kind of hold over her. Neither Caesar, nor Antony, chose to have him removed from power, when they became involved with Cleopatra so perhaps they also depended upon him. Sadly we shall never know all we can do is speculate."

"The oils found in his tomb, you said you could let me have a copy of their chemical analysis."

"Yes I did, Herbert, so I did."

The Professor rose. He walked to the door, opened it and stuck his head out. "Could one of you ladies please locate the Meryneith file? It is probably under expeditions—Egypt, last year. I only want the section relating to analysis of liquid substances. It will form an addendum page to the report." He closed the door and returned to his desk. "It should not take them more than a few minutes. Now do tell me how did this . . . this substance come into your hands?"

"Raymond, I'd rather not say. It was Lucien in fact who brought it to me."

"How is that old faggot? I'm amazed you've stuck with him for so long. I think I met him once and that was enough."

"Lucien, oh he's alright. I hardly ever see him except when he wants some special fragrance for one of his friends."

There was a knock on the door. "Come in," called out the Professor. A young woman entered clutching a file. "Ah, Angelique, I see you have brought me the copy of your thesis, thank you very much." She handed the slim file to the Professor then quickly left the room. His phone rang.

Herbert sat watching. He checked his watch. It was time to go. He needed to get back to the shop or he would be late in meeting an important customer. There was a problem. His friend's posture had changed. The Professor had stiffened, his voice had become firmer. Finally he replaced the receiver.

"I'm sorry, Herbert."

"Something wrong, Raymond?"

"Yes, the Meryneith file—it appears to have disappeared. They cannot locate it in the computer and the hard copy has been removed."

# Chapter Twenty-Nine

## North Wales

He badly needed a break. Life had become intolerable. His urge, his need was driving him crazy. It was taking over his mind making it difficult for him to concentrate. He had even begun to snap at Mrs. Wainright which was most out of character. Since the wretched trial his mother had become more and more domineering. He was finding it increasingly difficult to escape from her. If he were not leaving for the shop she demanded to know where he was going and whom he was going to see every time he made some excuse to leave the cottage. She reminded him, no nagged him, about the stranger which the boys and Oliver had caught spying on the cottage. "They're watching you, Archibald. You must listen to your mother. This thing is not over yet. You must be careful." Her words repeated over and over in his mind.

In the past he had always had Sam to fall back on but now she too had deserted him. He had thought of trying to phone her again. Perhaps she had a friend or an acquaintance she could recommend to him but each time he picked up the phone he somehow lacked the courage to make the call. The camper had been driven only once in two weeks and that was to Altringham. There was a street frequented by prostitutes. He could easily have bought one for an hour's pleasure. He had driven slowly down the road, cruised, was the word used in the films he watched. There were plenty of girls to choose—tall ones, short ones, black ones, white ones, peroxide blondes, red heads, thin ones and even fat ones but it wasn't the same. On slowing down they had pushed themselves forward, pouted their lips, lifted a skirt to reveal a white thigh, or touched their breasts to encourage him. But, this had the opposite affect. It scared him off. Each time he had accelerated away—to safety.

The last time he had picked up a hooker they had hardly got started when her pimp had attacked him. It was a set up. They had taken his watch, his wallet, even his new leather jacket. He had pleaded with them not to hurt him. It was not the pain which terrified him. It was how he would explain away any bruises or cuts to his mother. He would never trust one of them again. Plus, they never satisfied him. They just wanted to get it over with as fast as possible. It was all too clinical. There was no passion and he certainly was not going to waste anymore of his precious perfume. He was beginning to believe his mother's threat not to make anymore.

The decision to get away for twenty-four hours was thanks to the Antiques Road Show. He had watched a recording of the program filmed in the grounds of Chirk Castle located on the border of England and North Wales. Often in the past he had accompanied old Mr. Donaldson on a weekend buying trip to North Wales where they had attended auctions of old farm houses. Together they had explored numerous Welsh villages for antique bargains. He searched the web. Fortune had it. There was an auction taking place in Llandudno in the ballroom of the Grand Hotel. He printed it out to show his mother. The catalogue included Welsh dressers, Carlton Ware and Moorcroft pottery. He told her if the prices were right he had ready buyers eager to scoop them up. Surprisingly enough she accepted what he said. He even suggested she come with him for the ride. "It will do you the world of good, mother, to get away for a night. How long is it since the last time?" She never answered. He did not expect her to. It was so many years he could not remember. Mrs. Wainright was happy to run the shop in his absence. She needed the money. Her husband, Robbie, was unemployed again.

The Volkswagen camper was running well. The engine was a bit noisy. The old girl struggled to climb some of the hills, which necessitated him changing down to second, a task requiring some concentration and skill. The long stick-gear-change required a firm strong push or pull, which stretched his short arms while the clutch felt as though it needed thrusting down as far as the tarmac.

Twenty miles before Llandudno he pulled off the A55 following a signpost to Rhyl. Many years back, as a teenager, he had spent a fun three days in the town in the company of a youth group. Even then Rhyl had seen better days. Up to the mid-sixties it had been a popular resort for working class low-budget holiday makers from around Merseyside—the poor man's Blackpool. It even boasted a tower, 80-metres high. But Blackpool had survived the loss of its traditional holiday market. For less money, people chose to fly off to exotic destinations such as Majorca or Ibiza. There, they could still guzzle draught English beer; scoff greasy fish and chips whilst enjoying a game of bingo, complain about the locals, kick a ball around and end up having a senseless punch-up over nothing. Plus, the weather was guaranteed. The sun always shone not like in poor old Rhyl.

As the camper rumbled into the town familiar sights from a distant youth flashed past. The marine lake where he had spent many happy hours driving an electric motor boat had long dried up. A number of buildings were boarded up, abandoned by their owners. Empty plots showed were the council had exercised their right in pulling down such condemned buildings before they collapsed on their latest inhabitants—squatters.

Yet, there was still hope. Gaudy neon lights flashed on and off, advertising all-day poker and slot machines. A revue bar boasted the assets of Olga and Katrina who had ventured all the way from the Ural Mountains to share their voluptuous charms with the visitors to Rhyl. On every second block the ubiquitous public house stood firm, a stalwart against changing times and a monument to British culture. "The Gulls Nest", "Sea Breeze", "Linga Longa", and a plethora of other exotic names announced they had vacancies. But he did not seek a bed and breakfast establishment, but rather one of the numerous caravan parks which dotted the coastline. They were cheap, but of greater importance you could come and go freely as you wish and, he had the van to sleep in. All that was needed was a clean toilet and shower block. The first two camps he pulled into informed "No, sorry, no mobile campers" but they would happily rent him one of their superior vans for the night. Archibald declined the offer.

Six miles out of town and he had crossed the River Clwyd. He thought of turning back when a small sign attracted his attention—"Heulwen Farm, Caravan Park, half a mile". It was worth a try. He turned into the narrow lane. The driver of the silver Audi who had been following the camper since he had left home chose to drive on before turning around and stopping.

Being so far out of town and set way back from the sea "Happiness Farm Caravan Park" was cheaper not that this concerned him. A dozen large caravans stood in a row. Some even boasted small manicured gardens around them indicating that their occupants were permanent residents. For only twenty pounds they welcomed him for the night telling him to park behind the ablutions block.

It was still school holidays. Gangs of unruly youths in search of something to do hung around the arcades. Young girls giggled and flaunted their white bodies as they pretended to inhale an offered cigarette. Purple hair, studs and rings pierced flesh, high plastic boots in summer, brassiere straps and rolls of stomach fat flashed before his eyes. Archibald moved on. The night was young. He was enjoying the freedom of walking along the strip. Nobody knew him. He was lost in the crowd. The camper was parked in the public car park. As additional security he had purchased a Krook-Lock which tied the steering wheel to the clutch pedal. It would not prevent a professional thief from stealing the vehicle but might give joy-rider-thieves second thoughts. He was not to know a silver Audi was parked observing the vehicle.

Jimmy's Jumbo Prawns—he felt like something different. It was almost eight o'clock. The large open-plan restaurant was half-full he wondered if it even bothered to open out of season. A pretty young girl showed him to a table. He did not like it preferring to sit where he had a better view of the room with his back against the far wall. It was a table for four. He lied about some friends possibly joining him later.

The Greek salad was bland. The feta cheese could have been soap and he almost broke a tooth on one of the olives. It so annoyed him when the kitchen could not be bothered to remove the stones. The soggy basmati rice was tepid, tasteless and overcooked. The queen prawns, the specialty of the house, were mushy inside, while the burnt outer shells were inedible. Jimmy's *world famous prawn sauce,* consisted of minute specks of what possibly could have been chilly, floating on the surface of a dark insipid oily liquid.

He had asked for some bread. It had taken a while. Two slices cut in half of white processed bread, posed inside a cheap straw basket, with a packet of miniature butter which had obviously been well hidden in the back of the deep freeze making it impossible to spread. The sweet white house wine was warm but he did not complain. What was the point? And, it would only draw attention, the last thing he needed.

The service had been slow. The prawns had taken ages to arrive but he was in no hurry. He enjoyed just sitting and watching the people. Two young waitresses attracted his attention. He guessed they were students earning extra money during their holidays. He enjoyed watching their slim bodies run between the tables as they went about their duties. A table, four youths—two males, two females—in the middle of the room, was creating an inordinate amount of noise. He analyzed them to be football louts. They were giving one of the waitresses a difficult time. He despised them—shortly cropped hair, skinheads, his mother would have called them—silly childish tattoos adorned their muscular arms. One had a silver stud protruding out of his right eyebrow, the other, a series of rings dangling from his ears. They drank directly from the mouths of their beer bottles, banging them down hard on the table to attract attention as soon as they were empty, which was often.

He sat watching them shout and blaspheme whilst arguing amongst themselves. He detested the uncouth way they held their knives and forks waving them in the air, pointing with them to emphasize some senseless point. The girls were no better. He could not see their faces but their hair was cut in that spiky unfeminine way he so loathed. They both wore low-slung tight-fitting jeans with short vest-like tops which exposed the top of their white buttocks. One wore red string underwear the other black. The sight infuriated him but it kept drawing his eyes.

Old Mr. Donaldson had the answer. Archibald could hear his voice as though he were present at the table. "You see, young Archibald," he would say. "We need a war, a damn good war that would sort out these louts. You young people are so lucky. In my day we had first, the Great War, then twenty-one years later Hitler came along. A good war helps to cull overpopulation. What we're looking at is cannon fodder, that's all these louts are worth."

He would have so loved to have confronted them. He imagined himself approaching the table, telling the bigger of the two men to shut up or get out. The man would jump to his feet swear foully at Archibald before attempting to hit him. Archibald easily ducked the wild swing forcing the huge arm up in a sweeping arc which dislocated the brute's shoulder. For good measure he broke his wrist in a second twisting movement. The man screamed in pain as he crashed helplessly to the floor. The second youth was now on his feet. He grabbed Archibald from behind but Archibald easily slipped out of the grip. Grabbing an arm he twisted it up behind the man's back. He too screamed in pain. In a deep steady voice Archibald announced to the astonished restaurant that table 17 wanted their bill as they were leaving. The terrified waitress ran to the table. The two tarts stared down at the tab in its cheap plastic folder. Archibald tightened his grip. The man screamed out. "Pay the bill, pay it damn you." One of the tarts opened her handbag, the other followed. Their trembling fingers fumbled to pull out bank notes.

"Don't forget to leave a generous tip," announced Archibald sternly.

The tart on the left emptied her purse onto the table. The waitress scooped up the money while all the time Archibald held the second youth in an excruciating arm lock. She checked it then smiled in admiration at Archibald. "Thank you," she whispered before scampering off to the safety of the bar. Still maintaining a vice like grip on the man's arm Archibald pushed him forward towards the door. The two girls struggled to lift the first man who yelled with pain. The door to the street was opened. Archibald gave a final twist to the arm before propelling the man forward. Using his right foot he lashed out. His boot made contact with the small of the man's back causing him to fall heavily onto his face where he lay moaning in the road. The two girls half-carried the other beast out. The doors closed. Archibald walked calmly back to his table as though nothing had happened. People stood up to applaud him. Somewhat embarrassed Archibald sipped his wine. It was all so easy after all he had seen Chuck Norris do it so many times in the films.

"You're bill, luv."

Archibald stared at the waitress as she placed the plastic bill folder in front of him. The table of four was now making more noise than ever. Even the girls were drunk. There was going to be trouble. It was time for him to go.

The passenger door of the silver Audi opened and a man slipped inside. "Well, find anything?" asked his partner behind the wheel.

"Nothing, if he really does have it then he must be carrying it on him. The camper is clean. There is absolutely no place inside where he could have concealed it."

"I'd better get back to the restaurant then. He should be coming out soon."

"Don't bother. There's no need to follow him. If, and when, he does pick up a woman he will bring her back here.

That's why he bought the camper. That's what it's for. It's his passion wagon."

"So? We just wait here."

"No. You wait here. I need to stretch my legs and get something to eat. Phone me the minute you spot him I'll be over there by those takeaway outlets."

The light was fading it was ten o'clock. Archibald had been in and out of three bars. There were no single women. They were either in big groups or with partners. The arcades were no good. They were frequented by the teenagers. He was beginning to think that perhaps Rhyl was not such a good place to find a partner. Perhaps it was too down market. He could drive on to Colwyn Bay or even Llandudno but the hour was late. Tiredness was beginning to overcome him. He supposed it was his age compounded by the fact he was not really a night person. Ten was usually his bedtime.

Deep in thought he returned to the camper. It was exactly where he had parked it except it stood alone. The car park was empty except for a handful of vehicles. For good measure he walked around it. Everything appeared normal. Sitting in the passenger seat he clutched the steering wheel. Where to? Where now? He turned the ignition to light up the instruments. The clock showed 10:15. He fired up the engine, turned on the lights, selected first gear and drove slowly out.

It was the strong smell of popcorn wafting through the open passenger window which first caught his attention. His mother had strictly forbidden him ever sampling such a thing. It was on her list of *forbidden fruits*. He could not even remember when he had last tasted it or even if he had enjoyed it. Forced to slow down for traffic lights his eyes followed the direction of the aroma. A gaudily painted caravan was strategically placed on a corner. Some girls were buying candy floss. Turning left at the lights he pulled into an open space.

After locking the camper he strolled back towards the caravan. The candy floss purchasers had departed. A light flicked off. A door in the back opened. A young woman stepped down onto the street and walked around to the front where she picked up a sandwich board advertising the specials of the day. Picking it up she turned to renter the van. Archibald waited for her at the open counter.

"Sorry, luv, I'm closed."

Archibald liked what he saw—short black hair, nice face, not caked in makeup. He estimated her age to be somewhere close to thirty, "Any chance of some popcorn?"

"Sorry, like I said; I'm closed, anyway the machines off."

Archibald looked around. "Can you sell me a coke and . . . a chocolate mint bar?" Two more forbidden foods. His mother would not have approved.

The girl quickly turned around. From an under-bar deep freeze she pulled out a wrapped chocolate mint. "Small or large Coke?" She asked.

Archibald had expected a can. The girl held up a paper cup. He had no idea of the size. The girl had long elegant fingers. The nails were painted black. "That's fine thank you," he smiled. He watched as she expertly poured the coke.

"Eight fifty, please."

Archibald placed a ten-pound note on the counter. "Keep the change . . . for your bother."

"Ta very much," she replied then busied herself in closing down the caravan.

Archibald sipped the coke. He watched her move busily turning off appliances. She leaned over the open front to pull up the serving hatch. Under her white serving coat she wore a black tight-fitting top. She was struggling to reach the release catch. Her ample breasts were pushing down on the counter. Archibald swallowed hard. He put down the coke. "Can I help you?" Without waiting for a reply he reached up to release the first of two catches locking down the hatch. He helped push the hatch up and was rewarded with a lovely smile before the hatch imprisoned her in the caravan.

He finished the coke throwing the empty carton into a rubbish bin. He looked at the ice cream unsure whether or not to open it. A banging sound came from the back of the caravan quickly followed by the grating of a key and the snapping of a padlock. The girl appeared in front of him. Over her shoulder she carried a bag. She appeared smaller, more or less the same height as Archibald. She checked her watch. She frowned then fumbled into her bag for her cell phone. Archibald tried not to watch. With great difficulty he pulled the paper off the ice cream throwing it into the bin but missing. As he stooped down to retrieve it he heard her shouting into the phone—"What do you mean you can't come for another hour—sod off!"

She threw the phone into the bag. Pulled it tight over her shoulder and turned to march off. "Excuse me, Miss . . . could I . . . could I give you a lift somewhere? My van is only parked there," and Archibald pointed to the camper.

The girl stopped to face him. He could see by her face she was enraged. This excited him. "Thank you but *no*." She turned to walk off.

Archibald threw the unfinished ice cream away onto the pavement. "It's really no trouble. Do you have far to walk?"

She hesitated. "Which way you going?"

Archibald shrugged his shoulders. "I'm passing through. Where can I drop you? It's really no problem."

"What's your name?"

"Archie."

"Where you from?"

"Manchester," he lied. "I'm on my way to Llandudno to a . . . see some friends, tomorrow."

"I'm Liz, pleased to meet you. Yes, you can give me a lift. Are you sure you don't mind? It's on the Prestatyn road."

They walked together towards the camper. He unlocked the passenger door then quickly ran around to the driver's door. From his trouser pocket he removed a small glass phial. Quickly, he unscrewed the glass top. He poured a small quantity of the liquid onto his left hand then rubbed into his face and neck. He opened two buttons on his shirt and poured a small drop onto the skin of his chest rubbing it in roughly. He struggled with the key in the door. "Sorry to keep you, I always have trouble with the lock; have been meaning to have it replaced for a long time."

"Have you had the van long?"

"Ages. I used to use it a lot for camping." Archibald leaned towards her. "Please put your seat belt on. Here, let me help you." His arm reached over her.

"I can manage," and she pulled the belt across her body. Her nose twitched. "What's the aftershave, you're wearing?" Archibald turned the ignition key. The engine coughed once before starting.

"Do you like it?"

"Yes, it's quite strong, different."

Archibald held out his left hand. "Here, have a sniff it's also very good for clearing the sinuses." She hesitated feeling somewhat stupid she touched his arm bringing it closer to his skin.

Archibald withdrew his arm. He engaged first gear. He indicated right, checked the side mirror and began to pull out. The girl sneezed twice. "My handbag," she muttered, "need a bloody tissue."

"Here, take my handkerchief it is clean." The girl at first refused but Archibald shoved into her hands. She blew strongly into it.

The silver Audi followed from a safe distance. "He's either drunk or something is happening the strange way he's snaking all over the road. How does he do it? What's his secret? Apart from the drug I mean." The driver remained silent. "He's turning left, must be taking her to the camp sight. What shall we do?" The driver pulled over into a lay-by at the side of the road and turned off the headlights.

"Give him fifteen minutes and we'll follow."

For once the sky was clear and the half-moon provided sufficient light for them to drive slowly up the narrow lane without using the car's headlights. They had arrived at the farm gates. The engine was turned off and they both exited the car.

"There's the camper, right in front." Stealthily, they slipped through the gate in the direction of the camper. The vehicle was rocking on its suspension. Groans emanated from inside.

# Chapter Thirty

## Leipzig

Sweat had drenched his shirt. He no longer bothered to mop his brow. There was simply no time. The perspiration dripping down his face no longer concerned him, only his hands—these he needed to keep dry if he was to affect an escape. He had found nothing remotely long enough in the cellar or tunnel with which to reach the button. Eight, maybe nine-meters, was the distance he needed to cover if he were to reach it on the far wall, which he assumed released the barrier imprisoning him.

His first option had been to try his phone but of course no signal could penetrate so deep underground. The old man had not moved. He lay on his side in the fetal position, his right hand locked firmly around the handles of the money bag. Once satisfied there was no broom or pole Gerhard set about ripping apart the nearest shelf. It had not been an easy task. They were German built which meant they were constructed to last. First he had to clear away the boxes. That was the easy part. Lacking any tools he had only his brute strength with which to wrench the shelves off the legs which supported them. He estimated their height to be approximately four-meters. Two legs lashed together might just do the trick.

Concentrating on the task he had worked feverously. Time was of the essence. First he had broken a nail then the first of many splinters pierced his skin. His knuckles were grazed where they had come into rough contact with the stone wall. The heat was oppressive. He was not sure if it was due to his physical exertions or if the oxygen in the tunnel was beginning to run out. Either way, there was no time to worry about it.

He had no idea how long it had taken him to finally demolish the first set of shelves. Bent double, with perspiration pouring down his face, his lungs fought to suck in air. His back ached, his muscles throbbed. Blood covered his hands. Three finger nails were ripped, but there was no time to waste. His mouth was dry. He longed for a cool refreshing glass of water, not beer, but ordinary water.

The question now was how to join the two wooden shelf legs to make them long enough to reach the button. He thought of using his jacket but for once in his life he had forgotten to carry a knife. The material was too strong, the stitching too close, to rip using only his bare hands. This left his shirt but, there were the glass jars. Many of them held articles of clothing. A dozen jars now lay shattered on the stone floor. They had yielded two belts, three neckties, underpants, socks, shirts and a pullover.

The first few attempts to reach the button were abysmal failures. His makeshift pole was too short. He needed to retie the two legs so as to increase the length. But now he could no longer control it. With his hands stretched out between the bars the pole was impossible to manipulate. Each time it came close to the button it bounced off. He simply could not apply sufficient pressure.

More time was consumed in cannibalizing a third leg. Additional material needed to be sourced which resulted in another six jars revealing their secret contents. Exhausted but now confident he would succeed, his aching arms stretched out through the openings in the portcullis. The mark III pole was heavier. He willed his tortured wrists not to collapse.

"Slowly, slowly," he murmured encouraging himself to succeed. He pushed the pole out through the metal bars sliding it up the stairs, careful not catch the bindings on the edges. On the fourth attempt his aching arms had informed this was the easiest way. Use the steps to defy gravity. Then, using every last ounce of strength lift it up to make contact with the green button.

It was working. "Easy does it . . . easy does it." He began to slowly lift the pole. It was not wobbling as much as the previous two. The muscles in his arms were screaming. His wrists threatened to collapse. It rested on the wall only 10-centimetres from the button. Carefully he dragged it closer. Eight, six, four, now it was resting against the square metal frame containing the button. All that was required was to bring it away from the wall by two-centimeters then . . .

The generator coughed then spluttered. The lights dimmed, brightened, dimmed, flickered and went out as the generator died. "No! No! No!" Screamed Gerhard as darkness engulfed the cellar. Knowing it was futile he stabbed at the button, once, twice, again. Nothing happened except, the pole dropped onto the steps as his wrists finally surrendered to the weight. He let go.

His lungs gasped. His heart beat loudly. It was the only audible sound other than the pinking of the generator as it cooled down. Crawling on his knees with his hands outstretched he felt through the darkness—his goal the torch. It was somewhere near the table, so he thought. Seconds became minutes. Minutes seemed to last for hours. He banged his left-side against a solid object. His hands felt the wall. Where was the table—to the left or to the right? "Think . . . don't panic," he told himself.

More bumps, he continued left. This time his forehead touched something hard. It was the table. His hands swept the floor—boxes, papers—where had he left the torch—on top? Feeling with his fingers he touched the flat surface, more papers then—the torch. "Careful, don't knock it over," he whispered to himself. He finally grasped it. His thumb found the button. He pressed it firmly. A beam of light rewarded him.

With a big sigh he stood up. He shone the torch in the direction of the generator. Next to it stood a jerry can and a funnel. He transferred the torch to his left hand. With his right he lifted up the can. He shook it. It was empty. "Damn damn," he cursed.

He shone the torch around as though willing to find another—this time full. He heard a noise, a shuffling—rats? It was coming from the stairs. He moved quickly back to the portcullis. The old man had moved. "Ha! You! Open this bloody gate. Come on. I'll make it worth you're while."

The door at the top of the stairs was opening. Light from above shone through. A low shadow was forcing its way through the crack. "You fucking bastard come back. Don't leave me here?" The crack in the door widened. A wedge of light brightened the top of the stairs. Gerhard reached down to his ankle. He pulled out the Walther. Two quick shots hit the door just as it slammed shut. The shape had gone. The light extinguished; except for the torch in his left hand which was already beginning to fade. The gun fell from Gerhard's fingers. It clattered on the stone floor. The battery in the torch was fast running out. There was no time to waste. Gerhard first wedged the torch so its fading beam was focused on the green button. He picked up the pole. Step by step he maneuvered it upwards. He had five, ten minutes of light and then?

Wilhelm Voigtländer sat with his back to the door allowing his breathing to return to normal. Leaning with his back against the stout wooden door he forced himself to stand. He turned. With trembling fingers he slid first the top bolt then the second to secure the door. Even if Colonel Boch managed to lift the portcullis he would not be able to force the entrance door.

Wilhelm was no longer gasping for breath. He was alive. He had survived. He had outwitted his enemy. He felt euphoric. Slowly, he undid the buttons on his jacket. Still leaning against the wall he eased it off. Turning it around he looked at the hole made by the bullet. Pity, he thought, the jacket was ruined. It could be repaired, but why bother, not with €95,000 in cash at his disposal. With great difficulty he pulled the heavy bullet-proof jacket over his head. It dropped to the floor with a clatter. He felt suddenly lighter almost younger. Bending down he picked up the jacket pressing his finger into the indentation made by the bullet. He had been lucky—no prudent. Of course Colonel Gerhard Bock of the former STASI would attempt to cheat him. It was the nature of the beast. The force of the bullet had indeed knocked him over. He was lucky it was a low caliber projectile. He had estimated that the fuel needed to power the generator would not last more than 15 minutes. Only then could he attempt to open the door and make his escape.

Clutching the money bag he returned to the front room. He relit the paraffin lamp. The electricity to the house had been disconnected years ago. It was a poor neighborhood. People kept to themselves. It was better that way. Everyone had a secret they were guarding. Back in the lounge he went directly to a cupboard. He opened the doors to reveal an array of bottles. For a moment he hesitated then poured himself a large Kroatzbeere, an herb flavored liqueur from Silesia distilled from blackberries.

Collapsing into an armchair he sipped the rich sweet liquid savoring the flavor of summer berries as they exploded on his palate. The money bag was at his feet. Tomorrow he would return to Berlin, to the new flat he had just leased. Berlin was vibrant. There was life there. Leipzig was drab. It contained too many sad memories of a bygone era.

The money made all things possible. Perhaps he would do some traveling. He had always had the desire but the system forbade it. But then the system collapsed. But then he lacked the money. But now things were different. South America, the Brazilian jungle, the place had always fascinated him. He closed his eyes. Giant anacondas, man-eating caimans, richly colored macaw parrots, tropical rainforests, isolated Indian tribes—he had dreamed about it. He had devoured books and watched films. In a way his subconscious mind had already been there. And now it was all possible—or was it? He would need a passport.

The glass was empty. It was time to go—time to leave the house which had once been his home. He walked to the kitchen. He must wash the glass, dry it and return it to the cupboard. The chair he had sat in. The cushion must be pumped up, straightened. It was important to leave the house just as he had found it—inside in a pristine condition. He would return. He always did, perhaps in a week, a month, in several months. He picked up the money bag and walked back to the cellar door. He placed his ear against the wood. He held his breath—silence—all was quiet.

Finally, he extinguished the paraffin lamp placing it on the table in the lounge where it lived. Once more the house was dark and soundless. Instinctively, he felt his way to the front door. Automatically his fingers reached for the first of three locks. The door opened. It was drizzling. The quiet street was grey and drab. There was no sign of life.

Halfway down the road a Trabant trundled towards him belching out clouds of black smoke. "I wonder if they drive Trabants in Brazil. No, I rather think they make Beetles."

# Chapter Thirty One

# Paris

Herbert Siebert rushed into the shop. An elegantly dressed couple was seated in the far corner by the window. The man looked thoroughly bored while the woman was flicking through a back copy of Paris Match. The young shop assistant was busy serving a customer, while another potential buyer was browsing.

"Mademoiselle Convers, Monsieur LeGreves, do forgive me. I am so sorry to have kept you waiting." The man stood up. The women placed the magazine down on the small table. Without waiting for a reply Herbert ushered them through a side door into a small office.

He was ten minutes late. Professor Chapel had delayed his departure from the Louvre. He had insisted Herbert wait as the Professor searched in vain for the missing file on the Egyptian priest Meryneith. "I am so terribly sorry. Files like this just don't go missing. I'll phone you as soon . . ." but the Professor's parting words were lost as Herbert pounded down the corridor.

He battled to find a taxi. Then the traffic was terrible. It had taken more than twenty minutes to get from the Louvre to the shop at Montparnasse. *"Toutes est bloquée, rien marché"*, explained the frustrated taxi driver. Roads had been closed to allow the swift passage of yet another visiting head of state. *"C'est encore les Arabes"* spat out the driver.

The side office, or sampling room, was small. Two ornate Louis XIV chairs faced a small wooden desk whose top was covered with a black granite slab. One wall consisted of wooden cupboards, while behind the desk, a glass showcase exhibited exotic perfume bottles.

"Please take a seat," and Herbert indicated with his arm towards the two chairs as he sat himself down behind the desk. "Mademoiselle, I believe you are searching for your own very special fragrance. Well, let me tell you: you have come to the right place, for here, at L' Artisan Parfumeur, that is what we specialize in creating. Our list of clients is a veritable whose who of European society, but of course you already know this, otherwise you would not be here. So, in order to create your bespoke fragrance may I commence by asking you a number of important questions."

Herbert open a leather bound executive notepad. He selected a fountain pen from one of four pens standing in an antique gold penholder. Let me start by enquiring, "What is your preferred dress color?"

"Black verging on the darker shades of blue," she quickly replied.

"And for casual wear?"

"Um, I suppose red sometimes green, I avoid busy patterns preferring a more plain or one-color garment."

"What is your favorite jewel?"

"Emeralds, I believe."

"Followed by?"

She paused for a moment before responding. "I'm not really a jewellery person but my second choice would be rubies."

"And not diamonds—a girl's best friend?"

"Absolutely not; I find them far too common."

Herbet paused to scribble more notes. He looked up. "Just one more question, Mademoiselle. Would you prefer staying at home to read a good book or attending a social gathering?"

She looked towards her partner as though seeking a definitive answer. "It would depend, wouldn't it," she answered, "as to who was throwing the party and what book I was reading at the time? Does that answer your question?"

"Thank you, Mademoiselle, and what book are you currently reading? I promise you this is my final question."

"The Lost Stradivarius by Martin Fine; it's brilliant. I can't put it down."

"Yes, I too have read it and found it most intriguing. Now, you are probably asking yourself *why* I am asking you all these questions. What is the point? You see: I have just taken your *confession* from which I shall *distil* your brief." He paused to consult his notes. "You are, Mademoiselle, a very private person, someone who knows precisely what they want. You see something—you like it—you must have it. You are not someone who needs time to think before making an important decision. You cannot tolerate fools and people who are indecisive. Your personality is more introvert than extrovert although if motivated correctly you can easily become the life and soul of the party." Herbert paused before smiling. "I trust, Mademoiselle, I have not offended you."

There was silence. Only the murmur of traffic noise emanating from the street disturbed the tranquility in the small office.

"Well . . . well, I'm not sure what to reply. Yes. Yes, I suppose you are correct . . . partially. I rather thought you would start by asking me *what* my favorite fragrances were. *What* sort of flowers I like; *that* type of question then you would thrust a series of bottles for me to sniff."

"Mademoiselle Convers, rest assured we will soon come to the bottles. To create a perfume I have at my disposal over 2,000 notes." He saw a vague impression come over her. "Notes are what we call fragrances—smells to be precise. My brief . . . our brief," and he looked intently at her, "is to create for you a unique . . . your own personalized fragrance. It must be crisp, elegant, sophisticated. Above all it must not shout. It must not be floral rather woody perhaps, breathing a suggestion of cardamom, even cinnamon implying perhaps saffron. Roses, lavender, tuberose and jasmine are all definitely ruled out."

For the first time during the conversation her partner spoke. "You make it sound, Monsieur Sibert, more complicated than choosing a favorite wine."

"Indeed it is, Monsieur. Indeed it is. 'Quality in wine is not a matter of fact but a matter of sensual impact. The brain gives the verdict, only after hearing from the three senses—sight, smell and taste'. I believe the great André Simon said that. A fragrance must rise beyond this as only two of the body's senses come into play and sight of course plays a very minor if not insignificant part."

"And by asking Mademoiselle Convers these questions this helps you to select her perfume?"

"Very much so, a bespoke fragrance is a very personal statement. It is an extension of one's personality. Very active women, who pursue careers in business, are attracted to fresh, spring-like floral notes such as hyacinth, lily of the valley and freesia. Younger women, who tend to be cautious and reserved, are drawn to heavy sweeter perfumes. Older women gravitate to more powdery style notes combined with balsamic intrigue. Impulsive spontaneous women who thrive on action prefer citrus oils such as pineapple, raspberry, peach and blackcurrant in the top note. Then we come to the emotionally stable extrovert women, for her, we look to chypre fragrances using bergamot or oak moss. But I digress; Mademoiselle Convers is unique, so for her perhaps, we will create a combination of personalities."

Herbert stood up from behind his desk. He crossed the room towards a series of cupboards on the far wall. Taking his time he selected a number of small bottles placing each carefully on a white plastic tray. Lifting the tray he carried it over to his desk. After sitting back in his chair he delicately posed each bottle in front of Mademoiselle Convers. He pointed to a white ceramic jar containing cotton wool ear-buds.

"We have arrived at our initial sampling. In front of you, Mademoiselle, are six fragrances. I want you to test each one. Take your time. You can smell directly from the bottle but I advise you to rather dab a small portion on your arm which will allow the natural oils of the perfume to react with your skin. The difficult part is: I require you to place them in order of preference, starting on your left and finishing on the right with the one you least enjoyed. Do not stress yourself if none appeal to your olfactory senses. These are just a start from which I can build upon." Again he stood up. "I shall be just outside in the shop so please take as much time as is needed."

His assistant was busy serving a customer. A young man was standing waiting to be served. Herbert approached him from behind the counter. "Can I help you, Monsieur?"

The young man appeared nervous. He had not shaved. A two-day black stubble adorned his face—something which Herbert frowned upon. The man had clearly not entered the shop to purchase an aftershave.

"Thank you, my name is Pierre Nimier and I am trying to locate a friend who has disappeared. I wondered if you might have seen him."

Herbert stood back from the glass counter. "I hardly think that . . ."

"Please! All I ask is that you take a look. You see my friend was . . . is involved in manufacturing a special perfume and I wondered if he might have contacted you for advice."

"Nobody has come here seeking help of that I can assure you. Now, if you will kindly excuse me I have an important customer in the back requiring my attention." Herbert moved away but the young man persisted.

His voice rose. "Please . . . it won't take a second of your time, just take a quick glance." The raise in pitch had distracted the customer who was now looking towards them. The sales assistant appeared to be embarrassed at the disturbance.

"Very well then." Herbert reached over to snatch the sheet of paper from the young man. He froze. A cold shiver ran down his spine. The young man's words were lost upon him: "He hasn't been seen for 10-days. Nobody knows where he is. The police have even opened a missing person's docket."

He found himself staring at the face of Jacques Gavotte, a face he had last seen in the basement over a week ago when he had spied through the keyhole."

# Chapter Thirty Two

## Manchester

"What do you mean you don't know?" Lancelot Slim sat at his desk pressing the phone tightly to his ear. The signal was not strong. In his right hand he held a pen. It was to record any facts but all he was doing was doodling on the paper—drawing senseless shapes and coloring them in—wasting ink and paper—something he would reprimand his staff if he caught them doing the same. "He can't just have disappeared not with 100,000 Euros of *my money*. Somebody must know something. Trace his steps. Go to Berlin . . . yes, I know he did not tell anyone what precisely his movements were . . . yes, I know there's no file to follow. Wait a minute. Don't go away. I might just have something . . . a lead perhaps."

Lancelot placed the phone down on the desk. Swiveling around on his executive chair he pulled out a drawer from which he extracted a leather bound diary. He picked up the phone. "Are you still there? Good! Give me a minute." He put down the phone. Flicking back through the pages he mumbled out aloud to himself. "What was the date of that meeting with Gerhard? It was after his return from Moscow . . . two . . . three weeks back." His habit of jotting down odd pieces of information—names, places and then recording them in his diary was a habit which had stood him in good stead over the years. "Got it," he announced triumphantly.

He picked up the phone again. "Jorgen, are you still there? Good! Now listen to me . . . write this name down—Wilhelm Voigtländer, yes, I'll spell it for you . . . you've got that . . . Ok! Apparently, he was the head of some scientific section of the STASI which specialized in smells . . . yes smells—odors. They used it to train sniffer dogs. Gerhard mentioned his name. He is either in Berlin or Leipzig, or possibly both. Go there and track him down. Keep me posted on this number." Lancelot terminated the call before dropping the phone into his jacket pocket.

100,000 Euros, against his better judgment he had arranged the money for Gerhard. It was never intended to be paid over. "I just need to show it to him," Gerhard had assured him. "I'll let him keep ten, that'll be enough to shut the old fool up. He'll be more than happy with that."

"And, if he isn't?" Lancelot distinctly remembered asking the question.

"He will be. Trust Me."

Lancelot stood up. He walked to the window. The water from the canal glistened in the sunshine far below. People, ordinary people, were walking along the quays. A woman was being pulled by a large dog. His phone rang. He reached into his pocket. He listened. "Let me get this straight. Crumpet's gone missing. You don't know where he is. Jesus . . . and I have the client coming to see me. She's probably waiting in my outer office right now. You are sure he hasn't found the bug on his car? Good. You've traced it to a lock up garage. You are certain his car is inside it. You have opened the door. It's definitely his car and the bug? In Place. He must have acquired a second vehicle, probably a van of sorts. Ask questions. Find out everything you can and *don't* lose him again. Understand?"

Returning to his desk he checked his diary. His next appointment was due in five minutes. It was the Lisa Evans girl. He wondered what he was going to say to her. He picked up the office phone. "Joyce, has Lisa Evans arrived yet? She has. Well, show her in then." He removed a slim file from his desk, stood up and stretched. The office door opened. Lisa Evans walked in. Lancelot met her halfway into the office. He held out his hand. "Lisa, good of you to pop in. Come; let us sit at the couch. Has Joyce offered you some tea or coffee?" Lisa shook his hand then sat herself on the black leather couch. Lancelot sat opposite in a chair.

"Thanks for seeing me, Commander Slim, and yes, your secretary did organize me a glass of water. Kylie asked me to contact you to find out what was happening. Do you have anything to report?"

"How is Kylie?"

"She's very well, frightfully busy of course. She is in Paris doing a fashion shoot for some famous cosmetic company. That is why she asked me to follow up the case."

Lancelot sat back in his chair. He took a moment before replying. The clock on the wall behind Lisa told him he was running late. He needed to conclude the briefing as quickly as possible but without appearing rude. "I'm afraid there is not a lot to report. It is still early days. I did warn that the surveillance of a subject can be a prolonged activity. It is only in films where things happen quickly." He opened the file. "I see it is not quite a month since we first started surveillance. I did write a progress report to Kylie after the second week. I explained," and he consulted the notes in front of him, "we have established Crumpet's regular routine. He departs from his mother's cottage about seven-thirty each morning, except Sundays, to drive to his antique shop in Beeston. There, he spends his day unless visiting an auction or sale. He does not appear to have any friends or enjoy much of a social life. His mother rarely leaves her cottage where she runs a small homeopathic business supplying herbal cures and the like to local health shops."

He paused as he skipped over the incident with the four cats preferring not to mention it. "One of my people was able to gain entrance to the cottage where they were able to have a good look around. They have also visited the shop. We have stopped observing the cottage, likewise the shop, as it would be impossible not to be noticed if we maintained a continuous presence in such a remote place. Instead we have chosen to place a tracer on Crumpet's car so we know where he is going." Lancelot put down the file.

"Lisa, what we have done is illegal. It is against the law. Therefore, you must not mention this to anyone. I must have your word."

Lisa nodded her head. "Absolutely, I shall not mention it to a living person."

"Thank you, if we are to catch Crumpet—in the act so to say—we shall have to make it appear almost a coincidence. His next victim, assuming of course she agrees, will provide the missing piece with which to entrap him. We shall also be able to lay our hands on his so-called mysterious fragrance. Without this and a chemical analysis, we cannot link him to both you and Kylie."

"Why can't you just go and search his mother's cottage and the shop to find the substance?"

"Lisa, I only wish it were that simple. To do it legally we require a search warrant. No magistrate will issue such a document with only the flimsiest of evidence. And, even with the right papers what are we actually looking for—bottles of perfume? We are sure his mother manufactures the substance. It would be most unlikely if she were to carry a stock in the cottage. It would take an entire army weeks to uncover everything in that garden which is more of a farm. Again, the antique shop must have a hundred places where Crumpet could hide his bottles.

"No, searching is not the answer. Crumpet is not venturing out much. He is probably keeping a low profile for the moment. But, I am working on a plan to entice him out into the open. You just have to be patient, both of you. Now, unless you have any more questions for me." Lancelot's eyes shifted to the clock behind Lisa.

"No, thank you, Commander. I will be speaking with Kylie this evening so will brief her about our meeting. Will you contact me as soon as you have something new to report?"

"I most certainly will. I never like to raise expectations but I very much hope to have concluded this matter by the end of the month."

# Chapter Thirty Three

# Paris

"What's wrong with you? You look terrible. Are you ill or something?" Denise Vergé released Pierre from her welcome hug. She pushed him away while still holding onto his arms. "I thought you'd be pleased to see me back in Paris."

"I am it's just . . ."

"Have you eaten?"

"No."

"Good, neither have I and I'm starving. Let's go to my hotel and then we'll find a nice bistro somewhere."

The express train from Nice was on time. They chose to take the Metro. It was quicker and a lot cheaper than finding a taxi. Her hotel, La Paix, was located two blocks from the Pompidou Centre where her meeting with Hands on Advertising was to take place the following morning. He insisted on carrying her overnight bag. She did not resist. They spoke little during the journey having to change trains twice. At that hour of the evening the carriages were crowded. They both sensed they needed privacy to properly communicate.

The three-star hotel was old but clean and functional. After signing the register Denise ran up to her room, threw her bag on the bed, made use of the bathroom, adjusted her face then ran down the stairs to the small foyer.

"That was quick," remarked Pierre. "I always thought girls needed more time."

"Not this one. Where shall we go any ideas?"

"Yes, the concierge recommends an Italian restaurant. It's just around the corner."

They walked arm in arm. "Mama Roma" was busy but they were in luck. A table for two was just leaving. They stood at the tiny bar perusing the menu while the waiter quickly changed the tablecloth and relayed the table. They sat down, ordered their food together with a bottle of red Chianti—the house wine. The tables were tightly packed along the walls leaving barely sufficient space to move between them. But they had their privacy. Everyone in the room was too busy eating, drinking and talking—all concentrating on their food or their partners. Waiters danced in between the tables reaching over diners to serve steaming hot platters of pasta or giant cartwheels of pizza.

"What's the problem, Pierre?"

He held her hand. "I'm worried . . . no, shit scared about Jacques?"

"Jacques?"

"Yes, you know Jacques Gavotte, my friend, who made up the perfume."

"What's . . . ?"

The waiter arrived with a basket full of baguette and their wine. They waited for him to depart before continuing the conversation.

"Cheers"

"Cheers." Pierre sipped the wine savoring the rich tannins on his palate. "Good choice," he put down the glass. "Jacques has disappeared. No one has seen him for two weeks. The police have opened a missing person file. I suspect he is dead—murdered."

"No! It can't be. Why would anyone want to kill him?"

"The fragrance—it must be the fragrance—it's the only explanation."

"But who? Who would go to that extreme . . . to murder someone . . . for a smell? There must be a simple explanation."

"I only wish there was. None of his family has heard from him. His employer, the Sorbonne, has all but given up. The strange thing is I visited his flat. His phone was there plus his wallet together with his ID. Nobody goes out without money and a cell phone, plus his laptop was missing."

"And the flat, how did that appear?"

"A mess, as usual—otherwise normal. The only thing out of place was a dining room chair facing the door in the middle of the room."

"Gnocchi alla romana?"

Denise indicated it was for her. The waiter leaned across the table to place the steaming dish of pasta before her.

"Spaghetti con vongole. I bring you a bowl for the shells." The waiter disappeared. Denise reached for the parmesan cheese then sprinkled it liberally over her gnocchi. She passed it on to Pierre. They agreed to concentrate on their food both deep in thought.

Too full to contemplate dessert they ordered flaming sambuca with the coffee. "You see, Denise, I have a horrible feeling. Jacques is dead. Nobody just disappears like that. If he had succumbed to some unfortunate accident his body would have been found by now."

"You are sure it has something to do with the fragrance?"

"It must. There is no other solution. Jacques had no enemies. He was popular at work. He was . . . hell, I'm using the past tense *was* a regular sort of guy. I have even visited as many perfume houses as I can to show them his picture on the off chance he visited them."

"Why would he do that?"

"We discussed the need to possibly involve an organization which already had an established clientele and distribution base, that sort of thing. After all that is why I gave you a sample. On that subject do you have anything to report?"

Denise sipped her coffee. "Michel Ramonet has been analyzing the fragrance. He has discovered another attribute of it. In certain cases it turns on gays."

"I know," replied Pierre and he relayed his experience at La Reine Rules.

Denise struggled to suppress her laughter. "Sorry, I should not be laughing but the thought of you running away from an enraged queen—it's just too much."

"It wasn't funny," he replied sternly. "I have never been so scared in my life. Anyway, we escaped and I remain pure, intact so to say."

"Michel is worried. He says the fragrance is more of a drug. It is far too dangerous to ever be used as a perfume. There are substances in it which he has failed to identify so these have been sent off to a laboratory for further analysis. I wrote down what he told me." She leaned under the chair to retrieve her bag from which she removed a small notebook. "In addition to ambergris, nutmeg, mimosa, vetivert, cinnamon, pepper, sandalwood oil, ylang-ylang, lavender, citrus amber and spicy fougère, it contains calamus, henna, spikenard, frankincense, myrrh, cypress and terebinth. The last one is apparently pistachio."

"Means very little to me. All I know is that Jacques experimented with a whole assortment of different ingredients."

"Where did he get them from?"

"Some he bought from pharmacies and health shops but the more exotic, particularly the ambergris, he obtained from the lab at the Sorbonne where he worked. He told me they were working on a project funded by one of the large pharmaceutical companies. It had something to do with research into how the body's olfactory senses relate to pheromones, the biological substances which affect biorhythms, whatever that is meant to be."

"That's interesting; Michel said he was sending the sample to a lab at the Sorbonne. I wonder if it is the same one. You don't happen to know the name by any chance?"

"Jacques did mention it but I suppose I never took it in. I can find out if you like."

"No, don't bother. You know I think it is best you forget this fragrance project. As I said, Michel believes it is too dangerous to ever be used as a perfume. However, it could interest a drug company if, that is; he can identify exactly what causes the reaction. Anyway, there are just too many fragrances chasing too few consumers in an overtraded market.

You have no idea how much I have learnt about the perfume business. It is not all sweet smells like people believe."

The waiter hovered to remove their coffee cups. A continuous stream of hungry diners had entered the busy restaurant forming an impatient queue around the tiny bar, each waiting for tables. They had stopped consuming, stopped ordering—their table was needed. Pierre looked into Denise's eyes. He nodded in agreement. "Same again please, waiter, two double espresso and two sambucas." He turned to face Denise. "Go on, you were saying."

"Have you any idea, Pierre, how many new fragrances are launched each year?"

He shook his head.

"Hundreds and the number which make the big time—well you can count them on one hand, if that. To launch a new product you require a budget of not less than half a million Euros, double would be better. We are spending a paltry two-hundred-thousand on our latest campaign and that is over a three-year period. The total bill for Chanel using Nicole Kidman to promote Chanel No. 5, the best selling perfume ever created, is over twenty million Euros. Jennifer Lopez, Paris Hilton, Britney Spears are just three big names which were launched with massive publicity but simply dropped off the charts due to lack of sales. That's why I would not bother launching any new perfume. The business risk is just too high."

The couple seated at the adjacent table was leaving. As soon as they had squeezed out a waiter descended with a clean tablecloth and cutlery. In less than a minute the table was ready to receive the next diners. A large middle-aged woman arrived; being somewhat stout it proved too difficult for her to squeeze through the narrow gap separating the two tables. With an enormous sigh she collapsed into the chair facing the wall. Her stubby fingers wasted no time in picking up the menu as her partner squeezed through to sit with his back against the wall alongside Denise. He too picked up a menu.

Pierre glanced at the man. He quickly withdrew his eyes. He looked again. A puzzled look came over him. Denise stared at Pierre. She was about to ask what was wrong when her concentration was disturbed by the booming voice of the woman just arrived at the adjoining table.

"I told you, Herbert, we should have come earlier. You know how I hate waiting. It's not good for my legs to be standing so long." She dropped the menu onto the table. It fell knocking over the empty wine glass, which she ignored. "Where's that silly waiter? I'm ready to order: entrecôte steak with cheese sauce. I want extra French fries not spaghetti, and you?"

Her partner lowered his menu. For the first time his eyes looked across the table. His mouth opened but no words came out. His glance caught Pierre's. The man's pale face blushed. "Well, Herbert, what are you having? Answer me." Her neck turned to attract a waiter but the rolls of fat hindered its progress.

"We must go. I can't stay here. Come Lilia." Dropping his menu he tried to stand up but it first required his partner to move her chair back. He was imprisoned.

"What on earth has come over you, Herbert? You've been spending too much time in that laboratory of yours. My mother always said: breathing those vapors all day is bad for the brain."

He pushed the table forward. It moved a few centimeters but just enough to release him. "Really, Herbert," the fat woman exclaimed. The table was pressing into her bulging stomach.

"Come! I'm going. You stay if you must."

The commotion had drawn the attention of other diners. The woman scrapped her chair back. With a huge effort she lifted herself up just as her partner pushed by. "Is something wrong, Madam?" inquired a waiter as he skillfully avoided dropping the three plates of food in his hands as the woman's beamy backside engaged with him.

"It's my husband . . . he's . . . he's not feeling well."

The waiter disappeared. Pierre turned to watch the woman waddle out. The empty table was quickly tidied as two men waited to be seated.

"Well I never, did you see that?" Whispered Denise across the table.

"Yes, and I recognized him. I'm the reason he would not stay."

"What on earth do you mean?"

"I've met him before. I visited his shop, L'Artisan Parfumeur, in Montparnasse. I showed him Jacques's photograph. Of course he claimed never to have seen the face but there was something strange about the way he denied it. I couldn't argue with him of course but I had a definite feeling he was lying."

"Why would he do that?"

"The shop is owned by the queer whom we had the problem with, the one who owns the gay club. The one who tried to pick up Jacques."

"Oh! My God."

# Chapter Thirty Four

## North Wales

"He's got stamina. I'll give that to him. The bastard was at it for bloody hours. How many times do you think they did it?"

"Shut up. I'm thinking."

"Pardon me for living," muttered the younger man as he reclined the car seat back. He yawned loudly. "I don't know about you but I'm buggered."

His partner said nothing. His eyes were heavy. He too was fighting off sleep. He fought to focus on the road ahead avoiding getting too close to the rear lights of the Camper. "He's slowing down. He's stopping."

The man in the passenger seat brought his seat forward. Suddenly he was wide awake. "Looks like the girl is getting out. Shall I follow her?"

"No, there is no point she won't take us to what we want." They watched in silence as the girl jumped out of the passenger door slamming it hard behind her. Then, turning around she walked purposely away disappearing into the shadows cast by the street lamps down the long street of terraced houses. The camper indicated right and continued down the deserted road. The Audi followed a safe distance behind.

"No goodbye kiss, no farewell fond embrace, how strange? He didn't even drop her outside her door, whichever one it is. It's as though she suddenly wanted to get away from him."

"Where do you think he is going?"

"How the hell am I supposed to know? I'm not bloody clairvoyant," snapped back the driver. "What time is it?"

"One-fifteen. Christ I'm tired."

"Put your seat back. You get some sleep. I'll wake you if I need you to drive."

Archibald glanced at the clock on the dashboard. It was 13:15. He felt energized. The sex had been good. Liz, he thought her name was, had performed very well. He knew that he had too. Her cries of passion were not faked. The problem was there came a time when the hallucinogenic property of the fragrance wore off. Sometimes it happened as quickly as it started. The mood swing was frightening. One minute they craved for more, not a thing inhibited them, the next; they wanted nothing to do with you. He would never understand women. Normally, he timed it to no more than an hour, just to be safe. Drop them off while they still felt the affects. It was always safer that way.

But tonight he had been greedy. He really thought she might spend the entire night with him. It would have been nice. He had left it too late. By the time he was halfway to her house she was threatening to call the police. She had accused him of drugging her, of taking advantage of her. He had tried his best to calm her and when she had tried to hit him, well he had no choice. He told the bitch to get out.

A signpost indicated Llandudno twenty-eight miles. He decided to carry on. He could return to the camp site in Rhyl and sleep but he was not tired. He could pull over into a lay-by. It was what lorry drivers did. But no, there was always the chance a police car might come to investigate. It was too risky. He needed to put some distance between the girl in Rhyl, just in case. The camper was too conspicuous with its hand-painted floral patterns. It was too hippie. At first he thought it would make him appear younger—more attractive. It was a mistake he should have had it spray-painted a dull white. He would attend to that next week.

The roads were deserted. The traffic lights nearly always green as he drove down the A55 maintaining a steady speed always 10 miles per hour below the statutory limit. He passed through Abergele, the pebbly beach he had visited once as a child. Next came Colwyn Bay—neat suburbs where the residents of darkened houses slumbered peacefully. Leaving the A55 he chose the more picturesque coastal road passed Rhos on Sea and finally into the majestic sweeping bay of Llandudno.

The Queen of Victorian resorts had also gone to bed. Once the summer playground of well-heeled upper class families the long rows of Georgian-style terraced houses, where an army of servants scurried attending to the every need of their master and mistress, where now guest houses of various quality. The very servants' quarters deep down in the bowels or high up in the attics had long been converted into habitable rooms for renting. Following the Great War, the class distinction, upon which the sedate resort had been founded, quickly began to disintegrate. Now, only a few remaining four-star hotels were left to pamper to the needs of a wealthy minority.

Five minutes past two and Archibald pulled into the narrow entrance of the Grand Hotel. The front door was locked. He rang the bell. Nothing happened. He waited patiently. The pinking of the camper's engine, as hot metal cooled, was the only other sound. He knocked on the glass. He rang the bell again, this time holding his finger on the button. Finally, he was rewarded by the sight of an elderly Asian man.

"What do you want?"

"I would like a room please," replied Archibald politely.

"Have you got a booking?"

"No."

"It's late."

"Is it? Are you full or are you going to let me in?"

The man mumbled something which Archibald failed to comprehend. He fumbled with a catch on the side door. The door opened. "We don't normally get people arriving this late."

Archibald followed him to the reception desk. He looked around the shabby foyer. *The Grand Hotel* he thought, *you're not living up to your name.* An old photograph behind the reception announced the hotel had opened in 1901. Elegant horse drawn carriages were pictured outside the front entrance disembarking lavishly dressed gentry. For the men, tall top hats, long frockcoats, stiff white collars were the order of the day. The women's ridiculously broad bustles, worn under a mountain of somber material, seemed better suited to a funeral than a seaside resort hotel in the height of summer. Another old print showed the hotel at the entrance to the pier itself. It was constructed in 1876 and extended in 1884, a task which took two years to complete. First the money ran out and then a severe winter delayed the work.

"£75."

"I beg your pardon."

"You want a room? Its £75 for the night includes breakfast of course."

"Is this where the antique auction is taking place tomorrow, in the ballroom?"

"I don't know. I work nights. Here, you'll have to fill this in."

The porter slid a registration card across the desk. Archibald began to complete it. Just for good measure he misspelled his name. Crumpet became Crammer and the address was fictitious. He couldn't remember the registration number of the camper.

"Don't worry about that. Just sign at the bottom." The porter was in more of a hurry than Archibald. "I don't know why they need all this information. Nobody ever looks at it."

Archibald said nothing.

"You'll have to move your bus. Park it down towards the pier long as you move it by nine, it'll be alright there."

Twenty minutes later Archibald found his room on the fifth floor. The night porter was unable to take him up. "Not allowed to leave the reception, management orders," the man explained. The room had a magnificent view overlooking the bay. He opened the window to breath in the fresh sea air. The street lights twinkled highlighting the curvature of the beach. Suddenly he was tired. Not bothering to wash, not wishing to remove the smell of the girl from his body he climbed into the single bed nearest the wall. He closed his eyes trying to relive the pleasurable experience of the evening but sleep quickly overcame him. He was happy and content.

Five floors below with his head resting on the reception desk the night porter had fallen back into a deep sleep. But it did not last for long. The front door bell was ringing again. He lifted his head and opened his eyes. The noise had stopped. He thought he must be dreaming. He lowered his head. His eyelids closed. The bell rang again. Cursing loudly he struggled to find his shoes before shuffling off to the front door. Two men were standing outside.

"We need a room," one of them shouted through the glass.

"Go away, we are full," shouted back the night porter angrily.

# Chapter Thirty Five

## Leipzig—Berlin

Wilhelm Voigtländer tried his best to control the shaking in his hands as he fumbled to insert the slim key into the padlock. Next, there was the heavy mortise lock, it turned with difficulty. He pulled open the weighty door. A stale smell wafted up the stairs. Placing the lantern on the floor he removed the metal handle hidden behind the door and pushed it into a socket indented in the wall. He felt the head fit tightly onto the shaft. With his feet spread apart he took the L-shaped handle in both hands. Using his shoulders to maximize the strength of his body he began to wind the handle in a clockwise direction. As it turned a clanging grating sound broke the silence. Four turns and he needed to rest. His chest was heaving. Four more turns and rest again. Sweat began to drip down his brow. The back of his shirt was damp.

It took the best part of an hour, but finally, he had raised the heavy portcullis and locked it back in place. Had the electricity been connected he could have used the button on the wall. He needed to rest. There was no rush. He had all the time in the world except—he wanted to complete the distasteful task as quickly as possible. There was a man searching for him asking after Colonel Gerhard Bock and that meant the €100,000. He knew it could not be that easy.

He returned to the lounge where he switched on a small portable radio. The sounds of Wagner's Tannhäuser Overture immediately filled the silent room. He poured himself a large Kroatzbeere, his favorite herb flavored liqueur, distilled from blackberries grown wild in Silesia. He must have dozed off because the music had changed to a Beethoven symphony.

Carrying the lantern he descended the stone steps. For a second his heart skipped a beat. There was no sign of a body but he knew it must be somewhere. There was the smell. Stepping over a discarded makeshift pole he smiled. So, the bastard had tried to use it to escape having figured the button on the wall opened the portcullis. He was not to know without electricity it would not function. A shadow revealed a body curled up in the fetal position against a wall in the corner. Wilhelm placed the lantern on the table and returned upstairs.

He was glad he had only filled the twenty-five-liter can with ten-liters of diesel; otherwise he would have struggled to have carried it downstairs. The generator started on the fifth pull but this was enough to exhaust him again. With the lights in the cellar once more burning he sat at the small desk and surveyed the damage. Dozens of glass jars lay shattered on the floor. The first row of shelves had collapsed. He understood where Colonel Bock had found the wood to make his pole.

He turned to look at the body. The face was hidden under an arm. He wondered how long it had taken the man to die—a day, two days maybe three—but without water in total darkness not longer. Had he collapsed out of exhaustion, perhaps dehydration? Or had he screamed himself to death out of shear fear or frustration? Had he first gone mad? Solitary confinement in pitch blackness did that. Bock should know. The STASI had used it as a severe form of punishment. He needed to clear up the mess. The broken shelves and glass jars, even the files were of no value now, except the honey files.

They lay scattered on the floor; some of the papers had been trampled upon. His mind was made up. First the honey files, then the body, and finally the mess. Everything must look normal just in case. It would take him several days. The first task was easy. It was accomplished in half an hour. He repacked the cardboard box containing the honey files together with the two glass phials placing them in a wardrobe in the second bedroom. It was time to deal with the corpse. He knew it would be unpleasant but the body had to be disposed of. Therefore he had come prepared.

Going into the bedroom he removed his clothes before stepping into the decontamination suit and rubber boots he had bought from a medical supply company. He placed goggles over his eyes and a heavy surgical mask over his face. Movement became even more difficult. At first he had planned to slowly drag the body up the stairs using a rope. He now knew this would never work. He simply did not have the necessary strength.

He plodded slowly down the stairs taking his time, conserving energy. Standing over the corpse he tried to roll it over onto its back. He so desperately wanted to see the face of the man who had tried to kill him. Rigor mortis had long worn off. The body flopped over. "You bastard," he cried. "You fucking bastard." He stepped back. There was a neat round hole in the middle of the forehead. A pistol was still grasped in the right hand. Colonel Gerhard Bock had not suffered a long, drawn-out, slow death in darkness. He had taken the easy way out. Wilhelm felt cheated.

The rope was easy to tie around the feet but he battled to drag the dead weight across the floor to the foot of the stairs. The body had started decomposing. A greenish-brown, foul-smelling liquid was leaking out staining the stone floor. Using a stiff brush, hot water and lots of detergent he scrubbed the area clean. He was finally ready to commence the dissection. By now he should have been exhausted but instead found himself with sufficient energy to continue. Returning upstairs he unpacked the petrol-powered garden saw he had bought from a hardware shop. The salesman had assured him it could tackle the thickest of trees. Just to be safe he read the instructions again. "Don't overfill with petrol—always hold the machine away from the body at an angle of 45°—make sure the safety catch is on otherwise it won't start—*important*, do not push or pull—let the blade do the work". He had read enough. "The sooner you start the sooner you finish," he told himself.

He carried the chainsaw downstairs. He returned for the plastic butcher's tray, lining it with two heavy-duty black plastic bags. "Safety catch on—half a tank of petrol," he was surprised how little it held. "Hold the saw away from the body with the left hand. Firmly pull the starter cord back in one quick movement," he repeated the instructions out loud. The saw powered up first time. "My God, it's so easy." His voice was lost in the din.

Kneeling at right angles to the body he held out the saw. It was now heavy. With his thumb he flicked the safety switch off. The rotating blade immediately began to turn. The vibration shook him. The weight compelled him to lower his arms. The blade easily tore through the trouser cloth. The sound changed as it came into contact with bone. Within seconds the left ankle was detached except for some sinew. The blade started to grind into the stone floor. Sparks flew. Wilhelm jumped. He pulled the saw up swinging it to the side. His thumb fumbled to flick the safety catch back on. The blade stopped turning. Next he pushed the stop button before placing the saw down safely on the floor.

He stood up. His plan of how to dispose of the body was going to work but he needed to make a modification. He had read somewhere in a detective story that a serial killer always cut his victims' bodies up fully clothed as this helped to contain the splashing of body liquids. The ankle had been relatively easy he knew when he reached the torso things would be less pleasant. The problem was the angle of the cut and to avoid damaging the blade on the stone floor.

The damaged shelving provided the answer. He would drag a number of planks over and slide them under the body; this way he could create his own butcher's block. The blade would not be damaged when it cut into the wood.

His arms were aching. Two ankles complete with shoes, two legs severed just below the knee lay in the plastic bag. Surprisingly there was less blood and body fluids than he had expected. He switched off the saw and stood up. He was stiff. For a moment he wondered if he should cover the raw leg bones. But what was the point. The corpse, he no longer thought of it as Colonel Gerhard Bock, was not going anywhere.

Wearily he switched the lantern on before killing the generator. A strange silence suddenly descended. Bizarre shadows leaped amongst the shelves and walls. With his left hand he snatched up the plastic bag containing the body parts and with the lantern in his right, wearily plodded up the stone stairs back into the house.

His bladder was bursting. He dropped the bag by the kitchen door. It was still daylight. He would wait for darkness before venturing out into the jungle of a back garden. The old dried-up well was as good a place as any for disposing of the body parts. He seemed to think it was over twenty-meters deep. On removing the metal grid, which protected the open top, he had dropped stones down it. It seemed like ages before he heard a sound.

His tired fingers fumbled with the outer zip of his decontamination suit. Sitting on the edge of the bath he struggled to pull it off. Finally, standing in only his socks and underwear he stood over the toilet to urinate. As his bladder emptied his mind cleared. After getting dressed he would cook himself a nice meal—a juicy rump steak. He would eat it rare. First throw more wood on the stove. Boil a kettle of water. Place two potatoes in the oven. He would open a bottle of Cabernet Franc from the Schwarzerwald valley near Baden-Baden, costing almost €100 a bottle, he had never been able to afford it before but now, thanks to Colonel Gerhard Bock, he had bought several cases.

Jorgen Schaller had no trouble locating the bar. Although he had never visited it before, it was infamous as a meeting place where shady people had often met to exchange secrets. Throughout the cold war and a divided Germany, it had served as a convenient half-way house where informal communication could take place between opposing ideologies. Throughout the years, the police had never once chosen to raid it. Rumor had it that its true owner was the family of Walter Ulbricht, the First Secretary of the United Socialist Party, the man who was instrumental in constructing the Berlin Wall.

Located in a quiet square around the corner from the notorious Hohenschönhausen Prison it was surrounded by the ubiquitous high-rise, characterless apartment buildings, which so typified socialist Europe. He doubted if they had ever seen a coat of paint since they were constructed sometime in the late fifties. Plaster peeled from walls, wooden shutters hung at precarious angles from their straining hinges. The entire area remained trapped in a time warp, a monument to communist folly. It was a far move from his modern, tenth floor, comfortable office, located in the prestigious business centre, once the site of Checkpoint Charlie, where in 1961, American and Russian tanks stared down each other's gun barrels.

His business card described him as a private security consultant. After serving ten years in the Munich police, a wife and three children necessitated him seeking more remunerative employment. He had subsequently resigned to join an industrial security company. This had brought him into contact with Lancelot Slim. Their two companies had worked closely together over the years.

Feeling somewhat too conspicuous in his expensive dark-blue mohair suit tailored by Eberhards of the Kurfürstendamm he walked slowly into the square. A dozen shabbily dressed old men sat nursing an empty beer glass or coffee cup, a drooping cigarette hanging from their mouths. Two tables were playing chess, another cards. He felt their eyes scrutinize him as walked past them. He pulled open the door to the bar. Only one table was occupied by a man reading the newspaper. Clouds of blue smoke rose and circled above him as he puffed away at a brier pipe clenched firmly between his brown stained teeth. Jorgen sat at a small steel round table near the bar. An elderly barman nodded to him. He consulted his watch. It was 11:35, too early really to be consuming alcohol, but beer seemed to somehow suit the atmosphere. He ordered a *Berliner Weisse* not so much for its pale tart flavor but because it was low in alcohol.

The barman brought over the beer. "I wonder," asked Jorgen, "if you might know this man." From his inside pocket he pulled out a photograph of Gerhard Bock. It was passport size taken from a file scanned to him by Lancelot.

The barman picked up the photograph. He studied it for a moment then handed it back to Jorgen. He shook his head. "It's difficult. My memory isn't what it was." The barman returned to behind the bar. Jorgen was about to speak but the barman flashed his eyes in the direction of the man reading the newspaper then back at Jorgen.

Jorgen sipped the beer. From his wallet he removed a 100-Euro note. He placed it down on the table sliding it under the beer mat. Twenty minutes passed before the man with the pipe folded the newspaper under his arm. He stood up, threw some coins on the table and shuffled out without saying a word. Jorgen was becoming impatient. He had better things to do than waste time in a shabby rundown bar. He pointed to the note on the table. "Well, do you know him? Yes or no?"

"Let me take a second look. Like I said my memories not what it used to be—age you know."

Jorgen showed him the picture again.

"Yes, I might know him. The face does ring a bell—somewhere?"

Jorgen pulled out a second 100-Euro note placing it deliberately on top of the first.

"Colonel Gerhard Bock."

"When did you last see him?"

"Difficult to say, I see so many people coming and going all day." His eyes roamed around the deserted room. The barman had returned to his place behind the bar. His mind was working on overtime. The stranger was obviously not ex-STASI. He was too western. He had probably not visited East Berlin until long after the wall had come down. The question was: just how much money was he prepared to pay for information?

Jorgen understood the game. It was not his money he was spending. Lancelot Slim was paying. He pulled another note from his wallet.

"He was here ten days ago."

Jorgen stood up from the table. He removed the €300 from the table and walked up to the bar placing the money on the counter. From his wallet he removed another bill which he added to the other three. "Oh dear, it looks as though I have no more, but I can always come back. I want to know the name of the person he met. Here, let me help you remember." Jorgen opened a notebook. "I suspect it was a man called Wilhelm Voigtländer."

The barman remained expressionless.

"Thank you, your silence confirms it. Now, if either man returns, or if you know where I can contact them you will phone me immediately. That's worth another €300. Do we have a deal?"

"€500."

"€400."

"€500." Jorgen smiled. He offered his hand. "€500 it is. Shall we shake?"

The barman took his hand and for the first time he smiled. "Yes, I'll phone you the minute I see either of them."

Jorgen turned around leaving his half-empty glass on the table. "Thanks for the beer. I assume it's on the house," and he exited the room.

The barman walked over to the window to watch him leave. As soon as Jorgen had crossed the square and disappeared from sight he returned to behind the bar. He picked up the phone and dialed a number from memory. It rang for a full minute before a man's voice answered. "Wilhelm, its Karl. I think you should know. A man has just been asking for you and that Bock bastard . . . no, definitely not STASI . . .

no, not police either . . . he didn't say. He gave me a number to phone. Obviously, he wants to meet with you . . . you'll be in for lunch . . . the day after tomorrow . . . the usual pork knuckle . . . good, I'll have it ready for you and we can talk." He put down the phone. So far it had been a good day, €400 with another €500 to come. Wilhelm had suddenly come into money and was now his best customer eating in the bar practically everyday and even occasionally buying for others. The door opened. Four men entered the bar—locals, he knew exactly what they would order.

# Chapter Thirty Six

## Paris

Having first phoned the main number for the Préfecture de Police Judiciare, Pierre Nimier was directed to contact the 15iéme Arrondisement Station on the Rue Rémy Dumoncel. After informing the case officer, a lady, that he may have some fresh information regarding the disappearance of Jacques Gavotte he was requested to come in as soon as possible.

An hour later found him being shown into a small office containing two desks on the third floor of the building. Inspectrice Daguerre was not what he expected. For a start she was a woman. As he was shown into her office, she stood up. She appeared to be small in stature, not the Amazon he had anticipated. Pierre estimated her to be somewhere in the mid-forties. She wore a wedding band on her left hand. A small framed picture of a man together with two teenage children stood on the corner of her neat and tidy desk.

After inviting him to sit she requested he tell her what he knew.

Pierre hesitated. "It is difficult to know really where to begin. You see, I have a gut feeling about the man who runs a perfumery, L'Artisan Parfumeur, in Montparnasse. He may know something about Jacques's disappearance. Purely by chance I saw him last night in a restaurant and when he saw me, he immediately departed even after sitting down and perusing the menu. He was either terribly embarrassed or, frightened of something. It was so bizarre."

"Monsieur Nimier, why should this man have something to do with your missing friend? I do not think you are telling me everything. Why don't you start at the very beginning?" Her voice and attitude was stern.

"Yes . . . yes you're right . . . sorry. It's a bit embarrassing . . . sort of."

Pierre would have much preferred to have confided in a man. It would have been easier. Taking a deep breath he started with the stag night of eight months back and the dare to create a "passion fragrance". It was all a big joke, a bit of harmless fun, but. He related his nights of passion with unsuspecting partners, which he now deeply regretted then, the night that Jacques insisted on trying out the fragrance in a gay club.

"You say the club was called La Reine Rules. It is off the Champs Elysees, if I am not mistaken."

He watched her write the name down. "Yes, at the top, near *L'Arc de Triomphe*."

"Do you still have any of this . . . perfume in your possession?"

He explained how he had given his remaining sample to Michel Ramonet at L'Essence de la Grasse for analysis and how they had met through Denise Vergé. He stopped at informing her that he and Denise were currently dating. He watched as she made more notes then, she put away her pen.

"Thank you, Monsieur Nimier; may I have a number where I can contact you?"

Pierre handed her his business card. "What happens now?"

"We shall pay a visit to this," and she consulted her notes, "L'Artisan Parfumeur, in Montparnasse and see what they have to say. I have one more question. What made you visit them in the first place?"

"The yellow pages. I selected sixteen similar perfumers whom I thought Jacques might just have visited. It was just a long shot really. I felt I had to try and do something."

The young boy slipped out from under the duvet and tiptoed over to the window. Pulling hard on the rope cord, he allowed the midday sun to burst through the heavy drapes, flooding the large bedroom with light. He basked in its warmth on his naked body. A disgruntled noise emanated from the bed. A small white Maltese poodle jumped down onto the carpeted floor. It shook itself. The silver nametag attached to its collar rattled loudly.

"Take Max out and *do* put some clothes on. Come away from that window before someone sees you," the voice mumbled from beneath the duvet.

The youth quickly dressed into a pair of jeans then grabbed a shirt hanging over an armchair. Onto his feet he slipped a pair of leather moccasins. "Come, you," he called to the dog but it scampered away as he tried to pick it up. He pushed open the heavy door of the bedroom. The dog charged through his feet.

"Close the door," came the irritated voice from inside the room.

"Is Monsieur Bourboché awake?"

The boy nodded to the manservant, "Sort of . . . I suppose."

The manservant glared down at the boy. "Well! Off you go. Do as you are told. Take Max out to do his duties before he defecates on my clean carpets."

The boy waved a finger at the manservant who attempted to grab him but the boy was too quick. The manservant tapped twice on the bedroom door before pushing it open a jar. "Monsieur . . . Monsieur, are you ready for your tea?"

At first there was no response. The manservant waited patiently by the open door. He was finally rewarded with a grunt. "What time is it?"

"Its twelve-thirty, Monsieur."

"Half an hour, Claude," came the feeble reply.

Claude Pic gently closed the door to return to the kitchen where he put the final arrangements to his master's breakfast tray—one fresh croissant, a brioche, soft butter in a silver dish, runny honey, not out of the fridge, a glass bowl containing a dissected blood grapefruit and a silver tea pot containing jasmine tea—no milk and definitely no sugar. All he had to do was add the boiling water.

There was a bang. The front door opened and closed. Max came scampering into the kitchen to stop at Claude's feet. Raising himself on his hind legs he jumped up and down emitting a high-pitched bark.

"That's enough," ordered Claude and he reached for the silver dog dish with "Max" engraved on the outer edge. "Here's your Rice Krispies, try not to make too much of a mess," and he placed the bowl on the floor.

"I'm hungry. What have you got?" The boy had returned.

"For you, nothing. I suggest you leave before Monsieur Bourboché rises. You know he does not approve you hanging around the place during the day.

"No he doesn't. He loves me." Claude, who towered over the youth, grabbed him by the arm. The youth began to squirm. "Don't you hurt me. I'll tell Lucien."

"No you won't," and Claude tightened his grip. "Now go, if you know what is good for you. He'll phone you if he requires your services tonight."

"I haven't been paid. I need money."

"Tough, it's a cruel world." Gripping him tightly he frog marched the youth to the door where he shoved him outside. The door closed with a bang. Fifteen minutes later, Claude carried the silver breakfast tray into the bedroom, placing it on a large pedestal table next to the giant four-poster bed.

Lucien sat up. Claude puffed up the pillows to make him more comfortable. Lucien slipped the eye-mask off his head.

"Your breakfast, Sir." Claude placed the tray on the bed after first unfolding the short stumpy legs.

"Has Carlos gone?"

"Yes Sir."

"Did you give him some breakfast?"

"He did not appear to want any, Sir. He was in rather a hurry to leave. Shall I draw your bath, Sir?"

"Yes, Claude. Have there been any messengers for me?"

"A few, Sir. None of which are pressing, except for Monsieur Siebert. He has phoned four times. He says it is most urgent."

"What did you tell him?"

"That you were otherwise engaged and that you would return his call at the first opportunity."

Herbert Siebert was having difficulty concentrating. His wife had refused to speak to him after the debacle in the Italian bistro. They had ended up eating in a Vietnamese restaurant. It was all they could find at that late hour. She swore the steak, she insisted on ordering, was horse meat. The restaurant could not even provide a proper steak knife which made matters worse. Ignoring her protests he had thoroughly enjoyed his bowl of *Bun thang*, rice noodles, shredded chicken, fried egg and prawns served in a spicy broth. His insistence on using chopsticks had further added to her discomfort. They ate in silence, other than his unavoidably having to listen to her continuous complaints about the disgusting foreign food she was being forced to eat. They had driven home in silence, gone to bed in silence and, woken up this morning in silence.

Not that this really worried him. He had hardly opened the shop when his morning was destroyed by a visit from the police. This time there were two of them—detectives enquiring about the missing man—Jacques Gavotte. Was he sure he had never seen the man? Would he mind if they took a look around? He had taken them to his office. He had exclaimed how he crafted fragrances. They had asked so many questions he lost count.

As soon as they departed he had phoned Lucien. He knew it was futile. The man was never contactable before the afternoon. Protected by his bodyguard-manservant there was nothing Herbert could do.

The call was finally returned at 14:15. "Lucien, I am worried sick. The police have been around *again* asking questions and . . ."

The response gave him little comfort. "I was rather expecting some good news from you, Herbert. So, have you finally succeeded in duplicating the formula for me?"

"No, I am still working on it. I told you these things take time. Lucien, the police—twice they have been to see me. I think they suspect that . . ."

"Shut up! Don't talk such nonsense. I refuse to speak with you over the phone like this. You had better come around and see me—now!" screamed the voice, before the line went dead.

Herbert pressed the bell. Claude's voice answered. The door clicked. Herbert pushed it open and entered the marble foyer. He climbed the ornate staircase to the third floor which belonged to Lucien. Claude admitted him. "He is not in a very good mood," he whispered.

Herbert was shown into the drawing room as Lucien liked to refer to it. The large salon resembled a museum. Antique furniture occupied every square meter of floor. Each highly polished surface supported some *objets d'art* giant Ming vases, heavy bronze sculptures, intricate glass ornaments, delicate porcelain figurines and imposing marble busts. Louis X1V, Louis XV, Louis XV1, and Napoleonic into the twentieth century—every period of French history was covered. Lucien, wearing a purple and gold dressing gown embroidered with Chinese dragons was seated in the far corner in his favorite chair—A large eighteenth century chaise which he boasted came from le Petit Trianon in the palace of Versailles. Max was posed on Lucien's lap.

Fully prepared for an unpleasant meeting Herbert felt as though he was being summoned to an Emperor's court. But much to his surprise Lucien was all smiles. He offered Herbert some refreshment to which he declined. He enquired about Lilia's health. Herbert informed, somewhat abruptly, that his wife was fine. For several minutes they discussed the business. How was the market for expensive fragrances holding up? Were rocketing fuel prices, which were pushing up the cost of living, having any affect on demand? Was

Herbert still able to secure adequate supplies of ambergris, saffron, musk and other rare ingredients? New customers; were any celebrities? Who had introduced them? Throughout the polite discussion Herbert remained on his guard. Finally, Lucien had run out of topics. The two men sat facing each other. Lucien was stroking Max. The large diamond on his finger glittered in the light.

Herbert chose his moment. "Lucien, the police, I came here to discuss why the police have twice visited me to ask about Jacques Gavotte. What have you . . . your people done with him? I must know."

Lucien lifted Max off his lap placing him gently on the floor. "Off you run, you naughty boy, go and play." He turned to address Herbert. "All this business talk must bore him so." The dog remained at his feet not moving. Lucien waved his hands. "Off you go . . . go on . . . shoo." Max moved—hesitated—looked at Lucien in amazement and trotted off.

"Oh that! You must not concern yourself. It is probably just routine enquiries."

"Lucien, you have *not* answered my question. What happened to him when he left the shop?"

Lucien pulled out a pink linen handkerchief from under his left sleeve. He blew his nose vigorously. Gesticulating with the handkerchief he explained loudly, "How am I supposed to know these things? Hugo and Monty took him home I suppose. Look, if it makes you feel any better I'll ask them."

"But Lucien, what do I say to the police if they come back? What about the other one? What if he returns asking questions?"

"Very simple, my dear, you say *nothing*. You have never seen him, never spoken to him. The fact is you do not know what all this fuss is about and, do *not* talk on the phone to me about this again. As far as I am concerned the subject is closed." Lucien picked up a small bell. He rang it loudly before standing up. From the shadows the manservant mysteriously appeared. "Claude, Monsieur Sibert is leaving. Be so kind as to show him out."

Herbert stood up. His audience was concluded, but his mind was confused as he followed Claude out into the hall. Neither man spoke. Claude opened and closed the apartment door. Herbert descended the marble staircase. He felt he now knew what had happened to Jacques Gavotte and the knowledge terrified him. Butterflies filled his stomach. Should he go to the police and make a clean breast of it? After all he had done nothing wrong. He had committed no crime other than perhaps remain silent during his incarceration. Kidnapping what would be his sentence—ten years, more? He knew he could never survive a term in prison. It would kill him. But what was the alternative? Run away, but to where? How? He pressed the button. The door opened. He entered out into the street and fresh air. He had money, his secret savings built up over the years. What had he said to his friend Raymond at the Louvre? He would enjoy retiring to the country to paint.

Deep in thought as he turned the corner he bumped into someone. He apologized. It was a large woman. Unforgiving, she snapped back at him. His wife's image flashed before his eyes. What about her? Suddenly, the thought of just disappearing creating a new life for himself seemed clearer. He needed to think—how, when could he make it happen?

"Claude . . . Claude."

The manservant re-entered the drawing room, "Sir?"

"Bring me my phone."

"Certainly, Sir."

Claude quickly returned presenting the phone posed on a silver message tray. Lucien waited for Claude to vacate the room before dialing a number. "Hugo, we need to sort out the problem of the other one. Yes, that's right dispose of the matter as soon as possible."

# Chapter Thirty Seven

## North Wales—Manchester

"He's having breakfast in the dining room. We checked into the same hotel half an hour after him. What do you want us to do?" The man listened intently. "OK, I understood. I'll phone you back either way." He terminated the call. Slipping the phone into his pocket he leaned out over the rail to admire the view over the bay. He breathed in deeply. A seagull flew overhead squawking loudly. "It looks as though it's going to be another beautiful day. You know I could quite easily . . ."

Impatiently his younger companion interrupted him. "So, tell me, what happens now? Are we just going to stand here on Llandudno pier all day and admire the view?"

"That's not a bad idea. I might just do that I need to improve my tan, but not you. Go back into the hotel and keep an eye on Crumpet. I want to know why he has driven all this way. There must be a reason. Find out what room he is in and when he is checking out. The boss is keen to know who he contacts."

By right Detective Superintendent Donald Bradley should have been at home cutting the lawn. He had, after all, given a firm commitment to his wife that it would be completed today. Her parents, brother and sister were coming around tomorrow for Sunday lunch. It was his wife's turn to do the catering. Carmine, their daughter, was swimming in a gala. He had promised faithfully to be there. It started at 11:00 and would take him at least half an hour to drive to the pool. He glanced at his watch, 09:30 and the briefing had still not started. They were waiting for the Commissioner to arrive. Subconsciously, the fingers of his right hand began to scratch the eczema on his left knuckles. It was something he found himself doing when he was nervous or worried about something.

It was his weekend off but an emergency meeting had been called. A spate of ATM robberies was plaguing the greater Manchester area. The latest was splashed all over the morning newspapers. Questions were being asked. Why were the police not able to catch the culprits? Rumors were circulating. It was a terrorist gang with links to al-Qaeda. No, it was the Russian Mafia. The room was full. It seemed that the entire detective force from as far away as Liverpool had been summoned. The noise of pounding feet echoed down the corridor. It quickly grew louder.

"Looks as though he's finally here."

Donald turned to the man seated on his left. "I hope so. It's my weekend off."

Surrounded by a phalanx of senior officers the chief constable strode into the room. All conversation immediately terminated. Every eye was focused on him as he took his chair behind the briefing table. No sooner had he sat down than he stood up.

"Gentlemen, thank you for coming at such short notice. We are all busy so I shall come straight to the point."

"Some of us are bloody well on leave," murmured a voice behind Donald.

"As you all know for the past month a number of ATMs have been blown up. Yesterday's explosion resulted in the death of an innocent bystander."

"A bloody junkie, who choice the wrong place to kip," murmured the voice again.

"This drastically changes things. We are now dealing with murder. However, forensics has come up with a lead for us. The explosives are of South African origin. They are used exclusively in a platinum mine in a place called Rustenburg near Johannesburg. We have always suspected these robberies were not the work of a local gang. They are simply too violent, too brazen. So gentlemen, dig deep. Contact your sources. Put the word out we are looking for new faces on the block—South African, possibly Nigerian. Someone out there knows something. Someone has seen or heard of a new gang, probably black. This enquiry now takes priority over all others. Is that understood?"

For a moment there was silence until the question was asked. "What about the press? Have they been informed of this new information?"

"No, not as yet and we would prefer to keep it this way. The last thing we want is the press stirring up racial tensions which could lead to fresh attacks of xenophobia. Are there any more questions?" And he looked around the room. "No. Good, so let's get out there and find these bastards."

The meeting was over. The chief constable and his entourage quickly left the room. Donald stood up as did the men seated either side of him. The detective on his right was clutching a brown case file.

"Looks as though I can finally put this one back in the cupboard and concentrate on some real police work."

"Interesting case?" Asked Donald as they shuffled out.

"Not really, just some alleged serial rapist that landed on my desk. There's no real evidence or substance to make a case."

"May I take a look?"

"Certainly, you can have it," and he handed the file to Donald. The shuffle out of the briefing room had come to a halt. They waited patiently in line. Donald opened the folder. A face stared back at him.

"I know this character. I've met him." The vision of his daughter entering the shop to buy her mother a set of antique sherry glasses flashed through his mind. He had said it then. "I pride myself in my line of work I never forget a face." He had not been wrong. The only difference was that he had not met the face in person but only as a picture in a file. The queue was moving forward. He closed the file. "Can I keep it? I might just have an angle on this one."

"Be my guest, I'll tell admin you've got it."

"Do that. I have a funny feeling about this Archibald Crumpet character."

Archibald walked into the Grand Hotel ballroom. The auction was not due to start for another hour. This gave him sufficient time to peruse the lots on offer. A few pieces of furniture interested him: a George III inlaid bureau bookcase with a reserve price of £15,000 and a mahogany corner cabinet, a Beiremeier mahogany kidney-shaped desk, several guilt-framed wall mirrors and a Regency rosewood suite upholstered in green. The problem was one of transportation—the cost of hiring a van to transport the bulk items to Beeston. However, a Royal Winton chintz dinner service, a number of Victorian decanters and a series of Charlotte Watson cream jugs might be worth bidding for.

Shaun Formby watched the chambermaid push the loaded trolley down the deserted hotel corridor. Stopping at a room she knocked twice then waited a few seconds before inserting her card into the door. Two minutes later she reappeared to bundle used bed linen into the trolley's canvas container. Shaun chose the moment. "Excuse me, love, can you let me into room 517. I don't seem able to find me card."

She looked up at the young man addressing her. The rules stated that only the floor housekeeper could open a room. This would necessitate her explaining this to the man then she would need to ask the switchboard to page Dorothy who could be anywhere. It was a big hotel. Today she was working alone. She had two floors to clean which was totally unfair as it was changeover day. She hated the job but, it was a job, and she so desperately needed the money being a single parent with a teenage boy to bring up.

"517, you said?"

The man smiled. "That's right, love, sorry to bother you like this but I need to use the toilet—urgently," and his faced grimaced.

## The Devil's Fragrance 279

It was all so easy. Shaun closed the door then double locked it. He worked quickly starting first with the bathroom. It revealed nothing. One by one he pulled open the drawers. They were empty. The cupboard was next, followed by the suitcase. It was not locked. Careful not to disturb anything he lifted up the neatly folded clothes. He felt something—a leather wallet. It contained credit cards and money—£300. For a moment he hesitated then, removing the notes he stuffed them into his pocket. The credit cards were tempting particularly the visa. He could use it once maybe twice but cards left a trail. He should know, having served two out of a five-year sentence for possession of stolen property, robbery and committing grievous bodily harm. He was only just out on parole for good behavior. Snapping the wallet shut he slid it back under the shirts.

Closing the suitcase he stood up. Under the bed, under the mattress, behind the cushion of the chair, where else was there to hide something? He opened the wardrobe door again to ensure he had not missed anything. His eyes fell upon a pair of black shoes. He knelt down to examine them. "Bingo," he expressed out aloud. Pulling the small perfume bottle from the toe of the shoe he unscrewed the top. "Nice, so this is what all the fuss is about?"

Dropping the bottle into his jacket pocket he stood up. The job was complete it was time to leave. Halfway towards the door he hesitated. A thought had suddenly crossed his mind. He returned to the bathroom. "That'll do," his eyes focused on a small plastic bottle containing the hotel's all-in-one luxury lavender shower-gel. Opening the bottle he poured the contents into the sink. He ran the hot water tap into the open neck; bubbles poured out frothing down his hand. He emptied out the contents again. More bubbles and more foam remained. He repeated the process again and again. "Come on you bastard," he hissed anxiously. Finally, the tiny bottle appeared void of bubbles. He smelt it, still a cheap lavender fragrance lingered. It would have to do. Taking the ornate perfume bottle he poured some of the fragrance into the empty hotel bottle.

It was time for Archibald to register for the auction. He had decided to only bid for smaller items those which he could easily carry back in the camper. A wooden Victorian paper rack and an 8-day rosewood clock by James Smith had further attracted his interest. After the auction he planned to check out of the hotel and drive on to the town of Carnarvon. There would be more night life there and a better chance of meeting women. He was halfway through filling in the bidder's form. He had arrived at the section—method of payment. He wrote VISA, reached into his inside pocket when he suddenly realized he had left his wallet in the bedroom.

The auctioneer's clerk took his completed form and quickly perused it. "We'll need to take an imprint of your credit card, Sir, before we can issue you with a paddle."

"That's quite alright," responded Archibald. "I'm staying in the hotel. I just need to retrieve it from my room. I shall also give you my business card. I am a registered dealer. If you could just complete everything and I'll be back in ten minutes."

Archibald walked quickly towards the lift. He failed to notice the man seated in reception pretending to read the newspaper. The man was holding a phone in his hand. On seeing Archibald he brought it to his ear as he dialed a number.

The lift landed with a jerk on the fifth floor. Archibald exited the carriage and walked quickly down the corridor. A man bumped him as he rushed past. A phone was ringing loudly. "Sorry," muttered Archibald apologetically. The man either ignored him or simply had not heard him as he continued down the corridor. "Bloody rude bastard," muttered Archibald under his breath. He had arrived at his room. He opened the door and went directly to his suitcase. His heart skipped a beat when he realized he had not even locked it. He opened the lid and felt for his wallet. It was still there.

Shaun Formby bounded down the stairs into the hotel foyer. "I got it," he beamed to the seated man.

"Shut up you fool. You'll draw attention to us. Show me . . . slowly."

Shaun reached into his pocket. He had placed the plastic bottle in his left pocket; the heavier glass bottle was in his right. Making sure he had the right one he pulled it out. It was not prudent to cross Stewart Wilson if one wanted to live a healthy life.

"Give it to me." Stewart held out his hand. He opened the top and smelt it. "I suppose that's it. Come, let's get out. I don't want him seeing us. You made sure you did not disturb anything?" They quickly walked out of the hotel in the direction of the pier.

"Absolutely, boss. I did exactly as you told me."

"You didn't take anything else."

"No, on my mother's life, I swear," lied Shaun.

Stewart was dialing a number. "Mr. Fujimoto . . . yes, it's Stewy . . . good news . . . I've got it." He pulled the bottle out of his pocket to closer examine it. "Describe it? Well its small . . . old fashioned glass bottle with flowers engraved . . . the inside? Smells of strong aftershave . . . no, can't make out the color . . . about 2 maybe 3 ounces . . . yes that's all I'm afraid. OK, understood," and he terminated the call.

"Shaun you get the car. I'm going back inside to clear the room and pay the bill. We are going home."

# Chapter Thirty Eight

## Paris

The large Citroen was parked on a red line. The engine was running as the two men watched the couple mount the stone stairs to the conference hall. More people followed. "Looks as though he is attending some form of meeting. You nip out and find out when it finishes. We can't stay here we'll attract the attention of the police."

Monty nimbly stepped out onto the pavement closing the car door behind him. He walked slowly melting into the crowd of pedestrians. The car moved off.

Denise Vergé presented her invitation to the smartly dressed man who barely glanced at it. They made their way into the auditorium. "Where do you want to sit?" enquired Pierre.

"I think somewhere in the middle. I hope more people will come. It will be a bit embarrassing if only a handful is present."

"Saturday morning is not the ideal time to attend a lecture."

"Apparently, it was the only time Dr. Schultz had available."

"Who exactly is he and why are we here?" asked Pierre.

"Dr. Schultz is a leading dermatologist and scientist. He is an advisor to NASA. The Manufacturer's Perfume Association, on learning that he was in Paris, invited him to address its members. And, as I was in Paris the company asked me to represent them. Anyway, I am told he is very entertaining."

"Show me the invitation again."

Denise handed it to Pierre. "I see he is talking about the sun and its effect on the human body."

The room was slowly beginning to fill up. A further fifteen minutes passed before usherettes began to close the side doors. A man walked onto the centre stage introducing himself as the president of the association. He began by reading out a long introduction of Dr. Schultz, explaining how he had taken time out from his punishing schedule to address the members. A joke was cracked. The audience did their best to laugh. Finally, he ended by asking for a round of applause as he invited the Doctor onto the stage. The side doors to the auditorium opened as late comers squeezed in. A tall thin man in his mid-thirties dressed in jeans and short-sleeved stripped shirt walked onto the stage.

"He's young. I expected an Einstein-type character," whispered Pierre.

"Shush," echoed Denise pinching his arm.

"Ladies and gentlemen," began the Doctor. "I have been asked to talk this morning about the sun and its affect on the human body. It is a vast subject so all I can attempt to do in the time allocated is to highlight certain points and hopefully leave you with much to ponder. Please feel free to ask any questions. After all, it is your job to create the many creams and ointments used both to protect and repair the skin from damage caused by our sun.

"Let me start off by asking ourselves a question. Why did all ancient civilizations worship the sun? Not just the Egyptians, the Vedic people of ancient India, the Jomons of Japan, the Mayans of Central America and closer to home the ancient Celts all built their civilizations around the sun. Was this just a coincidence or simply superstitions of a primitive people? Or, did they have access to knowledge, which we today have still to garner?

"Even the most unsophisticated understand that when the sun shines it warms our planet and when it doesn't—well, we feel cold. Everyone understands the power of the sun's rays. *Nature* or natural human evolution, depending upon one's point of view, has genetically provided some homo sapiens, who inhabit regions of intense sunshine, black skins to better protect them."

"So how do you explain the yellow skin of the Bushman of the Kalahari? They are not black. What about the Arabs? The Middle East is one of the hottest places on earth."

Dr. Schultz smiled at the young man asking the question. "I said *some* homo sapiens *not* all. The Bushmen are unique. Arabs from the beginning of time have covered their bodies with cloth from head to toe. But permit me to move on. Let us not become embroiled in how different races have adapted to climate. That is a topic for another day.

"In summer, local news media broadcasts not just the weather, so we know what to best wear or what to do, but they also warn us about the UV factor for the day. What does all this mean? And why *warn* us? Why not simply advise? It has always amused me how Caucasians with pale skins spend fortunes in summer sun-tanning. Are they simply trying to look more like black-skinned people?

"You may laugh. Throughout the twentieth century it was generally believed it was *good* for the skin to be exposed to the sun's rays. We now know that far from this being beneficial it is in fact detrimental contributing to the formation of skin cancer. The old days of families holidaying on the beach and mother rubbing her own mixture of oils to protect their children have long gone. As you well know fortunes are now spent purchasing exotic creams stating they provide 10—20—40 and up to 60+ UVA protection factor. If you take the time, and your eyesight is good enough, the creams even tell you what goes into these magical potions—Ethylhexyl p-Methoxycinnamat—Titanium Dioxide—Dihydroxycetkl Phosphate and oh yes, substances we understand such as ascorbic acid, aloe and yeast extract to name but a few.

"I see some of you trying to write all this down. Don't. It's not worth it. I only threw in these scientific words to impress you. If you wish to know what goes into that soothing lotion you pay so much for then obtain a magnifying glass and read it for yourself.

"The sun affects our daily lives, whether it shines or not. Let's take a moment to study it. What are sun rays? What are they composed of? Every second of every minute of every day, since our planet came into existence, we have been bombarded by solar particles—we call the solar wind. The sun spins on its axis causing the equator to revolve every 28 days as seen from earth. However, because the sun is not solid, being composed of gaseous substances, the Polar Regions take 40 days to complete one revolution. So, as the sun spins it is throwing out radiation in the form of both positive and negative charged particles. Scientists refer to this *unbalanced* spin as "the differential rotation of the sun's magnetic field.""

Dr. Schultz paused in his presentation to look around the room. "Are you all with me? Nobody dozed off yet? Good." Polite laughter emanated. "Then I shall continue. Who can tell me: what are Sunspots?"

There was silence for a moment, before a hand rose in the second row. Dr. Schultz pointed. "Go on tell us."

"Because radiation varies across the surface of the sun, and because the top, middle and bottom portions are spinning at different speeds, every now again the magnetism becomes confused. This causes explosions which shoot out. I am not sure if I have explained it properly."

"Very good, excellent. You are almost there. Sunspots are believed to be regions on the sun's surface which have been pierced by magnetic loops emerging from the interior. These supercharged bursts of radiation, or magnetized gas to put it another way, bombard the earth causing radio blackouts, compasses to spin and power stations to trip. They can contain masses of upwards of a few billion tons and travel at speeds of up to 2,000 kilometers a second. The results can be catastrophic. Planes can literary fall out of the sky. Entire regions can be without electrical power for days. The damage caused can run into millions of Euros.

"Because the sun is molten, unlike the earth, it turns faster at its equator than at the poles. This phenomenon creates a confusion of sorts in the magnetism, causing magnetic waves to move faster so they become twisted and almost entwined. I can best describe this momentum, as a bit like twirling my hair around on a fork until it becomes so entangled it is almost impossible to separate without ripping out my roots. This action in the sun generates intense radiation, which is projected outwards creating, what we call sunspots.

"The sunlight, which is beaming down upon us at this very moment and is the catalyst of life here on earth, is also composed of radio, infra-red, visible, ultraviolet and X-rays, as well as charged particles known as ions. These, we commonly refer to as the solar wind. These particles come both positively and negatively charged in varying degrees of intensity. Most are harmless as they are absorbed by the "Van Allen Belts", which I can best describe as zones of radiation encircling our planet. These belts act as a form of shield protecting us from severe bursts of radiation. During periods of intense solar activity the charged particles are directed downwards towards the poles producing the spectacular illuminations known as the Aurora Borealis—the Northern Lights."

Dr. Schultz paused to clear his throat. "This is interesting stuff," whispered Pierre out of the corner of his mouth.

The Doctor continued. "However, the solar wind if super-charged, one-way or the other can reap havoc with our planet. Violent magnetic storms create chaos with our modern forms of communication, which we have come to rely upon. The loss of your favorite television program is nothing compared to ships' compasses, which no longer read accurately or, entire electricity generating plants exploding in a ball of fire. Sophisticated satellites are fried to a sizzle while aircraft become lost and disorientated with disastrous consequences.

"Scientists have calculated that the sunspot cycle lasts approximately 187 years. Further to this they now know the sun's magnetic field reverses every 3,740 years or 1,366,040 days. Do we have any students of Mesoamerican culture in the room?" No hands were visible. "Interestingly, the Mayan Long Count, which was the third calendar used by the ancient Mayans of South America counted out 1,366,560 days. You see, they did not take into account our leap year. How did they arrive at this knowledge? But I digress.

"The questions: we must ask ourselves are—how does this affect our planet? The changing magnetic field will probably cause the earth to twist upon its axis. This will cause volcanoes to erupt, faults in the earth's crust to open, resulting in massive earthquakes releasing gargantuan volumes of water. All in all, if any of us are fortunate enough to survive, we shall witness the end of our world, as we know it.

"The good news is that the solar wind particles first encounter the Van Allen radiation belts which encircle the earth. They are reflected north and south towards the poles spiraling back and forth. More commonly referred to as the Ozone layer it is this belt which our carbon dioxide emissions are destroying. You are probably asking yourselves by now: "but what has all this to do with the skin?" Well, the simple answer is *everything*.

"In 1984, research in the United States showed that fluctuations in magnetic fields cause genetic mutations in test tube babies at the time of conception. The polarity of the sun's radiation changes twelve times during a one-year earth cycle. Could this be the basis of the twelve types of personality so preached by astrologists?

"The average duration of the female menstruation cycle is 28-days. This coincides with the 28-day rotation cycle of the sun's equator—coincidence? But of course there are variations to this time period. The duration can vary if the polar magnetic field interferes with the equatorial magnetic field. Remember the poles are turning slower—40-days. The 28-day *average* cycle can be shortened or lengthened by up to 4-days.

"Ladies, let me not embarrass you. Just think for a moment. Say nothing but just ask yourselves this question. How often does my *monthly curse* come early or late?" Have you ever asked yourself why? Perhaps I have now given you a reason. Yes, I know artificial stimulants such as tobacco, alcohol, narcotics or even coffee if taken in excess can affect the regular cycle. But, scientific experiments have proved conclusively that females shielded from the sun by being placed under ground for extended periods of time will stop menstruating. Their biological clocks simply malfunction. This of course presents a whole new series of problems which will have to be solved before you ladies can safely enter into deep space exploration. Assuming that is, mankind wishes to colonize outer space using our conventional means of reproduction.

"But let us come back to earth. *Jetlag*. What is jetlag?"

This time a dozen hands shot up. "You, lady in the front row."

She hesitated. "When you've been flying for say twelve hours or more having crossed several time zones your body feels lethargic—strange sort of."

"Why? Someone tell me why?"

"Because the airline seats are designed to provide you with no leg room," a young man shouted out. Laughter filled the room. Dr. Schultz allowed it to die before continuing.

"We know that rapid movement across the earth's magnetic field creates a symptom scientist's call, behavioral inertia. Rapid changes in the magnetic field disturb the body's production of the hormone—melatonin. A study, completed in 1989, confirmed sunspots, which severely change magnetism in the surrounding environment, affect the body's endocrine system. The Pituitary and Hypothalamus Pineal, the Thyroid, the Pancreas and in ladies—the ovaries are susceptible to the solar wind.

"Travel by train, car or ship, the magnetic field is changing slowly so the body can easily cope. Jump on an aircraft in an environment where high-positive rays are bombarding earth. Disembark say two hours later in a place where low-negative rays prevail. The result—some people may feel a bit queasy until their bodies adapt—call it jetlag or homesickness. If your immune system is under attack with the flue or, you are carrying some unknown mild infection—it can suddenly be triggered. Why do young children always choose to be ill when they go on holiday with their parents?" A number of people laughed. "I can see the people who have children," joked the Doctor.

"Pregnant women are advised not to fly after their 28$^{th}$ week of confinement. Most airlines will only accept them with a doctor's note practically guaranteeing they will not give birth 20,000 feet up in the air. One of the answers lies in how a rapidly changing magnetic field affects the fetus in the womb.

"But all this is not new. The Mayan civilization of Central America understood thousands of years ago how our sun affects our personalities and how it controls female menstruation. We have now moved into the field of astrogenetics. Anyone care to define it?"

There was silence.

"Astrogenetics is the scientific study of how the astronomical forces of the universe, particularly our sun, affect and influence life forms on earth. It is believed the magnetic field of the earth somehow disturbs, or perhaps plays an intrinsic role in the creation of human life. To put it more bluntly; you are affected at the point of conception by the strength of the magnetic field of the earth, which in turn is altered by the solar wind emitted from the rays of our sun.

"Your personality or character is molded at that precise moment of conception. The position of the planets in the night sky then, or nine months later, at the time of your birth has got absolutely nothing to do with the makeup of your personality. In a nutshell, the astrologists have got it horribly wrong. It is now scientifically proven that the local magnetic field strength can cause mutation in cells, which are undergoing mitosis—cell division.

"Why is the first three months in the creation of a new human life form, the most critical, or should I say delicate?

Could it be that during this period the fetus which, let us say, was conceived at a high positive radiation period is being bombarded in the womb by negative emissions? On reaching the two hundred and seventy-fifth day, the exact level of radiation has returned to that of the moment of conception. The result is the child, now completely formed, is ready to be born. Recent studies show that many premature babies are born early because the polarity of the emissions arrives early. Conversely, babies, which need to be physically induced, because they are overdue, can be the result of the exact polarity arriving late. Therefore, the moment of birth is in direct relation to the moment of conception, with regards to the radiation levels from the sun.

"Could this be one of the reasons why our ancient ancestors worshipped the sun? Only now are we beginning to comprehend this incredible knowledge of how the Mayan civilization of Central America was controlled by a small number of people."

Dr. Schultz paused. He consulted his watch then glanced at the chairman. "It would appear I have over-run my time. My apologies, ladies and gentlemen, it is difficult to condense a three day paper into an hour's presentation. Do we have time for some questions?"

The president had joined the doctor on stage. "Perhaps a few," he responded.

Pierre's hand shot up. The doctor immediately pointed to him. Pierre stood up. "Dr. Schultz, you mentioned the Mayans and their intimate knowledge of the sun. Didn't they have a calendar which predicts the end of the world?"

"You are referring to the Mayan Long Count. The Mayans in fact possessed three calendars, one, very like our Gregorian calendar, counted out 365 days and was used by the common man. A second, sacred calendar, counting 260 days was used by their priests. Every 52 years these two calendars coincided as though commencing a new cycle. However, the third one, the Long Count, which you refer to was based upon the cycles of the sun and measures a staggering 1,366,560 days or 3,744 years. If they are correct then we are living in the end of the fifth cycle which translates to 21st December 2012."

"What happens then?" shouted a voice.

"Our world will come to an end."

More hands shot up.

Denise turned to touch Pierre. She whispered in his ear. "You never told me you were interested in this sort of thing?"

"You never asked. There are lots of things you don't know about me yet," and he pecked her lightly on the cheek.

The Doctor had finished answering another question.

"Sorry everyone, that's all we have time for," announced the president. "So, fellow members, I believe a big round of applause is necessary." Instantaneously the entire room clapped. A woman stepped onto the stage holding a box wrapped in gift paper. "We have a little something for you, Doctor Schultz, a token of our appreciation."

They waited for the crowds to shuffle out. "I am off to the ad agency, Pierre? Do you want to come with me or shall we meet afterwards?"

They were finally out of the auditorium standing at the top of the stairs leading down to the street. "How long will you be?"

"No more than two hours. We could meet for a late lunch," replied Denise.

"Where?"

"I don't know," she answered. They stood on the pavement facing each other.

"Denise, SMS me when you think you will be free. I'll meet you there." They kissed. Denise turned left, Pierre right. He glanced down the road. It was clear of traffic as the lights on the corner were red. Rather than walk on towards the crossing he began to cross the road. He turned to glance at Denise but she was already lost in the crowd. Something attracted his attention a large grey shape had jumped the lights and was charging towards him. For a moment Pierre froze then he ran for the safety of the centre island.

Denise heard a scream. A voice cried out. "Oh my God, there's been an accident. Someone has been knocked down." She turned as did another dozen faces. A large Citroen flashed passed ignoring the red lights. It swerved to avoid hitting an oncoming car. With a squeal of breaks it turned the corner and disappeared from view.

# Chapter Thirty Nine

## Berlin

Jorgen Schaller walked into the square. It was as though time had stood still, nothing ever seemed to change. Outside the bar, the same old men sat nursing their empty glasses. Some read dog-eared newspapers, others played chess or draughts. Nobody bothered to glance at him as he passed by. He opened the door and was surprised to see three tables occupied in the small room. Again no attention was paid to him other than the barman who acknowledged his presence with a nod. Jorgen approached the bar. The barman put down the glass he was polishing. From inside his jacket pocket Jorgen removed a plain white envelope which he dropped on the bar sliding it towards the barman.

"A *Berliner Weisse, bitter*." Jorgen chose to sit at a vacant table near the door away from the bar.

The barman opened the envelope. It contained five crisp new €100 notes. The barman coughed as though to clear his throat before attending to the beer. A man sitting at a table slowly stood up. Without uttering a word to his two companions he exited the bar. Using a tin tray the barman brought the beer to Jorgen. "He'll be ten minutes," the man whispered out of the corner of his mouth before returning to his place behind the counter.

Jorgen sipped his beer. To pass the time he scrolled through the messages on his phone deleting those he no longer needed. This finished, he commenced tiding up the other menus. The room remained silent. Nobody spoke. The barman slowly polished glasses. Jorgen glanced at the four tables. At one, sat two men, both reading a newspaper. They did not appear to show any interest in their half-drunk glasses of beer. The three men were playing cards only their eyes did the communicating. Seated on the third table were two more men. They just sat there. Jorgen was beginning to feel uncomfortable when the door opened and an elderly man stepped in carrying a dark sports bag.

Again, no eyes other than Jorgen showed any interest in who was the newcomer. The man was better dressed than the others. His clothes were new and the black jacket he wore smelt of fresh leather. He sat at the table opposite Jorgen. "Herr Schaller?"

"Herr Voigtländer?"

For a moment there was silence. "You have something for me?" Asked Jorgen.

"And you have something for me?"

Jorgen reached into his inside jacket pocket and removed a bulging envelope.

"€10,000, it's all there." He placed his hand down on the envelope.

Wilhelm reached down. He slid the sports bag across the floor towards Jorgen. The barman arrived at the table with another beer. Jorgen lifted the bag onto the banquette next to him. He unzipped it. He pulled out a small glass jar protected with bubble rap. "This?"

"A sample."

"Is this all?"

"It's all that remains," lied Wilhelm, who chose the moment to pick up the envelope.

Jorgen returned the jar to the bag. He pulled out four brown foolscap envelopes each bulging with papers. "These?" asked Jorgen.

"The files. They are all there, the list of experiments, formulas and the recorded results."

"How do I know they are genuine and if the thing works?"

Jorgen sipped his beer. He was enjoying the moment. Deliberately, taking his time he put down the glass then wiped the foam from his mouth with his sleeve. "You don't, but all the relative detail is there. I have excluded the tons of memos, meetings and reports. They are of no real value. You can have them if you insist but you will need a truck to carry them away." He picked up his beer again.

"You have not answered my question. What guarantees do I have? After all, you have taken €110,000 of our money."

"You asked for and I have sold to you the Honey Files that was the deal."

"Yes, but I am sure you would live to enjoy the money, Herr Voigtländer. What is to stop me shooting you here and now?"

Wilhelm smiled for the first time. "Go ahead but you will never leave this room alive." He moved his body sideways to give Jorgen a better view of the bar. Each of the seven men seated was aiming a firearm at him. The barman continued polishing glasses with a faceless expression.

"You've made your point. Enjoy the money."

"I will."

"Just one more thing. What happened to Gerhard Bock?"

"He made a mistake."

"What sort of mistake?"

"He tried to cheat me by killing me."

# Chapter Forty

## Grasse

Michel Ramonet opened the boardroom door. He never felt comfortable with its austere white décor. He particularly hated the expensive white plastic chairs which always made him feel as though he was sliding off them and, as for the imported glass table from Murano, no matter what it cost, he would gladly dispose of it for something more traditional and comfortable. Fortunately, he rarely visited the boardroom, as being the *nose,* he was more or less left alone, if the Chairman wanted to discuss a point with him then it was the Chairman who visited him. He was an artist, a creator of exotic smells. Meetings bored him but, the meeting today was of such a serious nature that he himself had suggested calling it.

They were all in place waiting for him. The chairman, Alan Thulier, was seated in his usual seat at the head of the table. On his left the financial director, Eugène Delacroix and on his right was Charles Seberg, the managing director. Also present were Marguerite Bise as secretary, Jean-Luc Picard, the marketing director and Edmund Bajulaz who headed up market research.

Michel chose to place himself one seat removed away from Jean-Luc. He pulled out the chair dropping the file he was carrying onto the glass table.

"Gentlemen and lady now we are all here let us get started," began the Chairman. "I thought it prudent to call this meeting following on from the talk I had with Michel last week. As we all know Michel has been working on a number of new fragrances in preparation for our new launch, which I am happy to say is on schedule. However, I have not summoned you all here to discuss that subject. Michel has brought to my attention a somewhat delicate matter which I felt prudent to share with you." The Chairman paused focusing his eyes directly on Michel. "Michel, I wonder . . . would you like to start the ball rolling?"

Michel opened the file in front of him. He cleared his throat as he glanced at each person present. "It is difficult to know precisely where to start. Several weeks ago I was asked to examine a fragrance. This is not something which I normally do. However, it immediately became obvious that it contained some mysterious substance with powerful aphrodisiac properties." He watched the body language of the assembled group suddenly change as each in turn appeared to focus their attention on him.

"Where did this . . . this substance come from?" enquired Edmund Bajulaz.

"From the young man who installed our new computer system."

"Really, how odd," added Eugène Delacroix.

"Apparently, his friend, whose name escapes me, is a chemist. He had been experimenting in making fragrances as a hobby. I suppose I examined it out of politeness. It was pleasant, quite robust and lingering, but nothing out of the extraordinary. However, its affect upon one of my young laboratory assistants was nothing short of frightening."

"How do you mean?" interrupted Jean-Luc Picard.

"Well . . . she became quite . . . quite emotional if I may put it in a delicate way."

"You mean sexy?" added Jean-Luc.

"Yes. Yes, I suppose you could say that."

Jean-Luc glanced at the Chairman. "So, what are we waiting for? Let's go into production. There is a fortune to be made. It's every perfumery's dream to create such a product. We will clean up the market."

"I was thinking on those very same lines," contributed Eugène, "presupposing of course we are not breaking any laws. Naturally, I would assume you would dilute the . . . the aphrodisiac portion to a controllable amount."

"Perhaps," replied Michel. "That may be possible but, and it is a big but—what about the ethics of producing such a substance? When does a perfume cease being an exotic fragrance to become a drug, if it produces a metabolic change, not on the wearer but on a person coming into contact with it?"

"Before we get into the moral aspect of producing such a perfume can you please tell us, Michel, about your findings?"

"Thank you, Chairman, yes, I was coming to that." Michel opened the file in front of him. He withdrew a single sheet of paper, adjusted his spectacles and began to read out aloud. "An initial analysis of the fragrance indicates the presence of: ambergris, nutmeg, mimosa, vetivert, cinnamon, pepper, sandalwood oil, ylang-ylang, lavender, citrus amber and spicy fougère. There is nothing out of the ordinary there except the concentration of ambergris was very high. This substance as you all know is both difficult to obtain and very expensive.

"Further chemical analysis reveals a list of chemical substances and trace elements which I shall not bore you with. They are all naturally occurring and being present in such minute quantities would not contribute to the side affects I mentioned. However, two ingredients are, or perhaps I should say *might,* be significant. These are Cantharides and Ginko Biloba."

Michel put down the paper to pick up another. "Cantharides—commonly known as Spanish Fly. It is made by crushing the dried remains of an emerald-green beetle into a powder which becomes a yellowish-brown-olive in color. The taste is bitter and the smell horrendous. Traditionally, it has been used in animal husbandry to encourage livestock to mate. The farmers simply add a prescribed dosage to the food. It is banned for human consumption in the United States and UK. During the sixties it became fashionable for certain hippie cultures to experiment with it as a sexual stimulant. Too small a dosage has no affect, but too much can cause permanent damage to the kidneys and genital organs. The difference between too little and too much is infinite. In order to prescribe the exact dosage the imbiber's age, weight, metabolism and body mass has to be accurately calculated."

Michel put down the paper. "Any questions before I continue?" He quickly glanced around the table. Nobody spoke. "Ginko Biloba, commonly known as the Maidenhair Tree. It grows in Eastern China but is now found in certain areas of Europe, namely Belgium. The tree grows very slowly but lives to a great age achieving a height of 35-metres. Dendrochronologists date the oldest recorded tree still living as being 2,500 years old. The bark gives off a fine hair-like substance, hence the common name, Maidenhair. When ground down into a fine powder Chinese apothecaries sold it as an aphrodisiac."

Michel paused as he held the paper closer to his eyes. "I am not even going to attempt to pronounce the scientific name but the substance produced, after a somewhat complex treatment process, increases the body's production of testosterone. In the case of men it helps to prolong sexual activity, and in woman, it stimulates the theca-ovary cells and the zona reticularis located in the adrenal cortex. It targets tissues in the blood and is transmitted as plasma-protein sex-hormone-binding globulin. There is a lot more scientific detail but I shall not continue. The adverse affects are that it accelerates the growth of pubic hair, contributes to breast cancer and the build up of subcutaneous fat in the muscles. On the positive side, tests are currently being run on its property to restore damaged brain cells to counteract the affect of Alzheimer's disease." Michel put the paper down and looked towards the Chairman.

"Thank you, Michel, so, Quo Vadis? Where do we go from here? Do we invest time and money with a view to bringing this product to the market or do we drop it here and now?"

For a minute nobody spoke. Jean-Luc was the first to break the silence. "I would like to know Michel's opinion. What do you recommend, Michel?"

"To terminate the subject here and now. For a start, we do not own the copyright not that any exists at this stage. Secondly, we manufacture fragrances not drugs. You all know as well as I do the time it takes to bring a new product onto the market. It is a long drawn-out journey—laboratory testing, clinical testing—then the need to gain approval from the various authorities. In this case we even know before commencing that two of the ingredients produce negative affects."

"What I would like to know is: what precise affect did the substance have on your technician? It was one of the girls I take?"

Michel sat back in his chair his hands were on the table. "It was quite extraordinary. In the bottle, when smelt, there was no immediate obvious affect. When worn by the man and sniffed off his skin quite the reverse happened. I noticed a twitching of the girl's nostrils as though they were agitated. I suppose this emboldened her to sniff closer—longer, until she was practically licking the man's hand. It all happened very quickly. Afterwards, she informed she suddenly felt very . . . very concupiscent."

"How long did this feeling last?" enquired the Charles Seberg. His mind was elsewhere. He was beginning to wonder if it might be possible to try some of this magical potion on Madeleine. Considering the money she was costing him—the flat, clothes, jewellery, presents—he was beginning to doubt his investment. The last two occasions spent with her had proved to be somewhat fruitless, first migraine then the monthly curse, not even a hand job had been offered.

He failed to hear the answer. "We made her drink water and wash her face. The affect quickly wore off. She did mention afterwards feeling somewhat detumescent."

Up until that moment Edmund Bajulaz had remained silent. "Michel, would I be correct in saying that this substance, I am referring to the unknown component, could be isolated? The actual fragrance is insignificant. It is simply the vehicle in which to transport the aphrodisiac."

"Yes, that is correct."

"Therefore, I am inclined to believe we should not simply jettison this opportunity. Just imagine if we could bring to the market a range of cosmetics which could stimulate sexual arousal, improve sexual performance, of course in a perfectly controlled state."

The Managing Director was lying on his back—fully erect. Madeleine was kissing his chest. Her fingers were fumbling to unfasten the buckle on the belt of his trousers. When finally she succeeded in her endeavors he heard her gasp, "Oh my God!"

"What do you think, Charles? Should we perhaps allocate a budget for preliminary research and development?"

"Oh yes," expressed the Managing Director somewhat loudly.

"Sorry, Charles, I take it then that you confer?"

"Yes, err . . . yes of course," he replied. Madeleine had suddenly disappeared.

"How much?" asked Eugène. "There is not much left in the research budget. It will probably mean us allocating money from one of the other projects."

The Chairman was back in command. "Gentlemen, do I take it we want to continue with this . . . this project."

"I have made my views very clear."

"Yes, Michel, I fully understand your point of view. The fact is this no longer forms part of your portfolio. You have played your part. You have analyzed a fragrance and have identified certain unique components. It is now up to the chemists to work on it. We do not carry the necessary people or equipment to perform this function, Edmund, do you have any ideas?"

"We shall have to be very careful whom we approach, Chairman. Let me give it some thought. My brother-in-law heads up the chemistry research department at the Sorbonne. He told me they were currently working on a project for one of the giant pharmaceutical companies. Apparently, they are conducting research into how the body's olfactory senses relate to pheromones, the biological substances which affect biorhythms. I shall have a discrete chat with him. See what he advises. Who could run such tests? What sort of costs will we incur that sort of thing then I shall report back to you?"

"Very well, do we all confer?"

There was silence and a gentle nodding of heads.

"Thank you, then I shall close this meeting."

# Chapter Forty One

# Manchester

"Shit that's strong. What you got on?"

Shaun Formby entered the small lounge from the bathroom. The three lads whom he shared the council flat with were seated, two on the couch, one in the armchair. Half a dozen empty beer cans and potato crisp packets lay scattered about on the floor. Their eyes were glued to the television. Manchester City was playing Liverpool.

"What's the score?" asked Shaun.

"Nil-nil with twenty minutes into the first half," came the automatic reply. "You going out? Got a date?"

"Maybe? What's it to you?"

"Foul! Did you see that? Come on. Book the bastard, ref."

Shaun slipped out of the room leaving the experts to argue the rules of football. For once he still had a few pounds left in his pocket, thanks to his visit to Llandudno. The lifts were not working. They had been out of order for months. The council had given up competing with the vandals. He skipped down the seven flights of stairs ignoring the Nigerian drug peddlers whose turf the estate had now become.

Shirley Williams had chosen to sit at a corner table where she could keep a close eye on the door. She was not happy. It was not the first time her fiancé, Craig, was late. In fact, it had become the norm of late, ever since he had been accepted into the Manchester CID. At least when he wore a uniform his hours were more or less normal unless an emergency arose. For the umpteenth time she glanced at her watch. It was now passed seven. Craig was thirty-five minutes late. She sipped her bitter-lemon. The pub was beginning to fill up. Being an attractive young woman she was beginning to feel vulnerable. It would only be a matter of time before some idiot decided she was fair game to be chatted up. The Keg, as the pub was called, was not the most salubrious of places, but it was a convenient meeting place. From here they were supposed to move on to see a film and then supper.

Shaun pushed open the door of the Keg. He saw some familiar faces at the bar. Their eyes were glued to the large plasma screen raised above the bar. The game was still on. The score remained nil-nil with only ten minutes left to play. Shaun ordered a pint of the local bitter. It was the one thing he had truly missed during his time in prison—beer and the pub. The food inside had been passable, and the boredom had not worried him. The important thing had been to blend in, not to become conspicuous so as to attract the eye of any of the gang leaders. Keep your head down, your mouth shut and above all, see nothing was the advice given to him by one of the old lags with whom he had shared a cell with. For once Shaun had listened to the guidance of an older person.

A shout, followed by groans, erupted. The Manchester City striker, Felipe Caicedo, had sidestepped two Liverpool defenders only to hit the left goal post. A defender quickly booted the ball back down the field. Another chance was lost.

Over in the far corner Shirley Williams glanced in the direction of the noise. The television was too far away for her to watch the game even if she had wanted to. Anyway, football bored her. Rugby was her preferred game. Craig played for the police XV and she enjoyed watching him. The difference was there was always something happening in rugby whereas football; as far as she was concerned soccer players were all overpaid prima donna pansies. And how could you decide an important championship by penalties? It did not happen in any other sport. The teams should play on until a goal is scored or they drop down dead with exhaustion. Her glass was empty. She did not really want another drink. She glanced again at her watch. In two minds whether to stay or leave, the phone in her bag began to ring. It was an SMS from Craig, he was ten minutes away.

The game had finished in a goalless draw. Shaun was on his second pint. Some of the men left leaving half a dozen stalwarts to analyze the game. Shaun joined in the conversation.

"The problem: is the Liverpool defense was just too strong."

"No, it's our mid-fielders, they kept loosing the ball."

"He's right; the strikers need clean ball if they are going to stand any chance of scoring."

"I think we should change the playing formation."

"Bollocks."

Finally, the last of the analytical minds had dried up which resulted in the conversation moving onto more mundane things—sex. Shaun downed his third pint.

"Take that bird sitting over there."

"Where?"

"There by the door, the brunette, nice pair of tits."

"What of her?"

"Well, why is she sitting all alone?"

"Probably waiting for her boyfriend to arrive."

"Suppose she's waiting for a bloke to chat her up, for all you know she's begging for some bugger to give her one. Maybe she's just ditched someone. Why else would a bird come into a pub on her own?"

Shaun placed his half-empty pint on the counter. It was his fourth. He burped loudly. "Needs a good fuck if you ask me," he slurred.

"Think you can give her one, do you?"

"Piece of cake," he bragged loudly.

"Twenty quid says you've got no chance." The man slapped a £20 note on the counter.

Shaun swayed slightly on his feet. "What's that, £20 for, chatting her up?"

"No arsehole. That says you won't walk out that door with her."

Shaun reached into his pocket. He peeled off a £50 note. "That says I will. Match it."

For a moment the man hesitated then, egged on by the others, he reluctantly removed the £20 only to replace it on the bar with a £50.

Shirley was fuming. She was starting to compose an SMS—a rude one—to Craig. He was now 45-minutes late. She looked up. A man had seated himself next to her.

"Hallo darling; thought you might like some company. Boyfriend stood you up as he? Can I buy you a drink?"

Shirley looked up at the young man who had suddenly invaded her space. Normally, she would have told him to go. He certainly was not her type. She hesitated. The thought crossed her mind that if Craig was to arrive and see her in conversation with another man it would make him jealous. Serve him right for neglecting her again.

"What'll you have, a gin?"

"Nothing, thank you."

"Come on, I shan't bight you." Shaun leaned closer. He picked up her empty glass. Shirley moved to stop him. Their hands touched. Shaun won. "A gin and tonic or . . ."

"I'm expecting my fiancé."

"Lucky bugger, silly sod for making you wait like this." With the glass in hand he disappeared off to the bar.

"Back so soon," came a sarcastic voice. "Told you where to jump, has she?" The man reached for the two bank notes which sat prominently in a glass on the counter.

"Not so fast," retorted Shaun. He ordered the drink. "First I'm buying the lady a drink."

"You shouldn't have."

Shaun placed the drink in front of Shirley. He held out his hand. "Shaun."

"Shirley," she replied somewhat reluctantly.

Shaun moved closer to her. "You're not from round here, are you?"

Shirley said nothing. She was confused. She didn't know whether to get up or . . .

"That's a lovely ring. Mind if I take a closer look?" Shaun was touching her hand. He was pulling it closer to him. Shirley smelt his strong aftershave. "Nice diamond must be a carat at least."

Detective Sergeant Craig Samson cursed the red lights. They must be faulty. They changed to green then seconds later flashed back to red allowing no more than three cars to cross over the busy intersection. The traffic had been horrendous. The station had received a tip-off from a woman in Salford. The rented house next door; it was full of blacks coming and going at all hours of the day and night. They were so noisy. She suspected drugs or worse. His boss, Detective Superintendent Donald Bradley, had asked him to investigate. There might just be a connection with the ATM bombers.

Because of the racial issue it was considered prudent to first obtain a search warrant as well as picking up a number of Black uniforms for backup. This had all taken time. They had searched the house finding only two illegals from Ghana and a small quantity of marihuana, but nothing to link the occupants to the bombers.

The lights had changed again, four cars this time, managed to get away. He would have to wait for the next change. He glanced at the clock on the dashboard. Shirley was going to kill him.

From the distant bar six pairs of eyes focused on Shaun. "The bastard is holding her hand. Jesus, Fred, your money is slipping away."

"Bollocks," came the abrupt reply. "He'll not crack that one. She's got too much class for the likes of him."

Shirley felt uncomfortable. By right she should have pulled her hand away, even slapped the man, but she did not. Shaun was leaning forward holding her hand, pretending to admire the engagement ring. He noticed her nose had begun to twitch and more important she was not putting up any resistance as he moved closer to her.

Craig opened his driver window. Leaning out he attached the blue flashing police light to the roof of the car. It was against regulations but, what was worse, a reprimand from the station or Shirley's wrath? He touched the remote and a wailing sound added to the confusion. The lights changed to green. He pushed his way forward. The car in front was letting him pass. He estimated he was five minutes away not more.

Shirley was not listening. The man facing her was talking incessantly—diamonds, jewellery—the words meant nothing. Something was drawing her to him. Her nose was practically touching him.

Shaun could not believe his luck. The girl was virtually licking his neck. She was asking to be kissed. He was beginning to feel the start of an erection coming on. It was now or never.

Across the bar six mouths dropped in unison. "Bloody Hell," a voice swore.

"Well bugger me," added a second.

Fred was speechless. He was beginning to regret having made the bet.

Shirley found herself standing. She still had not touched her drink. Shaun was leading her by the hand. She felt weak. She tried to scratch her itching nose but one hand grasped her bag while the other held Shaun's hand. They were heading towards the door, where to? She did not know, nor for once did she care.

# Chapter Forty Two

## Paris

Herbert Sibert looked around his small office for the last time. Everything was in place, just as it should be. The files, his precious recipes, nothing had been touched; even the petty cash was complete. It balanced to the Euro. Over the past few days he had photocopied the information he needed to take with him for his new life.

Taking out the second mortgage on the house had proved more difficult than he first imagined. The bank demanded his wife's signature, even though everything was registered in his name. He had carefully chosen his timing. She was on her way out to visit her sick mother—not that there was anything wrong with the woman. Herbert was convinced she would outlive them all. His wife demanded to know: "Why now? Why can't it wait until tomorrow when I will have sufficient time to read what it is you want me to sign?"

"I need to take it today, before they close, otherwise . . ."

"Why do you always leave things to the last moment, Herbert? It's so typical of you. Sometimes you make me so mad."

"It's for insurance purposes, dear. We don't want to make the mistake of underinsuring, now do we? What would happen if there was a fire tonight? God forbid, you would never–."

She grabbed the papers from him, barking, "Oh very well, where . . . show me where I must sign?"

Patiently, he pointed to the relevant places, turning over the pages as quickly as he could. Finally, having completed the operation she grabbed her bag and rushed out mumbling. "My poor mother, you know how unfair you are when . . ."

The door then swung shut with a loud bang leaving Herbert alone clutching the signed document.

He had told the bank he required the additional €800,000 in cash to buy a quarter-share in L'Artisan Parfumeur. They hadn't even blinked. His preparations were well underway. He had made discreet enquiries. He hoped to procure false identity documents. There was nothing from the house he would take, not even his clothes. It was all part of the plan. He had to make it appear that he had simply disappeared—perhaps murdered. But now, his timetable, if one had ever existed, had been brought forward. The front page of the evening newspaper had necessitated he leave Paris tonight, never to return. Picking up the paper he shoved it into his bag after having glanced once more at the headline. "Hit and run accident on Paris streets" and the picture of Pierre Nimier stared back to haunt him.

Denise Vergé was still in a state of shock. Time had lost all meaning. She sat staring. The question—why? Why Pierre? One moment they were together—the next? The room was silent except for the ping emanating from the heart machine which indicated Pierre was still alive—only just. Wires and tubes were attached to his broken body. His head was swathed in a multitude of bandages.

"There is nothing you can do? Go home. Get some rest. We will contact you the moment there is a change."

Denise looked up as though awaking from a trance. It was the Sister.

"Look, he is young and healthy. The human body is a miraculous machine. It has the ability to cure itself and, with as much help as we can give it, time will tell."

Denise stood up. "When do you think he might . . .?"

"We really can't say. He is in a coma. His body has shut down and is concentrating on healing its injured parts. If you are religious pray for him otherwise . . . it is best you leave. We have contacted his parents in Bayonne they are on their way to Paris as we now speak. Do you know them?"

Denise shook her head.

"Very well, I will make a note in the file for the hospital to contact you the moment they arrive."

"You are very kind," muttered Denise, as they walked out together into the corridor.

"Mademoiselle Vergé? You are Denise Vergé?"

Denise turned towards the voice calling her name. A short middle-aged woman dressed in a charcoal colour trouser suit was walking down the corridor. A younger man accompanied her. The woman held out an ID badge.

"Inspectrice Daguerre, Préfecture de Police Judiciare, may we have a few words with you?"

"You can use my office," volunteered the Sister.

Denise followed. For the first time she noted the blood stains on her clothes—Pierre's blood when she had held his head on the street as they waited for the ambulance. They squeezed into the tiny office. There were only two chairs. "I'll get another," volunteered the Sister.

The Inspectrice sat behind the desk. She indicated for Denise to occupy the other chair. The man remained standing. "What is your relationship with Monsieur Nimier?"

"We are friends . . . good friends."

"How long have you known him?"

"Not long, a few months I suppose."

"Do you know anyone who might want to kill him?"

Denise began to sob. The policeman offered her a tissue. "Thanks," she muttered. "Sorry, it's just . . ."

"Take your time, would you like a coffee perhaps?"

"Yes, thank you."

The Inspectrice addressed the man. "Anton, nip out and see if you can find us some coffee." Turning to Denise she continued. "Take your time, in your own words; tell me anything you might think is relevant."

"You don't think then that this was just a tragic accident?"

"No, I do not. I believe it was a premeditated attempt of murder and that is why I am posting a twenty-four hour police watch over Monsieur Nimier. Now, start by telling me how you both met."

Takao Fujimoto picked up the phone. His secretary was calling him. "Lancelot Slim is on the line again. He says he must speak with you."

"Tell him I am out . . . tell him I am in Japan. No, wait, he will find out. Tell him I am away . . . in the countryside and you will get the message to me." He replaced the receiver then stood up from his desk to walk over to the window. He looked out. It was a beautiful day. In the far distance he could just make out the parapets of the Palais de Versailles.

Lancelot Slim was fast becoming a problem. He knew he would be stupid to cross the man. He could be dangerous, but the fact was, he no longer needed him. He had obtained the sample fragrance without his involvement, all that was needed now was for his chemists to analyze and reproduce it. Lancelot need never find out. If however he did produce another sample Takao could stall it, eventually, to inform Lancelot that it simply did not work. There was too much at stake, nothing less than a fortune was at his finger tips—his for the taking. He could finally leave Shiseido and start his own company. But first he needed to know. Walking back to his desk he checked the number for the laboratory before phoning it. He spoke in Japanese.

Fifteen minutes later the chief chemist, Kimura-san, was knocking on his door. "Enter," he shouted in Japanese. The meeting would be conducted in that language, his secretary and none of the French staff had ever bothered to learn his native tongue. "Tell me," he ordered, "what have you discovered about this mysterious fragrance?"

Kimura-san bowed his head. "A great deal, Takao Fujimoto. I have identified over two hundred different trace elements all of which are derived from various plants. However, I suspect the animal protein, honey, is what creates the stimulating affect. We are busy trying to analyze the specific type."

"What do you mean? Honey is honey, surely?"

"I wish it were that simple, Takao Fujimoto. As you well know honey is the oldest sweetener known to mankind. Bushman cave paintings found in Spain, dating back over 100,000 years show that our ancestors had discovered the many properties of honey. Starting life as a drop of nectar in the flower it is transformed by the bee into grape sugar, aided by the scented gums and oils of the plant source. It contains iron, phosphorous, manganese, lime and sulphur all of which are easily digested. Today sugar has replaced honey that is why we all suffer with gastric nervous disorders and tooth decay."

Takao Fujimoto sat back in his chair allowing his chief chemist to waffle on. He thought of interrupting but decided against it. Kimura-san was a perfectionist that is why he had insisted on bringing him to France from Japan. The man lived for his science.

"What we are now trying to do is determine the exact type of honey. I suspect it might come from the wild almond tree which renders it poisonous. It is used to treat rheumatism and a derivative goes into the making of certain cough medicines. Together with castor oil it has been known to help relieve the symptoms of asthma and catarrh. Alternatively, a more common lime blossom honey, affective against insomnia, may have been used. It is common in many mild laxatives and diuretics, because it stimulates the appetite but rarely contributes to obesity."

Takao Fujimoto marveled at how Kimura-san never made use of notes. All this knowledge was stored away in his phenomenal memory.

"As well as determining the precise source of the honey it is equally important to ascertain which bee is responsible. I suspect it might be the South Africa Black Bee with its viscous deadly sting. This strain is hard working producing good quality honey. Alternatively, the more common Brown Bee with the yellow stripes might be the culprit. They were endemic to ancient cultures, pictures of them are commonly found in ancient Egyptian tombs. I need a few more days then I should have the answers for you. Is it possible to obtain another sample, as I could then let one of my assistants run some additional tests, without of course them knowing the reasons?"

"That might be possible but I would prefer you to make use of what you have. Do you think you will be able to replicate its hypnotic affect? The smell is of no importance. It is the reaction it has which concerns me."

"I understand perfectly. It will not be easy. It will take time but as usual I shall succeed. Will that be all, Takao Fujimoto? May I now return to my laboratory?"

"Yes of course, Kimura-san, just keep me up to date with your progress."

Kimura-san stood up. He bowed politely then turned and left the room. Takao Fujimoto waited a few moments before telephoning Lancelot Slim. He now knew what to say to him.

# Chapter Forty Three

## Manchester

The car screeched to a halt outside the Keg. Craig Sampson jumped out locking the vehicle with the remote as he ran into the pub. The noise of the busy bar struck him immediately. He looked at all the tables and around every corner. Shirley was nowhere to be seen. For a second he thought of asking someone, but whom? It was obvious she had gone but where? Had she called a taxi? "Damn damn," he muttered under his breath. He turned to leave the pub. Once outside in the car park he pulled out his phone to dial her again. The number just rang and rang. Slowly he walked back to the car.

"The subscriber you have dialed is not available please try again later."

"I know that you stupid bitch." He cursed the automatic voice. Maybe she was just slow in retrieving the phone from the confines of her bag. Standing beside the car he dialed the number again.

Shirley was confused. She had walked out of a bar with a complete stranger. Something she had never done. Something she would never dream of doing. What was wrong with her? They had walked as far as a side entrance of the building which was closed. His hand was pulling down her knickers. He had already fumbled with her breasts. His breath stank of beer. It repulsed her yet—she could not stop kissing him. Her phone rang. It was in her bag on the floor beside her knickers. She tried to mumble something but he was smothering her. The phone stopped ringing then it started again—Craig.

"Leave it," he ordered.

Craig stared at the phone. It informed it was ringing Shirley, but the sound, it was somehow different. Then he understood. He could hear it ringing elsewhere. There were two ringing sounds. Shirley must be very close. He ran to the corner of the building. There in the shadows—two people. It was obvious what they were doing. "Shirley . . . Shirley," he called out.

"Craig . . ."

"Fuck off, cunt," a man's voice threatened.

Craig rushed forward. The man turned fumbling to zip himself up. "Fuck off I said."

The man hit out with his right hand. Craig easily side-stepped the blow. "Shirley, what the hell?"

"Craig, watch out he's got a knife."

Craig turned to see his adversary advancing on him something glistened in his right hand. "Don't be stupid, put that away," Craig shouted.

But there was no stopping Shaun. He began to circle Craig closing in on him, the knife wavering in his right hand just like he had seen it done a hundred times in the movies. "Go for the soft belly," that was what Rambo, his hero, had always done.

Craig did not see Shirley pull her knickers up or stuff her breasts back into her brassiere. His eyes were focused on the shiny object. He pivoted on the balls of his feet waiting for the lunge. It came. He moved away catching the attacking arm in a locking movement. Shaun screamed in pain as his arm was twisted up and over. The knife dropped to the ground. Craig released him. Shaun dropped to the floor hugging his aching arm. Craig kicked him in the solar plexus causing Shaun to vomit stale beer.

"Are you alright, darling, did he . . .?"

"No," she cried, the tears running down her eyes. "I'm so sorry."

"Rubbish, it's not your fault, not with scum like this on the streets. Go to my car. It's parked around the corner, while I call for a squad car.

Lancelot Slim was working late. It had been a long day and not a particularly good one. He knew Takao Fujimoto was avoiding his calls and when he finally managed to communicate the man sounded somewhat vague. From being highly enthusiastic about obtaining a sample of the fragrance he now gave the impression he no longer cared. Lancelot did not believe for one moment his story about Tokyo putting pressure on him which was occupying all his time.

'Do not wait for things to happen. Make them happen.' This had always been his motto. He had phoned an associate in Paris to call up an old favor. The man had responded that he would ask some discrete questions about what Takao Fujimoto was up to. Lancelot checked his watch. It was seven in the evening. His secretary had long gone home. He opened the door to his office. "Come in both of you," he ordered.

Sandra Robinson, followed by Terry Bagshaw, entered first. "Take a seat. How is the face, Terry?"

They both sat down on the couch. Lancelot chose to sit opposite them. "The face is fine. It's the cuts on the hands which have taken the longest to heal."

"Good, I am pleased to hear that," replied Lancelot. "Now, Sandra, have you given this entrapment idea any consideration? This thing has dragged out for far too long. We need to obtain a sample of this substance as quickly as possible."

Terry answered first. "I am sorry about loosing Crumpet the other weekend. I had no idea he had gone and bought a second vehicle but at least I now know where he went—Llandudno, North Wales and, that he was being followed."

"Are you sure?"

"Absolutely, Commander, ever heard of a Stuart Wilson?"

"I can not say I have," responded Lancelot.

"Stuart Wilson is a small-time crook in the Manchester area. His specialty is debt collection and running errands for the bigger boys. He has form and is not the sort of person you would invite home to tea with your mother. Together with a second man," Terry stopped to consult his notes, "Shaun Formby, another regular offender, they were employed to follow Crumpet and to obtain from him, guess what—a mystery perfume?"

Lancelot leaned forward in his chair. "How did you find all this out, Terry, and, more important, who hired them?"

"It was easy. Once I knew Crumpet had driven off in a second vehicle I phoned the shop." Again Terry consulted his notebook. "He uses a Mrs. Wainright to mind the business when he is away. On asking for Crumpet she informed he had departed for Llandudno to attend an auction of antiques at the Grand Hotel. I drove to Llandudno to learn that Crumpet had checked into the hotel at 02:05 using the name Crammer with a false address."

"Strange, why would he do that?" muttered Sandra.

"He is probably being extra cautious after the trial and his unwanted notoriety. Why he checked in so late remains a mystery, but what is of interest, is that thirty minutes after him two more men arrived asking for rooms. Nobody had made a reservation. Crumpet departed the following day after lunch having purchased a number of items at the auction. The two men, Wilson and Formby, checked out at 10:20 according to the hotel."

"That is interesting," interrupted Lancelot, "that must mean they had achieved their objective of obtaining the substance. They probably gained entry to his room while he was attending the auction. But who engaged Wilson and Formby that is what I want to know?"

"I'm coming to that, Sir," responded Terry. "Wilson runs errands for the Hanratty Brothers. They control much of the drug traffic and prostitution around the greater Manchester area. My source inside informed that a Chinese had engaged the Hanratty Brothers to obtain the substance."

"Could the Chinese in fact be Japanese?"

"Possibly," replied Terry. "I do know. Whoever he was lives outside the country."

"Well that explains that then," murmured Lancelot. He looked across at Sandra. "Ok, now tell me how you propose to entrap our friend Crumpet."

# Chapter Forty Four

## Manchester

The door opened and a man walked in. The door banged shut. "Well well well, Shaun Formby, fancy having you as our guest again. You must really like it here. How long have you been out; a week or is it two? Never mind, lad, you'll soon be going back to see your friends and this time for a very long time."

"I ain't done anything. You've got nothing on me."

"Only attempted rape, attacking a police officer with a knife, that should put you away for a good twenty-years, plus of course your previous form will be taken into account, so lets call it a nice round twenty-five years."

Detective Superintendent Donald Bradley pulled back the chair. He sat down facing Shaun across the bare table in the small police interview room. "I thought we'd have a little chat—off the record—just for old-time sakes, Shaun, seeing as we are such good friends."

"I've got nothing to say to you, not without my lawyer present."

"Got your own mouthpiece, have you? I am impressed. Moving up in the world, last time it was legal aid." Bradley pulled a plastic bag from his pocket placing it on the table between the two of them. "What can you tell me about this?"

Shaun said nothing.

Inspector Bradley opened the bag. "Here, let me help you." A small round plastic bottle fell onto the table. "Recognize this?"

"Never seen it before," and Shaun turned his head away.

"Course you have, Son. It was in your pocket."

"I dunno?"

Inspector Bradley picked up the bottle holding it out in front of him. "Says, Shower-Gel-Shampoo, Grand Hotel."

"So what!"

"You are so right, Shaun, The bottle—so what—it means nothing but, it is what is inside which interests me."

"It's fucking empty."

"Ah! So you do recognize it, Shaun. I thought you might."

"I'm saying nothing until I get a lawyer. I know my rights." Shaun sat back in the chair and folded his arms in a defiant manner.

The Inspector continued. "It's the substance inside which intrigues me the most." He unscrewed the small plastic top then brought the open bottle up to his nose. "Nice, smells expensive, want a sniff?" He passed the open bottle to Shaun who simply ignored him.

"I forgot. You want your lawyer." The Inspector replaced the top on the bottle then returned it to the plastic bag. "I am hoping the substance—you see, Shaun, the bottle is not empty, there is enough remaining for us to do a chemical analysis—contains an illegal substance, because then I can get you another five-years. That adds up to? Let me see . . . thirty-years. Christ, you'd be sixty by the time they let you out. That's assuming of course you survive the time because I somehow feel your good friend, Stuart Wilson, will somehow not appreciate you dragging his good name into this mess you've created for yourself. He will no doubt ask himself: "Just how did young Shaun obtain a sample of this exotic perfume to use on himself?"

The Inspector watched a sudden change come over Shaun, although he remained seated with his arms folded, staring away into the far corner of the tiny room. Bradley picked up the little bottle in the plastic bag. "Now this," and he dangled the bottle in the air, "leads me to the Grand Hotel, Llandudno, where *you* and Stuart Wilson stayed last Saturday night. You both checked in at 02:45 in the morning—why so late? What on earth were the two of you doing in such a respectable conservative seaside resort at such an hour, surely not enjoying the nightlife, or partaking in the sea air? However, what is even more amazing is that you both arrived thirty-minutes behind this man." The Inspector reached into his inside pocket to remove a photograph which he laid out on the table.

"Take a good look. His name is Archibald Crumpet."

Shaun defiantly crossed his legs, tightened his arms and shifted his gaze to the other corner of the room.

The Inspector stood up. "Take your time, Shaun; in fact you have all the time in the world—thirty years if my math's is correct. Tell me why you were following this man. I want to know what he did, who he met and who engaged you two? I am going off for a nice cup of tea and when I return we can continue this conversation and, if I am fully satisfied you have told me everything then you can go. I might just be able to convince my detective sergeant to drop all the charges against you."

Detective Superintendent Donald Bradley exited the room leaving Shaun alone. He opened a second door leading off the passage to enter a small observation cubicle which surveyed the interview room through closed circuit television cameras. "Well Craig, what do you think?"

Detective Sergeant Craig Samson was seated at the narrow desk watching the three television monitors. "He'd be a fool not to accept your offer, boss."

"It is still your call, Sergeant. You were the one he attacked with a knife. It was your fiancé whom he tried to rape, so, if you wish to go ahead and press charges I fully support you. However, a lot depends upon your Shirley. You know as well as I do the trauma she must go through when that bastard in there gets a smart lawyer to tell the world how she was a willing party." Craig was about to speak but the Inspector was too quick. "That is what a defense council will say in court. There is no smoke without a fire. Fortunately, no penetration had taken place, thanks to your intervention, and as for this bastard? Once we let Stewart Wilson know that young Shaun here has helped himself to some of the substance—well, you can imagine how that will go down, particularly if my hunch is correct that Wilson was probably doing a job for the Hanratty Brothers. They are behind this. Wilson is too small a fish to wriggle without first obtaining their permission. This way we get closer to Crumpet. We need to put him away if only to protect more young women and as for my friend Shaun, Wilson will take care of him, if not, it will only be a matter of time before he is back in that room."

"I am happy with that. Shirley certainly does not want to press charges. She just wants to forget the unfortunate incident and as for me, I rather like the idea of the Hanratty Brothers learning that young Shaun has double-crossed them."

# Chapter Forty Five

# France

Cardamom, cinnamon, nutmeg, oregano, paprika, turmeric, and chili—the exotic aroma of freshly ground and newly picked spices scented the air. Open wooden barrels, intricately woven baskets each displayed the products of nature in every color of the rainbow—blood red, emerald green, lemon yellow, coal black. Balanced precariously on a large table posed a veritable mountain of garlic and next to it an even greater tumbling tower of purple onions. Aubergine, cauliflower, broccoli, runner beans, French beans, broad beans, lettuce, spinach, monstrous artichokes and trees of asparagus were all on offer. "Organically grown", *"disposition naturelle"*, *"sans produits chimiques"* boasted the labels.

It was the celebrated Saturday market in the ancient Roman town of Arles located in the south of France. Farmers, vegetable growers, creators of cheese, butter, honey and just about everything edible—picklers of shallots, courgettes and beetroot—of every conceivable delicacy had brought the results of their labors to tempt the army of fervent shoppers.

Housewives straining with bulging shopping baskets dangling from an exhausted arm, stern faced professional buyers, curious visitors, ambling tourists, in fact, the complete spectrum of humanity had come—to look, to smell, to taste, to sample, to criticize—with the ultimate goal of purchasing the freshest, the biggest and always at the lowest price. A cacophony of questions and answers bounced back and forth between the buyers and sellers adding sound to the multitude of fragrances in the air. Deals were swiftly concluded. The price was reduced by a Euro, an extra peach, plum or bunch of grapes was added to conclude the sale.

Herbert Siebert carefully selected a Granny Smith. He inspected the color of its green skin for bruises. It was firm and hard. Once satisfied, he placed it gently into a plastic bag with two others, being careful not to crush the cheese. The cheese selection was enormous. It was difficult to know where to start. After much deliberation and sampling he had settled for a small wedge of pungent Münster, a creamy Saint-Marcellin and a semi-soft Tomme de Savoie all produced locally by a rather garrulous farmer's wife. He enjoyed this new experience of shopping.

In his previous life, of only five days ago, it was his wife, Lilia, who performed this essential function. If and when he had purchased anything it was invariably the wrong item or the price he had paid was too high. He would have liked to have bought much more but what was the point. There was no cooking facility in the small quiet hotel he had selected from the list supplied by the local tourist office. Anyway, he enjoyed walking around the ancient town of Arles discovering its many culinary secrets hidden amongst a multitude of bistros and stylish auberges.

Why Arles, he had asked himself? Well, it was far enough away from Paris. Being still the tourist season he could easily loose himself amongst the crowds. It was important not to stand out. The false passport and identity documents had cost him a small fortune but he was yet to collect them. "Another week. It will take five more working days. It is not my fault you have brought the date forward," the shifty-looking man had informed. Then, he could leave the country—but where? He was still undecided. He would cross that bridge as and when he had the documents in his hand. Canada sounded promising. At least there they spoke French. In the meantime he was enjoying playing at being a tourist.

But why Arles? Why not Marseilles or Nice? It was surely easier to remain incognito in a big city. He blamed Vincent Van Gogh for his choice. The great artist's *Café terrace at Night* painted in 1888 had always fascinated him. *The Postman Roulin, The Bedroom at Arles* and his personal favorite,

*Starry Night* were all painted in Arles. He now understood why. There was a certain timeless romantic charm about the place.

So engrossed by visiting the numerous places of historic interest he had hardly given a thought to what might be happening in Paris. Would they be frantically searching for him—dragging the river or combing the backstreets?

He was walking past the Church of Saint Trophime, once a cathedral and now famous for its garish Romanesque architecture, displaying the representation of the last judgment engraved on its portal, when his feet told him they might enjoy a slight respite. Across the road stood a small café, choosing an outside table he ordered himself a coffee and a slice of strawberry cheesecake.

The cake proved delicious, Lilia would definitely have approved. He was halfway through when two tall men dressed in rather somber dark suits approached his table.

"Monsieur Herbert Siebert . . . you are, Monsieur Herbert Siebert?"

Herbert looked up. A portion of cheese cake dropped from his fork landing with a plop on the plate. One of the men flashed a badge at him. It was presented inside a leather folder.

"You are under arrest for the murder of a Monsieur Jacques Gavotte anything you say may be . . ."

He was not listening. "Could I finish my cake first before I come with you?" Herbert asked somewhat shocked.

# Chapter Forty Six

## Beeston

The Welsh Dresser was heavy. Archibald watched as the four furniture removers struggled to carry it out of the shop. He had protected the corners with cardboard to avoid any scuff marks. Once out on the road they placed it on the ground before lifting it up into the van. It was the final piece of the order to go. They had left this one for last. The foreman slammed shut the door. They were ready to depart. All that was needed was Archibald's signature on the document and they could be on their way.

The shop suddenly looked empty. Archibald went directly to the crowded back room. He looked around deciding which items he should next move in. The smaller ones he could do on his own, for the Regency cabinet, he would have to ask Mrs. Wainright to bring her husband, Robbie, in to help him. He picked up a small Edwardian coffee table to carry into the shop. The bell rang. A middle-aged couple had entered the shop. Archibald greeted them.

"Just browsing," the woman replied.

"Be my guest, shout if I can be of any assistance," responded Archibald politely.

The phone on the desk in the shop rang. Archibald walked over to answer it. He listened intensively.

"Yes, of course I remember you," he lied. "The late-nineteenth-century Scottish mahogany dresser in the style of George Walton; the one with the large centre drawer, yes it is still available . . . that's correct £4,000 . . . certainly . . . I look forward to seeing you."

Archibald put down the phone. He was puzzled then he suddenly remembered. Attractive, brunette, hair neatly trimmed to above the shoulder. She had worn a three-quarter-length, tight-fitting white trousers which showed off her slender figure. She was shopping for large antique furniture with which to furnish her recently acquired farmhouse. She had wanted to know if she could visit him after five o'clock, the day after tomorrow. "It will be closer to six. It is the only time I have free." and her husband? He had asked. "No, he won't be coming. He is overseas and I have no idea when he will be back."

"I wonder," he mumbled to himself. Rhyl had been the last time—in the camper van. Caernarvon had been a disaster. Foolishly, he had mislaid his fragrance bottle and without it he was lost. He had literally stripped the camper apart in a futile attempt to find it but it was nowhere to be found. Plus, £300 was missing from his wallet. He wondered if the girl had somehow taken it. His mind returned to the caller, Sandra, she had said her name was, Sandra Robinson. She had quite a sexy name. He seemed to remember she had worn quite a strong perfume that afternoon she first came into the shop.

"Can you help us please?"

Archibald looked up. It was the woman shopper. She was holding up a silver teapot.

"Certainly Madam, that is early Victorian, part of a set, functional but very collectable. Silver is on the way up as I am sure you know."

Detective Superintendent Donald Bradley stopped the car. He stared at the small cottage. The gate was open. Four black cats sat in a row watching him. He scratched the eczema on the knuckles of his left hand as he threw ideas around his mind—the best way to confront the subject. The skin began to bleed. "Stop that," he told himself. He made a mental note to see his doctor at the first opportunity. He checked his watch. It was 03:30 in the afternoon. He opened the car door. "In for a penny in for a pound—nothing ventured nothing gained." He was keen to meet Mrs. Crumpet, Archibald's mother. After what Shaun had told him about the mysterious fragrance with its powerful aphrodisiac properties he had studied the transcript of Archibald's trial.

Without hesitating he marched boldly through the open gate. Four black cats barred his way. Their backs arched. Teeth glared. A hissing sound emanated from the cat on the extreme right. The others quickly followed suit. Ignoring the threat Superintendent Bradley placed his size twelve boot firmly down on the ground and marched stealthily forward. The law was on his side.

At the very last moment the cats moved. The door to the cottage opened. An elderly woman's face appeared. The cats hissed louder. "Yes," she called out.

"Detective Superintendent Donald Bradley, Manchester CID, may I have a few words with you, Madam?"

"Your badge?"

"Certainly, Mrs. Crumpet, it is Mrs. Crumpet?"

The Inspector had arrived at the door. He showed her his identification.

"You had better come in." Turning to the cats she informed, "It's alright, boys, the gentleman is a friend." The hissing ceased. The cats dispersed.

Superintendent Bradley followed her into the cluttered kitchen. "Take a seat, Mr . . . what should I call you?"

"Superintendent will do nicely, Madam"

"Superintendent, would you like some tea?"

"That would be nice, Mrs. Crumpet, but don't go to any trouble."

"I do not receive many visitors, but when I do, I like to make them feel at home. Will dandelion tea be alright? I take it with a spoon of honey."

"That will do nicely, Mrs. Crumpet." He quickly glanced around the busy kitchen. Pots, pans, bundles of dried flowers—herbs he guessed—hung or lay everywhere. After busying herself at the stove she placed an old-fashioned steaming-hot kettle followed by a large breakfast cup and saucer in front of him.

"Help yourself to the honey. I do not use sugar. It is not good for you." A big glass jar was pushed towards him. She sat across the wooden table and began to sip her tea. He tasted his. He added some honey and gave the mixture a vigorous stir. He tried it again then added more honey.

"It is an acquired taste. Dandelion possesses excellent diuretic and digestive qualities. It is good for the liver and the gall-bladder. I have also added some dried cowslip it helps to calm one you know."

He said nothing as he sipped the tea. The way she had conveyed this information clearly indicated she was an intelligent woman. He hoped it would make his unpleasant task easier. He decided to come straight to the point.

"Do you know why I am here, Mrs. Crumpet?"

"It's about Archibald, isn't it?" she replied softly.

"Yes, I am afraid it is."

He found himself scratching his eczema again. He pulled his hand away. "I know all about the after shave you make for him, Mrs. Crumpet. You don't supply anyone else, do you?"

"Of course not, Superintendent, it is just that Archibald has difficulty in making friends."

"This perfume . . . you are aware the affect it can have on say . . . a young woman?"

"I feed it to my chickens and ducks. It is amazing how it helps them to lay. Of course they take it in a dry form but do not worry yourself, since that awful trial I have stopped making it. Archibald will get no more."

"That's just the problem, Mrs. Crumpet. I suspect he has kept a stock of it."

"Oh he hasn't, the naughty boy, he told me he had used it all up."

"Are you aware he has recently purchased a camping van?"

She rose from the table clutching in both hands the heavy iron kettle. She walked over to the stove. The room was silent. Finally, she returned. "Some more tea?"

"No thanks, I'm doing fine." He was beginning to feel somewhat relaxed—perhaps too calm for the job. He watched as she filled up her cup.

"Mrs. Crumpet, I have come here to warn you—not officially you might say—but rather as your friendly Copper—*if,* Mr. Crumpet, Archibald, persists in his ways then he *will* go to prison and, it will be for a very long time. Because, I shall personally see to it and I feel certain that is the very last thing you wish to happen. You see, Mrs. Crumpet, I have a daughter. She is just seventeen. I strongly suspect that your son might have attempted to seduce her when she visited his shop two Saturdays ago. I may be wrong but, I cannot take the chance of him trying this with other young women. We will be watching and the next time–".

"He takes after his father," she interrupted. "His father couldn't keep his hands off other women that's why he had to go. I have brought Archibald up on my own since he was five-years-old and I do not intend to lose him now. Superintendent, you have my word. Archibald will never touch a woman again of that I promise you."

"I only hope you are right, Mrs. Crumpet, because–".

"Oh Superintendent," and she stood up, "your hand, let me see your hand."

"What?"

She had moved quickly to his side of the table. "Your hand, permit me to take a look." Very gently she lifted up his left hand. You have been scratching it. You mustn't, but of course you know that. Is the rash just on the hand or do you have it elsewhere on your body?"

"On my elbows and behind my knees," he answered softly not really knowing why.

She left the kitchen leaving him to ponder why he had disclosed his skin complaint to a complete stranger. It was a subject which greatly embarrassed him and one he preferred not to discuss openly. She returned clutching a small jar. She opened the lid and taking his left hand again began to gently rub a white lotion into the cracked skin.

"This will help. It contains zinc, sulphur and selenium, as well as geranium and lavender. You don't smoke do you?"

He shook his head.

"I thought not. Smoking destroys vitamin C that is why heavy smokers develop such deep facial cracks. I drummed this into Archibald as soon as he became adolescent." She closed the jar placing it in front of him. "Rub that into the affected areas in the morning and before you go to bed at night. It won't cure you but will help to control the irritation. When the skin has healed only use it once a day and then maybe every second or third day unless the dryness returns."

He looked at the knuckles on his hand. The cream was beginning to dry out and already the persistent itchiness had gone. "Thank you, Mrs. Crumpet. You make this yourself do you?"

She smiled knowingly.

"May I pay you?"

"Absolutely not, Superintendent, I am most appreciative to you for coming around to see me like this. Like I said, the cream will not cure your eczema it will only keep it under control so consider it a sample. The health shop in the village stocks it or, you are more than welcome to visit me whenever you require more."

"That is very kind of you, Mrs. Crumpet, but let us not forget the purpose of my visit—your son, Archibald."

"Oh you won't have to worry about him. He will not give you any more problems. Now a final cup of tea and do try one of my scones. I put a little cannabis into the mixture it is an excellent preventative against headaches and back pain."

"I will pretend I did not hear that, Mrs. Crumpet."

Three scones and a second cup of dandelion tea later, Detective Superintendent Donald Bradley stood at the doorway of the cottage to bid Mrs. Crumpet goodbye. One by one each of the four cats came to rub themselves against his leg. They followed him proudly down the driveway to his vehicle. He opened the car door. Mrs. Crumpet had entered her cottage but sitting in a line were the four cats. As he glanced back at them they each meowed as though bidding him farewell.

# Chapter Forty Seven

# Paris

A loud knocking at the door surprised Claude Pic. He was just beginning to enjoy the first of his three-minute boiled eggs in the kitchen. He glanced up at the wall clock. It was nine o'clock in the morning. The knocking persisted only this time louder. It would wake his master, the last thing he wanted. *"Merde,"* he swore loudly, dropping his spoon onto the table. He stood up, untying his apron so as to put on his black jacket. The banging started all over again. *"Je viens, je viens, doucement,"* he shouted.

He was puzzled. Normally any visitor wishing to enter the building rang the bell in the street. There was a camera as well as an intercom so Claude could press a button in the apartment which opened the street door. Security was very strict. There were five luxury apartments in the building each one occupied an entire floor.

Claude peered through the spy hole. *"Oui,"* he called out. *"Est-ce qui?"* He could make out several shapes. He heard the word—"police—open up"—he saw the uniforms. They pushed their way into the lobby. A woman flashed a badge at him. She asked for Lucien Bourboché.

"He is asleep in bed you can't . . ."

The woman nodded to the three policemen. They rushed through into the flat.

"I demand to know . . ."

"Take us to him," ordered the woman.

The door to Lucien's bedroom was already open. The woman turned to her assistant. "Anton, you go in, get him dressed, remember to read him his rights."

Claude had recovered his composure. "Madam, I believe it would be prudent if you allowed me to assist in the waking of Monsieur Bourboché."

She nodded her head.

"Who are you? How dare you? Claude? Claude," the shouts emanated from the giant four-poster bed.

"Who is this?" asked one of the policemen. The bedcovers had been pulled off and a young boy, naked, stared up at them.

Claude walked over to the window and began to pull open the heavy drapes. "I think you had better get up, sir. These gentlemen wish to talk with you."

"Claude . . . Claude what is going on?"

Claude pulled the young boy to his feet. "*You*, get dressed quickly." Turning to the policemen Claude advised, "May I suggest you let me assist Monsieur Bourboché. It will be much quicker for us all. The three policemen looked at each other. The young detective nodded his head. They moved back. Claude held out a bathrobe. "Here, let's put this on shall we and get you dressed, Sir."

"Phone Robert, I want my lawyer, get him straight away," barked Lucien. "He will sort this out."

"Very well, Sir."

Lucien pushed Claude away. He staggered off towards the bathroom. Two policemen shadowed him. The boy ran out of the room. "Just a minute, who are you? What's your name?"

The boy looked defiantly at the woman.

"How old are you?"

"I am eighteen. Leave me alone. I have done nothing," the boy replied in a foreign accent.

"Probably not, if you are telling the truth, but, if you are under age and perhaps illegal in this country then that is an entirely different matter." She turned to face the policeman standing beside her. "Take him away."

The atmosphere in the small interrogation room was tense. Lucien sat very subdued behind the small table. Nervously, he played continuously with the large diamond ring on his finger turning it around and around. His lawyer, Robert, seated next to him, was doing all the talking. Claude had forced him to wear a dark pinstripe suit, the one he so disliked. He had only worn it once and that was to a funeral. Claude had advised him about wearing his normal pink or light blue—"Not for the police," he had advised.

"This is outrageous. You have absolutely no proof that my client here, Monsieur Bourboché, was involved in any way with this missing . . . what did you say his name was?"

"Jacques Gavotte," replied Inspectrice Daguerre calmly.

"And as for this other person, you claim Monsieur Bourboché ordered to be killed. The whole thing is quite preposterous. I demand that you release him immediately with a formal apology. Monsieur Bourboché is a prominent businessman. Many important people are his personal friends. I am afraid, Madame, you have gone over your head this time. This could very likely cost you your career."

"Thank you for that advice but let me ask you one final time, Monsieur Bourboché, have you ever seen this man before?" Inspectrice Daguerre slid the photograph back across the table.

Lucien turned his head in the opposite direction. His lawyer touched him on the arm. Lucien shook his head. "My client says *no*. Now, may we please go?"

Inspectrice Daguerre opened a file which she had deliberately refrained from opening. "Do you know a Monsieur Herbert Sibert?"

The lawyer nudged Lucien. Reluctantly he answered. "Of course I know Sibert. The bastard used to work for me until he disappeared with all my money."

"Good," replied Inspectrice Daguerre, "because I have here a written statement signed by him in which he claims you held Jacques Gavotte prisoner in the cellar of your shop, L'Artisan Parfumeur, in Montparnasse."

"That's a bloody lie," snapped back Lucian. "I know absolutely nothing."

"So you say. So you say, Monsieur. It is just that we have found traces of Monsieur Gavotte's DNA in a small room in the basement. It is where Hugo and Monty, they also are your employees, are they not, killed him?"

"Do you have a body?" asked the lawyer.

"No, and we do not need one."

"Then you only have this word of a . . . petty *thief,* associating my client with this alleged incident. The fact is you do not possess any substantive evidence associating Monsieur Bourboché with this unfortunate missing person. The fact is Monsieur Bourboché rarely visits the shop so whatever Siebert is claiming is totally unfounded."

"I do not think so." She paused to extract two more sheets of paper. "You see, I have two more signed statements, one from Hugo, the other from Monty." She held them up to emphasis the point. They have sung to us like two performing canaries once we pointed out they would each serve a life sentence while their boss, the man who instructed them to *dispose* of Jacques Gavotte and Pierre Nimier, continued to live his life of luxury. They have agreed to cooperate fully with us in return for the possibility of receiving a lighter sentence which is something your client here has clearly not done."

Inspectrice Daguerre pushed her chair back. She stood up. Turning to her assistant she ordered, "Book him, murder and attempted murder and naturally we oppose any bail."

Lucien turned to his lawyer. Tears began to flood his eyes. "Do something, Robert. You can not let this happen to me. What about Max? I cannot rely on Claude to walk him and anyway, I have only got this horrid suit to wear. No, you must insist they release me. I want to go home."

# Chapter Forty Eight

# Beeston

Using the driver's rear-view mirror Sandra Robinson checked her makeup one final time. Just a touch of mascara, a mere suggestion of rouge on the cheeks and a soft orange-pink lipstick, which complemented her flowing brunette hair, was all that was necessary. The white blouse with its plunging V-neck, worn together with a specially purchased new, black, uplifting Wonder-Bra—she made a mental note to charge the company for it—it had not come cheap—would be her main armament.

She spoke softly to test the miniature microphone built into the buckle of her belt. "Testing . . . testing 1 . . . 2 . . . 3 . . . Do you read me, Terry?"

Parked around the corner in a silver grey Vauxhall, Terry adjusted the squelch switch. "I hear you, Sandra, over."

"Terry, I am going to drive up, will park across the road—should be in place in three minutes."

"Sandra—Roger that."

Archibald Crumpet was busy revaluing his stock. It was something he did every six months, especially those items which had not moved. Furniture prices remained relatively constant but silver, which had been fetching low prices, was on the up. Two large late-nineteenth century Chinese vases had still not been sold. The market was flooded with them and oriental pieces were no longer in vogue. He checked what he had paid for them. He could afford to lower the price. How much, was the question? The door bell rang.

He looked up from the desk. It was the woman, his appointment. He rose and walked towards her holding out his hand in welcome. She was wearing the shortest of mini skirts. His eyes were drawn immediately to her cleavage. He liked what he saw.

"Mr. Crumpet?"

"Call me, Archie."

"Archie, sorry I am a little late." She gripped his hand firmly, perhaps longer than usual.

Her perfume was strong. He breathed deeply savoring its fragrance. "The late-nineteenth-century Scottish mahogany dresser in the style of George Walton, the one with the large centre drawer"—he guided her to it. He opened up the drawers then stood back allowing her to examine it for herself. She leaned forward. His eyes were immediately drawn to her plunging cleavage. It would appear she had small but firm round breasts—the type he most preferred. She was rubbing her hand along the varnished edge of the dresser in a somewhat erotic manner.

"It's so firm and hard to touch."

Outside the shop, hidden around the corner, Terry almost choked on the biscuit he had begun to munch on. It was obviously time for him to move.

Archibald said nothing.

"I like it. I really like it," she continued, "what other pieces do you have which might go with it? Do you have something in the back?"

Archibald smiled. "Why certainly, if you would come this way please." He turned around. "Please follow me."

"You are taking me to the room in the back are you, Archie?" she said loudly, hoping the microphone in her belt buckle was accurately relaying the information.

Terry returned the packet of biscuits to the glove compartment before stepping out of the vehicle.

"I have a number of items which might interest you, Sandra. I apologize for the state of the room. I only use it for storage and repairs. Be careful, some pieces are a bit dusty so mind your clothes."

She followed closely behind him. He stopped to show her a four-poster bed. Their bodies touched. Again, he enjoyed the fragrance of her perfume.

She laughed loudly, "Why it's enormous—obscene almost."

Terry quickened his pace.

"Of course I would have to assemble it properly but you can see from the ornate headboard exactly how big it is. The design is George III. I estimate its age to be around 250-years-old. I advise you to replace the mattress, finding a suitable manufacturer should not prove too difficult." He watched her rub her hand up and down the top of the rounded leg post. She moved sensuously closer too him.

"One could have a lot of fun on a bed this size," she purred.

Terry was finally in position outside the shop.

"Indeed one could," replied Archibald. "Now, I have here an interesting armoire. Unfortunately, it is not of the same period but the color of the wood does match." He moved away halting at a large antique wardrobe. Sandra followed him. Her hips touched his. She saw his eyes focus on her cleavage. She pushed out her chest. Archibald moved away.

Terry glanced at his watch. Sandra had been in the shop for fifteen minutes and so far nothing was happening. He touched the tiny earphone attached to his right ear. Apparently, Crumpet was offering to show her an ottoman, which he claimed, came with the bed. Terry wondered what on earth that could be. From his jacket pocket he removed a small camera. He checked the battery. It was fully charged and the memory card was empty. He was rapidly becoming bored.

Fifteen minutes later, Sandra walked out of the shop. "Well?" he asked.

"Nothing, absolutely nothing, he showed no interest in me whatsoever."

"Yes, but what about his aftershave? What did he smell of?"

"Carbolic soap."

# Chapter Forty Nine

## One Year Later

Lancelot Slim put the lengthy report down. He had finally finished reading it. "So", he muttered to himself. "Not a complete write-off." Removing his spectacles he rubbed his eyes. A red light flashed on his desk phone. It was his secretary.

"I have the newspaper, sir. May I bring it in?"

"Yes, please do, Joyce."

Yesterday he had received the call from France. The job had been done—successfully. He had even read about the incident on the internet. He waited for Joyce to leave his office before picking up the paper—*Le Monde*. The article appeared on page three. His French was almost fluent but there were still certain words which eluded him.

> "A fire in the early hours of this morning destroyed a laboratory complex, on the outskirts of Versailles, belonging to the Shiseido Company of Japan. According to a company spokesman nobody was injured as the building was unoccupied at the time. A forensic expert from the fire department stated that the intensity of the blaze was due to the storage of volatile liquids, apparently used in various scientific experiments. It is believed that a faulty gas pipe may have caused the fire."

Lancelot put down the newspaper. There had been no communication with Takao Fujimoto for over a year but his spies in France had kept him well informed. His instructions had been explicit. "There must be no loss of life." That way, any routine investigation undertaken by the fire department, would be cursory. Takao would not pursue the matter. His Japanese chemist was working on too many projects that Japan knew nothing about.

He returned to the report opening the file at the summary page.

"The so-called STAZI Honey Files failed to produce any magic aphrodisiac formula. However, I have summarized for your easy reading those items which may be of interest to you.

1. Dog breeding report to improve the olfactory senses in canines together with training methods.
2. Chemical formula for prolonging the storage life of odors.
3. Four derivates using Sodium Thiopental—truth serum short acting barbiturate—suitable for conducting interrogation where the victim is unaware of being questioned—administered through tea or coffee.
4. Twenty-two experimental recipes for concocting fragrances with alleged stimulating properties—see addendum X1.

Lancelot closed the file pushing it to the side of his desk. He needed to make one final call before going out. He would lock the file in his walk-in safe. For the moment he would do nothing. He had too many other pressing matters to attend to. The information it contained was secure. He had no doubt an opportunity to put it to good use would arrive sooner than later.

Kylie Moon picked up the gold Schaffer fountain pen. It was heavy in her hand. "You sign here and here," pointed Jean-Luc Picard, "just below my signature as Director of Marketing. The contract has been extended for another five years and all changes requested by your new manager have been affected. She drove a hard bargain," he joked.

Kylie looked at Lisa Evans who nodded her agreement. Kylie signed the first of her signatures. Jean-Luc turned over the page. "And again here, here and here." Finally the task was completed. "Now, all that remains is for us to celebrate with a glass of champagne."

"Not for me thank you," replied Kylie. "Lisa and I are flying off to New York this evening and I need to commence packing."

"Very well," responded Jean-Luc. "On behalf of Essence de la Grasse I look forward to welcoming you to Grasse. Our advertising agency has proposed we commence production of the launch of *"Diable"* next month, beginning with a series of photographs featuring the countryside around Grasse where the perfume is made. I am glad you like the design of the bottles. After much deliberation we chose to go for this elegant wine-decanter design for the perfume. For the eau de Cologne and eau de vie we shall use the plainer square bottle which will help to keep the price down."

Lisa Evans glanced at her watch. "I am sorry to be rude but we really must be going, Jean-Luc. Kylie has a meeting at the film studio in two hours. It is not yet public knowledge but she has been cast to play the new Bond girl in the "Devil's Fragrance" to be launched next year. It is based upon the best selling novel by Martin Fine. Filming starts in three months so it is important we complete the Grasse shooting before the film production commences."

"Congratulations to you both. That is wonderful news." Jean-Luc stood up to guide the two ladies out. His mind was awhirl. Kylie Moon, the new face of Essence de la Grasse, chosen to launch their new range of fragrances, was to star in the latest James Bond film. He could not wait to tell the board. They would need to double production—no treble it.

Lucien Bourboché lay prone in the tiny hospital cot. Through bleary eyes he stared upwards at the dirty grey ceiling. Layers of flaking paint were threatening to fall off. The plastic tube attached to his arm no longer irritated him. His chest heaved as his blocked lungs struggled to inhale and exhale the stale air. From an overweight—bordering on obese—120-kilograms, his weight had plumaged to a mere sixty kilos.

At least he no longer pined for his former life. He had finally stopped asking the questions—*why*? And *how,* had he ended up in this dreadful place—La Santé? Built in 1875, overcrowded, disease ridden, it ranked as one of the worst *Establissements pour peines* in the French penal system. The modern day Devil's Island on French soil; it had been condemned by the European Union who ranked it as one of the most outdated of France's 102 prisons.

His trial had been quick. His lawyer had been ineffective. The evidence against him was insurmountable. Hugo and Monty had each received 25-years instead of life in return for testifying against him and as for Herbert, that bastard. Lucien choked at the thought of the man. Pain shot through his body. Finally it subsided. His breathing returned to normal that is, as normal as it would ever be.

Herbert had received five-years for assisting in the kidnapping, three of which were suspended. His sentence was being served out in a *centres de detention*—a prison for mild offenders where the cell doors were left open and prisoners were free to move around, not like Lucien. He began to choke again. His eyes were moist but no tears flowed. Locked up for twenty-two-hours a day in a cell no bigger than a broom closet with three other hardened criminals, but it was the Muslim gangs whom he most feared. They despised his type, as did the judge at his trial. All his friends, his so-called powerful associates, had deserted him. He heard voices. They came from the foot of the bed. They were talking about him, discussing him as though he was not there. It was so disgusting so impersonal. They treated him like a specimen.

The elderly prison doctor turned to address the four young interns who had unluckily been allocated to assist at La Santé. "This one has not long to go. He is in the advanced stages of full blown AIDS. His immune system has all but collapsed. We did have him on Atazanvir, the antiretroviral, but that is no longer coping. Bloody promiscuous homosexuals, it serves them right."

The voices dissipated leaving Lucien to his little world of the crumbling ceiling. "This one has not got long to go." The words reverberated around his mind. For him it was good news. He closed his eyes. He so missed his Max.

Claude Pic and his partner, Josephine, sat on a bench in the Bois de Boulogne watching Max playing with new Max. The sun was shining. It was a glorious sunny morning. "We'll give them another ten minutes together then we'll go. Where would you like to have lunch today?"

"I'm easy, you choose," she replied. "I'm so pleased Max is getting on with new Max. It would have been terrible if they had fought, then what would we have done?"

"Bought a Max-3, just so long as there is a Max in the apartment we can continue to live there and collect the money. I have a feeling Max will enjoy a very long life—forty years at least. Did I tell you the replica of the Napoleon wall clock is ready for collection? You can not tell it from the original."

"How much did it cost?"

"Five Thousand Euros."

"*Mon dieu*, that is a lot."

"Not if you consider I have a buyer for the original—eighty thousand Euros. Max won't complain."

She laughed. "Just how anyone can leave the apartment, with all those valuable antiques, to a dog amazes me."

"Do not forget the trust fund to pay for Max's daily fillet steak and visit to the poodle parlor, not to mention the vet bills. It all costs money. As long as we present Max to the lawyer once a year all is well."

"And when Max eventually dies?"

"Then the flat and its contents will go to animal welfare."

"We can't allow that to happen. Can we?"

"Absolutely not, come on, put Max and Max on the lead. It is time for lunch. I fancy a fresh lobster at Fouquet's today."

Nothing had changed. The cottage was exactly the same except that is for the welcoming committee. As soon as Detective Superintendent Donald Bradley stepped out of his car in the direction of the open gate, four black cats were there to greet him. There was no spitting, no arched backs and no show of razor-sharp teeth instead—a gentle purring as one by one they came to rub themselves against his legs. He would have some clever explaining to do when the family Labrador picked up the scent on his trousers. It was a year since he had visited the cottage but being in the vicinity a sudden urge came over him to make a call. He could purchase more cream for his eczema, not that he needed to use it much these days.

Just like before he was halfway down the path when the door to the cottage suddenly opened. It was uncanny. "Good afternoon, Superintendent, this is a pleasant surprise, do come in. I see the boys *are* pleased to see you."

He followed her into the cluttered kitchen. Large cast-iron pots bubbled away on the old wood-fired stove. She indicated he sit at the kitchen table. She apologized for the mess as she swept up an assortment of herbs in her arms. "Some tea? I am sorry I can't offer you any scones but I do have freshly baked biscuits. She placed an ancient round tin of Bauman's Biscuits on the table and removed the lid. "Do help yourself."

Together they sipped their tea. He munched on the biscuits. They were delicious. He wondered what weird and wonderful ingredients had gone into them. As though reading his mind she volunteered. "They have quite a bit of ginger in them. It helps to disguise the bitter taste of nettle. I always like to include it as it is an excellent blood cleanser." She glanced at his hands. "I see your skin has cleared up. You are still using my lotion."

"Yes, Mrs. Crumpet, in fact that is my reason for popping in, to obtain another jar from you, but this time I insist on paying for it."

"I knew you had not come to discuss Archibald. He is a good boy now. These days he rarely goes out because he is spending more and more time restoring old pieces of furniture. He does it here in one of the outbuildings. Some nights he is still working away at midnight. He is ever so clever with his hands."

"I am pleased to hear that, Mrs. Crumpet."

A loud cackling sound disturbed their conversation. "Oh my, it's Walter, I completely forgot."

Bradley turned his neck in the direction of the noise. A large white goose had entered the kitchen. Big, pink, webbed-feet stamped up and down on the stone floor. White feathered wings rose and fell while a viscous beak opened and shut. The old lady stood up. "Alright, Walter, I'm coming now."

The goose intensified its dance.

Bradley stood up. The goose hissed loudly and went to charge him.

"Stop that, Walter, the Superintendent is a friend."

The angry bird braked. It pivoted, turned and waddled out leaving a white feather behind. The old lady followed. Bradley, not really knowing why, followed behind. The goose led them through the house and out of a back door into an exotic garden. They weaved there way passed shrubs and trees to an open space where a series of chicken runs stood. At the second enclosure the old lady stopped. The goose continued through the open gate to disappear inside a small shed. Immediately, loud squawks and a rustling sound were followed by a number of tiny chicks scampering out into the open, closely fussed over by a second goose and finally, Walter emerged bringing up the rear. Bradley counted ten.

The second goose came waddling over. "Well done, Lesley, you clever girl." The old lady put her hand deep into her apron pocket. Opening her clenched fist she threw tiny pellets in the direction of the geese. Lesley wasted no time in going for them, the chicks following closely behind.

Bradley was about to ask but was cut short.

"They have all hatched today. I've been so busy in the kitchen I forgot to visit them that was why Walter was so cross. He came to tell me off for neglecting them. He wanted to boast about his knew family."

"Of course," replied Detective Superintendent Donald Bradley wondering if he dare tell his family when he returned home.

The church was three hundred years old. It was built into the side of the mountain on the outskirts of town. Having survived the physical ravages of time it was now battling to survive with an ever-dwindling, aging congregation. However, because of its romantic setting it was a popular venue for weddings.

Hervé Duronzier fussed around the altar putting the final unnecessary touches to the panoply of flowers decorating the church. The exquisite floral arrangements had been his personal contribution to the occasion. The combined creative skills of his multi-talented merchandising staff had been allowed to blossom. With a final touch to a yellow rose, a delicate adjustment to a fern leaf, he pivoted around to face the groom. The sound of the Mendelssohn Wedding March blasted out from the ancient organ filling the small church with sound.

"That's it, I can't do another thing. I think she's coming. I'd better take my place."

"Thank you, Hervé. You've done a marvelous job. Nobody could have done better," replied the groom.

"Oh! You really think so." Hervé ducked into the fourth row on the bride's side of the aisle next to Michel Ramonet.

All heads were turned towards the entrance to the church.

"Oh doesn't she look lovely," contributed Madam Pommé, dabbing her eyes with a lace handkerchief.

"Radiant,"

"Stunning," added another voice.

The bride on her father's arm had entered the church. The groom's father leaned forward touching his son on the shoulder. "Good luck, son,"

"Thanks dad."

The bride slowly made her way down the aisle until she arrived beside her husband to be. The organ stopped. The bride's father released his daughter's arm. He lifted her veil. Denise Vergé turned to face the groom, Pierre Nimier. Their eyes sparkled as they both smiled. The priest broke the silence.

# Other Books by Martin Fine

### THE CRYSTAL SKULL

According to the lost Mayan civilization of South America our present world will end on the 20th December 2012. The native tribes of both North and South America all talk of the 13 crystal skulls brought to the continent at the beginning of time by the founders of civilization.

A pure quartz crystal skull surfaces in Belize. It is transported to the British Museum in London for analysis. Suddenly, alarm bells are sounded throughout the religious world. Is this the skull, which will unlock the true origin of mankind, or is it simply another hoax? Can the skull be a depository of Mayan knowledge given to us by a past civilization, or even an ingenious form of communication, and if so to whom?

This riveting thriller transports the reader from the ancient world of Mesoamerican civilizations to the inner-secrets of the Vatican and the Muslim Brotherhood who are intent on capturing it. Will the skull confirm the existence of God, or will it finally prove we are not alone in the universe?

## THE RHODES DIAMOND

A mysterious black-diamond, once the property of billionaire South African diamond magnate Cecil John Rhodes—enclosed in a priceless gold-crafted egg, created by Carl Fabergé, imperial jeweler to the Tsar of Russia is auctioned in London.

A descendent of the Polish Princess, Catherine Radziwell, suddenly emerges to claim the egg. Who was this mysterious Princess, and what was her involvement with Rhodes? Who is the rightful owner of this precious *objets d'art*?

A powerful Ukrainian Oligarch vies with an unscrupulous Chinese billionaire industrialist, against descendents of the holocaust in a desperate - no holds barred fight - to gain possession of this valuable work of art.

## CHILDREN OF APARTHEID

Powerful leaders in the Kremlin, Washington and Cuba manipulated the politics of intrigue and power-broking in Africa. The demise of colonial rule transforms the face of Africa, and brings the Cold War—in which the forces of capitalism and communism confront each other—to the very borders of South Africa.

From the picturesque vineyards of the Cape to the bloody battlefields of Angola, fate entwines two young South Africans, one black and one white, on opposite sides of the conflict.

The legalization of the liberation movements and the release of Nelson Mandela bring the opposing ideologies to the brink of civil war. This history—of the bitterness and hatred of different cultures ultimately blending together over three decades to create the Rainbow Nation of South Africa—is told through their eyes.

## THE LOST STRADIVARIUS

Entombed with its creator for almost two hundred years - together with the secret formula of how Antonio Stradivari created his ultimate masterpiece, the violin is discovered - only to be lost, until it surfaces in Nazi occupied Europe, where yet again it mysteriously disappears.

A quirk of fate pits a young British violin virtuoso against ruthless, powerful men in Ukraine and China, in a desperate search to recover the lost *Francisca-Antonia* - the Holy Grail of stringed instruments.

Through the streets of modern day Moscow to the hidden mysteries of Shanghai and Wuhan, the hunt leads to the old Jewish East End of London, where a secret code must be deciphered in order to reveal its abstruse location.

## FOREVER AFRICA

The year is 1970 and independence brings to an end British colonial rule in the small East African State of Gondwanaland.

The winds of change blowing through Africa lead to the build up for independence and the birth of a new nation. The election is stolen—the newly elected Prime Minister cunningly declares himself *President for Life* - whilst exploiting the naiveté of donor countries - in order to enrich himself.

From the colonial dominated golf club to the Asian traders and indigenous African people the story of Africa is told. Gondwanaland gradually sinks into the quagmire of a one-party corrupt African state until an ingenious plot emerges to depose the despot and offer fresh hope to its people for the future.

## BIRKENHEAD REVISTED

One of the greatest maritime tragedies of the nineteenth century occurred when HMS Birkenhead struck an un-chartered rock off Danger Point on the coast of South Africa. Of the 638 persons on board, 445 perished, the legend of the *Birkenhead Drill* was born.

It was a beautiful clear night in February 1852, at the Cape of Storms. How could one of Queen Victoria's latest iron-ships sink less than two miles from the shore with such terrible loss of life?

The reader is transported on an historical journey through the smoky, industrial Birkenhead shipyard of Cammel Lairds—an impoverished famine struck Ireland—to the baronial homes of the aristocracy and a Colonial War in far-flung Africa.

It is a story of love and human passion relating the arduous times in which people lived and the many lives, which the great ship influenced

CPSIA information can be obtained at www.ICGtesting.com
Printed in the USA
LVOW06*1230111013

356498LV00005B/311/P